"Miss Sloane, I think you misunderstand something about what's going on here."

Sheridan's heart skipped. Why was Rashid so beautiful? And why was he such a contrast? He was fire and ice in one person. Hot eyes, cold heart. It almost made her sad. But why should it? She did not know him, and what she did know so far hadn't endeared him to her.

"Do I?"

"Indeed. I am not Mr. Rashid."

"Then who are you?"

He looked haughty and her stomach threatened to heave again. Because there was something familiar about that face, she realised. She'd seen it on the news a few weeks ago.

He spoke, his voice clear and firm and lightly accented. "I am King Rashid bin Zaid al-Hassan, the Great Protector of my people, Lion of Kyr and Defender of the Throne. And you, Miss Sloane, may be carrying my heir."

HEIRS TO THE THRONE OF KYR

*Two brothers, one crown, and a royal duty
that cannot be denied…*

The desert kingdom of Kyr needs a new ruler.

Prince Kadir al-Hassan, the Eagle of Kyr:
the world's most notorious playboy.

Prince Rashid al-Hassan, the Lion of Kyr:
as dark-hearted as the desert itself.

These sheikh princes share the same blood,
but they couldn't be more different. So now there's
only one question on everyone's lips…

Who will be crowned the new desert king?

Don't miss this thrilling new duet from
Lynn Raye Harris—where duty and desire
collide against a sizzling desert landscape!

GAMBLING WITH THE CROWN
May 2014

CARRYING THE SHEIKH'S HEIR
July 2014

CARRYING THE SHEIKH'S HEIR

BY
LYNN RAYE HARRIS

MILLS & BOON

Published in Great Britain 2014
by Mills & Boon, an imprint of Harlequin (UK) Limited,
Eton House, 18-24 Paradise Road, Richmond, Surrey, TW9 1SR

© 2014 Lynn Raye Harris

ISBN: 978 0 263 24667 4

Printed and bound in Spain
by Blackprint CPI, Barcelona

USA TODAY bestselling author **Lynn Raye Harris** burst onto the scene when she won a writing contest held by Mills & Boon®. The prize was an editor for a year—but only six months later Lynn sold her first novel. A former finalist for the Romance Writers of America's Golden Heart Award, Lynn lives in Alabama with her handsome husband and two crazy cats. Her stories have been called 'exceptional and emotional', 'intense' and 'sizzling'.

You can visit her at www.lynnrayeharris.com

Recent titles by the same author:

GAMBLING WITH THE CROWN
   (Heirs to the Throne of Kyr)
A GAME WITH ONE WINNER
   (Scandal in the Spotlight)
REVELATIONS OF THE NIGHT BEFORE
UNNOTICED AND UNTOUCHED

Did you know these are also available as eBooks?
Visit www.millsandboon.co.uk

To my brainstorming partners,
Jean Hovey and Stephanie Jones,
who write together as Alicia Hunter Pace.
They calmly listen to my ideas, toss out helpful
suggestions, and don't get offended when I don't use
a single one. And when I tell them there might be
jackals, they reply that you can never have too many
jackals. Thanks for having my back, ladies.

CHAPTER ONE

"A MISTAKE? How is this possible?"

King Rashid bin Zaid al-Hassan glared daggers at the stuttering secretary who stood in front of him. The man swallowed visibly.

"The clinic says they have made a mistake, Your Majesty. A woman…" Mostafa looked down at the note in his hand. "A woman in America was supposed to receive her brother-in-law's sperm. She received yours instead."

Rashid's blood ran hot and then cold. He felt… violated. Rage coursed through him like a flame from a blast furnace, melting the ice around his heart for only a moment before it hardened again. He knew from experience that nothing could thaw that ice for long. In five years, nothing had penetrated the darkness surrounding him.

His hands clenched into fists on his desk. This was too much. Too outrageous.

How dare they? How dare anyone take that choice away from him? He wasn't ready for a child in his life. He didn't know if he would ever be ready, though eventually he had to provide Kyr with an heir. It was his duty, but he wasn't prepared to do it quite yet.

The prospect of marrying and producing children

brought up too many memories, too much pain. He preferred the ice to the sharpness of loss and despair that would envelop him if he let the ice thaw.

He'd obeyed the law that required him to deposit sperm in two banks for the preservation of his line, but he'd never dreamed it could go so horribly wrong. A random woman had been impregnated with his sperm. He could even now be an expectant father, his seed growing into a tiny life that could break him anew.

An icy wash of terror crested inside him, left him reeling in its wake. He would be physically ill in another moment.

Rashid pushed himself up from his chair and turned away so Mostafa wouldn't see the utter desolation that he knew was on his face. This was not an auspicious beginning to his reign as Kyr's king.

Hell, as if this was the only thing that had gone wrong. His stomach churned with fresh fury.

Since his father died two months ago and his brother abdicated before he'd ever been crowned, it was now Rashid's duty to rule this nation. But nothing was the way it was supposed to be. As the eldest, he should have been the crown prince, but he'd been the despised son, a pawn in his father's game of cat and mouse. In Kyr, the king could name his successor from amongst his sons. There was no law that said it had to be the eldest, though tradition usually dictated that it was.

But not for King Zaid al-Hassan. He'd been a cruel and manipulative man, the kind who ruled his sons—and his wives—with fear and harsh punishments. He'd dangled the possibility of the throne over his sons' heads for far too long. Kadir had never wanted to rule, but it hadn't mattered to their father. It was simply a way to control his eldest son. But Rashid had refused to play, instead leaving Kyr when he was twenty-five and vowing never to come back again.

He had come back, however. And now he wore a crown he'd never expected to have. His father, the old snake, was probably spinning in his grave right this minute. King Zaid had not wanted Rashid to rule. He had only wanted to hold out the hope of it before snatching the crown away in a final act of spite. That he'd died without naming his successor didn't fill Rashid with the kind of peace that Kadir felt. Kadir wanted to believe their father had desired a reconciliation, and Rashid would not take that away from him.

But Rashid knew better. He'd had a lifetime of his father's scorn and disapproval and he just simply knew better.

Yet here he was. Rashid's gaze scanned the desert landscape, rolling over the sandstone hills in the distance, the red sand dunes, the palms and fountains that lined the ornate gardens of the palace. The sun was high and most people were inside at this hour. The horizon shimmered with heat. A primitive satisfaction rolled through him at the sight of all he loved.

He'd missed Kyr. He'd missed her perfumed night breezes, her blazing heat and her hardy people. He'd missed the call to prayer ringing from the mosque in the dawn hour, and he'd missed riding across the desert on his Arabian stallion, a hawk on his arm, hunting the small animals that were the hawk's chosen prey.

Until two months ago, he'd not set foot in Kyr in ten years. He'd thought he never would again, but then his father had called with news of his illness and demanded

Rashid's presence. Even then, Rashid had resisted. For Kadir's sake, he had finally relented.

And now he was a king when he'd given up on the idea years ago. Kadir was gone again, married to his former personal assistant and giddy with love. For Kadir, the world was a bright, happy place filled with possibilities.

Desolation swept through Rashid. It was an old and familiar companion, and his hands clenched into helpless fists. He'd been in love once and he'd been happy. But happiness was ephemeral and love didn't last. Love meant loss, and loss meant pain that never healed.

He'd been powerless to save Daria and the baby. So powerless. Who knew such a thing was possible in this day and age? A woman dying in childbirth seemed impossible, and yet it was not. It was, in fact, ridiculously easy. Rashid knew it far too well.

He stood there awhile longer, facing the windswept dunes in the distance, gathering his thoughts before he turned back to his secretary. His voice, when he spoke, was dangerously measured. He would *not* let this thing rule him.

"We chose this facility in Atlanta as the repository of the second sample for a reason. You will call them and demand to know this woman's name and where she lives. Or they will suffer the very public consequences of their mistake."

Mostafa bowed his head. "Yes, Your Majesty." He sank to his knees then and touched his forehead to the ornate carpet that graced the floor in front of Rashid's desk. "It is my fault, Your Majesty. I chose the facility. I will resign my position and leave the capital in disgrace."

Rashid gritted his teeth. Sometimes he forgot how

rigidly prideful Kyrians could be. He'd spent so many
years away. But if he'd stayed, he would be a different
man. A less damaged man. Or not. His mother and father
had been willing to use any weapon in their protracted
war against each other, and he had been the favorite. The
damage had been done years before he'd ever left Kyr.

"You will do no such thing," he snapped. "I have no
time to wait while you train a new secretary. The fault
lies elsewhere."

Rashid stalked back to his desk and sat down again.
He had many things to do and a new problem to deal
with. If this American woman had truly been impregnated with his sperm, then she could very well be carrying the heir to the throne of Kyr.

His fingers tightened on the pen he'd picked up again.
If he thought of the child that way, as his heir, and of the
woman as a functionary performing a duty—or a vessel
carrying a cargo—then he could get through these next
few days. Beyond that, he did not know.

An image of Daria's pale face swam in his head,
twisting the knife deep in his soul. He was not ready
to do this again, to watch a woman grow big with his
child and know that it could all go wrong in an instant.

And yet he had no choice. If the woman was pregnant, she was his.

"Find this woman by the end of the hour," he ordered. "Or you may yet find yourself tending camels in
the Kyrian Waste."

Mostafa's color drained as he backed away. "Yes,
Your Majesty."

There was a snapping sound at precisely the moment
the door closed behind the secretary. Pain bloomed in
Rashid's palm. He looked down to find a pen in his hand.

Or, rather, half a pen. The other half lay on the desk, dark ink spilling into a pattern on the wood like a psychologist's test blot.

A cut in his skin dripped red blood onto the black ink. He watched it drip for a long moment before there was a knock on his door and a servant entered with afternoon tea. Rashid stood and went into the nearby restroom in order to wash away the blood and tape up the cut. When he returned to his desk, the blood and ink had been wiped away. Cleaned up as if it had never happened.

He flexed his hand and felt the sting of the cut against his palm. You could sweep up messes, patch up wounds and try to forget they ever happened.

But Rashid knew the truth. The cut would heal, but there were things that never went away, no matter how deeply you buried them.

"Please stop crying, Annie." Sheridan sat at her desk with her phone to her ear and her heart in her throat. Her sister was sobbing on the other end of the line at the news from the clinic. Sheridan was still too stunned to process it. "We'll get through this. Somehow, we'll get through. I *am* having a baby for you. I promise it will happen."

Annie sobbed and wailed for twenty minutes while Sheridan tried to soothe her. Annie, the oldest by a year, was so fragile, and Sheridan felt her pain keenly. Sheridan had always been the strong one. She was still the strong one. Still the one looking out for her sister and wishing that she could give Annie some of her strength.

She felt so guilty every time Annie fell apart. It wasn't her fault, and yet she couldn't help but feel responsible. There'd only been enough money in their family for one daughter to go to college, and Sheridan had better grades. Annie had been shy and reclusive while Sheridan was outgoing. The choice had been evident to all of them, but it was yet another thing Sheridan felt guilty over. Maybe if their parents had tried harder to encourage Annie, to support her decisions, she would be stronger than she was. Instead, she let everyone else make her choices.

The one thing she wanted in this life was the one thing she couldn't have. But Sheridan could give it to her. And she was determined to do just that, in spite of this latest wrinkle in the plan.

Eventually, Annie's husband came home and took the phone away. Sheridan talked to Chris for a few minutes and then the line went dead.

She leaned back in her chair and blinked. Her eyes were gritty and swollen from the crying she'd been doing along with her sister. She snatched up a tissue from the holder on her desk and dabbed at her eyes.

How had this all gone wrong? It was supposed to be so easy. Annie couldn't carry a baby to term, but Sheridan could. So she'd offered to have a baby for her sister, knowing that it would make Annie happy and fulfill her deepest desire. It would have also made their parents happy, if they were still alive, to know they'd have a grandchild on the way. They'd had Annie and Sheridan late in life, and they'd desperately wanted grandchildren. But Annie hadn't been able to provide them, and Sheridan hadn't been ready.

Now Sheridan wished she'd had this baby earlier so her parents could have held their grandchild before they died. Though the child wouldn't be Annie's biologically, it would still share her DNA. The Sloane DNA.

Sheridan had gone in for the insemination a week

ago. They still didn't know whether it had worked or not, but now that she knew it wasn't Chris's sperm, she fervently hoped it hadn't.

She'd been given sperm from a different donor. A foreigner. The sperm bank would give them no other information beyond the physical facts. An Arab male, six-two, black hair, dark eyes, healthy.

Sheridan put her hand on her belly and drew in a deep breath. They couldn't test for another week yet. Another week of Annie crying her eyes out. Another week until Sheridan knew if she was having an anonymous man's baby or if they would try again with Chris's sperm.

But what if she was pregnant this time? Then what?

There was a knock on her door, and her partner popped her head in. Sheridan swiped her eyes again and smiled as Kelly came inside the small office at the back of the space they rented for their business.

"Hey, you okay?"

Sheridan sniffed. "Not exactly." She waved a hand. "I will be, but it's just a lot to process."

Kelly came over and took her hand, squeezed it before she sat in a chair nearby and leaned forward to look Sheridan in the eye. "Want to talk about it?"

Sheridan thought she didn't, but then she spilled the news almost as if she couldn't quite help herself. And it felt good to tell someone else. Someone who wouldn't sob and fall apart and need more reassurance than Sheridan knew how to give. If her mother was still alive, she'd know what to say to Annie. But Sheridan so often didn't.

Kelly didn't interrupt, but her eyes grew bigger as the story unfolded. Then she sat back in the chair with her jaw hanging open.

"Wow. So you might be pregnant with another man's baby. Poor Annie! She must be devastated."

Sheridan's heart throbbed. "She is. She'd pinned all her hopes on me having a baby for her and Chris. After so many disappointments, so many treatments and failed attempts of her own, she's fragile right now...." Sheridan sucked in a breath. "This was just a bad time for it to happen."

"I'm so sorry, sweetie. But maybe it won't take, and then you can try again."

"That's what I'm hoping." The doctor had said that sometimes they had to repeat the process two or three times before it was successful. And while it seemed wrong on some level to hope for failure this time, it would also be the best outcome. Sheridan stood and straightened her skirt. "Well, don't we have a party to cater? Mrs. Lands will be expecting her crab puffs and roast beef in a couple of hours."

"It's under control, Sheri. Why don't you just go home and rest? You look like hell, you know."

Sheridan laughed. "Gee, thanks." But then she shook her head. "I'll freshen up, but I'd really like to work. It'll keep my mind occupied."

Kelly looked doubtful. "All right. But if you find yourself crying in the soup, you have to go."

The party was a success. The guests loved the food, the waitstaff did a superb job and once everything was under control, Sheridan went back to the office to work on the menus for the next party they were catering in a few days' time. Kelly stayed behind to make sure there were no last-minute issues, but Sheridan knew her partner would come back to the office after it was over.

They were a great team. Had been since the first moment they'd met in school. Kelly was the cooking talent, and Sheridan was the architect behind the business. Literally the architect, Sheridan thought with a wry smile. She'd gone to the Savannah College of Art and Design for a degree in historical preservation architecture, but it was her talent at organizing parties that helped make Dixie Doin's—they'd left the *g* off *doing* on purpose, which worked well in the South but not so much when visiting Yankees called it *doynes*—into the growing business it was today.

They'd rented a building with a large commercial kitchen, hired a staff and maintained a storefront where people could come in and browse through specialty items that included table linens, dishes, gourmet oils and salts and various teas and teapots.

Sheridan settled in her office to scroll through the requirements for the next event. She had no idea how much time had passed when she heard the buzzer for the shop door. She automatically glanced up at the screen where the camera feed showed different angles of the store. Tiffany, the teenager they'd hired for the summer, was nowhere to be seen. A man stood inside the shop, looking around the room as if he had no clue what he was doing there.

Probably his wife had sent him to buy something and he had no idea what it looked like. Sheridan got up from her desk when Tiffany still hadn't appeared and went out to see if she could help him. Yes, it was annoying, and yes, she would have to speak to the girl again about not leaving the floor, but no way would she let a potential customer walk away when she could do the job herself.

The man was standing with his back to her. He was

tall, black haired and dressed in a business suit. There was something about him that seemed to dwarf the room, but then she shook that thought away. He was just a man. She'd never yet met one who impressed her all that much. Well, maybe Chris, her sister's husband. He loved Annie so much that he would do anything for her.

In Sheridan's experience, most men were far too fickle. And the better looking they were, the worse they seemed to be. On some level, she always fell for it, though. Because she was too trusting of people, and because she liked to believe the best of them. Her mother had always said she was too sunny and sweet. She was working on it, darn it, but what was the point in believing the worst of everyone you met? It was a depressing way to live—even if her last boyfriend had proved that she'd have been better off believing the worst of him from the start.

"Welcome to Dixie Doin's," she said brightly. "Can we help you today, sir?"

The man seemed to stiffen slightly. And then he turned, slowly, until Sheridan found herself holding her breath as she gazed into the most coldly handsome face she'd ever seen. There wasn't an ounce of friendliness in his dark eyes—yet, incongruously, there was an abundance of heat.

Her heart kicked up a level, pounding hard in her chest. She told herself it was the hormones from all the shots and the stress of waiting to see whether or not the fertilization had succeeded.

But it wasn't that. It wasn't even that he was breathtakingly handsome.

It was the fact he was an Arab, when she'd just been told the news of the clinic's mistake. It seemed a cruel joke to be faced with a man like him when she didn't know whether she was pregnant with a stranger's baby or if she could try again for her sister.

"You are Sheridan Sloane."

He said it without even a hint of uncertainty, as if he knew her. But she did not know him—and she didn't like the way he stood there sizing her up as if she was something he might step in on a sidewalk.

She was predisposed to like everyone she met. But this man already rubbed her the wrong way.

"I am." She folded her arms beneath her breasts and tilted her chin up. "And you are?"

She imbued those words with every last ounce of Southern haughtiness she could manage. Sometimes having a family who descended from the *Mayflower* and who boasted a signer of the Declaration of Independence, as well as at least six Patriots who'd fought in the American War of Independence was a good thing. Even if her family had sunk into that sort of gentile poverty that had hit generations of Southerners after Reconstruction, she had her pride and her heritage—and her mother's refined voice telling her that no one had the right to make her feel as if she wasn't good enough for them.

He did something very odd then. He bent slightly at the waist before touching his forehead, lips and heart. Then he stood there so straight and tall and, well, stately, that she got a tingle in her belly. She imagined him in desert robes, doing that very same thing, and gooey warmth flooded her in places that hadn't gotten warm in a very long time.

"I am Rashid bin Zaid al-Hassan."

The door opened again and this time another man entered. He was also in a suit, but he was wearing a headset and she realized with a start that he must be a bodyguard. A quick glance at the street in front of the shop revealed a long, black limousine and another man in a suit. And another stationed on the far side of the street, dark sunglasses covering his eyes as he looked up and down for any signs of trouble.

The one who'd just entered the shop stood by the door without moving. The man before her didn't even seem to notice his presence. Or, more likely, he was so accustomed to it that he ignored it on purpose.

"What can I help you with Mr., er, Rashid." It was the only name she could remember from that string of names he'd spoken.

The man at the door stiffened, but the man before her lifted an eyebrow as if he were somehow amused.

"You have something of mine, Miss Sloane. And I want it back."

A fine sheen of sweat broke out on her upper lip. She hoped like hell he couldn't see it. First of all, it wasn't ladylike. Second, she sensed that any nervousness on her part would be an advantage for him. This was the kind of man who pounced on weakness like a ravenous cat.

"I don't believe we've ever done business with any Rashids, but if we accidentally packed up some of your wife's good silver with our own, you may, of course, have it back."

He no longer looked amused. In fact, he looked downright furious. "You do not have my silver, Miss Sloane."

He took a step toward her then, his large form as graceful and silent as a cat. He was so close she could smell him. He wasn't wearing heavy cologne, but he had a scent like hot summer breezes and crisp spices. Her fanciful imagination conjured up a desert oasis, waving palm trees, a cool spring, an Arabian stallion—and this man, dressed in desert robes like Omar Sharif or Peter O'Toole.

It was a delicious mirage. And disconcerting as hell.

Sheridan put her hand out and smoothed it over the edge of the counter as she tried to appear casual. "If you could just inform me what it is, I'll take a l-look and see if I can find it."

Damn her voice for quavering.

"I doubt you could."

His gaze dropped to her middle, lingered. It took several moments, but then her stomach began a long, slow free fall into nothingness. He couldn't possibly mean—

Oh, no. No, no, no...

But his head lifted and his eyes met hers and she knew he was not here for the family silver.

"How...?" she began. Sheridan swallowed hard. This was unbelievable. An incredible breach of confidentiality. She would sue that clinic into the next millennium. "They wouldn't tell me a thing about you. How did you get them to reveal my information?"

For one wild moment, she hoped he didn't know what she was talking about. That this was indeed some sort of misunderstanding with a tall, beautiful Arab male who meant something entirely different than she thought. He would blink, shake his head, inform her that she had accidentally packed a small family heirloom—though she'd never done such a thing before—when she'd catered his event. Then he would describe it and she would go searching for it as though her life depended on it. Anything to be rid of him and quiet this flame raging inside her as he moved even closer than before.

But she knew, deep down, that he did know what she meant. That there was no misunderstanding.

"I am a powerful man, Miss Sloane. I get what I want. Besides, imagine the scandal were it to become known that an American facility had made such a mistake." His voice dripped of self-righteousness. "Impregnating some random woman with a potential heir to the throne of Kyr? And then refusing to inform the king of the child's whereabouts?"

He shook his head while her insides turned to ice as she tried to process what he'd just said.

"It would not happen," he continued. "It did not happen. As you see."

Sheridan found herself slumping against the counter, her eyes glued to this man's face while the rest of the room began to darken and fade. "D-did you say *king*? They gave me a king's sperm?"

She pressed a shaky hand to her forehead. Her throat was dry, so dry. And her belly wanted to heave. She'd thought this couldn't possibly get worse. She'd been wrong. She swallowed the acidic bitterness and focused on the man before her.

"They did, Miss Sloane."

Oh, my God. Her brain stopped working. She'd thought he was the one whose sperm she'd gotten— he'd said she had something of his, right?—but a king would not come to her shop and tell her these things. A king would also not look so dark and dangerous.

This was someone else. An official. Perhaps even an ambassador. Or an enforcer.

It was easy to believe this man could be hired muscle. He was tall and broad, and his eyes were chips of dark ice. His voice was frosty and utterly compelling. He had come to tell her about this king and to—to...?

She couldn't imagine what he'd come here for. What he expected of her.

Sheridan worked hard to force out the words before the nausea overwhelmed her. "Please tell the king that I'm sorry. I understand how difficult this must be, but he's not the only one affected. My sister—"

She pressed her hand to her mouth as bile rose in her throat. What would she say to Annie? Her fragile sister would implode, she just knew it.

"Sorry is not enough, Miss Sloane. It is not nearly enough."

She swallowed the nausea. Her voice was thready when she spoke. "Then I don't—"

"Are you quite all right?" He was beginning to look alarmed. A much more intriguing look than the angry one he'd been giving her a moment ago.

"I'm fine." Except she didn't feel fine. She felt hot and sweaty and sick to her stomach.

"You look green."

"It's the heat. And the hormones," she added. She pushed away from the counter, her limbs shaking with the effort of holding herself upright. "I should sit down, I think."

She started to take a step, but her knees didn't want to function quite right. Mr. Rashid—or whatever his name was—lashed out and wrapped an arm around her. She found herself wedged tightly against a firm, hard, warm body. Her nerve endings started to crackle and snap with fresh heat.

It was too much, too much, and yet she couldn't get

away. Briefly, a small corner of her brain admitted that she didn't *want* to get away.

He spoke, his voice seeming farther away than before. The words were beautiful, musical, but he did not seem to be speaking them to her. And then he swept her up into his arms as if she weighed nothing and strode across her store on long legs. Her office door opened and he went and sat her down on the small couch she kept for meeting with clients.

She didn't want to let him go, but she did. Her gaze fluttered over to the entry, where saw a wide-eyed Tiffany standing there, and one of the suit-clad men, who reached in and closed the door, leaving Sheridan alone with Mr. Rashid.

He sank down on one knee beside the couch and pressed a hand to her head. She knew what he would find. She was clammy and hot and she uttered a feeble protest. The door opened again and Tiffany appeared with a glass of ice water and a folded cloth.

Sheridan took it and sipped gratefully, letting the coolness wash through her as she closed her eyes and breathed. Someone put the cool cloth on her forehead and she reached up to clutch it because it felt so nice.

She didn't know how long she sat there, holding the cloth and sipping the water, but when she finally opened her eyes and looked up, Mr. Rashid was still there, sitting across from her in one of the pretty Queen Anne chairs she'd bought from a local antiques shop. He looked ridiculous in it, far too big and masculine, but he also looked as if he didn't care.

"What happened?" His voice was not as hard as it had been. She didn't think he was capable of gentleness, and this was as close to it as he got.

"Too much stress, too many hormones, too much summer heat." She shrugged. "Take your pick, Mr. Rashid. It could be any of them."

He muttered something in Arabic and then he was looking at her, his burning gaze penetrating deep. There was frost in his voice. "Miss Sloane, I think you misunderstand something about what's going on here."

Her heart skipped. Why was he so beautiful? And why was he such a contrast? He was fire and ice in one person. Hot eyes, cold heart. It almost made her sad. But why should it? She did not know him, and what she did know so far hadn't endeared him to her. "Do I?"

"Indeed. I am not Mr. Rashid."

"Then who are you?"

He looked haughty and her stomach threatened to heave again. Because there was something familiar about that face, she realized. She'd seen it on the news a few weeks ago.

He spoke, his voice clear and firm and lightly accented. "I am King Rashid bin Zaid al-Hassan, the Great Protector of my people, the Lion of Kyr and Defender of the Throne. And you, Miss Sloane, may be carrying my heir."

CHAPTER TWO

THE WOMAN LOOKED positively frightened. Rashid did not relish making her so, but perhaps it was better if he did. Better if she agreed without question to what she must do. She could not be allowed to stay here in this…this *shop*…and work as if she did not potentially carry the next king of Kyr in her womb.

He had spent the long hours of the flight researching Sheridan Sloane. She was twenty-six, unmarried and part owner of this business that planned and catered various parties in the local area. She had one older sister, a woman named Ann Sloane Campbell, who had been trying to conceive a child for six years now.

Sheridan was supposed to carry the baby her sister could not conceive. It was an admirable enough thing to do, he supposed, but since he'd now been dragged into it, he had his own legacy to protect. If her sister was upset about it, then he could not help that.

Sheridan Sloane was a pretty woman, though not especially striking in any way. She was of average height and small boned, with golden-blond hair of indeterminate length since it was wrapped in a coil on her head. Her eyes, wide as she gazed at him, were a blue so dark they were almost violet. There were bruises under them, marring her pale skin.

She was tired and overwhelmed and no match for him. She was the sort of woman who did what she was told, in spite of her small rebellion earlier. She was a pleaser, and he was not. He would order her to come with him, and she would do it.

But, as he watched her, her body seemed to grow stiff. He could see the shutters closing, the walls rising. It was an unpleasant surprise to find she had a backbone after all. Still, he'd broken stronger people—men, usually—than her.

She shifted until she was sitting fully upright, her feet swinging onto the floor now. She faced him across a small tea table, her eyes snapping with fresh sparks. He was intrigued in spite of himself.

"*You* are the king? You could have said that right away, you know, and saved us a few steps."

He arched an eyebrow. "Yes, but what would you have done then? You nearly fainted when I informed you that you had been inseminated with a king's sperm."

Her lips pursed. "I nearly fainted because it's been a long, stressful day. Do you have any idea how my sister took the news, Mr.—oh, hell, I have no idea what to call you."

"*Your Majesty* will work."

Her face flooded with color. And there went that little chin again, thrusting into the air. Who was she trying to convince that she was a tigress? Him, or herself? Before he could ask, she imbued her voice with steel.

"I realize we find ourselves in an untenable situation, but someone inserted your sperm into my body a few days ago. I think that warrants a first-name basis, don't you? At least until this is resolved."

Rashid would have coughed if he'd been drinking anything. As it was, he could only glare at her. She shocked him. Oddly, she also amused him. It was this last that should alarm him, but in fact it was the first normal thing that had happened to him since he'd taken the throne two months ago.

He shouldn't allow any familiarity between them. But she might be carrying his child—*his child!*—and it seemed wrong to treat her as a complete stranger. He thought of Daria, of her soft brown eyes and swollen belly, and he wanted to stand up and flee this room. But of course he could not do so. He was a king now, and he had a responsibility to his nation. To his people.

And to his child.

Daria would want him to be kind to this woman. So he would try, though it went against his nature to be kind to anyone. He was not cruel; he was indifferent. He'd learned to be so over the hellish years of his childhood. If you did not care, people couldn't hurt you.

When you did... Well, he knew what happened when you cared. He had the scars on his soul to prove it. The only person he cared about these days was Kadir, and that was as much as he was capable of.

He inclined his head briefly. "You may call me Rashid." And then he added, "I suggest, however, you do not do it in front of my staff. They will not understand the informality."

She wrapped her arms around herself and rubbed her upper arms almost absently. "You can call me Sheridan, then. And I don't see why you need worry about your staff. We won't know for another week if there's a baby.

I can call you with the information, if you'd like. Then we can decide what to do if it's necessary."

He blinked at her. She truly did not understand. Or she was being stubbornly obtuse on purpose. His temper rose anew.

"You will not call me."

She frowned at his tone. "Fine. You can call me. Either way, we'll work it out."

He clenched his fingers into fists in his lap. Stubborn woman!

"There is nothing to work out. You have been artificially inseminated with my sperm. You might be carrying the next king of Kyr. There is no possible choice other than the one I offer you now."

"I honestly don't think—"

"Silence, Miss Sloane," he snapped, coming to the end of his tether. "You are not here to think. You will accompany me to the airport, where you will board the royal jet. We will be in Kyr by morning, and you will be shown every courtesy while we await the results. Should you fail to conceive my child, you will be escorted home again."

Her jaw had dropped as he talked. He tried not to focus on the pink curve of her lower lip. It glistened with moisture and he found himself wanting to lean forward and touch his tongue just there to see if she tasted as sweet and delicate as she looked.

The thought shocked him. And angered him. He did not want this woman.

She was shaking her head almost violently now. A lock of hair dropped from her twist and curved in front of her cheekbone. She impatiently tucked it behind an ear.

"I can't drop everything and go away with you! I have a business to run. And my bank account, unlike yours, I'm sure, isn't bursting with money. No way. No way in hell."

Her response stunned him. He shot to his feet then, his temper beginning to boil. He had a country to run and one crisis after another to solve these days. He had a council waiting for him, a stack of dossiers on potential brides to scour through and an upcoming meeting with kings from surrounding nations to discuss oil production, mineral rights and reciprocity agreements.

And yet he was being thwarted by one small, irritating woman who refused to give an inch of ground in this battle. A people pleaser? She didn't look as if she cared one bit about pleasing him at the moment.

Rashid gave her the look that made the palace staff tremble. "I wasn't giving you a choice, Miss Sloane."

She sucked in a breath, and he knew he had her.

But then her face reddened and her eyes flashed purple fire and Rashid stood there in shock.

"You think you have the right to make decisions for me? This is America and I don't have to go anywhere with you. Not only that, but I *won't* go. If I'm pregnant, we'll figure it out. But as of this moment, we do not know that. I can't just leave because you wish it. Nor do I intend to."

His entire body vibrated with fury. He was not accustomed to being told no. Not by his employees at Hassan Oil—a company he'd built on his own and still owned to this day, even if he'd had to turn over the day-to-day operations to a CEO—not by his staff in the palace, not by anyone anywhere in the past several years. He was an al-Hassan, with money and influence, and people did not tell him no.

And now he was a king, and they *really* did not tell him no.

But Sheridan Sloane had. She sat there on her couch, looking pale and delicate and too small to safely carry a baby for nine months, and spoke to him like he was her gardener. It infuriated him. And stunned him, too, if he was willing to admit it.

No matter how much he admired her fighting spirit, he would not be merciful. He'd left mercy behind a long time ago.

"Miss Sloane," he said, very coolly and clearly. "It would be unwise to anger me. This business you run?" He snapped his fingers. "I could destroy it in a moment. I could destroy *you* in a moment. Continue to defy me, and I shall."

Sheridan's pulse skipped and slid like it was tumbling down a hill and couldn't find purchase. He'd just threatened her. Threatened Dixie Doin's. At first she wanted to laugh him off. But then she looked at him standing there, at his tall, dark form and the dark glitter of his eyes, and knew he was not only perfectly serious, but that he was also probably capable of accomplishing it.

He was a king. *A king!*

Of an incredibly rich, oil-producing nation in the Arabian Desert. She knew where Kyr was. Hadn't they just had a crisis that was plastered all over the news? The king had been very ill and no one had known who his successor was going to be.

She'd found it fascinating that a monarch could choose his successor from among his sons, and puzzling that he had not done so by that point. They were grown after all, and he must surely know which of them was best suited to the job.

The fact he had not done so surely spoke volumes about him—or about his children. She wasn't sure which.

But the crisis had passed and Kyr had a king. This man. Rashid bin Zaid al-Hassan. Oh, yes, his name was imprinted on her memory now. She would never forget it again as long as she lived.

Still, she had not been raised to blindly follow orders and she would not start now. Even though he terrified her on some level. He was so cold and angry, and he was a king. But he was not *her* king. Hadn't her ancestors fought to divest themselves of kings?

Sheridan cleared her throat. "It's only seven more days until the test. You could stay in Savannah. Or maybe you could come back when the results are due. It seems far simpler than what you're proposing."

He did not look in the least bit appeased. "Does it, now? Because your business, which has another owner and employees to help, needs your presence far more than a nation needs her king, yes? How extraordinary, Miss Sloane."

Sheridan pushed the stray lock of hair behind her ear again. How did he manage to make her feel petty when all she wanted was to continue to live her life as normally as possible until the moment when she found out if everything was going to change or not? She didn't even want to contemplate what it would mean if she *were* carrying this man's child.

A royal baby. Madness.

She twisted the cloth that she'd earlier pressed to her

forehead. "I didn't mean to suggest any such thing. But yes, my business is important to me, and I can't leave Kelly to do everything by herself. I have menus to plan, and supplies to buy—"

"And I have a peace agreement to broker and a nation to run." He'd already dismissed her, she realized. He slipped a phone from his pocket and put it to his ear. And then he was speaking in mellifluous Arabic to someone on the other end. When he finished, cool dark eyes raked over her again. "You will come, Miss Sloane, and you will do it now. My lawyer has instructions to purchase your loan from the bank. I assure you he will accomplish this, as I am willing to offer far more than this business is worth."

Sheridan's jaw dropped even as a fine sheen of sweat broke out between her breasts. He was quite easily the most obnoxious man she'd ever met. And the most attractive.

No. The most evil man. Yes, definitely that. Evil.

Because she knew he was not bluffing. A man who had the power to obtain her information from the fertility clinic—information protected by law—as if it was freely available to anyone who asked, was not a man to make bluffs.

He had the power to buy Dixie Doin's and do whatever he wanted with it. Close the doors. Put people out of work. Ruin hers and Kelly's dream. She didn't care so much for herself right now, but Kelly? Kelly had been so kind when Sheridan told her she wanted to have a baby for Chris and Annie, even though it would impact the business for her to be pregnant.

Not to mention the impact while Sheridan went through the insemination process. You just didn't show up at the clinic one day and ask for sperm after all, and Kelly had stoically accepted it all without even a hint of disapproval or fear.

So how could she allow this overbearing, rude tyrant of a man to ruin Kelly's dream just because Sheridan wanted so very desperately to defy him?

She couldn't.

She rose on shaky feet and faced him. He was so very tall, so overwhelming, but she faced him head on with her chin up and her back straight. She pulled in a breath that shook with anger.

"Am I to be allowed to collect any clothing? Surely I need my passport."

She thought he would look satisfied or triumphant at her capitulation, but he in fact looked bored. As if he'd never doubted she would agree. She hated him in that moment, and Sheridan had never hated anyone in her life.

"You do not need a passport if you are traveling with me. But we will make a brief stop at your home. You will get what you need for the next week."

Fear skirted the edges of her anger. Was she truly proposing to board a plane to a far-off nation where she didn't speak the language and didn't understand the customs? But how could she refuse? If she did, he would ruin Dixie Doin's and put them out of business. All the money she and Kelly had invested would be gone.

But what happened in a week? Would he force her to stay in Kyr forever if she were carrying his child?

Sheridan put a hand to her mouth to press back the sudden cry welling up in her throat. In reality, she was being kidnapped by a desert king, forced into a harem for all she knew, and there was nothing she could do about it.

Not if she wanted to protect her friend and her employees. Not to mention Annie and Chris. What would this man do to them if she didn't comply? Could he get Chris fired? He could certainly buy the loan on their house—they'd mortgaged it to the hilt to pay for one failed fertility treatment after another—and then what?

Ice formed in her veins. He would throw them out of their home with no sympathy or shame. She could see it in his eyes, in the hard set to his jaw. This man was ruthless and incapable of empathy.

"How do I know I'll be safe?" Sheridan asked, her voice smaller than she would have liked.

His brows drew down swiftly as his anger flared. "Safe? Do you think me a barbarian, Miss Sloane? A terrorist? I am a king and you are my honored guest. You will have every luxury for the duration of your stay in Kyr."

She swallowed at the vehemence in his tone. "And what if I'm pregnant? What then?"

Because she had to know. For herself, for the child. She had to know what this man would do, what he would expect.

His icy gaze sharpened in a way that sent a shiver rippling through her. "You were planning to give the child away. Why would this change?"

An unexpected arrow of pain dived into her belly, hollowing out a space there. Yes, she'd been planning to give the baby up. But to her sister. Carrying a child for Annie and Chris was one thing. She would not be the baby's mother, even if she was the biological mother, but she would still be part of his or her life. An aunt who would spoil the child of her body rotten, kiss and hug him, buy him presents, shower him with love.

But to give her baby to a stranger, even if the stranger was the other half of the child's DNA?

It went against everything she felt inside.

"I won't give up my baby." Her voice was hoarse. But what choice did she have? He would destroy everyone she loved.

His eyes glittered like ice and she trembled inside. "Yes, I see," he murmured after a long moment. "I am a king, and my son will be a king. Why would you willingly relinquish a child so valuable?"

Sheridan had never wanted to harm another human being in her life, but if she could slap this one and get away with it, she would. He was evil, hateful. Her face flooded with heat and her stomach flipped, but this time it wasn't a sickening flip so much as an angry one.

"You're disgusting," she spat. "I don't care how amazing and fabulous you think you are, but until today I'd never heard of you." *A small lie.* "My feelings about this baby have nothing to do with who you are and everything to do with the fact he *or* she is half mine."

She lifted a shaking finger and pointed at the door. He didn't own her, and until they knew whether or not she was pregnant, she wasn't going anywhere with him. It was a risk, but she needed time to figure out what to do, time to consult an attorney and talk to her family. If she left the country with him, it was over. He would own her and any baby within her.

"You should leave."

He stared at her for a long moment, that handsome

countenance wreathed in dark anger. And then he burst out laughing. It shocked her. The sound was so rich, so beautiful. And chilling in a way.

"I don't see what's so funny," she said, her heart fluttering like a hummingbird's wings. "I am perfectly serious. I'll see you in court, *Your Majesty.*"

The door opened behind her. She turned, hoping it was Kelly or even Tiffany coming to save her, but it was merely one of the bodyguards.

"The car is ready, Your Majesty."

"Excellent."

Sheridan turned toward the king, but he'd moved when she'd been looking at his bodyguard. Before she knew what he was about, he swept an arm behind her knees and jerked her into his arms. Once more, she was pressed against his hard, taut body, his scent in her nostrils, conjuring images of heat and sand and cool water. A hot, tight feeling flared beneath her skin, burning through her and stopping the breath in her chest until he was halfway across the storefront.

There were customers, she noted vaguely. And Tiffany, who looked up as Rashid al-Hassan walked by with Sheridan in his arms. Tiffany didn't even look surprised, the silly girl. She just looked bored, like always.

Sheridan knew she needed to scream. She needed to get these people's attention and get this man to put her down immediately. She felt her lungs working again—of course they'd never stopped, but she hadn't felt them, hadn't felt anything but heat and unbearable want when he'd picked her up—and she sucked in air, preparing to release it in the most eardrum-shattering cry she could manage.

But she never got the chance because Rashid al-

Hassan—the Great Protector of his people, the Lion of Kyr and Defender of the Throne—dropped his mouth over hers and silenced her.

CHAPTER THREE

RASHID HADN'T MEANT to kiss her. But the damned woman was going to scream and he could not allow it. So he'd silenced her in the only way he could.

Her mouth was soft and pliant and sweet. He took advantage of the fact her lips were open to slip his tongue inside and stroke across the velvety softness of her mouth. She didn't move for a long moment and he began to wonder if she would bite him.

She was certainly capable of it. He'd not encountered a woman such as this one in…well, ever. Usually, women softened around him. Their eyes got big and wide and their mouths fell open invitingly. They sighed. They purred. They pouted.

They did not act as if he were poison. They did not glare daggers at him and spit fire and tell him to get out in prim little voices that belonged to the starchy librarians he'd encountered when he'd gone to university.

Sheridan's breath hitched in and he knew he had her. Knew she was his, for the moment.

He deepened the kiss, demanding more of a response from her. He had to keep her mouth busy and her thoughts focused on him until he could get her out of the store and into the car. It was a mercenary act on his part and he had no trouble pushing it as far as he needed in order to keep the fool woman silenced.

Her mouth opened a little wider, her tongue stroking tentatively against his.

Rashid's body turned to stone in a heartbeat. He had not expected that. But then he reminded himself there was a reason for his reaction. It had been a while since he'd had a woman. Being king had taken all his time these past couple of months. He was no longer a private citizen. No longer a man who could walk into a club, spot a gorgeous woman and take her home for a night of hot sex and no recriminations.

He was a king, and kings did not go anywhere without an entourage. They also did not pick up women and take them back to the palace for sex.

Certainly, he could have sent for a woman. But what kind of man would he be if he sent others to pick out women for him for the express purpose of having sex?

He was no prude, and he figured what people did with their bodies was their own business, but he'd never paid for sex in his life and he wasn't going to start now. Because that was what it would be if he ordered a woman for the evening as if she were an item on a room service menu.

Oh, she would not be a common prostitute. She wouldn't be a prostitute at all. But that didn't make it any better in his mind.

Another reason why he was going to have to choose a wife soon from the handful of princesses and heiresses his council had recommended. And yet he couldn't imagine having sex with any of the women whose dossiers he'd been sent thus far, much less facing one of them across a breakfast table for the rest of his life.

Damn Kadir for forcing him to take the throne. Yes, Rashid had always wanted to be king, but he hadn't quite realized how very confined he would feel. He was a ruler, a man with the power of life and death over his subjects, a man with absolute authority—and he had no private life to speak of. No one with whom he could share the simple pleasures.

He had not thought that would bother him so much, but it did. He missed Daria. Missed having someone in his life who loved him because of his flaws, not in spite of them. But Daria was gone, and there was no one.

Sheridan shifted in his arms and he felt her confusion, her hesitation. She was fighting herself, fighting her nature, and if he'd learned anything about her in these last few minutes, he knew she would conquer her baser instincts and fight against him soon enough.

A people pleaser? Perhaps she was, but she was not a Rashid pleaser. He knew that well enough now.

Because he was angry, because he was frustrated, he took the kiss to another level, ravaged her mouth like a man starved. He wanted to confuse her, wanted to keep her quiet and, hell, yes, he wanted to disconcert her. How dare she disobey him?

She gripped his lapels, twisted her fists in them. And then she met him as savagely as he met her. His body responded with a surge of heat he'd not felt in a long time. Her breath grew shallower and she made a sound in her throat.

He broke the kiss then, uncertain if he was pushing her too far too fast. Alarmed at his body's reaction to her, he tucked her head against his chest before she could speak.

"Quiet, *habibti*. Let me get you home." He smiled

at the women in the shop who threw them astonished looks and then strode outside and down the front steps before Sheridan could regain her ability to think clearly.

The car door swung smoothly open and Rashid bent to place Sheridan on the seat. She was so small and light that it was like handling a piece of china. He didn't want to break her, but he also knew she was stronger than she looked.

He got in beside her, the door sealed shut, and the car slid smoothly away from the curb and down the sun-dappled streets. The partition was up between them and the driver, and silence hung heavy in the car.

"You kidnapped me." Her voice was small and frightened and Rashid swung to look at her. Her golden hair gleamed in the sunlight that filtered into the car and her eyes were wide with fear. He did not enjoy that, but he told himself it was necessary. Whatever it took to force her to obey.

Rashid sat back and tugged a sleeve into place. He was not precisely pleased with himself, and yet he'd done what had to be done. A man like him claimed his child. And the woman carrying it.

"I did warn you."

"You said you weren't a barbarian." Her hands clenched into fists in her lap. She wore a pink dress and smelled like cotton candy and Rashid wanted to lean into her and press his nose to her hair.

"Indeed."

"Then I must be confused, because I thought barbarians did precisely what you just did. Or did you perhaps say you weren't a *barber* and I simply misunderstood?"

And there was the attitude. Clearly, she was not

damaged in any way. It gave his temper permission to emerge.

"I am a desert king. Of course I'm a barbarian. Isn't that what you believe? Because I speak Arabic and come from a nation where the men wear robes and the women are veiled, that I must surely be less civilized than you?"

Her lips pressed into a tight, white line. "Even if I didn't believe it, don't you think you just proved it? What kind of man kidnaps a woman he's never met just because there's been a mix-up in the clinic?"

Her eyes were flashing purple fire again. For some reason, that intrigued him almost as much as it angered him.

"A man who has no time for arguments. A man who holds the lives of an entire nation in his hands and who needs to get back to his duties. A man who has no reason whatsoever to trust that the woman carrying his heir will turn over the child when it is time."

Her eyes darkened with anger. "I won't give up my baby just because you wish it."

"You were willing to do so for your sister."

"That's different and you know it. I would still be part of the child's life. A beloved aunt." She shook her head suddenly. "Why are we arguing about this? There's no guarantee I'm pregnant. It doesn't always work the first time."

"Perhaps not, but I will take no chances. My child will be a king one day, Sheridan Sloane. He will not be raised in an apartment in America by a woman who works sixteen-hour days and ignores him in favor of her own interests."

Her skin flushed bright red. "How dare you?" she growled. "How dare you act as if you know me when you don't have the faintest clue? I would never ignore my child. Never!"

He infuriated her. No, she'd not planned for a child in her life—the baby was supposed to be Annie's—but the fact he would sit there and smugly inform her that he believed she would neglect her baby in favor of her business made her defensive and angry. Of course she would still have to work, but she would figure it out.

Except there would be no figuring it out. This man was a king, and if she was pregnant, he wasn't going to abandon her to raise the child alone. He would be a part of her life from now on.

Sheridan shivered at the thought. How did one work out custody with a king?

"This baby is supposed to be Annie's," she said, working hard to keep the panic from her voice. "I hadn't planned on a baby of my own, but that doesn't mean I would be a bad or neglectful mother. And I won't let you steamroll right over me just because you're a king. I have rights, too."

His eyes were hooded as he studied her. Did he have to be so damned beautiful? She'd never seen hair so black or eyes so fathomless. If he was an actor, she'd wonder if his cheekbones were the work of a plastic surgeon. His face was a study in perfection, angles and planes and smooth, bronzed skin. He was golden, as if he spent long hours under the sun, and there were fine lines at the corners of his eyes where they crinkled as he studied her.

Her gaze focused on his mouth, those firm, beautiful lips that had pressed against hers. She felt a fresh wave of heat creeping up her throat. He'd only kissed her to shut her up, but she'd forgotten for long minutes why that was a bad thing. His mouth had ravaged hers and she'd only wanted more. Even now, her lips tingled with the memory of his assault on them. She was bruised and swollen, but in a good way. In the kind of way that said a woman had been well kissed and had enjoyed every moment of it.

Sheridan dropped her gaze from his, suddenly self-conscious. It had been a long time since she'd kissed anyone. A long time since she'd lain in bed with a man and felt the heat and wonder of joining her body with another. She hadn't thought she was deprived. Rather, she'd thought she was busy and that she just didn't have time to invest in a relationship.

But now that he'd kissed her, she felt as if she'd been starving for affection. As if the drought in her sex life was suddenly much larger than she'd thought it was. How could he make her feel this way when he was not a nice man?

After her last relationship, a short-lived romance with a womanizing accountant who'd made her feel like the only woman in his life until the moment she'd caught him with his tongue down someone else's throat, she'd vowed to only date nice, trustworthy men.

Rashid al-Hassan was definitely not a nice man. Or trustworthy. But he made things hum and spark inside her, damn him. She'd only kissed him once, but already she wanted to lean forward, tunnel her fingers through that thick mane of hair and claim his lips for another round.

Insanity, Sheridan.

"Surely there is something you want more than this child," he said smoothly, cutting into her thoughts, and her heart began to beat a crazy rhythm.

"No."

He lifted an eyebrow in that superior arch she despised. "Money? I can give you quite a lot of it, you know. Once our divorce is final, you could be a wealthy woman."

Divorce? Her stomach fell to the floor at the thought of being married to this man for even an hour.

"I don't want your money. And I'm definitely not going to marry you." There was only one thing she wanted. It also wasn't something he could give. Unless he had the power of miracles.

She was certain he did not. If a dozen doctors couldn't fix Annie's fertility issues, then neither could a king, no matter how arrogant and entitled.

"Everyone has a price, Sheridan. And if you are pregnant, you most certainly *will* be my wife. In name only, of course. My child will not be born illegitimate."

Her name on his lips was too exotic, too sensual. It stroked over her senses, set up a drumbeat in her veins. And embarrassed her because he clearly wasn't suffering from an unwanted attraction, too. *In name only.*

"All I want is a baby for my sister. And I intend to give her one."

"After you give me my heir, of course."

Her lips tightened. "You make it sound so cold and clinical. As if you're selecting a prized broodmare to give you a champion foal."

The car glided through the streets. Outside the windows, people behaved as usual. Tourists chattered excitedly and pointed from their seats in the horse-drawn carriages that traveled through Savannah's historic district. Part of Sheridan wanted to open the door and run when the car came to a standstill in traffic.

But there was no escape. Not like this anyway. The only way to fight a man like him was with lawyers, and even that was no guarantee because he could afford far better representation than she could.

"It is a clinical thing, is it not?" His voice was rich and smooth and crusted in ice. "We have never been intimate, and yet you may be pregnant with my child. Put there with a syringe in a doctor's office. How is this not clinical?"

Sheridan swallowed the lump in her throat. "I was supposed to be having a baby for my sister. With my brother-in-law's sperm. What would you propose we do differently?"

Of course, it would have been cheaper and easier for her and Chris to just sleep together until she was pregnant, but what a horrifying thought that was. He was her sister's husband and her friend, and there was no way in hell. Lying on a table with her feet in stirrups might be clinical, but it was the only solution.

He ignored the question. "Nevertheless, it is my sperm you received. How do you think this makes me feel?"

She swung around to look at him. Up to this point, she hadn't thought of how it must have affected him. She was almost ashamed of herself for the lapse. Almost.

That ended when she met his gaze. He was looking at her as coldly as ever. King Rashid al-Hassan was a block of ice. A block of ice that had burned strangely hot when he'd pressed his mouth to hers.

Sheridan nervously smoothed the fabric of her dress. "I admit I hadn't thought of it. I imagine you're angry."

"That is one way of putting it." His dark eyes flashed. "I am a king and my country has laws I must obey. You may think us barbarians, but there is a certain logic to the king depositing sperm in a bank outside his nation. It was never meant to be used. Or not under normal circumstances."

She didn't want to think about what kind of circumstances would precipitate using the sperm, but she imagined it would involve his untimely death and no heir to follow him to the throne. She might not like him, but she wouldn't wish him dead.

Yet.

"No, I can see how it might be useful. It's forward thinking to do such a thing."

"Apparently not, when mistakes such as this are allowed to occur."

Sheridan put her hand over her middle instinctively. Fresh anger swirled in her belly. "Calling this baby a mistake is unlikely to inspire my confidence, don't you think? You want me to give him or her up, but you speak as if you don't care about him other than as your heir."

"He will be my heir. Until there is another child, at least."

Her heart thumped. "Because you can choose your successor in Kyr. Of course." Her fingers tightened over her flat belly. She didn't even know if there was a baby in there yet, but already she felt protective and angry.

"It is the way of our people."

Maybe so, but it seemed a horrible way for children to grow up. Talk about an unhealthy sense of competition. "You weren't chosen until right before your father died. How did that make you feel?"

His eyes glittered hot and she had the feeling she'd tweaked the lion's tail. He looked at her as if he would snap her in two with one fierce bite. Yet his voice was still as icy as ever.

"You push me too far, Sheridan Sloane. You should be more cautious."

Maybe she should, but she couldn't seem to do so. "Why? Because you might kidnap me or something?"

His dark eyes raked over her. "Or something."

CHAPTER FOUR

KYR WAS HOT. Savannah was hot, too, but it was also muggy because they were so near the ocean. Kyr was not muggy, though the Persian Gulf was nearby. It was just hot, with the kind of heat that sucked all the moisture right out of you and left you gasping for breath. It was also beautiful, which Sheridan had not expected.

The desert sands were almost red and the dunes rose high in the distance, undulating like waves on the ocean. As they'd approached the city from the airport, she'd viewed tall date palms that grew in ordered rows. Sheridan had been in the same car with Rashid, but once they'd arrived at the palace she'd been taken to what appeared to be a lonely wing with no one else in it. If he had a harem, this was not it.

She still couldn't believe she was here. She paced around the cavernous room of the suite she'd been shown to and marveled at the architecture. There were soaring arches, mosaics of delicate and colorful tile and painted walls and ceilings. There was a sunken area in the middle of the room, lined with colorful cushions, and above her the ceiling soared into a dome shape that was punctuated with small windows, which let light filter down to the floor and spread in warm puddles across its gleaming tiles.

It was a beautiful and lonely space. Sheridan sank onto the cushions and sat by herself in that big room, listening to nothing. There was no television, no radio, no telephone that she could find. She had her cell phone, but no signal.

She leaned back against the cushions and swore she wouldn't cry. For someone like her, a person who craved light and sound and activity, this silent cavern was torture. Just yesterday—had it really been only yesterday?—she'd been surrounded by people at Mrs. Lands's party. And then she'd been in her office, with her beautiful store outside her door, listening to the sounds of people on the street and the low hum of her radio as it played the latest top-forty hits.

She hadn't exactly been happy, not after the news from the clinic and Annie's reaction, but she'd been far more content than she'd given herself credit for. Tears pushed against her eyes at the thought of all she'd left behind, but she didn't let them fall.

Rashid al-Hassan was a tyrant. He'd swept into her life, swept her up against her will and deposited her here alone. And all because the stupid sperm bank had used the wrong sperm. She'd wanted to give her sister a precious gift, but she was here, a veritable prisoner to a rude, arrogant, sinfully attractive man who had all the warmth and friendliness of an iceberg.

He hadn't let her call anyone until they were on his plane. She was still astounded at the opulence of the royal jet. It was one of the most amazing things she'd ever seen, with leather and gold and fine carpets. The bath had even been made of marble. Marble on a jet!

LYNN RAYE HARRIS   51

It had also been bigger than her bathroom in her apartment. There were uniformed flight attendants who performed their duties with bright smiles and soft words—and deep bows to their king. She could hardly forget that sight. Any time anyone on that plane had come close to Rashid al-Hassan, they'd dipped almost to the floor. He hadn't even deigned to notice half the time.

It stunned her and unnerved her. She kept telling herself he was just a man, but there hadn't been a single person on that plane who'd acted like he was. When she'd finally been allowed to phone Kelly and Chris—not Annie, goodness, no—she'd held the phone tightly in her hand and explained as best she could that she would be gone for the next week.

They'd taken the news of Rashid much better than she had. Kelly, always a hopeless romantic, had wanted to know if he was handsome and if she would have to marry him. Sheridan had clutched the phone tight and hadn't told her friend that even though Rashid expected her to marry him, she'd rather marry a shark. She'd just said they were taking this one day at a time and would deal with a pregnancy when and if it happened. As if Rashid was reasonable and kind instead of an unfeeling block of stone.

Chris had told her to be strong, and not to worry about Annie. It would all be fine, he'd said. She'd had to bite her lip to keep from crying at the thought of Chris telling her sister the news, but she'd thanked him and told him she'd be in touch.

She spread her fingers over her abdomen. What would become of her if there were a baby inside here?

She stared up at the beam of sunlight filtering into her prison and pressed her fist to her mouth to contain her sob. Nine months as his wife in name only, his prisoner, shut away from the world—and then he would coldly divorce her and send her on her way with empty arms.

Despair filled her until she thought she would choke with it. Soon there was a noise at the entrance to her prison. A woman in a dress and wearing a scarf over her head came in and sat a tray down on a table nearby. Sheridan shot to her feet and went over to where the woman was removing covers from dishes.

"That smells lovely." She was surprised when her stomach growled, especially considering how queasy she'd been feeling since Rashid had come to the store yesterday.

The woman gave her a polite smile. "His Majesty says you must eat, miss."

Must. Of course he did. And as much as she would love to defy him, she wasn't so stupid as to starve herself just to prove a point.

"Can you please tell me where His Majesty is? I would like to speak with him."

Because she was going to go quietly insane if she had to remain in this room alone with no stimulation. The books—and there were plenty of them—were written in Arabic.

The woman shook her head and kept smiling. "Eat, miss."

She gave Sheridan a half bow and glided gracefully toward the door. Sheridan thought about it for two seconds and then followed her. But the woman was through the door and the door shut before Sheridan could reach it.

She jerked it open only to be confronted with the same thing she'd been confronted with earlier: a man in desert robes standing in the corridor, arms crossed, sword strapped to his side. He looked at her no less coolly than his boss had.

"I want to speak to King Rashid," she said.

The man didn't move or speak.

Anger welled up inside her, pressing hard against the confines of her skin until she thought she might burst with it. She started toward the guard. He was big and broad, but she was determined that she would walk past him and keep going until she found people.

The man stepped into her path and she had to stop abruptly or collide nose first with his chest.

"Get out of my way." She glared up at him, but he didn't seem in the least bit concerned. She gathered her courage and ducked the other way. But he was there, in front of her, his big body blocking her progress.

Fury howled deep in her gut. She was in a strange place, being guarded by a huge man who wouldn't speak to her, and she was lonely and furious and scared all at once.

So she did something she had never done in her life. She stomped on his foot.

And gasped. Whatever he was wearing, it was a lot harder than her delicate little sandal. She resisted the urge to clutch her foot and hop around in circles. Barely. The mountain of a man didn't even make a noise. He just took her firmly by the arm and steered her back into the suite. And then he shut the door on her so that she stood there staring at the carved wood with her jaw hanging open. Her foot and her pride stung. She thought about yanking open the door and trying again, like an annoying fly, but she knew she'd only get more of the same from him.

She stood with her hands on her hips, her gaze moving around the room, her brain churning. And then she halted on the tray of food. The tray was big, solid, possibly made of silver. It would be heavy.

Sheridan closed her eyes and pulled in a deep breath. She wasn't really thinking of sneaking into the hall and braining the poor guard, was she? That wasn't nice. He was only doing what he'd been ordered to do. It wasn't polite to smack him with the tray when she really wanted to smack Rashid al-Hassan instead.

She opened her eyes again, continued her circuit of the room. There were windows. All that glass would make a hell of a noise if she busted it. Part of her protested that it was an extreme idea, that a lady didn't go around breaking other people's property. Worse, an architect who specialized in historical preservation didn't go around breaking windows in old palaces, even if the glass was a modern addition to the structure. Which she could tell by the tint and finish.

But this could hardly be termed a normal circumstance. King Rashid al-Hassan had already made the first move, and it hadn't been polite or considerate. So why should she be polite in return?

Game on....

Rashid had just settled in for lunch after a long morning spent in meetings with his council when Mostafa hurried into his office, a wide-eyed look on his face. The man dropped into a deep bow before rising again.

"Speak," Rashid said, knowing Mostafa would not do so until told.

"Majesty, it's the woman."

Rashid went still, his hand hovering over a dish of rice and chicken. He set the spoon down. *The woman* was such an inadequate description for Sheridan Sloane, but if he tried to point that out to Mostafa, the man would think him cracked in the head.

"What about her, Mostafa?"

"She has, er, broken a window. And she is asking to see you."

A prickle of alarm slid through him. "Is she hurt?"

"A few small cuts."

Rashid was on his feet in a second. Steely anger hardened in his veins as he strode out the door and down the corridors of the palace toward the women's quarters. He'd placed her there because it was supposed to be safe—and also because he didn't quite know what to do with her now that he had her here. He'd sent his father's remaining two wives to homes of their own, ostensibly in preparation for taking his own wife—or wives—but in truth he'd wanted to rid the palace of their presence.

They were women his father had married later in life, and so they were much younger than King Zaid had been. Rashid had no idea what kind of relationship his father had had with either of them, but they made him think too often of his father's tempestuous relationship with his own mother. Rashid would not live with women who reminded him of those dark days.

Palace workers dropped to their knees as he passed, a giant wave of obeisance that he hardly noticed. He kept going until he reached the women's suite and the mountainous form of Daoud, the guard he'd placed here.

Daoud fell to his knees and pressed his forehead to the floor. "Forgive me, Your Majesty."

"What happened?"

Daoud looked up from the floor and Rashid made an impatient motion. The man had been with him for years now, long before Rashid became king. Daoud stood. "The woman tried to leave. I prevented her."

"Did you harm her?" His voice was a whip and Daoud paled.

"No, Your Majesty. I took her by the arm, placed her inside the room and closed the door. A few minutes later, I heard the crash."

Rashid brushed past him and went into the room. One tall window was open to the outside. Hot air and fine grains of sand rushed inside along with the sounds of activity on the palace grounds below. Two men worked to clean up the glass that had blown across the floor.

Sheridan sat on cushions in the middle of the room, looking small and dejected. There were a couple of small red lines on her arms and his heart clenched tight. But the ice he lived with on a daily basis didn't fail him. It rushed in, filled all the dark corners of his soul and hardened any sympathetic feelings he may have had for her.

Sheridan looked up then. "And the mighty king has come to call."

"Out," Rashid said to the room in general. The servants who were busy picking up the glass rose and hurried out the door. A woman appeared from the direction of the bath. She dropped a small bowl and cloth on the side table and then she left, as well.

The door behind him sealed shut. Rashid stalked toward the small woman on the cushions. Her golden-blond hair was down today. It hit him with a jolt that it was long and silky and perfectly straight. She was wearing flat white sandals with little jewels set on the bands and a light blue dress with tiny flowers on it. She did not look like a woman who might be carrying a royal baby.

She looked like a misbehaving girl, fresh and pretty and filled with mischief.

And sporting small cuts to her flesh. Cuts she'd caused, he reminded himself. She picked up the cloth and dabbed at her hand. The white fabric came away pink.

"What did you do, Miss Sloane?"

As if he couldn't tell. The window was open to the heat and a silver tray lay discarded to one side. Such violence in such a small package. It astonished him.

She wouldn't look at him. "I admit it was childish of me, but I was angry." Then her violet eyes lifted to his. "I don't ordinarily act this way, I assure you. But you put me here with nothing to do and no one to talk to."

"And this is how you behave when you don't get your way?"

Her gaze didn't waver. In fact, he thought it flickered with anger. Or maybe it was fear. That gave him pause. She had no reason to fear him. Daria would be ashamed of him for scaring this woman.

He tried to look unperturbed. He didn't think it was working based on the way her throat moved as he stared back at her.

"In fact, I realize that we can't always have our way," she said primly. "But this is my first time as a prisoner, and I thought perhaps the rules were different. So I decided to do something about it."

Rashid blinked. "Prisoner?" He spread his hands to encompass the room. It was plush and comfortable and feminine. He remembered it from when he was a child, but he'd not entered these quarters in many years. They hadn't changed much, he decided. "I've been in exclusive hotels that lacked accommodations this fine. You think this is a prison?"

A small shard of guilt pricked him even as he spoke. His rooms with Kadir had been opulent, too, and he'd always thought of them as a cage from which he couldn't wait to escape. Beautiful surroundings did not make a person happy. He knew that better than most.

And she looked decidedly unhappy. "Even the cheapest hotels tend to have televisions. And computers, radios, telephones. There are plenty of books here, I'll grant you that—but I can't read them because they aren't in English."

Rashid's brows drew down. He turned and looked around the room. And realized that she was correct. There was no television, no computer, nothing but furniture and fabric and walls. When the women left, they'd taken their belongings with them. Clearly, they'd considered the electronics to be theirs, too.

"I will have that corrected."

"Which part, Rashid?"

He nearly startled at the sound of his name on her lips. He hadn't forgotten that he'd told her she could call him by name, but he somehow hadn't expected it here and now. Her voice was soft, her accent buttery and sweet.

He suddenly wanted her to speak again, to say his name so he could marvel at how it sounded when she did. Deliciously foreign. Soft.

He shoved away such ridiculous thoughts. "I will have a television installed. And a computer. Whatever you need for your comfort."

"But I am still a prisoner."

He clenched his jaw. "You are not a prisoner. You are my guest. Your every comfort is assured."

"And what if I want to talk to people? Have things to do besides watch television all day? I'm a businesswoman, Rashid. I don't sit around my home and do nothing all day."

"I will find a companion for you."

She sighed heavily. And then she went back to dabbing the cuts on the back of her hand. His anger flared hot again.

"You could have hurt yourself far worse than you did," he growled. "Did you even consider the baby when you behaved so foolishly?"

Her head snapped up, guilt flashing in her gaze. "I've already admitted it was a mistake. And yes, I considered what I was doing before I acted. But I didn't expect the glass to shatter everywhere like that. I threw the tray from a distance, but I guess I threw it harder than I thought."

She'd thrown the tray. At the window. She could have been seriously hurt, the foolish woman. But she sat there looking contrite and dejected—and yes, defiant, too— and he wanted to shake her. And tell her he was sorry.

Now where had that come from? He had nothing to apologize for.

Don't I?

He had brought her to Kyr against her will, but what choice did he have? She could be pregnant with his child. Until he knew for certain, he was not about to let her stay in America, living alone and working. What if something happened? What if her store was robbed or someone broke into her apartment?

He'd seen how flimsy her door locks were. Oh, she thought they were state-of-the-art, no doubt, but he'd hired some of the best lock pickers in existence when he'd been building his business from scratch. He'd wanted to test his security, and he knew how easily locks could be breached.

If someone wanted to get to her, they could. And if it became known that she might carry an heir to the throne of Kyr? He shuddered to think of it.

"You will not do anything so foolish again, Miss Sloane."

"I don't intend to—but I also don't want a companion. I want my freedom to come and go from this room, to talk to whomever I want to. And I want to talk to you from time to time. If there's a baby, then I want to know its father as something more than an arrogant stranger. And if there isn't, then I'll go home and forget I ever met you."

Rashid stood stiffly and stared down at her sitting there like some sort of tiny potentate. She had nerve, this woman. But it was absolutely out of the question. He wanted nothing to do with her. If she was pregnant, he'd deal with it when the time came—he could hardly think the word *wife*—but for now she was safely stowed away and he could go about business and forget she existed.

"You may come and go if that is what you wish. But you will have a servant to guide you, and you will do what you are told. You will not wear that clothing, Miss Sloane. You will dress as a Kyrian woman and you will be respectful."

Her chin lifted again. "I am always respectful of those who are respectful of me. But I refuse to be swathed head to toe in black robes—"

His anger was swift as he cut her off. "Once more, you make dangerous assumptions about us. I will send a seamstress to you and you may choose your own colors. This is nonnegotiable."

Her mouth flattened for the barest moment. And then her lips were lush and pink again as she nibbled the bottom one. "And am I to see you, too? Have conversations with you that aren't about what I'm wearing or where I plan to live?"

He almost said yes. The word hovered on his tongue and he bit it back. Shock coursed through him at that near slip. Why would he want to spend any time with her? Why would he ever do such a thing? It was not in him. It was not what he did, regardless that he'd thought of that kiss for half the night during the flight home. He'd told himself it had simply been too long since he'd been with a woman and that was why he kept thinking about it.

But this woman was not the one he was going to break his fast with. That road was fraught with too many dangers. Too many complications.

"I think that is unnecessary," he said curtly. "I have a kingdom to run and very little time."

"I think it *is* necessary." Her voice was soft and filled with a hurt he didn't understand.

He refused to let her get to him. She was a stranger, a vessel who might be carrying his child. He did not care for her. He would not care for her.

"Yet this, too, is nonnegotiable," he told her before turning and striding from the room.

CHAPTER FIVE

SHERIDAN DIDN'T KNOW why it hurt so much to watch him walk out, but it did. She didn't care about him at all—she actively disliked him, in fact—but his rejection stung. She might be carrying his child and he didn't even care about who she was as a person. He didn't want to know her, and he didn't seem to want her to know him.

She didn't move when the workmen came back inside to continue cleaning the glass, or when Fatima—the woman who'd brought her food and had returned after Sheridan broke the window—came over and took the cloth from her to wipe the remaining cuts. They were small, but they stung.

Oh, she'd been so stupid. So emotional. She'd behaved crazily—but it had worked because he'd come. And he'd promised her a small measure of freedom. That had to be a triumph. Fatima dabbed some ointment on her cuts, and then disappeared into the bathroom to put everything away.

How had it come to this? Sheridan was a nice person. She was friendly to everyone, she loved talking to people and she'd never met anyone she didn't like. Until yesterday when Rashid al-Hassan had shown up, she hadn't even thought it was possible to dislike someone.

There were people she got mad at, certainly. She got mad at Annie for not being stronger, but that only made her feel guilty. Annie hadn't had all the advantages that Sheridan had—she wasn't as outgoing, she hadn't been popular, she didn't know how to talk to people and make friends and now she couldn't even have a baby—so it was wrong of Sheridan to get angry with her. Sheridan could hear her mother's answer when she'd been a teen complaining that it wasn't fair she had to stay home from the party because her friends hadn't invited Annie, too.

Annie's not like you, Sheri. We have to be gentle with her. We have to watch out for her.

Not for the first time, Sheridan wondered if maybe Annie would be tougher if everyone in her life hadn't coddled her. If she'd had to stand up for herself, make her own friends, fight her own battles.

Sheridan clenched her hand into a fist and sat there as still as a statue for what seemed the longest time. Even now, she felt like she should be calling Annie to ask how she was instead of worrying about her own situation.

She looked up to see yet more men arriving in her room. They chattered in fast, musical Arabic, dragging out measuring tapes and writing things down on paper. Then they disappeared.

Everything transpired quickly and efficiently over the next couple of hours. Sheridan didn't see the new glass going in because by that time she was in her bedchamber—seriously, it was a chamber, not a bedroom—with three seamstresses, several bolts of fabric and ready-made samples hanging from a portable rack. A young woman who spoke English had come along to translate.

"This one, miss?"

Sheridan looked at the satiny peach fabric and felt a rush of pleasure. "Definitely."

The clothing the women wore was beautiful. Sheridan felt another wash of heat roll through her as she thought about her preconceived notions. She'd expected they would wear black burkas covering them from head to foot, but that was not at all the case.

The garments these women wore were colorful, lightweight and beautiful. They were long, modestly fitted dresses with embroidery and beading on the necks and bodices. The hijab, or head covering, was optional. Two of the women wore them and two did not.

But the possibilities there were beautiful, as well. The fabric was gossamer, colorful and draped in such a way that it created a sense of mystery and beauty.

The women worked quickly, draping bolts of fabric over her body, slipping pins inside and pulling the fabric away only to replace it with a new bolt. Sheridan tried on two dresses they had on the rack—one a gorgeous coral and the other a pretty shade of lavender that brought out the color of her eyes. The seamstress in charge promised they could have those two ready in a matter of hours once they returned to their shop and got to work. The others would take a full day.

Sheridan didn't want to imagine that she needed many dresses for her stay, but how could she know for certain?

The women packed everything up and left just as two men came in with Fatima. They were carrying a box with a flat-screen television in it and they proceeded to set it up on one of the credenzas nearest the bed.

Sheridan wandered into the living area of the suite and found a new television there, too, as well as a state-of-the-art computer and a newly installed telephone. The new glass was set into the casement and the men were sweeping up.

Her throat grew tight. Rashid had done what he'd promised. Thus far. He'd seemed surprised she'd had no television or computer, and he'd worked fast to correct it. But, as nice as this was, she'd wanted more from him. She'd wanted *his* time, wanted to understand more about this man who might just be the father of her baby. He could not be wholly unlikable, could he?

But he seemed determined not to give it to her.

She picked up the remote and flipped on the television. The one in the living area was mounted to the wall, and it was huge—it was almost like having a movie screen when all the colors suddenly came to life and filled the surface. It didn't take too long to figure out how the satellite worked—and her throat tightened again as she landed on CNN International and English conversation filled her ears.

It was nice to hear, but it only brought home how alone she was here. How would she get through a week of this? Nine months of this?

Rashid had said she could come and go, but only with an escort and only when she had the proper clothing. Since she still didn't, she wouldn't attempt to leave her quarters yet. She'd already behaved abominably.

She could still see him standing there, looking at her with the most furious expression on his face. He'd also, for a moment, seemed not fearful…but, well, something besides angry. Maybe *wary* was the word. Like he didn't want to be in the same room with her, but knew he had to be.

It hit her then that not only was he not attracted to her, but she also revolted him. He was tall and handsome and kingly, and she was a short blond woman who organized parties for people. She was pale and slight compared to him. He was the Lion of Kyr, or some such thing like that, and she was an ordinary house cat.

Who might just be pregnant with the next king of the jungle.

She would have laughed if it wasn't so serious. Sheridan went over to where Fatima had set a fresh pot of tea and some pastries and poured a cup. Despite the nausea, which came and went, she decided to try a pastry and see if it stayed down. After she'd made an impulsive decision to throw the tray at the window, she'd not eaten any of the food that she'd carefully set aside to get to the tray. Things had happened so quickly after that and she hadn't had time.

Sheridan frowned as she nibbled on a pastry. Rashid was repulsed by her. It made sense, in a way, and it certainly explained the way he acted.

But then she thought of their kiss again, of the way it had slid down into her skin and made her want things she'd almost forgotten existed. Even now, the memory of it made her tremble. He'd slid his tongue into her mouth and she'd practically devoured him.

How embarrassing.

But she'd thought, dammit, at least for a minute anyway, that he'd been equally affected. He'd kissed her with such hunger, such passion, that she'd been swept up in the moment.

Yes, swept up enough so that he could carry her to the car before she managed to make a peep. Sheridan set the pastry down with disgust. He'd certainly known what he was doing. And she'd been just sensation deprived enough to let him.

"Miss?"

Sheridan looked up to find Fatima standing over her. The two men were leaving, carting the remnants of television and computer boxes with them.

"Yes?"

"Do you require anything else?"

That was a loaded question if ever she heard one. "Your English is good, Fatima."

"Thank you, miss. I studied in school."

"Have you worked in the palace long?"

"A few months."

"Do you know the king well?"

She shook her head. "No, miss. King Rashid, may Allah bless him, has come home again after many years away. We will prosper under his benevolent reign."

Sheridan wasn't going to laugh over that *benevolent reign* remark, though she wanted to. But she also felt a spark of curiosity. "Many years away?"

Fatima looked a little worried then. "I have heard this in the palace. I do not know for certain. If you will excuse me, miss. Unless you need something?" she added, her eyes wide and almost pleading with Sheridan not to ask anything more about Rashid.

"Thank you, but I'm fine," she replied, offering the woman a smile to reassure her.

Fatima curtsied and then hurried out of the room, closing the door behind her with one last fearful glance at Sheridan.

After a long day sorting through national problems, including one between two desert tribes arguing over who owned a water well, Rashid was glad to retire to his quarters. These rooms had once been his father's, but he'd gotten the decorators to work immediately so that they no longer bore any resemblance to the man who'd lived in them for thirty-seven years.

Gone were the ornate furnishings and narcissistic portraits, the statuary, the huge bed on a platform complete with heavy damask draperies. In their place, Rashid had asked for clean lines, comfortable furniture, paintings that didn't overwhelm with color or subject matter and breezy fabrics more in fitting with the desert. Certainly the desert was bitterly cold at night, but he didn't need damask draperies for that.

The palace had been modernized years ago and had working air and heat for those rare occasions when it was needed. Rashid slipped his headdress off and dropped it on a couch. Then he raked his hand through his hair and pulled out his phone. He stared at it for a long moment before he punched the button that would call up his favorites.

Kadir answered on the third ring. "Rashid, it's good to hear from you."

"*Salaam,* brother." He chewed the inside of his lip and stared off toward the dunes and the setting sun. It blazed bright orange as it sank like a stone. He'd debated for hours on whether or not to call Kadir. They weren't as close as they'd once been, and he found it hard to admit he needed people. "How are you?"

Kadir laughed. "Wonderful. Happy. Ecstatic."

"Marriage agrees with you." He tried not to let any bitterness slip into his voice, but he feared it did anyway. Still, Kadir took it like a blissfully happy man would: as the uninformed judgment of a bachelor.

"Apparently so. Emily keeps me on my toes. But she

forces me to eat kale, Rashid. Because it has micronutrients or some such thing, she says it's good for me."

"That doesn't sound so bad." It sounded horrible.

"She makes a healthy drink for breakfast. It's green. Looks disgusting, but thankfully doesn't taste as bad as it looks." He sighed. "I miss pancakes and bacon."

Rashid was familiar with pancakes, though he'd never developed a taste for them during the brief time he'd spent in America. He almost laughed, but then he thought of Daria cooking meals for him and swallowed. She used to make these wonderful savory pies from her native Ural Mountains. He'd loved them. He'd loved her.

Rashid swallowed. "I want you to build a skyscraper for me, Kadir."

He could practically hear Kadir's brain kick into gear. "You do? Is this a Kyrian project, or a personal one?"

"I need a building for Hassan Oil in Kyr. I want you to build it."

"Then I am happy to do so. Let me check the schedule and I'll see when we can come for a meeting."

"That would be good."

Kadir sighed, as if sensing there was more to the call. "I will come anyway, Rashid, if you wish it."

He did wish it. For the first time in a long time, he wanted a friend. And Kadir was the closest thing he had. But a lifetime of shutting people out was hard to overcome. He'd let in Daria, but look how that had turned out.

"Whenever you can make it is good. I'm busy with many things since you left."

"I'm sorry we didn't make the coronation. It was my intention, and then—"

"It's fine." He pulled in a breath. "Kadir, there is something I want to talk about."

"Then I will come immediately."

That Kadir would still do that, after everything that had passed between them, made an uncomfortable rush of feeling fill Rashid's chest. "No, that is not necessary. But there's a woman. A situation."

"A situation?" He could hear the confusion in his brother's voice.

Rashid sighed. And then he told Kadir what had happened—the sperm mix-up, the trip to America, the way he'd given Sheridan no choice but to return with him. Kadir was silent for a long moment. Rashid knew his brother was trying to grasp the ramifications of the situation. At any rate, he couldn't know half of why this unnerved Rashid so much. Rashid hadn't hidden his marriage to Daria, but he'd been living in Russia then and the information hadn't precisely filtered out.

And the baby? He did not talk of that to anyone.

"So she might be pregnant?"

The ice in his chest was brittle. "Yes."

"What will you do? Marry her?"

Rashid hated the way that single word ground into his brain. *Marry.* "I will have to, won't I? But once the child is born, she can leave him here and return to America."

Kadir blew out a breath. Rashid wondered for a moment if he might be laughing. But his voice, when he spoke, was even. "I don't know, Rashid. The American I married would put my balls in a vise before she agreed to such a thing. In fact, I think most women would."

"Not if you pay them enough to disappear."

Kadir might have groaned. Rashid wasn't certain, because his blood was rushing in his ears. "You could try. It would certainly make it easier with the council if she would agree to disappear afterward. If she's pregnant, they will have to accept her. But they won't like it."

Rashid growled. "I don't give a damn what the council likes."

And it was true. The council was old and traditional, but there were lines he would not allow them to cross. He was the king. They had power because he allowed it, not in spite of it. They wanted him to marry a Kyrian. But if he wanted to marry a dancing bear, he would. And if he wanted to marry an American girl, he would do that, too.

"At least be nice to the woman, Rashid. You *are* being nice to her, yes?"

"Of course I am." But a current of guilt sizzled through him. He could still see her eyes, so wide and wounded, looking up at him today when he'd told her there was no reason for them to spend time together. No reason to know each other.

And perhaps there wasn't. But the days were ticking down and they would soon know if she were pregnant. And then he would have to take her as his wife.

It made him want to howl.

"We will come for a visit soon," Kadir said. "Perhaps it would be good to have Emily there. The poor woman is probably confused and scared."

He didn't think Sheridan was all that scared. He could still see her standing up to him, spitting like a wet cat when he'd told her he would take the child and raise him in Kyr.

"I am nice to her," he said defensively. "She is my guest."

Kadir laughed softly. "Somehow, I don't think she sees it quite the same way."

They spoke for a few more minutes about other things, and then Rashid ended the call. He sighed and went out onto one of the many terraces that opened off his rooms. There was a soft breeze tonight, hot and scented with jasmine from the gardens. In another few hours, it would turn chilly, but for now it was still warm.

The minarets glowed ocher in the last rays of the setting sun. The sounds of vendors shouting in the streets filtered to him on the wind, along with the fresh scent of spicy meat and hot bread.

Rashid breathed it all in. This was home. Unbidden, an image of Sheridan Sloane came to mind. She had a home, too, and he'd forced her out of it. For her own protection, yes, but nevertheless she was here in a strange place and nothing was familiar.

Guilt pricked him. He should not care about her feelings at all, but if she was truly carrying his child, did he want her upset and stressed? Wasn't it better to make her welcome?

He sighed again, knowing what he had to do. Tomorrow, he would take lunch with her. They would talk, she would be happy and he would leave again, content in the knowledge he'd done his part.

It was only an hour—and he could be nice to anyone for an hour.

Sheridan awoke in the middle of the night. It was dark and still and she was cold. She sat up, intending to pull the blanket up from the bottom of the bed, but she wasn't all that tired now. Her sleep was erratic because of the time difference. She checked her phone for the time—

still no signal—and calculated that it was midafternoon at home. She never napped during the day, so it was no wonder she was messed up.

She got up and pulled on her silky robe over her night-gown before going into the bathroom. Hair combed, teeth brushed, she wandered into the living area. And then, because she was curious, she went and opened the door to her suite. The guard was not there. She stood there for a moment in shock, and then she crept into the corridor.

She didn't know where she was going or what she ex-pected, but she kept moving along, thinking someone would stop her at any moment. But no one did. The cor-ridors were quiet, as if everyone was asleep. She didn't know how it usually worked in palaces, but it made sense they were all in bed.

When she reached the end of a corridor and came up against a firmly locked door, she turned and went back the way she'd come. There were doors off the corridor, and she tentatively opened one. It was a space with seat-ing, but it wasn't quite as ornate as hers. It was, not plain precisely, but modern. Personally, she preferred some antiques, but this space was intended for someone who liked little fuss.

She thought perhaps she'd stumbled into a meeting area since it was so sterile. A breeze came in through doors that were open to the night air and she headed toward them. She hadn't been outside since she'd ar-rived, and she wondered what it would be like in the desert at night.

She stepped onto a wide terrace. The city lights spread out around her and, in the distance, the dark-ness of the desert was like a crouching tiger waiting for an excuse to pounce. She moved to the railing and stood, gripping it and sucking in the clean night air. It was chilly now, which amazed her considering how hot it had been when she'd arrived.

A frisson of excitement dripped down her spine. It surprised her, but in some ways it didn't. She'd never been to the desert before. Never been to an Arab country with dunes and palaces and camels and men who wore headdresses and robes. It was foreign, exotic and, yes, exciting in a way. She wanted to explore. She wanted to ride a horse into that desert and see what was out there.

She heard a noise behind her, footsteps across tile, and she whirled with her heart in her throat. How would she explain her presence here to her guard? To anyone?

But it wasn't just anyone standing there. It was a man she recognized on a level that stunned her. Rashid al-Hassan stood in a shaft of light, his chest and legs bare. He looked like an underwear model, she thought crazily, all lean muscle and golden flesh. He was not soft—not that she'd expected he would be after he'd pressed her against him—but the corrugated muscle over his abdomen was a bit of a sensual shock. Real men weren't supposed to look like that.

"What are you doing here, Miss Sloane?" he demanded, his voice hard and cold and so very dangerous.

The warmth that had been undulating through her like a gentle wave abruptly shut off.

Run! That was the single word that echoed in her brain.

But she couldn't move. Her limbs were frozen. Not only that, but Rashid al-Hassan also stood between her and escape....

CHAPTER SIX

SHERIDAN SUCKED IN a deep breath and pulled her robe tighter, even though it couldn't protect her from the fury in his dark eyes. She thought of Fatima's fearful look earlier today and wondered if perhaps this man was more frightening than she'd thought. Her blood ran cold.

"The door was open. I—I wanted to see outside."

"You are in my quarters, Miss Sloane."

Oh, dear. "I'm sorry. I didn't know."

He still hadn't moved. He stood in the door, his broad frame imposing. She told herself not to look below the level of his chin. She failed.

"So you decided to wander in the middle of the night and open random doors?"

She twisted the tie of her robe. "Something like that. I'm on a different schedule than you, I'm afraid. Wide-awake and nothing to do."

"Nothing to do." His voice was somehow full of meaning. Or perhaps she imagined it.

"I didn't mean to disturb you."

He still looked imposing and impossible. And then he shoved his hand through his hair and moved out of the doorway and onto the terrace. Sheridan stood frozen.

"You didn't disturb me. I was awake."

"You should try hot milk. It helps with insomnia." Oh, no, she was babbling. Sheridan bit her lip and told herself to shut up. This man was dangerous, for heaven's sake. Not at all the sort to put up with babbling in the middle of the night.

"I don't need much sleep," he said. "And I don't like hot milk."

"I don't either, actually. But I understand it works for some."

He went and leaned on the railing, near her. She thought she should take this opportunity to escape, and yet she was curious enough to want to stay. He made her nerves pop and sing. It was an interesting sensation.

"When it's light, you can see all the way to the gulf from here," he said. He lifted his hand. "In that direction, you can see the dunes of the Kyrian Desert. The Waste is out there, too."

"The Waste?" She moved closer, reached for the railing and wound her fingers around the iron.

He turned his head toward her. "A very harsh, very hot part of the desert. There is no water for one hundred miles. The sands are baked during the day, and at night they give up their heat and turn cool. You can freeze out there, if you don't die of heatstroke during the day."

It was hard to imagine such a place in this day and age. "Surely there are ways to bring water into it."

"There are. But there is no reason to do so. It would be cost prohibitive, for one thing. And who would live there? There are nomads, but the people who are accustomed to the cities would never go."

"Have you been there?"

He didn't speak for a long moment. "I have. There is an oasis midway. It was once part of a trade route across the desert. I went as a boy. It was part of my training as an al-Hassan."

She could imagine this harsh, dark man out there now. But as a child? It seemed so dangerous and uncertain. "I've never been to a desert before. I've never been anywhere but the Caribbean. Until now, I mean."

He looked at her. "Are you more comfortable now that you have a television and internet access?"

"It helps. But I'm still used to doing more than I have the last day. I like to be busy."

"Consider it a vacation."

"That would be easier if it actually were."

"Miss Sloane—"

"Sheridan. Please." Because she felt so out of place when he called her Miss Sloane. She needed him to acknowledge her as more than a random stranger. Because, regardless of whether or not there was a baby, they'd shared something incredibly intimate. Even if it had been clinical.

"Sheridan."

She shivered at the sound of her name on his lips. Why? Because it sounded like a silken caress. "Thank you," she said.

"I was going to say that I realize this is not easy for you. It is not easy for me, either."

"I know."

He turned to look out at the city lights and she watched the play of the wind in his hair and the soft glow of moonlight on his profile. He was a very beautiful man. And a lonely one. She didn't know why she thought he was lonely, but she did.

"I have decided to give you what you've requested," he said, and her heart thrummed. "I want your stay to be pleasant. If it pleases you to talk to me, then I will grant it."

She was surprised and pleased at once. "I appreciate that very much."

They stood there in silence for a long moment. "It is an extraordinary length to go to, to have a baby for someone else."

She felt a touch defensive. "It's not just for anyone. Annie is my sister."

"I am aware of this."

Sheridan sighed. The night breeze whipped up then, just for a moment, and she shivered. "She and Chris have tried and tried. They've seen doctors and been through one treatment after another. Nothing seems to work." She gripped the railing tightly, staring off toward the flickering lights of the city. "There was one doctor who mentioned an experimental treatment in Europe. Annie wanted to do it, and Chris would do anything for her. But the cost... Well, it's a lot. And there are no guarantees. They would have to sell everything and then hope..." She swallowed the lump in her throat. "I offered to step in before they went deeper into debt."

"So you would put your own life on hold to have this child for your sister. And then you would hand him or her over as if the previous nine months had happened to her instead of you."

The lump in her throat wouldn't go away. She hugged her arms around herself to keep from shivering. The air seemed colder now. "I didn't say it would be easy, but it's what you do when you love someone. You make sacrifices."

He seemed very quiet and still as he watched her. She'd expected him to make some sort of remark, but he said nothing at all. It began to worry her, though she didn't quite know why. She cleared her throat softly and told him the truth.

"I don't quite know what to say to you," she admitted. "I never know if you're angry or if you're just the kind of man who doesn't speak much."

He was looking at her with renewed interest. "I'm not angry. I'm frustrated."

"We're both frustrated."

"Are we?"

"I…" She sensed that this conversation had moved out of her control somehow. His eyes glittered in the night. He seemed suddenly very intense. And very— dear heaven—*naked*. "Yes, uh, of course. Why wouldn't we be? This is a frustrating circumstance."

"I find it very interesting that you could be carrying my child, and yet we've never been intimate. I've never undressed you, never tasted your skin."

She was growing hot now. So very hot. "Well, er…"

"Have you thought of it, Sheridan? After that kiss, have you wondered?"

Her heart hammered hard. Another moment and she would be dizzy. Yes she'd thought of that kiss. And she'd thought of her flesh pressed against his, nothing between them but skin and heat. She'd wondered what it would be like to be this man's lover. This dynamic, incredible man.

"Of course I have," she said, shocking herself with the admission. And him, too, if the way his muscles seemed to coil tight beneath his skin was any indication. He was like a great cat ready to pounce. The Lion of Kyr, indeed. "But that doesn't mean I want to do anything about it."

Liar.

"Then I think perhaps you should be more careful which rooms you wander into in the middle of the night."

His voice was icy again, yet it was somehow hot, too. Not menacing, but promising in a way that had her limbs quivering.

"I didn't know this was your room. And I didn't come here for...for..."

She couldn't finish the sentence. Her ears were hot, which was ridiculous because she wasn't a naive virgin. She hadn't had many lovers—well, only two, in fact—but that didn't mean she didn't know what happened when a man and a woman got naked together.

But it was the imagining that was killing her here. Rashid was beautiful, dark and dangerous and mysterious, and the idea of him completely focused on her body was more arousing than she could have imagined possible. She reminded herself that she didn't like him, but her body didn't seem to care. *So what?* That was the message throbbing in her sex, her veins, her belly. A relentless throb of tension and yearning that would only be broken if this man took her to his bed.

"Perhaps you did not," he said smoothly, "but you want it nevertheless. I can see it in your eyes, Sheridan."

She tried to stiffen in outrage. She was fully aware her nipples had beaded tight against the silk of the robe. Instead of trying to hide them, she wrapped her arms beneath her breasts and hugged herself against the chill air. Not that she was all that cold with Rashid al-Hassan looking at her like he might devour her. Which was a bit of a shock since she'd convinced herself that he wasn't really attracted to her.

Apparently she was wrong....

"You're being too polite, Rashid. You mean to say you can see it in my nipples, but the truth is it's cold out here," she said brazenly. "It has nothing to do with you."

"I'm not the kind of man one issues challenges to, *habibti*. I have a pathological need to prove the issuer wrong."

She took a step backward. "We don't know each other well enough. Touch me and I'll scream."

He laughed. It was completely unexpected. She didn't like the warmth dripping into her limbs at the sound. "You forget this is the royal palace of Kyr and I am the king. If I wish to tie you to my bed and have my way with you on a nightly basis, there is no one who will stop me."

Her heart hammered. She wasn't supposed to be titillated by the idea of being tied to Rashid's bed. And yet she was.

He moved then, toward her, and she didn't even try to get away. She was frozen like a gazelle, waiting for the big cat to strike. And strike he did. He tugged her against him, her body in the thin silk robe flush to his naked flesh, and spread his hands over her backside.

Yet he didn't hold her tight. She could escape if she wished. She knew it and he knew it—and she didn't even try.

He laughed again, softly, triumphantly. "Such a liar, Sheridan," he said thickly. And then his mouth came down on hers.

If the kiss in her store had been surprising in its intensity, this one was downright earth-shattering. Rashid's tongue traced the seam of her lips and she opened to him, tangling her tongue with his almost eagerly.

The sensations rioting through her were more intense than she ever recalled experiencing before. It was the hormones from the shots, she told herself—but it was also the man. He was more exciting than anyone she'd ever known. Which didn't make any sense because he was also the least likable person she'd ever known.

Not to mention she didn't even really know him at all. He was a king, a desert sheikh, an autocratic ruler accustomed to ordering people around and getting his way.

And she was giving him precisely what he expected.

But it felt so good. Their tongues fought a blistering duel, her skin grew moist and impossibly hot and wetness flooded her sex. Her limbs were weakened by the kiss and she lifted her arms to put them around his neck. The shock of his hot skin beneath hers made her whimper.

Rashid turned her until her back was against the railing—and then he untied her robe and slipped it off her shoulders. The next thing she knew, his hot mouth was tracing a path down the column of her throat while she threaded her fingers into his dark hair and clutched him to her.

His teeth bit down on her nipple through the silken fabric of her nightgown and she gasped. It wasn't a hard bite, but it had the effect of sending pleasure shooting straight to her core. Her body clenched hard with desire as she gripped his shoulders and thrust her breasts toward his mouth.

She wanted him to remove the thin tissue of silk between his mouth and her body, but he didn't. He licked her through the fabric, nibbled and sucked until she was wild with need. Her nipples were more sensitive than ever since she'd had the hormone shots. If he did nothing but this all night, she knew she would come from the stimulation.

But he had no intention of doing only that. He reached down and gathered the hem of her nightie, lifting it up her legs, exposing her. Sheridan thought she needed to protest, but some needy, wicked part of her really didn't want to.

Rashid's hands glided beneath her gown, up the flesh of her abdomen, until he was cupping her breasts beneath the fabric, his hot hands spanning her skin, making it burn.

His mouth claimed hers again. It wasn't a tender kiss, or even a teasing kiss. It was a full-out assault on her senses. He stepped in closer, pinning her body to the railing with his much bigger, much harder one.

And that was when she felt him. That insistently hard part of him that pressed into her, letting her know that he was every bit as affected by the tension and heat between them as she was.

Sheridan acted instinctively. She reached for him, cupped her hands over that hard part of him she shouldn't crave but did. It had been so long since she'd been with anyone and she was suddenly ravenous. Rashid made a noise, a growl of satisfaction or encouragement in his throat. A thrill shot through her.

She'd thought he'd be disgusted by her, but that clearly wasn't the case. He wanted her. And, right now, she wanted him. It was insane, but nothing about this situation was normal. If she slept with him, what would change? Not a damn thing.

She pushed her hands beneath his briefs, cupped him in her hands. He was big and full and so very ready that it almost scared her. She didn't know this man at all, and what she did know hadn't been very pleasant up until this point.

He'd threatened her, taken her against her will and brought her here and treated her as if she was someone he'd hired to do a job instead of a woman caught up in a mistake not of her own making. He'd been angry with her, and he'd started this to prove a point, to punish her.

Now he was in her hands, his body hard and taut and ready. He broke the kiss and stared down at her, his eyes dark and deep and so fathomless she was almost frightened. But he was just a man, she reminded herself, and he'd not harmed her. He'd never given a single indication that he would force her to do anything she didn't want to do.

"Sheridan," he growled, his voice as tight as she'd yet heard it. "If you don't mean to give yourself to me, you need to leave. Now. Because if you continue to touch me like that, I'm not stopping until I've tasted you as thoroughly as I desire."

Sheridan bit her lip as her heart skittered recklessly in her chest. A sane woman would leave right this instant. A sane woman would not give her body to a man she barely knew simply because he made her feel more excited than she'd ever felt before.

She was not precisely sane at this moment. Maybe it was the heat of the desert, or the sand, or the opulent palace. She had no idea, but she wanted things she shouldn't want.

"I don't want to leave. I don't want to stop touching you."

With a groan, he swept her up into his arms and carried her through the door.

CHAPTER SEVEN

SOMEWHERE ON THE trip to his bed, panic began to flood her system. But before she could react, he set her on the bed and stripped her nightgown from her body. And then he was hovering over her, kissing her until her fear melted and her body caught on fire again.

Oh, this was so wrong—and so right. Sheridan put her arms around him, ran her hands over his broad back, the thick muscles and tendons, down his biceps and over his pecs. He was magnificent, and he no doubt knew it.

He left her mouth to lick his way to her breasts again. He took his time, sliding his tongue around and around before he sucked one aching nipple into his mouth. Sheridan cried out with the intensity of the pleasure spiking through her.

"You are sensitive," he murmured, his breath hot against her skin and yet cold where it drifted over her wet nipple. "So sensitive."

Sheridan couldn't speak. Her stomach churned with anticipation and, yes, even fear. Because what was she doing? Part of her brain kept wondering, but the rest refused to entertain any alternatives to what was currently happening.

And then Rashid moved down her body, his hands

spanning her hips and peeling her panties down until he pulled them free and dropped them somewhere on the floor. She could see his beautiful face illuminated by moonlight, see the vaulted ceilings of the chamber, hear the exotic sounds of the Kyrian night drifting inside—and it made her feel as if she wasn't herself. As if this was a fantasy. A thousand and one Arabian nights with her own desert king.

Sheridan bowed up off the bed as he touched his mouth to the wet seam of her body. The pleasure was so intense, so spellbinding, that she practically sobbed his name. He gave her no relief from the feelings rocketing through her. He held her legs open and licked her until she was a shuddering mass of nerve endings.

Sheridan's world exploded in a white-hot blaze of light, her body tightening almost painfully before soaring over the edge. But before she could manage to come back to herself, Rashid was there, his mouth capturing hers, demanding her full attention. She melted into his kiss.

And then she felt him, big and hard and poised at her body's entrance. He put a hand under her bottom, lifted her toward him. She wrapped her legs around him, her heart pounding as she waited for what happened next.

He seemed to hesitate for a long moment. And then he said something in Arabic, some muttered phrase, before he pushed into her body. He didn't move fast, didn't jam himself inside her. He took his time. And then he was deep within her, the two of them joined in the most intimate of ways, and fresh panic began to unwind inside her belly.

What was she doing? What was wrong with her? Sex with a stranger wasn't like her at all!

Rashid's head dropped slowly toward hers and she closed her eyes, tilting her mouth up until he captured it. She sighed—or maybe that was him. But then he started to move and she no longer cared about anything except what he was doing to her.

He was gentle at first. But as she arched her body into his, he took her harder and harder, until they were moving into each other in an almost punishing rhythm. She ran her hands over his skin until he gripped her wrists and shoved her hands over her head, binding her.

It was erotic, sensual and utterly exhilarating. Their skin grew hot and moist as they tangled together and the tension inside her coiled tighter than the lid on a pressure cooker.

And then she couldn't hold on a moment longer. He was too good at this, too compelling, and she came in a rush of blinding intensity that left her gasping for air and crying his name at the same time.

She felt his body tighten inside hers, and then he flew over the edge with her, his breath a harsh groan in her ear. They lay together for a few moments, hearts pounding, skin slicked with perspiration, breaths razoring in and out. Sheridan's legs trembled from gripping his hips so tightly with her thighs. She eased them down and lay still beneath him, her eyes closed and her brain finally began to whir into consciousness again.

What did one say after sex like that? Especially with a man you hardly knew and definitely didn't like?

She didn't get a chance to find out.

He pushed off her and stood, and cool air wafted over her skin, chilling her. She wanted to grab the covers and pull them up, and yet she couldn't seem to move. Because he was staring down at her, his face stark in the darkness, his chest rising and falling with more than exertion.

He was angry. Or tormented. She wasn't sure which, and it alarmed her. She sat up and wrapped her arms around her knees, trying to hide herself.

"Thank you, Sheridan," he said, his voice so courteous and calm. And cold. Sheridan shivered at the frost in his tone. He bent down a moment and then straightened, laying her nightgown and underwear on the bed at her feet. "Get dressed and I will escort you back to your room."

Rashid was up at dawn. He'd tossed and turned for the past couple of hours in a bed that still smelled like the woman he'd shared it with. The corners of his mouth turned down in a frown as his stomach twisted with guilt.

But why should that be? He enjoyed sex as well as the next man. He'd only ever loved one woman with his heart, but he'd loved many women in the physical way. He was not a monk and he hadn't been celibate for the past five years. It had taken him over a year to take a woman to his bed again, but he'd done so.

Sex with Sheridan Sloane was nothing out of the ordinary for him. And yet it was. Because she might be carrying his child, and though he'd been so focused and intent on her body, on tasting her and enjoying her, he hadn't expected the gravity of that fact to hit him with such a jolt after he'd found his pleasure in her body.

He'd bedded the woman who could be pregnant with his heir. A woman he didn't love, but who he would have to take as his wife if she was.

Still, he should be happy he'd finally released some

of this pent-up tension. He was not. He was strangely restless. Keyed up.

Ready to explore Sheridan's creamy skin and secret recesses again and again.

That was the part that unnerved him. The sex had been pretty spectacular, hot and exciting and intense, and he'd been utterly focused on it, lost in it.

But then it was over and they'd lain there together, breathing hard, her heart throbbing against his own— and he'd wanted to escape. He didn't understand how he could be so cold and unemotional one minute and so gutted the next.

She'd gutted him. Sex with her had gotten into his head in a way that sex with other women did not—and he didn't like it one bit. So he'd risen and gone to get her robe from the terrace while she dressed. When he'd come back, he'd handed it to her silently. It had been cold from being outdoors, but she'd put it on anyway and belted it tight.

Then he'd escorted her back to her quarters because he hadn't been certain she could find her way alone. She hadn't spoken on the walk back down the corridors. He'd stopped in front of the door to the women's quarters, vowing to himself to station a guard there at night in the future instead of outside the entrance to the private wing.

There was another way to her rooms, through his own, but he'd refused to use it. It would be too easy to go through that entry again if he started now, so he simply didn't.

She'd hesitated at the door as if she wanted to say something to him, but he'd put his hands in her hair and held her face up for his kiss. To silence her. To end any awkwardness.

When she'd been rubbery and clinging to him, when his body was beginning to respond with fresh heat that he knew would ignite into a fire at any moment, he'd let her go, striding away without another word.

Her reaction had been a very resounding door slam. But it was for the best, really. He had too much to do, too many things to worry about, and no time to navigate the mire of repeatedly bedding a woman who might be carrying his heir. A woman who might soon be his wife.

If she was angry with him, so much the better. He'd intended to be nice to her, but he'd gone way overboard. And now he would have to stay away from her, as he'd intended in the first place.

Sheridan didn't believe that Rashid would come to see her that day. After the confusing—and paradigm changing—previous night, she didn't really think his decision to talk to her would stand.

And of course she was right. As the day wore into night, there was no sign of Rashid. She was allowed to wander the palace, as he'd promised, but she did not bump into him anywhere. She wore one of the dresses from the dressmaker, along with a hijab that covered her hair, and then she spent fascinating hours walking through the palace and studying the architecture.

But in spite of her enjoyment of everything the palace had to offer, she remained preoccupied with Rashid. With last night. She couldn't think of it without blushing. She'd had sex with him—hot, wild, crazy, passionate sex—after knowing him for two days.

Worse, she wanted more. She knew it wasn't going to

happen—that it *shouldn't* happen—but she couldn't help but imagine Rashid coming to her room in the night. He would peel her clothing away, and then use that magical mouth of his to drive her insane with wild need.

Sheridan fanned herself absently with her hand. The guard who strode silently along wherever she went didn't bat an eyelash. She'd tried to talk to him about mundane things, but he remained silent.

When she ventured out to the stables after dinner, he followed. But when she tried to touch one of the horses, just to pet its velvety nose, he stopped her.

"His Majesty would not want you to get bitten, miss."

"I've been around horses before," she said, more than a little surprised that he spoke English. She'd started to think he was ignoring her because he didn't speak her language. "I think I can tell when they're going to bite."

Still, she strolled along until they came to a room at the end of the stable. She looked over the top of the door and practically melted.

"Puppies!" She turned to her guard. "What kind of dogs are they?"

He seemed to hesitate, as if he didn't want to engage in conversation, but then he relented. "They are Canaan dogs, miss. A hardy and ancient breed."

The puppies were small and squat, and had curled tails. They almost looked like huskies, except they weren't gray and didn't have thick fur. The mother dog was nowhere to be seen at the moment.

"They're precious."

Sheridan stood and watched the puppies wiggling happily, playing and yipping, and wished she could go in and sit down and let them climb all over her. But she knew her guard wouldn't approve of that. Eventually, the sound of approaching hoofbeats made her turn her head. A man in desert robes sat astride a beautiful bay horse as it trotted toward the stable. When they reached the building, he swung down and handed the reins to a groom, who had appeared out of nowhere.

And then the man turned his head until dark glittering eyes met hers, boring into her with that combination of heat and anger that seemed unique to Rashid. Her belly clenched at the primal recognition that stirred to life inside her.

Beside her, her guard had dropped into a low bow. Sheridan, not quite knowing what to do, decided to curtsy. Oh, she was plenty angry with Rashid, but she would not create trouble by refusing to acknowledge his power over his subjects. She wasn't stupid and she knew it was important to have her guard's respect.

Rashid's eyes narrowed—and then he came toward her. His gaze raked over her, taking in the hijab and dress—which she'd realized weren't strictly necessary since she'd seen women in his palace dressed in Western business attire—before landing on her face again.

"Miss Sloane, isn't it a bit late to be touring the stables?"

Miss Sloane. As if he hadn't been inside her just a few hours ago. She lifted her chin. "I believe I already established that I'm still on a different sleep schedule than Kyr. Though it isn't quite eight o'clock here yet, which I would consider early even were I acclimated to your time zone."

Her heart thundered relentlessly in her breast as she stared at him. He was no longer quite the stranger he'd been before last night's passionate encounter, and it disconcerted her.

He turned his attention to the guard. "Leave us."

The guard rose and melted into the night. Sheridan felt a hot wash of anger move through her.

"I realize you're a king, but do you have to talk to people like that?"

His brows drew down. "Like what? I told him what he needed to know. Do you prefer I ask him politely to go?"

"It might be nice, but no, I don't really expect that out of you."

"You sound like my brother."

She blinked. "Do I? Is he a nice, sensible man?"

"Nicer than I am."

"So you admit you aren't very nice."

"I'm not trying to be." He shrugged. "I am who I am. I don't have to explain myself to anyone."

She dropped her gaze. It was an odd conversation in some respects. Odd because of what they'd done the night before, and odd because she could feel that fire beneath the surface. It was only waiting for ignition.

"After last night, I really didn't expect an explanation."

Oh, wow, had she really said that? She wanted to bite her tongue.

He searched her features. "You are upset because I did not allow you to stay in my bed."

"Allow?" She resisted the urge to poke him in the chest, but only barely. "What makes you think I wanted to stay? We were finished and it would have been awkward to stay. You don't strike me as the type for small talk, and I'd rather not have to attempt it. It was better that I left."

His dark eyes flashed with some unidentifiable emotion. "You continually surprise me. I thought you would be upset. Regretful. Wringing your hands and wishing you could undo the things we did together."

She shrugged as if casual sex was her thing when it really wasn't. "Why would I want to undo it? It was nice."

"Nice?" His voice was a growl and she suddenly wanted to laugh. Even superior kings had fragile egos when it came to their performance in bed. Hint that you were less than satisfied and you found yourself faced with a dangerously tense male animal with a point to prove.

"Unlike *you,* yes, it was nice. Very nice, if you insist."

He stiffened. And then he laughed softly. Once more, the sound of his laughter had a way of surprising her. It was as if he didn't laugh often enough and wasn't quite sure how. "You are baiting me. I see it now. If I said the moon was golden tonight, you'd say it was yellow."

That pesky warmth was flowing in her limbs again. Her body ached with his nearness, and though she had another, more immediate ache between her thighs to remind her of his possession, that didn't stop her from wanting it again.

"And what am I supposed to be baiting you into?" Her voice was huskier than she would have liked it. But he already knew how he affected her. One corner of his mouth lifted in a superior grin.

"Perhaps you want another demonstration of my niceness."

Heat flooded her cheeks. "Hardly. Once was enough, thank you."

Once was not enough. And that really worried her. Why did she want him? It wasn't like her to crave a man the way she craved him after only one night. Plus, this was too complicated. They weren't dating. This wasn't a man she'd met in Savannah, a man with the freedom and ability to pursue a relationship with her.

This was a king. A man who ruled a desert nation. A man who was so unlike any man she'd ever known that he confused her. He was arrogant, bossy and he already acted as if he owned her.

And she *let* him. She'd always thought she was a feminist, but the way he made her behave was decidedly not liberated. It was needy, physical and completely focused on sexual pleasure. If he threw her into a stall right now and had his way with her on the hay, she'd only urge him on.

He moved away from her and she tried not to let her disappointment show.

"Come, I will take you back to your quarters."

She threw another glance at the puppies before joining him. They walked side by side, but not touching, toward the palace.

"You like puppies?" he said.

"I love puppies. I've never had a dog, but I plan to get one some day."

"You've never had a dog?"

She shook her head as they walked across the courtyard. "My sister was bitten by a neighbor's dog when she was four. So we never got one because she was too scared."

"That hardly seems fair," he said.

Sheridan felt that old familiar prick of resentment flaring deep inside. It was followed, as always, by guilt. It wasn't Annie's fault.

"Maybe not, but she cried whenever my parents

talked about getting a dog for the family, so they gave up. We didn't even have a cat."

"Did a cat bite her, too?"

Sheridan stopped abruptly. Rashid was a few steps ahead when he turned toward her, waiting. "She had allergies," Sheridan said. "And it's not her fault."

He moved toward her again. She had to tilt her head back to look up at him. He bristled with a coiled energy that she was certain contained a hint of anger. At her? At Annie?

"Perhaps not, but it seems to me as if your sister's problems have done nothing but impact your life. Did you always give up everything you wanted for her sake?"

Sheridan's chest grew tight. The lump in her throat was huge. "Don't talk to me that way. You don't know my sister and you have no right to judge her. Annie's fragile. She needs me."

His gaze raked her face. "Yes, she needs you. She needs you to acquiesce to her demands, to give her what she wants, to provide the thing she believes she's been cheated out of."

Sheridan gasped. And then she reacted. She moved to slap him, but he caught her wrist and held it tight. His dark eyes were hard. And filled with a sympathy she'd not seen there before.

She was shaking deep inside. "How dare you? Annie didn't ask me to have this baby for her. I offered! And I'm going to do it, even if it takes another year to start again."

He ran his fingers down her cheek tenderly, and she trembled. "Of course you offered, *habibti*. Because you love her and because you were afraid for her. I don't fault you for this. I fault her for refusing to see what it might cost you."

She shook her head softly. "They are paying for the procedure and the birth. It's not costing me anything."

He let her go and stepped back. His mouth was a white line now. "It costs nine months of your life, it places a burden on your body and then there is the emotional impact of giving up the child at the end. That is not *nothing*."

He was confusing her. Just a couple of days ago he'd suggested she turn over any child to him and now he was talking about the emotional impact of that kind of decision. Who was this man?

"I knew that when I offered."

His expression was black. "Yes, but did you also know that you were offering to risk your life? Did you consider that? Did she?"

Sheridan's heart pounded. "Childbirth is safe. This isn't the eighteenth century."

He stood stone-still but she sensed his muscles had coiled tight. As if he was a nuclear reaction waiting to happen. But then he pulled in a deep breath and huffed it out again and she knew he'd found the switch to turn it off.

"Of course it's not. You are correct."

Sheridan had a strong urge to reach for him, but she didn't. Something was bothering him. Some dark emotion reflected in his gaze, but she wasn't quite sure what it was.

"What's this about, Rashid?"

"It's not about anything," he finally said.

Her voice was little more than a whisper. "I don't believe you."

He stood there for a long moment, as if he was fighting an internal battle. And then he turned and strode away without another word, disappearing into the long gallery running along the back of the palace.

CHAPTER EIGHT

THE DAYS PASSED too slowly. Sheridan kept hoping to see Rashid, but he seemed to be avoiding her. She emailed with Kelly, planned the menus for two upcoming parties and felt guilty for not being there to help with the physical preparations. But there was really no need. Dixie Doin's operated like the efficient party machine it was meant to be.

Sheridan had spent a lot of time making sure that was so when she'd decided to have a baby for her sister. Though she'd intended to work until the birth, there were never any guarantees and she'd wanted to be prepared for anything.

Kelly hardly missed her, though she assured Sheridan that she missed her personally. Emails from Annie were another story. Sheridan dreaded to open them. She knew Annie was upset, but the lack of understanding about the situation made her stomach hurt. Her sister actively hoped that the IUI had failed. Sheridan understood that wish, understood it would be the easiest thing for them all. She'd thought the same thing when she'd first been told, but now that she was here with Rashid and he was real to her, not just a random sperm donor, the situation was much more complicated.

She thought of the man who had touched her so sensually, the man who heated her blood and chilled her bones and confused her to no end. No, this situation was no longer random and impersonal. It had ceased to be so the instant he'd walked into her life.

If Rashid hadn't come looking for her in Savannah, what would Annie have wanted her to do? Sheridan didn't want to know, and yet she couldn't help thinking about it. Would Annie have wanted this baby, too? Or would she have wanted Sheridan to terminate the pregnancy so she could start fresh with Chris's sperm?

She didn't even know if she was pregnant yet, but already she was emotional over the idea of losing this baby. Would it have been simpler if she'd never met Rashid, never slept with him?

Probably, but it was too late for that.

Sheridan took her usual route through the palace, stopping in the kitchen to see the staff and find out what they were preparing. She was fascinated with the food here, the fresh olive oil and breads, the fruits and nuts, and the flavorful dishes made with chicken and goat. The staff seemed wary at first, but as her visits increased—and Daoud, her formerly silent guard, or Fatima translated for her—they began to look forward to her arrival.

She tasted food, oohed and aahed appropriately and discussed ingredients. She even made note of some things to try for Dixie Doin's. Not everything was Kyrian, however. There was plenty of French cuisine as well, which surprised her at first but not when she considered that the French had once sent colonists to Kyr.

If anyone found it odd that an American woman roamed the palace, they did not say so. In spite of the women she saw in business attire, she kept to the rules

Rashid had set and wore Kyrian clothing. She even wore the hijab, because when her blond hair was hidden people seemed less likely to see her as an outsider.

Not that all Kyrians had black hair—there were some brown and tawny gold heads she'd seen—but her hair was so pale as to be noticeable when uncovered.

She'd gone to see the puppies again. When there was no sign of the mother dog, she asked Daoud why. That was when she learned that the puppies were orphans. They were being bottle-fed and taken care of by the grooms. She'd had Daoud ask if she could feed them, though he'd seemed reluctant to let her.

But she'd done it, and then she'd found herself surrounded by yipping dogs while she giggled and petted them and watched them suck down the milk. They were so sweet and she loved spending time with them. It was the highlight of each day, especially as she never saw Rashid.

She thought about him. She lay in her bed at night with her hand over her belly and thought about the man she'd made love to only once. The man whose baby might be in her womb right now.

She wondered where he was, if he was in his own bed and thinking of her, or if that single night had been an aberration and he now gave her no more consideration than what he'd had for breakfast. Probably the latter, considering she hadn't seen him since that night when he'd left her standing in the darkened courtyard.

She'd considered walking down the corridor in the middle of the night again, opening his door and making him talk to her. But when she'd gotten brave enough to act on it, a guard had been stationed outside her own door. He'd looked up from his tablet computer, his eyes meeting hers steadily until she'd shut the door.

Clearly, Rashid had thought she might come looking for him and had taken steps to prevent it. She was somehow both embarrassed and furious at once at the notion.

Still, Sheridan went through the days and did not ask where Rashid was. If he thought she was pining for him, then she was going to prove she wasn't. How could she when he was still such a stranger?

An enigmatic, compelling stranger that she wanted to know better.

Soon it was the night before her pregnancy test and Sheridan couldn't seem to settle down. Her stomach was twisted in knots and nothing Fatima brought seemed appealing. She finally tried a little bread and some sparkling water and settled onto the couch to read for a bit when the door to her suite opened and Rashid walked in without preamble.

Emotion flooded her in an instant: happiness, anger, fear, sorrow. So many things it was hard to sort them all out, and all caused by this dark man who stood there in a smartly tailored gray suit and Kyrian headdress. Not for the first time, he made her heart skip a beat.

"Fatima says you aren't eating," he said, his voice tight and diamond edged. Just the way she expected it.

Of course he was getting reports about her. "I'm not hungry."

He came over and glared down at her. If he would put his hands on his hips, it would be the perfect admonishing parent pose.

"You have to eat. It's not good for you or the baby not to eat."

She put her hand over her belly automatically. "We don't know if there is a baby."

"We will know soon enough. Besides, it's better to assume there is a baby and do everything to take care of it properly."

She wanted to yell at him. "I didn't refuse, Rashid. I can't keep anything down right now. My stomach is upset." She set the book aside and matched his glare. "You promised we would spend some time together so we could know each other better, and yet I've not seen you in five days now."

His expression didn't ease. "I've been busy. This is what happens when one is a king."

"Yet you found time to come here tonight and chastise me for not eating."

He stripped off the *kaffiyeh* and tossed it aside. Then he raked a hand through his hair. "I came straight here from a meeting." He walked over to the table where Fatima had left food in chafing dishes and examined the contents. Then he picked up a plate and dished some things onto it.

Sheridan bristled. "If you think you're going to force me to eat—"

"Not at all," he said, picking up a fork and heading over to sit in a nearby chair. "I haven't eaten yet and I'm starving."

Sheridan blinked. After days of silence, he was planning to eat with her? He'd taken her to bed, made her feel things that excited and confused her and then when she'd been certain he was planning to do it again, he'd left her standing alone in the courtyard.

To say she didn't understand him was an understatement.

"Wow, I'm being graced with your majestic presence for dinner? I'm honored."

He looked up at her, his eyes gleaming. But not with anger. "You said you wanted to talk to me. Here I am. Talk. Bore me silly if you must."

She folded her arms. "Perhaps I'm a sparkling conversationalist. Did you ever consider that?"

"It has not been my experience with most women, but perhaps you will be different."

She told herself it would be unwise to throw a pillow at him. She chose instead to focus on one aspect of what he'd said. "Most women? Who has managed to please you conversationally?"

He took a bite of food, chewed and swallowed. She didn't think he would answer her, but then he looked up again and speared her with his hot gaze. "My wife did," he said. "Not always, it's true. But often enough. She died five years ago, in case you were wondering."

Her belly had tightened into a hot ball of nerves. Of all the things he could have said, she hadn't seen that one coming. Her heart ached for him. "I'm sorry, Rashid."

She didn't know what else to say. To lose someone you loved had to be such a tragedy. And someone so young, too. No wonder he sometimes seemed cold and lonely. It made sense now.

He set the plate aside. "This is not something I speak of, but if we are to marry, I thought you should know it."

Her throat was tight and her heart hammered in her stomach, her chest, her ears. "I appreciate you telling me. But I'm not certain marriage is the answer to our dilemma. Assuming there is one."

He frowned. "This child has to be born legitimate, Sheridan. It is the only way."

Panic bloomed inside her. She didn't want to take away a child's heritage, but she also didn't want to have to marry a man she hardly knew. They had sexual chemistry, but what if that was all they had? How could she live a lifetime with a man who'd only married her to claim a child?

"I assume I have no say in this?"

"You would prefer options? Marry me and be this child's mother, or go home after you give birth. Those are your options."

She figured it was a good thing there were no weapons nearby. "Those aren't options."

His eyes flashed. "They are the ones you have."

"I won't leave my child."

"No, I didn't think you would. I might have thought so once, but no longer."

Her head was beginning to ache. "And what brought about this blinding revelation?"

"Daoud tells me you've been playing with the puppies. Feeding them, taking care of them. And then there is my kitchen staff, Fatima and even the stable hands. They like you, and you like them. They all say how kind you are, how caring. Yet even without these things, there is this deed you set out to do for your sister. You are a giving person, Sheridan, but I don't believe you are so giving as to leave your child in Kyr. You will stay."

His words wrapped around her heart and squeezed. She liked Daoud, Fatima and the kitchen staff. To know they liked her, too, was touching. "There is every possibility I will go home tomorrow."

"Yes, there is."

Pain sliced into her at the thought. It confused her. She wanted to go home, wanted to go back to her life in Savannah, her business, her friends. She wanted her life the way it was before Rashid al-Hassan had walked into it.

And yet that thought filled her with despair. Never to see him again? Never to make love to him? He didn't seem much bothered either way, and that hurt, too.

"All this talk of marriage is premature," she said tightly.

"Is it? We will know tomorrow. If you are pregnant, things must be done quickly."

"And you've already decided everything. Without asking me what I might want."

It was just like him, of course. King Rashid acted. He did not consult a soul. He simply did what he deemed best. Just like when he'd scooped her up and brought her to Kyr against her will.

"I have told you your options." His voice was smooth and even, as if he was explaining things to a child.

Anger wrapped long fingers around her throat and squeezed. "I still have Annie to consider. What about her?"

His expression grew hard. Hard and cold and unapproachable. "What about her?"

That was the moment when the bile in Sheridan's stomach started swirling hard, pushing upward, demanding release. She got to her feet and staggered toward the bathroom. She barely made it in time, and then she was bending over the sink, retching.

There was a hand in her hair, holding it back. He put another hand on her back and rubbed gently while tears sprang to her eyes and she felt utterly miserable. She wanted to tell him to stop touching her, but in fact it felt nice to have him soothe her. She was a traitor even to herself.

"I'm not trying to be harsh," he said, his voice gentle for once. "But your sister cannot figure into my dynastic responsibilities. There are other solutions to her problem. You told me yourself about an experimental treatment."

Sheridan put her hands on the counter, bracing herself, her eyes squeezed shut as she prayed there was nothing else left to come up.

"They can't afford it," she said miserably when she could speak.

"I can."

Sheridan turned on the water and gulped some down before she straightened shakily and turned to face him. His beauty always hit her with a punch and now was no exception. A king had just held her hair while she'd thrown up the little bit of food she'd managed to eat.

If anyone had ever told her such a thing could happen, she'd have never believed them.

"You would do that for them?" Her heart was still pounding, but for a different reason now. It was everything she could have wanted for Annie. There were no guarantees the treatment would work, but it was a chance.

"I would not do it for them," Rashid said very softly. "I would do it for you."

Rashid watched her mouth fall open on a soft "oh" and was seized with a desire to claim her lips and take everything he desired. But she wasn't feeling well, and he hadn't come here for that anyway.

No, he'd come because Fatima had said she wasn't eating. And because he'd been getting endless reports about her roaming the palace, commenting on the architecture, talking with endless people, playing with orphaned puppies and spending time in the kitchen discussing recipes and food service.

At a recent lunch he'd attended with some visiting dignitaries, the napkins were folded in shapes. They had been lotus flowers, he'd realized, and he'd been so fascinated that he'd missed the first half of what one of the dignitaries had been saying to him about water rights and oil production.

When he'd asked about it afterward, someone had told him that Miss Sloane had taught the staff how to do it. Lotus napkins. Puppies. Even Daoud spoke her name with a quiet reverence that set Rashid's teeth on edge.

Everyone liked Miss Sloane, and that had made him think about her more than he wished. He liked her, too, but in a different way. He liked the way her body moved beneath his, the sounds she made when she came and the way her mouth tasted his so greedily. He'd thought about it for days now.

He'd deliberately stayed away because he didn't trust himself not to act upon the hot feelings she ignited in him.

He'd been right, considering that he was staring at her mouth and thinking about it drifting over his skin.

Her eyes filled with tears. It was almost a shock, considering that she'd been so strong from the moment he'd first seen her until now. One spilled down her cheek and she quickly dashed it away.

"I don't know what to say." She pulled in a breath and rubbed her hand over her mouth.

His throat was tight and he didn't know why. He cleared it. "You need to rest, *habibti.*"

She pushed a lock of golden hair behind her ear. Her fingers were trembling. "Yes, I probably should. I am quite tired."

She was sagging against the counter and he reached over and swept her into his arms.

"What are you doing?" she gasped.

She was so light, so small. She weighed nothing and it made something move deep in his chest as he thought of her huge with child. "Taking you to bed."

Her cheeks reddened. "I don't feel up to, to…"

He carried her into the bedroom and set her on the bed. "And that is not what I'm suggesting."

He picked up her gown from where it lay neatly folded on her pillow and handed it to her. She clutched it to her chest. On impulse, he ran his fingers over her cheek.

"Change. I'm going to finish eating. Then I will come back. If you still wish to talk, we will talk."

Her eyes were red rimmed. "All right."

He turned away and went back into the living area to finish eating while she changed. He didn't like the way she'd seemed so shattered just now. So stunned and confused. He preferred the Sheridan who stood up to him. The Sheridan who got spitting mad and told him there was no way she would give up her baby.

That Sheridan was strong and would survive anything he threw at her. Anything the world threw at her. But would she survive a baby? She was so small, so delicate.

Rashid couldn't help the memories crowding his head. They made him shiver, made him ache. He would not go through that again. His heart had to remain hard, no matter that Sheridan threatened to soften it.

When he figured she'd had enough time to change, he strode back toward her room, expecting her to pelt him with questions or rebuke him for making decisions for her. Perhaps he'd let her say whatever she wished, since her fire aroused him, and then maybe he'd undress and climb in bed with her. If one thing led to another, who was he to complain?

But when he got there, she was sound asleep in the middle of the bed.

CHAPTER NINE

"THE TEST IS POSITIVE."

The doctor, a lean, short man with glasses, was looking at the results on a printout. No peeing on a stick for
Sheridan. It had been far more involved, with urine and
blood samples and an excruciating wait while the lab
processed the results. "Your hCG levels are doubling
nicely and all looks normal at this stage."

Sheridan sat in her chair in Rashid's office and felt as
if her heart had stopped. Across from her, Rashid sat at
his desk, his lips compressed into a tight line. The doctor seemed oblivious to the undercurrents in the room
as he stood and bowed low.

"Congratulations, Your Majesty."

Rashid waved the man out and then they were alone.
But Rashid didn't speak. He simply sat there with that
bloodless look on his face until her belly was a tight
ball of nerves.

"I'm not sure I really believed it would happen the
first time." Her voice shook but Rashid didn't seem to
notice.

He looked up at her as if just realizing she was there.
"What?"

But he didn't wait for an answer. He sprang to his

feet and began pacing like a caged beast. He was wearing his desert robes today, complete with the headdress held in place by a golden *igal*. He was regal and magnificent and breathtaking. She watched him pacing, her hand over her stomach, and tried to come to grips with the fact she was having his baby.

"We'll marry immediately. The council will have to be informed and then we can sign the documents. We can have a wedding ceremony for the public, but that can be done in a few weeks. You won't be showing by then and—"

"Stop." Sheridan was on her feet, her blood pounding in her throat and temples. She didn't know why she'd spoken, but she felt as if her entire life was altering right before her eyes and there was nothing she could do to stop the tidal wave of change.

Rashid was looking at her now, his dark gaze dangerous and compelling. She reminded herself that he was capable of tenderness. He had touched her tenderly only last night when holding her hair and rubbing her back. And then there was the night he'd made love to her, so hot and intense and, yes, tender in his own way.

"You're making all these plans without asking me how I feel about any of them."

His brows drew down. "This is the way things are done in Kyr. How would you know what the arrangements should be?"

She dug her fingernails into her palms. She was sweating, but not from illness. From shock. And fear.

"I wasn't talking about how things are done in Kyr. I'm talking about this marriage."

As if she could refuse it. She was here, in his palace, and he was a king. This child had to be born legitimate.

And he'd said he would pay for Annie's treatment. What more could she want?

Love. Yes, she could want love. She could want to marry a man because she loved him, not because she had to.

His gaze narrowed. "You are pregnant—this marriage will take place."

She held her arms stiffly at her sides. "Maybe I want to be asked. Did you ever consider that? Maybe I wanted to get married in an old church somewhere, with my family surrounding me, and maybe I wanted to be in love with the man I marry."

Oh, why say that out loud? Why let him know what a hopeless romantic you are?

His expression grew hard. "Life does not always give us what we want. We have to take what's offered and do the best we can with it."

Her heart fell. He was infuriating. Cold and calculating and arrogant. She wanted him to care, at least a little bit, about what this meant for her. To him, she was a woman who carried a potential king. He wanted to order her about the way he ordered Daoud or Fatima or Mostafa.

And she knew, if she knew nothing else, that she couldn't allow him to do that without protest.

"I didn't say yes yet. You're making plans and I didn't say yes."

There was a huge lump in her throat now. Huge. It was like she'd swallowed all the pain she'd ever felt and was about to choke on it.

He picked up a pen on his desk and flipped it in his fingers as if he needed something to do. As if he was irritated. "You are carrying my child and we are going to marry. There's nothing to say yes to." He fixed her with a hard stare. "But if you could say no, would you? Knowing what's at stake for everyone involved, would you say no and deny your child the opportunity to be my heir? Or your sister the chance to have her own child?"

Sheridan's throat hurt. "I didn't say that."

He threw the pen down and sank into his chair again. "Then I fail to see the problem. You will be a princess consort, *habibti*. You will have a life of privilege. And you will be the mother of our child, which is what you've assured me you want. Or am I mistaken? Would you rather leave the child with me and return to America once he is born?"

Sheridan clenched her fists in her lap. Once more, it was a good thing there were no weapons handy. "This baby might be a girl, you know. And no, I don't want to leave her with you."

"Then we will marry immediately and be done with this matter."

This matter. As if marriage and children were the equivalent of deciding where to go on vacation or which carpet to order for the new house.

"Thank you for settling that." Sheridan got to her feet. She was shaking with rage and fear, and sick with the helplessness she felt. "I guess I'll return to my rooms now and await your next command. How I got through life for twenty-six years without you to tell me what to do is quite the mystery. I'm pleased I don't have to think for myself a moment longer."

"Careful, Sheridan," he growled.

A sensual shiver traveled down her spine at the sound. Oh, what was it about him growling at her that turned her on? She'd just told him off for being autocratic, so why did part of her thrill at the edge in his voice?

"Why? If I make a mistake, you'll just tell me what to do to correct it." She sank into the deepest curtsy she'd yet done and then turned and strode toward the door. He was there before her, his arm shooting out and wrapping around her before she could escape.

Her breath caught as he spun her around. "You dare to walk out on a king?"

"You aren't *my* king," she said hotly. But her body was melting where it touched his and that inconvenient fire was beginning to sizzle through her.

"Maybe I am," he said, his voice heavy and angry at once. "Maybe I am utterly *your* king."

Her reply was lost as he ripped the hijab from her hair. "You're mine now, Sheridan," he said hotly, backing her against the wall and pressing his body to hers. "And I keep what's mine."

And then he brought his mouth down on hers. Sheridan stiffened. She was determined to fight him, to keep her mouth closed to his invasion, to push him away.

But she did none of those things. Of course she didn't. Rashid al-Hassan was an unstoppable sensual force and he had a power over her that she couldn't deny. His tongue slid between her lips, demanding her response—and then they were kissing each other frantically, hotly, with all the pent-up passion of the past few days of deprivation. She'd never had such a physical connection to a man before. A connection that went against sense and reason and just *was*.

His hands spanned her rib cage, his thumbs grazing her nipples as he pinned her body to the wall with his own. Her pulse raced as her nipples tightened painfully. Her breasts were so sensitive now and they both knew why.

He found the closures to her dress and opened them deftly. Then he was pushing the garment off her shoulders, letting it fall to the floor. She wrapped her arms around his neck and arched into him until he growled again and stepped back to rip her panties down her legs. She stepped out of them as she fumbled with the soft trousers he wore beneath his *dishdasha,* trying to free him.

He helped her and soon she had her hands on his hot erection. But he didn't give her a chance to play. His broad hands went to her bottom, lifted her high against the wall—and then he plunged into her as they both gasped.

"Sheridan." His voice was a hot whisper in her ear and her heart twisted tight. "I need you."

"Kiss me, Rashid," she begged. Her skin was too tight, her belly too hollow, her body too hot. She needed the things he gave her, needed the connection and release. She didn't understand it, but she craved it. Craved him.

He fused his mouth to hers—and then he began to drive up into her, harder and faster and deeper than before, until her body was alive with sensation, until she had to wrench her mouth from his and sob his name as she splintered apart in his arms.

He didn't release her, though. He took her again and again, until she was a quivering mass of nerve endings, until her body couldn't take another moment's pleasure, until he finally let go of his rigid control and came, his seed filling her in warm jets.

He laid his forehead against the wall behind her, his

breath coming in gusts. His skin was hot and moist and so was hers. She turned her head into him, tasted the salt on his skin on impulse.

And found herself released. He stepped away from her and fixed his trousers, then reached down and picked up her gown for her. She snatched it out of his hand and he met her gaze evenly.

They stared at each other for a long moment, her clutching the dress in front of her like a shield, him clenching his fingers into tight fists at his side. As if he wanted to touch her again but had to force himself not to.

Her legs were weak and anger bubbled hot in her veins, but if he reached for her, if he kissed her again, she'd open to him like a flower.

And she really despised that about herself. There was such a thing as being delightfully impulsive, as being friendly and open, but this was too much.

"I don't understand you," she said. "If you don't like being with me, why do you touch me in the first place?"

She thought they had a chemistry that was unusual, but maybe she was fooling herself. Maybe he just saw her as an option for quick sex. He found his pleasure in her body and he was done. And she was just stupid enough to make the same mistake twice.

He shoved a hand through his hair. "I like being with you. But it's over and I have work to do."

She shook out her dress angrily and slipped into it. Then she turned her back on him. "I can't do this without your help."

He came over and stood behind her, his fingers brushing her skin as he zipped her up and fastened the hooks. When he finished, she turned around and glared at him.

"This can't happen again," she told him tightly. "I

have feelings, Rashid, and I won't let you stomp all over them just to get your way. And another thing," she added, pointing at him. "There are women in this palace in dresses and business suits and slacks. I've seen them, and while I played along with your commands to dress as a Kyrian woman, I won't blindly do it anymore. Kyrian women seem to represent a range of styles, which you purposely did not tell me. If I want to wear my jeans, I'm wearing them."

His expression was tightly controlled. "When you appear before the council, you will wear traditional clothing. Aside from that, I don't care."

She lifted her chin as she met his dark stare. "Oh, I already gathered that, Rashid. You don't care at all."

Rashid met with the council and informed them he would be marrying, and why. The council wasn't pleased that Sheridan wasn't Kyrian, but they could hardly argue with the fact she was carrying his child.

"And would you consider a Kyrian woman for a second wife, Your Majesty?" one of the men asked.

Rashid let his hard stare glide over the gathering. They were good men, wise men, men whose families had spent generations on the council. And while they had gotten far more progressive over the years, they still clung to some traditions. A pure Kyrian dynasty was one of those, though they all knew that past sheikhs had sometimes married foreigners and had children with them. Still, it cost him nothing to appease them. They would not accept Sheridan as queen, but as a princess consort. And with a future queen of Kyrian descent to be named, they would be happy.

"I will," he said coolly. "But not immediately."

That seemed to satisfy them and the council was dismissed. Rashid returned to his office to work, but he couldn't seem to stop picturing Sheridan up against the wall, her lovely legs wrapped around him, her sweet voice panting in his ear as he took her over the edge.

He pushed back from his desk and sat there staring at the place where they'd been. He'd taken her like a savage. Like a man for whom control was impossible to attain, when nothing could be further from the truth.

She wound him into knots and he didn't like it. She'd said he didn't care, but he very much feared he might. Not a lot, certainly, but more than he was comfortable with. Because he couldn't stop thinking about her, or about how it felt to lose himself in her body.

He was not the sort of man to become obsessed with a woman, yet she intrigued him. Had from the first moment he'd seen her standing in her shop, all small and blond and seemingly sweet.

But then he'd kissed her and his world had gone sideways. He'd wanted her every moment since.

And he hated that he did.

She was pregnant. Thinking the words sent that same cold chill through him, as always—but there was something else, too. Pride, possession, ownership. She was carrying his child and he was going to marry her. For Kyr.

Rashid got to his feet and left the office, striding through the palace until he came to his rooms. It wasn't quite dark yet, but the hour was growing late. He changed into jeans—not without thinking of her informing him that she would be wearing her jeans whenever she wanted, that defiant tilt to her chin—and a button-down shirt, and then went through his suite of rooms to the hidden door that connected to the women's quarters.

He stood there for a long moment, staring at the lock. And then he released it and stepped inside. She wasn't in bed so he moved through the rooms until he saw her at the computer. She was hunched over it, her head in her hands, and his heart squeezed.

Then she reached for a tissue and he knew she was crying. Damn it. His fault, no doubt. Because he'd pushed her away. But how could he explain to her that being in her arms after they had sex felt like a betrayal? Not because of the sex, but because of the way he wanted to linger, the way he wanted to know everything about her.

"Sheridan."

She startled, shooting up out of her chair and whirling to face him. Her nose was red. "My God, you scared me to death."

"I'm sorry."

She was wearing her jeans and a silky shirt and she looked so small and alone as she stood there with her shoulders bent. "How did you get in here?"

"There's a hidden door in the bedroom. It leads to my rooms."

"Oh," she said softly, and he knew she must be wondering why he hadn't used it to bring her back the other night. But there were more immediate things to think about.

"What is wrong?"

She gave a half shrug. "I was just reading email from my business partner. I think we're both realizing our dream is over now."

"I know you blame me for these things, but I am not

the one who caused this." And yet he did feel guilty for his part in changing her life.

"Believe it or not, I do know that. But it seems so odd that a single oversight could impact so many lives."

"This is quite often the case."

"For a king, I'm sure it is. For a girl from Savannah who just wanted to give her sister a gift, this is all a bit of a shock."

She walked over and put her hands on the back of a chair, gripping it so tightly that her knuckles whitened. He watched her, torn between going to her and holding her and staying where he was. In the end, he decided to stay. She would not welcome him at the moment.

She swiped the tissue over her nose again and stuffed it in her pocket. "So what did you come here to tell me to do now?"

Rashid's brows drew down. Why had he come? *Because you can't stay away. Because she has a brightness to her that draws you like a moth. Because you want to feel that brightness wrapped around you again.*

"I didn't come to tell you to do anything."

She waved a hand as if she were sweeping aside a bothersome fly. "Well, isn't that a relief? What can I help you with, then?"

For once in his life, he was left with nothing to say. He dug down into the recesses of his brain. "My brother is going to build a skyscraper for me. I understand you have architecture experience. Perhaps you could consult?"

She blinked at him. Several times. "I...well, I did train as an architect, but I worked on historical preservation. Old buildings. Skyscrapers aren't quite my thing. Not to mention I left the profession to start Dixie Doin's with Kelly."

"Why did you do that?" He truly wanted to know. She'd gone to school for one thing and ended up doing another.

She shrugged. "I enjoyed architecture, but it wasn't as fun as party planning. I like organizing things, making people happy. Preserving old buildings takes time, but making people happy with food and fun is instant gratification."

"Which explains why you spend so much time in the kitchen. I enjoyed the lotus-shaped napkins, by the way."

She smiled at him, a genuine smile for once, and his heart did that little hitch thing again. "I'm glad. I'll show them ferns next. Then maybe some swans."

"No swans at the state dinner, I beg you."

She laughed. "Fine, no swans." But then her smile faded and she slumped against the back of the chair. "Will I get to attend these functions, or am I to be kept shut away like that cousin you can't trust not to drink too much and dance on the tables?"

The way she said things amused him. "Do you drink too much or dance on tables?"

"Not since college." He must have looked surprised because she laughed again. "I'm kidding. I danced on the tables *without* drinking. Because it was fun sometimes to let loose."

He tried to imagine her on top of a table, dancing and having fun. "Do you let loose often?"

She hesitated a moment. "Too often where you're concerned."

The words hung in the air between them. He could feel his body hardening, and she hadn't said anything provocative. Or done anything provocative. But he knew

how she tasted, how she felt, and he wanted to unwrap
her and taste and feel her again.

And again.

"We've only been together twice," he pointed out.

"And if you hadn't avoided me for so long, I imagine
it would have been far more often than that. Though I
suppose it's a very good thing you did."

Okay, he was seriously hard now. Ready to walk over
there and take her in his arms. "You say the most unexpected things."

"I'm too honest for my own good sometimes. I've always been this way, but I like it because it beats keeping things inside."

"But you do keep some things inside." He was thinking of her sister and the way she defended the other
woman's weaknesses even when they affected her life.
He wondered why she did that, but he supposed he didn't
really have to ask. When he'd been a kid, he'd done everything he could to keep Kadir insulated from their
father's wrath. It hadn't always worked, but he'd tried.

She bowed her head. "I suppose I do. But everyone
needs a few secrets, right?"

Who was he to contradict her? He had secrets of his
own. "I don't know if *needs* is the right word. But yes,
I know what you mean."

Her blue eyes gleamed. "I'm still angry with you. But
if you walked over here and took me in your arms, you
could make me forget it all for a few hours."

He was poised to do just that when she continued.

"But I'm asking you not to." She shook her head. "I
need time to process this, Rashid. I need time to figure
out how to fit my life into this box you've handed me. I
can't do that if you confuse me with sex."

CHAPTER TEN

SHERIDAN'S HEART POUNDED as she gazed at the handsome sheikh standing across the room. Just a word from her and he would cross the distance separating them and make her feel as if she were the most important, wonderful thing in his life for a few hours.

But she couldn't let it happen again. Not after the way she'd felt this afternoon when they'd made love so urgently against a wall. After, when she'd felt shattered by the emotions he stirred inside her, when she'd needed tenderness and closeness, he'd pushed her away. Every effort she made to be close to him, he rebuffed. So why did she keep doing it?

And now she had to marry him. She didn't know how she was going to survive if she had to keep navigating a sexual minefield with him. They'd done everything backward. Baby, sex and now marriage, and she couldn't keep going down the same path without knowing who he was. Really knowing.

"The sex doesn't mean anything to you," she said. He did not contradict her, and her belly squeezed a little tighter. "And it doesn't mean anything to me either, but it could start to mean more than it should just because I feel so out of place here."

That was what truly frightened her. She was a stranger in a strange land, wholly dependent on this man, bound to him by ties greater than any devised by law. She had to keep her feelings grounded in reality. To do that, she couldn't fall into bed with him every time he came near her.

He shoved his hands into his pockets—God, he was delicious in faded jeans—and adopted a casual pose that belied the tension in the set of his shoulders. He was a man poised on the edge of action. Always. That he would attempt to hide that from her was encouraging.

Because they both knew who had the true power. That he would allow her to have her own both stunned and warmed her. It was progress.

"I am not trying to place you in a box. You seem not to realize how very privileged your life is about to become."

"A gilded box is still a box."

He rubbed a temple and came around to sink down on the cushions of a settee. "I do in fact know this." He leaned back and gazed up at the domed ceiling above them. "I hated living in this palace as a child. It was hell in many ways."

She came around the chair and perched on the edge of it, her heart in her throat and a dull pain stinging her eyes.

He shrugged. "My father was a harsh man, *habibti*. He did not believe in sparing the rod, so to speak."

She swallowed. Was he actually sharing things with her? Or was this an anomaly? "I heard that you only recently returned to Kyr. Is that why?"

His eyes glittered. "The palace is full of information, it would seem."

"The person I heard it from seemed rather terrified to impart it. As if you would be angry. As if you are a tyrant who punishes people for slights."

He looked rather stunned at that revelation. "I am a king, and I must be harsh at times. But I am not a tyrant. The only people who feel my wrath are the council and my immediate staff. I have no need to terrify maids or cooks, I assure you."

"Honestly, I didn't think you did." Because the people she'd met seemed happy to have him as their king, though they were also more than a little awestruck by him. He didn't speak much, they said. He kept to himself. He was serious and responsible and he didn't smile.

But he was fair. No one had yet claimed he wasn't.

One dark eyebrow arched as if he didn't quite believe her. "Really? I would imagine you were my greatest critic. Did I not kidnap you and force you to come to Kyr? Am I not forcing you to marry me against your will?"

She clasped her hands together in her lap. "Well, those things are pretty bad and you should feel quite ashamed of yourself. But you haven't been cruel. Exasperating and arrogant, but never cruel."

He held her gaze steadily. "I am intimately acquainted with cruelty, and therefore I have striven never to be the kind of man who resorts to it in order to achieve his aims."

Again, her heart twisted for the child he'd been. "I believe you."

He blew out a breath. "Well, we have progress, then." He stood suddenly. "Good night, Sheridan. Sleep well."

"Rashid, wait."

He turned back to her, a question in his expression.

Why had she stopped him? What did she want to say? Her heart beat hard and her throat ached and she didn't understand this urge to go to him and wrap her arms around him. Not for the sexual chemistry, but for the boy he'd once been. The boy who'd had a cruel father and hadn't known much love.

She wanted to know more. So much more. But he was finished and she didn't know how to make him start again.

"Sleep well," she said, her voice little more than a whisper.

He tilted his head in acknowledgment. And then he was gone.

Kadir al-Hassan arrived the next day with his wife, Emily. Sheridan had just returned from playing with the puppies when she found the palace staff in an uproar. Or the domestic staff anyway. She swallowed hard and hurried to her room to change out of her jeans and T-shirt. It was quite a relief to be able to dress in something she wasn't worried about getting dirty, though she'd chosen to wear the hijab, too. She liked the fabric covering her head when she went out into the hot Kyrian sunshine. It helped keep her cool.

Now she hesitated as she stood in her closet. She had her clothes from home and the Kyrian clothing. In the end, she chose to wear a blouse and trousers with the hijab. Then she checked her email and waited nervously for someone to decide she should be sent for.

Finally, there was a knock at her door and Emily al-Hassan was on the other side. She was a pretty girl, tall and slender and elegantly dressed in a designer suit and low heels. And she was smiling.

"You must be Sheridan," she said after she introduced herself. "I'm so pleased to meet you."

Sheridan was happy to meet her, too. Emily was American, and it was like having a visitor from home even though they'd never met before.

Emily took a seat and talked easily while Fatima arrived with tea. Once Fatima was gone, Emily's expression changed to something more sympathetic and concerned.

"How are you holding up?" she asked. "Is Rashid behaving himself?"

Sheridan felt a little odd talking about her life with a stranger, but then Emily was the only other person she knew who shared the novel experience of marrying a Kyrian royal.

"I'm not sure he knows how," Sheridan said, and Emily laughed.

"Truthfully, when I first met him, Rashid scared me half to death. He's so quiet. So intense." She frowned then. "I probably shouldn't say anything, but you are marrying him now and so I feel you should be armed with as much information as possible. Rashid and Kadir didn't have a good relationship with their father. He was very harsh."

"Rashid mentioned it."

Emily's eyes widened a bit. "Did he? How interesting. Did he also mention that their father refused to choose an heir? It should have always been Rashid, but King Zaid wanted to punish him. So he left the succession undecided."

"But he decided in the end."

Emily sipped her tea. "No. Kadir did. Rashid did not come when their father died, and so Kadir had to take the throne. But Rashid finally showed up before the formal declaration. And Kadir abdicated."

Sheridan blinked. "Why would he do that?"

Emily's cheeks reddened a bit then. "It's a long story, but he did it for me. I was too scandalous for Kyr, you see. And Kadir never wanted to be a king. He only married me to get out of it."

"But you're still married."

Emily laughed. "Oh, yes. Marrying Kadir for all the wrong reasons is still the best thing I ever did. Because it turns out the reasons were right in the end."

Sheridan's throat ached. It was clear that Emily al-Hassan loved her husband very much. And he must love her equally as much to have given up a throne. It was incredibly romantic. And it made her sad when she thought of her and Rashid and their impending marriage.

She shook her head as hot feelings welled up inside her. "I don't want to marry Rashid. I don't love him, and he doesn't love me. But there's the baby to consider. A baby born to an unmarried mother can't inherit a throne, apparently, even when the king of Kyr is most definitely the father. And forget shared custody." She waved a hand. "Not happening here."

"No, that is definitely Kyr for you." Emily leaned forward and squeezed her hand. Sheridan liked how sympathetic and friendly the other woman was. "Kyr has its charms, and the al-Hassan brothers have even more. I promise you they are worth it in the end. Even grouchy Rashid."

Sheridan laughed. She'd been on the edge of tears, but laughing helped to banish them. At least temporarily. God, she'd needed this. Someone who didn't think the sun rose and set on Rashid, who knew he was flawed and who didn't mind saying it.

"He is grouchy," she said. "And bossy."

Emily laughed. "Bossiness is an al-Hassan trait. But you have to admit they are devilishly handsome."

"I haven't seen your husband yet, but if he looks anything like Rashid, I'd say you're a very lucky woman."

Emily's eyebrows waggled. "I am a *very* lucky woman. And you will be, too, once you tame Rashid."

Sheridan sighed. The other woman was so certain everything would work out in the end. Sheridan didn't feel that way at all. She thought of Rashid pushing her away after sex and her heart wanted to break. "I don't know that he's tamable. Or that I want to. In truth, I wish I could just go home."

But that wasn't as true as she claimed, and she felt a blush stain her cheeks. Emily very politely didn't comment.

"Would you like more tea?" Emily asked instead, reaching for the pot.

"Please."

After they settled down with fresh cups, Emily looked at her very thoughtfully. "Kadir tells me that Rashid has always been intense, but he has not always been the sort of emotionally closed-off man he is now. Kadir does not know what happened, but he thinks something did. There were a few years when they only had the barest of contact. Kadir was building his business and Rashid was in Russia." Emily sipped her tea. "I've only known grouchy Rashid, so I can't say for certain. But Kadir loves his brother very much, and he would not do that if Rashid was not good."

Sheridan's heart thumped. She wouldn't have guessed

that Kadir didn't know about his brother's marriage and his wife's subsequent death, but clearly he did not. It wasn't her place to say anything, so she sipped her tea and kept silent. But she hurt for Rashid as she thought of him losing the woman he loved and having no one to turn to.

They sat there for another hour, chatting about many different things. Emily explained the Kyrian wedding procedure to Sheridan, who found it comfortingly sterile. Oh, she'd always wanted the big emotional wedding, but signing her name on a document and then watching Rashid do the same would be quite enough for her. It was like signing loan papers at the bank. She could handle that.

But when the time came to do just that later the same day, Sheridan found herself more emotional than she'd thought she would be. The signing took place in Rashid's office with Kadir and Emily for witnesses, along with the lawyers who presided over the entire thing. It lasted all of a few minutes as they sat on one side of a conference table with the lawyers on the other and Kadir and Emily at either end.

There was a translator who read the documents to Sheridan, and then she was directed to sign her name on a line. She could feel Rashid beside her, his gaze intent on her as if he expected her to refuse. She almost did. She almost stood and ran from the room, but in the end she knew it would merely be a stalling tactic.

She signed and put the pen down, then stared at her fingers clenched in her lap. Rashid scratched his signature across the document in a hasty scrawl, and then shoved the whole thing across the table.

He was angry, she realized, but she didn't know why.

She glanced over at Emily, who gave her a smile of encouragement and a firm nod, as if to say, "You can do this."

Another few moments and the men on the other side of the table were filing the documents into briefcases and rising. They left the room, and then Emily went to Kadir, who took her hand in his and gave her a look that could only be called hot. He was very handsome, of course. The al-Hassan brothers had been designed by God to make female hearts beat a little harder when they walked into a room.

"Congratulations, Rashid," Kadir said, shaking his brother's hand. "And Sheridan, welcome to the family."

He kissed her on both cheeks. Emily did the same while Kadir took his brother aside for a quick conversation at the other end of the room. Sheridan's heart was beating hard and her stomach fluttered.

"It'll be fine," Emily said. "He's a good man. He's just a little lost, I think. Kadir was, too, but we found our way." She squeezed Sheridan's shoulders. "You will, too. I'm certain of it."

Sheridan wished she shared Emily's confidence, but all she could do was smile wanly and thank the other woman for being there.

Kadir joined his wife then, his arm going around her shoulders. He couldn't seem to be near her without touching her. It made Sheridan wistful. Rashid touched her, but only to initiate sex. After he'd found his release, he was finished with the touching.

"We should leave them alone now, *habibti,*" Kadir said.

And then Kadir and Emily were gone and Sheridan was left standing in Rashid's private office—where they'd had mad sex against the wall—with the beautiful view of the sandstone cliffs in the distance on one side and the ocean on another. The room was quiet. Too quiet.

She turned to look at Rashid and found him watching her. He did not look pleased. She thought of him shoving the papers across the table and her belly tightened. He wanted to be married even less than she did, it would seem.

She thought of him last night, telling her about his wife. He'd said it plainly, unfeelingly, but she knew he must have been deeply affected by the death of the woman he'd loved.

And he must have loved her, since he'd married her willingly and not because she was pregnant with an heir to the throne.

Now he was married to her, and no matter how much he'd said it had to be done and there was no choice, he clearly wasn't happy about it now that it had taken place.

His frown deepened. "Kadir says you are frightened of me."

Sheridan shook her head. "I'm not."

"I didn't think you were. You've been giving me hell since the first moment I saw you. If you weren't frightened then, you could hardly be so now that I've made you a royal princess."

Her belly rolled with nerves. A princess, but not a queen. In order for there to be a queen, the king had to make a proclamation. That much she'd learned from Emily. And while it was silly to even think about the difference, it was quite obvious that Rashid did not intend to issue a proclamation. His father had never done so, either.

"I don't feel like a princess."

"You will soon enough. You'll have to go before the council, and then there are state functions to preside over, meetings to attend. You'll have a secretary and a staff. You will have to choose a cause to support, and then you will need to make appearances for it—"

"Rashid, please." He stopped speaking. There was no moisture in her throat at all. She thought of everything he'd just said and wanted to run and hide. She wasn't shy, but it was too much to process so soon. "Can I please get used to the idea of being married before you start throwing duties at me?"

He looked stiff. Formal. He was so incredibly handsome in his dark desert robes today. They were trimmed in fine gold embroidery that sparkled and shimmered as he moved. Her own dress—a deep purple silk gown with a cream hijab—was not as beautiful.

"Since you informed me you did not wish to be married, and that you did not like having nothing to do, I assumed you would be happy to do things that would take you away from me."

This conversation was like navigating a minefield. How did one respond? Did she ignore the jab about marriage and focus on the part about being busy? Or did she address them both?

"You know what my objections to this marriage are, so I'm not repeating them. And I *would* like to be busy, but the things you've mentioned are not like running a party-planning and catering business."

His mouth flattened. "Some of the skills are the same. You said you liked to make people happy. You will be doing the same as a royal princess. And there will be functions to plan, if you wish to be involved in that."

"I think you know I would."

"Then you will inform your secretary. She will arrange everything for you." He went over to his desk and shuffled through some papers while she stood there and felt like a kid who'd been called into the principal's office for misbehaving.

"Are you angry with me?" she finally asked, deciding that the only way to get anywhere with him was to speak her mind.

He looked up then, his dark gaze spearing her in place. Her blood thumped slowly in her veins at the heat she saw there.

"Angry? No."

He went back to what he was doing and she huffed a sigh. "Rashid, you don't act like someone who's not angry."

He dropped the papers he'd been going through and came around the desk. Then he leaned back on it and crossed his arms. "You looked like a lamb being dragged to the slaughter at that table just now."

Her blood was beginning to hum with irritation. It was a welcome feeling compared to the ones she'd been having. "You didn't seem all that happy, either. I don't think there was a person in this room who believed either of us wanted to get married, so don't you go blaming me for your mood."

"I do blame you, Sheridan. My mood is one of frustration. Because I could smell you beside me and I couldn't touch you. You've told me not to touch you and I won't. But it frustrates me greatly. A man should be able to touch his wife."

Her heart skipped. Of all the things she'd thought were bothering him…

The blood rushed wildly through her veins. He was

sexually frustrated, not angry. He wanted her. In spite of everything, little bubbles of excitement popped and fizzed in her tummy.

"I thought you said we would have a marriage in name only." Because he had said so in the car in Savannah, and though they'd already had sex twice, she wanted him to admit he'd changed his mind. Because she wasn't going to keep having wild encounters with him and then be sent away as if she'd somehow misbehaved.

His eyebrows shot up. "Do you honestly think after this past week that's going to happen?"

She shrugged. "You tell me. Both times we've been together, you couldn't wait to get away."

He put his forehead in one palm for a moment, his fingers spanning his temples. And then he was looking at her again.

"It's not you."

There was a pinch in her chest. "That's a cliché, Rashid. It's not you, it's me. It's also what people usually say right before they say something awful, like 'I think we need to take a break' or 'I just can't love you the way you deserve.'"

As soon as she said the word *love* she wished she could call it back. It had no place here, and judging by the way he was looking at her now, it never would.

"We are clearly not taking a break. We've only just started. And as for love…" His expression grew stony. "I'm not capable of it, Sheridan."

Sheridan swallowed hard. Why did it hurt to hear him say it? Did she really expect love to enter the equation?

Yes. Yes, she did. Maybe not now, but someday. How could you live with someone, have such undeniable sexual chemistry with them, and not fall in love at some point? It didn't seem possible. There was more heat between her and Rashid than there'd ever been in both of her other relationships combined.

But maybe that was just her. Maybe Rashid took that kind of response for granted.

Sheridan turned toward the door. "I think I should go now. You clearly have work to do."

"I'm not trying to hurt you, *habibti*." She thought of the way Kadir had said that word to his wife and tears welled behind her eyes.

"Why would I be hurt?" She lifted her chin. "We are nothing to each other, Rashid. Apparently, we're going to remain that way."

CHAPTER ELEVEN

THEY ATE DINNER in Rashid's private dining room with Kadir and Emily. That was an exercise in torture for Sheridan since those two were so clearly in love that it hurt to watch. Not because she expected Rashid to love her or because she wanted to love him, but when you found yourself pregnant and married without a mention of love, you felt rather cheated over the whole thing.

Why had she used that word earlier? Because she'd been hurt, that was why, and she'd tried to cover it up. She'd blundered, and then she'd found herself stumbling down a path where her new husband had informed her that he wasn't capable of love. It was not an auspicious beginning to a marriage.

She'd half expected Rashid to stop her when she'd walked out on him earlier, but he'd not done so. When she'd walked out of his office, Daoud was there. And for the first time ever, he dropped to his knees and bowed his head.

"Your Royal Highness."

Sheridan had started to shake then. "Daoud, please. Get up."

He'd done so, his dark eyes searching her face in a way that warmed her. As if he'd been looking for sadness and willing to pummel whomever had made her so. But then he'd dropped his head again and she'd realized that Rashid was in the hall behind her.

"Take Her Highness to her room, Daoud. She needs to rest."

"Yes, Your Majesty."

So she'd rested. And when she'd finished resting, she'd gone to the stables to check on the puppies again. They were getting bigger by the day. Soon, Daoud informed her, they would be given to new homes and she wouldn't get to see them anymore. She'd picked one up and held its soft furry body against her cheek before handing it back to the groom and returning to the palace.

And now they were at dinner and Sheridan was trying to follow the conversation, though not doing a good job. They were speaking English, because Emily didn't speak Arabic either, but the laughter and sound of voices just droned over her head while she wallowed in her own misery over her situation.

She'd spoken to Annie earlier, and Chris. Annie was over the moon with excitement about seeing the specialist. Chris was more subdued, as if he knew what this opportunity was costing Sheridan. But he was grateful nevertheless. He expressed it adequately enough for them both, though Sheridan might have liked her sister to realize how huge a change was occurring in her life.

For Annie, the prize was a baby of her own. Nothing and no one got in the way of that fact.

Kelly had been shocked, but she'd taken it all in and started making plans for the future of Dixie Doin's without Sheridan. That had hurt, but it was also necessary.

"Sheridan. Sheridan?"

She stirred after her name was repeated and looked up to find three sets of eyes looking back at her.

"Are you ill?" Rashid asked. "Do you need to lie down?"

She shook her head. "No, I'm fine. I was just thinking." She smiled as she picked up her water glass. "Please don't stop talking on my account."

Kadir shot his wife a look. "Actually, we were going to turn in. It's been a long day."

"Yes," Emily said. "I'm pretty tired. It's been a lovely day, though."

Everyone agreed it had been a lovely day. And then they took their leave of each other with hugs and kisses on the cheek. The room was quiet when Kadir and Emily were gone. Oppressively so, just like before.

"We keep finding ourselves alone together in spite of our best efforts," Sheridan said cheerfully as she turned toward Rashid.

"This is not necessarily a bad thing." Rashid's gaze was bright. Hot. And her stomach flipped even as her body began to melt at the promise in those eyes.

"I think I should go."

"And what if I said your place tonight is here? In my bed?"

She felt light-headed, dizzy. It was anticipation, fear and, yes, even a certain kind of joy she found astonishing.

"I don't think that's wise," she said, even though the voice in her head said something else entirely.

He moved toward her, took her hand and slowly pulled her into his arms. She went reluctantly, but she went. Her palms rested on his broad chest as his heat slid into her bones, her blood. Why did being held by

Rashid feel so right? And why did she want to wrap her arms around him and comfort him? She wanted to know why he had that haunted look in his eyes, and she wanted to know why he pushed her away in the most tender of moments.

"I think it's very wise," he told her. "The wisest thing possible."

His head dipped toward hers and her eyes drifted closed. But then she pictured how it would go. The delicious silkiness of his kiss, the inflammatory response of her own, the frantic revealing of bodies and the cataclysmic joining that would strip all her defenses and leave her heart bare.

And then the ice at the end. She couldn't take the ice.

"I'd rather talk," she blurted out.

He stopped, his lips a whisper away from hers. "Sheridan, you torture me."

Her fingers curled into his shirt. "We can't keep having wild sex like this, Rashid. We have to talk sometime."

He straightened, looking perfectly dejected. Like a kid who'd just had a treat taken away. "I don't see why we can't have sex first and then talk."

"Because you won't talk then. You'll run, or you'll take me back to my rooms, and nothing will ever get said."

He studied her very solemnly. And then he stepped back and drew her into the living area. She sank onto one of the couches and curled her feet beneath her. Rashid went to the opposite end of the couch.

"What do you wish to talk about?"

Sheridan bit her lip as she watched him. What did she wish to talk about? Anything. Everything. Only she'd never really expected he would do as she asked, so here she was with no leading question. No carefully thought-out phrase to begin prying into his life.

So she launched into it like a cannonball off a diving board.

"Why are you incapable of love?"

His eyes widened. And then his mouth flattened and she was certain he would brush her off. He did not, however, but she found herself almost wishing he had.

"Because it hurts. Because people die and you're left figuring out how to live your life without them. It's easier not to love."

"But choosing not to love and being incapable of it are two different things, right?"

He rubbed a hand over his face and looked away from her. "Maybe so. But I've chosen what works best for me."

"You will love this child, though." She wanted to understand him. He'd lost a wife and that had affected him greatly. But surely he would love their baby. She needed to know he was capable of that much at least.

"Sheridan." He didn't say anything else for a long moment. And then he closed his eyes and swallowed. "My wife was pregnant. She had a rare congenital defect that caused her to hemorrhage."

He swallowed and his skin paled visibly. Sheridan wished she could stop him, wished she could go over and pull his head to her chest and just hold him. But how could she do such a thing when he was talking about the death of a wife and child he'd loved?

"There was nothing the doctors could do. And the baby, who until that time had seemed healthy, was stillborn."

"Oh, Rashid." Her eyes filled with tears. What could

she say? What could she do? His anger over her having a baby for Annie made so much more sense now. He'd talked about risking her life that night. And when she'd asked him what was wrong, he'd told her it was nothing. She'd known it was not nothing.

She hadn't known it was anything so tragic, however.

"Yes, I will love this child. But I'm terrified to do so. Perhaps now you can understand why."

She clasped her hands tight in her lap. "I do."

"Kadir doesn't know about this. No one does. I was in Russia then, running my business, and had very little contact with anyone outside of the microcosm of my life."

It humbled her that he would share something with her that he hadn't even shared with his family. She thought of Emily telling her earlier that Kadir knew something had happened to his brother, but not what. "Maybe you should tell him. Maybe he has words of wisdom that I can't seem to find."

"There are no words of wisdom, Sheridan. You simply get through each day until the pain isn't as great. You never forget, but you learn how to live anyway."

She couldn't sit here any longer and not reach out to him. So she got up and moved closer, taking his hand and squeezing it in hers. That was all. Just a touch. He squeezed back and then they were looking at each other, their gazes tangling, searching, locking together for what seemed forever, but was probably only a few minutes.

"I'm sorry I pried. It wasn't my intention to make you share painful memories."

He lifted her hand to his mouth and kissed her knuckles. "You're very sweet. When you aren't telling me to go to hell, that is."

She smiled. It shook at the corners, but she held it together anyway. "If I didn't tell you, who would? You have far too many people bowing and scraping and bending over backward to serve you. You need someone to remind you that you aren't perfect."

"No, I am definitely not perfect. In this, you are very like Daria."

"That's very sweet of you to say."

"But also mercenary."

"Mercenary?" Her blood beat in her temples, her throat.

His eyes glittered hot. "Life is for the living. And I want you, Sheridan. Now, tonight. I want to take you to my bed and keep you there until you can't move a muscle. Until your body is liquid with pleasure, weak with desire and sated beyond your wildest imaginings."

Her breath caught. "That sounds quite amazing, Your Majesty. But I'm still not certain it's a good idea."

Because he made her heart thrum and her body melt and her eyes sting with tears. She was drawn to him physically, but it was also more than that. And that was what frightened her. How could she spend time with him and not be drawn deeper into that spell? He was so much more than an arrogant and entitled king.

He was a man who'd lived an imperfect life, who'd experienced pain and loss and incredible sadness. He was also lonely, and that loneliness called to her because it was so familiar. He took care of everyone else first—his nation, his duties—and whatever was left over he gave to himself. But it wasn't much.

For a man who was rich in material things, he was sorely lacking in emotional fulfillment.

"We have to start somewhere," he said softly.

Oh, how she wanted to accept, to let him know he didn't need to be alone. But the risk…

"I can't go to bed with you now only to have you freeze me out later."

"I don't want to freeze you out."

"But you do. You have."

"I know."

But he tugged her hand until she had to move right up against him. And then he speared his other hand into her hair and lowered his mouth to hers. She didn't stop him. She closed her eyes, and then his lips met hers and she sighed. He kissed her sweetly, so sweetly, and yet the heat swelled inside her, rolled through her, intensified with each gentle stroke of his tongue against hers.

"I won't get up and go back to my room in the middle of the night," she said between kisses. "I won't, Rashid."

"I understand." And then he kissed her deeper, harder, until the passion unfurled between them, until he pushed her back on the couch and shaped her body with his hands, exploring her curves endlessly.

She thought he would undress her there, but he soon lifted her up and pulled her outside onto the terrace. It was a beautiful night, not too cool yet, with stars winking over the dunes. He took her to the railing and stood there gazing out over the darkened desert. Behind them, the city lights tinted the sky, but it wasn't enough to drown out the vast darkness before them.

"I left Kyr for many years," he said, standing behind her at the railing and putting his arms around her, caging her in. "I gave up the expectation I would become king when I was a young man. I wandered the world, and I started my own business, which I built into the powerful oil company it is today. I became who I am because of my life here in Kyr. And one thing I vowed many years ago was that no child of mine would ever believe I did not love or approve of him. Or her."

He turned her in his arms then and she gazed up at him with eyes blurred with tears. "I believed you the first time you said it," she said softly.

"Yes, but I wanted you to know that I was certain. This child will not lack for love."

Sheridan swallowed the lump in her throat. She wanted to ask him if there could ever be love between them, but she knew it was not a question he wanted to hear. He'd told her he chose not to love, not that he was incapable of it, and so that gave her hope.

She put a hand to his cheek and watched his eyes darken. "You're a good man, Rashid. And I know you'll be a good father."

He turned his head and pressed a kiss into her palm. "You will want for nothing here, *habibti*. I know this is not the life you would have chosen, but I believe you will come to love Kyr as I do."

"I hope I do," she said, her heart pounding at the realization she could love so much more than Kyr if he would let her.

He kissed her suddenly. And this time he did not stop. This time, he kissed her until she was melting and pliant, and then he swept her into his arms—how many times had he done this now, and why did it thrill her every time he did?—and carried her into his bedroom, where he undressed her slowly, kissing and caressing each bit of skin he revealed, until she was quivering with anticipation, until she was ready to beg him for release.

He made love to her first with his mouth, and then, when she was sated and shattered, he settled between her thighs and entered her on a breath-stealing plunge. Sheridan wrapped her legs around him as he rode her, arched her body into his and let him take her over the edge of passion and into the depths of a pleasure so intense it made her cry his name again and again.

When she was shattered and spent again, when she couldn't lift a muscle, Rashid found his release in her body. He rolled away from her and she lay there with the cool air wafting over her heated skin and her brain racing, wondering if he would get up and hand her the clothing he'd dropped onto the floor.

She didn't dare reach out to him. Long minutes passed in which she worried and wondered and thought of what she would say if he withdrew again. And then she thought maybe she should just get up and go. Take the decision away from him. Show him she didn't care about his rejection.

Sheridan pushed herself upright and swung her legs off the bed. She fumbled for her clothes in the dark, her eyes stinging, as Rashid didn't say a word. He didn't care if she left. After everything he'd said, he didn't even care.

But then he was there, his hand smoothing over the curve of her back, her buttock, and she stopped what she was doing as her skin reacted with the same predictable flare of heat as always. Oh, it wasn't fair. It just wasn't fair.

"Don't go," he said. And then he pulled her down, into his arms, and she was lost all over again.

CHAPTER TWELVE

HE'D BEEN RIGHT about her, Rashid thought. She *was* a people pleaser. Sheridan was the kind of bright, sunny sort of person that he was not and never had been. She was light to his dark, sweet to his sour, sunshine to his ice. She made people happy. She spoke with everyone she met as if she was genuinely interested in them. She had to have a translator, but she was beginning to learn a few words and when she tried them out, no matter how badly she mangled them, even the council smiled indulgently.

He did not fool himself that would last, however. The council would eventually begin to demand he take a second wife. He'd told them he would, but he was in no hurry to do so.

Besides, when would he have time for another woman? He was busy enough with Sheridan. Not that she demanded his time, but he often found himself giving it. He went looking for her during the day, found her with her secretary or in the kitchen. Occasionally, he found her in the stables with the puppies.

He looked down at the basket that Mostafa had placed silently beside his desk and took a moment to wonder at himself. Was he going soft?

Soon there was a knock on his door, and Sheridan breezed into the room. She was wearing cream trousers and a red shirt today, and her hair tumbled in blond curls over her shoulders. She was fresh and pretty and glowing.

He glanced at her belly worriedly, but then he told himself it was silly. She wasn't even showing yet. There was nothing to worry about.

"You wanted to see me?" she said.

He stood and went to her side. "I did." He leaned in and kissed her cheek. And then he had to tell himself it was the middle of the day and he had appointments in a few minutes. But he was already hard. It surprised him how quickly she got to him.

As if she knew what kind of internal battle he was having, she slid her arms around him and brought her body against his.

"You smell good, Rashid."

"Stop flirting with me." He tried to sound stern but she only laughed. And then she stood on tiptoe and pulled his head down. He thought she was going to kiss him on the mouth, but she turned her head at the last moment and landed a kiss on his jaw. Then she laughed and pulled out of his arms.

He snatched her back and kissed her properly until she clung to him, until her body went soft and her tongue glided against his and she sighed.

He considered taking her on the desk when there was a noise. A whimper. Sheridan pushed him away and stood with her eyes wide. "What was that?"

"What was what?"

"That...that sound. Like a puppy—" And then her breath caught and her eyes brightened and Rashid reached for the basket. He opened the lid and a pale golden puppy sat there, blinking and yawning.

When it saw Sheridan, the little tail thumped. Sheridan squealed as she reached into the basket and took the puppy out. "Oh, sweet baby, what are you doing in the big, bad king's office? Are you hiding?"

She looked up at him, her eyes shining, and he couldn't remember why he wasn't supposed to feel a flood of warmth at that look. Why it was dangerous to do so.

"The puppies are old enough to go to permanent homes now. I thought you might like one of your own. Daoud said this one was your favorite."

"Oh, Rashid." She bent her head and put her face in the dog's fur. "Yes," she said softly. "He's a precious little guy."

Rashid was beginning to feel uncomfortable. Not in a bad way, but in a "what the hell do I do now" way. Why hadn't he just sent Daoud to her room with the puppy? Except that she wasn't staying in her room lately, was she?

No, she'd been in his every night for the past two weeks. He liked having her there. He thought back to that very first night when he'd found her on his terrace and made love to her. And then he'd jumped out of bed like he'd been singed and escorted her back to her room. He'd followed it up by doing the same thing the next time he'd lost control with her, and she'd thought that meant he didn't want to be touched.

Nothing was further from the truth. He loved when she touched him, loved the tenderness in her fingers, the sweetness in her tongue, the wickedness in her mouth when she took him between her lips. He was beginning to crave her touch.

She beamed at him, her sweet face lighting up with joy. His heart, that organ that was supposed to be encased in ice, kicked. He reached down deep, searching for the ice, jerked it back into place like a blanket.

He could smile, he could be warm and make love, but he could not let his heart be touched. That was the last battleground and the one he would not allow to be breached.

Rashid reached out and stroked the dog's head. "It will be good for the baby to grow up with a dog."

Her smile didn't waver. "It will be good for me, too. Thank you."

She stood on tiptoe to kiss him and then she wandered over to the seating area and set the dog on the floor. The little guy scampered around happily, and Rashid hoped he didn't pee on the rug.

"Are you prepared for the trip?" he asked. They were traveling out into the desert so that he could fulfill his duties to meet with some of the nomadic tribes that still ranged the vast Kyrian Desert. It was mostly ceremonial, but necessary. And while he could leave Sheridan behind for the week or so he would be gone, he wanted her to see the desert as he saw it. The beauty, the majesty, the overwhelming might of all that sand and sun. He wanted his child to feel it inside the womb, to become one with the land, the same as he was.

"I think so. My secretary has been telling me what to expect and what to take."

"How is Layla working out for you?"

He'd sent her a woman who'd trained in European universities and who had a fresh, open manner. Not that he supposed Sheridan would have had any trouble if Layla had been dour, considering how she'd wound Daoud around her finger. If Daoud didn't have a fiancée he adored, Rashid might be jealous.

"I like her. She never makes me feel stupid for not knowing what I'm supposed to do."

Layla had been teaching her protocol and schooling her on Kyrian history in preparation for their upcoming public wedding. Rashid had pushed that out as far as he could, simply because he hadn't wanted to deal with a long day of ceremony and pomp, but the day would arrive soon enough and they'd have to give the Kyrian people something to celebrate.

"I'm glad to hear it."

She frowned a little then. "I asked Annie and Chris if they would come for the formal wedding, but I don't think Annie wants to come."

"I'm sorry, Sheridan." He was predisposed to dislike her sister simply because the other woman seemed not to care how her actions hurt Sheridan, but he knew that it wasn't quite as simple as that. Annie was shy and frightened of new situations. He understood that now, but it didn't mean he liked the way it affected Sheridan.

"I knew it was a long shot. All the pomp and noise, the dignitaries, the heat and strangeness of a place she's never been. It would be too much for her."

He didn't point out that apparently the strangeness of Switzerland, where Annie would have her experimental treatment to try to give her a chance to conceive, didn't seem to bother her.

"We will bring them here another time, then. I will make it happen, I assure you."

She laughed. "Please tell me you're not going to kidnap my sister and her husband, Rashid. If you keep snatching people from the States, eventually you'll be caught, and then there'll be an international incident."

He came and sat down beside her while the puppy yipped and tried to chase his tail. "I won't kidnap them."

"Well, that's a relief."

He tugged her onto his lap because he couldn't quite control himself.

"But I'm not sorry I kidnapped you," he told her, pushing her blond hair back behind her ears and watching the way her eyes darkened with passion as he ghosted a thumb over one budding nipple.

Her voice was a purr. "I thought you had appointments?"

"I'm the king. I can reschedule if I want to." He reached for his phone and punched a button. Mostafa answered. "Reschedule everything for the next two hours."

Sheridan laughed as he tossed the phone aside again. "Such a bossy man. And so certain of yourself. What if I have appointments?"

He pulled her head down to his. "None are more important than this one."

Her mouth brushed his softly, sweetly, and his groin tightened.

"No," she agreed. "None are."

The car that would take Sheridan to her doctor's appointment was waiting for her the next morning. Daoud escorted her down the steps and out the door, but before he could help her into the car Rashid strode outside, looking regal and magnificent in his desert robes.

"I thought you had a meeting," Sheridan said.

Rashid grinned at her. "Did I not explain to you how this works? I am the king. I can reschedule meetings."

Sheridan settled onto the seat and Rashid climbed in beside her. Then the door sealed shut and the car started toward the city.

"It's not necessary for you to be there the first time."

He took her hand in his and butterflies soared in her belly. "I know you're trying to spare me any pain, but I feel as if I should be there for you."

Sheridan's heart squeezed tight as she gazed up at his handsome face. She'd spent every night for the past two weeks in his bed, and she still felt the same butterflies whenever he touched her. Butterflies, heat, need and a melting, aching, wonderful tension that suffused her whole being as he worshipped her body with his own.

And now he'd given her a dog. She'd named the little guy Leo because it just seemed to fit. He was the same tawny gold as a lion, plus he'd been given to her by the Lion of Kyr. Her husband. She dropped her gaze to their linked hands and felt a bittersweet happiness flood her.

Because she was falling for this man. So very hard. Sometimes she thought he cared about her, too, but then she'd catch him standing on the terrace in the middle of the night, leaning against the railing, caught up in thought. She didn't disturb him. She just watched and waited and when she couldn't stay awake any longer, she fell asleep in his bed alone. He never left her right after they made love anymore, but he did leave. Often.

And it hurt. She could admit that to herself. It hurt that he still felt the need to get away from her. She could never understand the depth of the loss he'd experienced, but he couldn't live his life mired in the past. That wasn't good for him. Or for their child.

Or for her, but then she felt as if that was a selfish thought to have. She knew she was not a replacement for his lost wife, a woman he'd loved very much, according to Daoud.

Daoud didn't talk about his king often, and never about anything private, but he had once let it slip to Sheridan that he'd been with Rashid in Russia and that he'd watched him change after the tragedy. Rashid had never been a bubbly person, but he'd closed down completely in the aftermath of his wife and child's death.

Sheridan squeezed Rashid's hand and hoped he didn't regret coming with her today.

They soon arrived at the Royal Kyrian Hospital and were ushered into a spotless examining room. There was no such thing as waiting to be seen when you were the king of Kyr, because the doctor and her staff were already there and waiting for Sheridan to arrive.

After being directed to change and then ushered onto the table, Sheridan lay there while the doctor used the ultrasound wand to search for a heartbeat. Rashid stood beside her, holding her hand, his eyes on the screen as the doctor found the tiny bean that was their baby.

And then the heartbeat filled the speaker and Sheridan couldn't contain a sob. She bit her lip, trembling from head to toe, while the doctor took photos. Rashid's grip tightened. She looked up at him, at the whiteness of his skin, and her heart skipped.

He was reliving an earlier moment just like this, she imagined, and she wished she could tell him it was okay, that it would all be okay. But she couldn't really guarantee such a thing, could she?

The doctor said something in Arabic that suddenly

had Rashid's fingers tightening even more. The wand stopped moving and the doctor stared at the screen.

"Twins," she said after a long moment. She turned to look at Sheridan. "You are having twins, Your Highness."

Rashid stood looking at the screen, his body as rigid as a board. "Twins? You are certain?"

The doctor smiled. "Yes, Your Majesty. There are two heartbeats." She turned the sound on again. And Sheridan could hear it, the faint beat of another heart beneath the pounding of the first.

"They're so fast," Sheridan said, worried at the quick tempo.

"This is perfectly normal," the doctor replied.

She finished up the exam and then they discussed things like vitamins, exercise and birthing classes. It all seemed so surreal to Sheridan. When it was finally over, the staff made another appointment for her and then she and Rashid were back in the car and returning to the palace.

The silence between them was uncomfortably thick. Sheridan searched for things to say, but discarded most of them. What did you say to a man who was staring out the window and ignoring you after hearing the heartbeats of his children? If he was any other man, she might ask him what was wrong.

But she knew, didn't she? It was the ones who didn't make it, the ones he'd loved and lost that were on his mind.

"Are you all right?" she finally asked when the silence stretched too thin. Outside the car, life went on as usual, but inside it was quiet and strained.

He turned to look at her. His eyes were bleak. "I'm fine."

"You shouldn't have come."

He was polite and distant at once. "You shouldn't have to go through this alone. I wanted to be there."

"But it causes you pain."

"I've been through this before, Sheridan. I knew what to expect when I went with you."

"You haven't said anything since we heard the heart-beats."

His jaw flexed. "It was a shock. I didn't expect two babies. I don't think you did, either."

"No. But twins run in my family, though in my aunts and cousins, not my mother. I didn't even consider it would happen to me."

His gaze raked her. "You are so slight. Are the other women in your family as small?"

"My Aunt Liz is, yes, and she had twins. No problems other than a bit of preeclampsia at the end." She sighed. "It will be fine, Rashid. What happened to your wife—well, it was uncommon. Tragic and terrible, but uncommon."

He seemed so detached and cold. "I am aware of this."

They reached the palace then and the doors swung open. Rashid helped her out of the car and led her inside while the palace guards saluted and other servants bowed as they passed. Her heart pounded as they walked through the ornate and beautiful corridors. She wanted to rewind the clock, to go back to the way things were before they'd gone to the hospital, but that was impossible now. She simply had to deal with the aloof man at her side and wait for him to thaw again.

When they reached the private wing, he stopped before the door. He looked as if he'd like nothing better than to escape. "The doctor said you should rest."

"Yes, but it's not even lunchtime yet and I just got up a couple of hours ago."

"Still. Two babies will sap your strength if you aren't careful."

"They are the size of beans, Rashid. I think I can handle some activity. Besides, I still have things to do before we go into the desert. Layla has promised to give me some more lessons this morning on protocol. I think it would be wise to learn as much as I can if I'm not to embarrass you out there."

He grew very still then and a tiny thread of unease uncoiled within her. She knew what he would say before he said it. "Perhaps you should not go with me, *habibti*. We'll be moving around a lot. Besides, it's dreadfully hot, and you might get ill. You should stay here and think about the public wedding. There is much to be done yet."

Sheridan put her hand on his arm. He stiffened beneath her touch and she dropped her hand, hurt by his rejection. Frustration pounded into her. She would not be silent.

"Why are you behaving like this? I'm not any *more* pregnant than when we left here this morning. Why is it suddenly too hot for me to go with you?"

He swallowed. "It's not suddenly too hot. It's always been too hot. I failed to consider it before."

Of course she knew what was wrong with him. She'd been worried about it since he'd insisted on going with her to the hospital. How could he contain his anxiety at what might happen to his children when his previous experience had been so tragic?

"So now that you've seen the babies and heard their

heartbeats, it's too hot? What else, Rashid? Is it too dangerous to have sex now, too? Too dark at night, too light during the day, too many steps between the bedroom and the kitchen? Is Leo too energetic for me? Should I lie down in bed and not get out for the next few months?"

She was on the edge of hysteria. She knew it, but she was just so furious. It was like she'd had him for a little while, had the beginnings of such a perfect life going with him, and now he was slipping away. Slipping into the past and the tragedy that had happened to him.

Slipping away from her.

Because he was afraid of caring and afraid of being hurt. Her heart ached so much for him. She wanted to slap him silly and she wanted to hold him close and tell him that he had to learn to feel again. For their family. Because he deserved to know love again.

She wanted him to know that *she* loved him. She couldn't help it. She'd tried not to fall, but how could she not?

The way he touched her, held her, the way he said her name when they were in bed together, and the way he reached out to her when she knew it was a difficult thing for him to do. He had feelings that went deep, and he was terrified of them.

But how could she love a man who didn't love her? How could she watch him with her children and know he would always keep part of himself separate from them?

At this moment, he'd retreated behind his barriers. He was aloof and cool and she wanted to scream.

"Don't be melodramatic, Sheridan," he snapped. "I'm thinking of your health and the babies. There is nothing wrong with this. You should be thankful I give a damn at all."

And that was it, the blow that had her reeling. The metaphorical slap to the face that reminded her of her place and jolted right down to her soul. She knew she wasn't a replacement wife, but she'd hoped—no, she'd begun to believe—that she might mean something to him in her own right.

But this sarcasm, this utter arrogance? She couldn't stomach it, no matter how she ached for him.

"I see," she said, quietly shaking inside. He was stiff and formal now, all trace of the thoughtful lover gone. It hurt so much. She'd be damned if she'd let him see it, though. "Thank you for letting me know. I am so fortunate that you care."

His nostrils flared, a single concession to emotion. She hoped he might break then, hoped he might tell her he was sorry, that he hadn't meant that the way it sounded.

He almost did.

"Sheridan, I—" He stopped, clenched his jaw, shook his head. And then he looked at her again with eyes that were cold and empty. Icy. "Go rest. I'll see you when I return in a week."

CHAPTER THIRTEEN

RASHID HAD BEEN gone for three days when the rumor reached her. Sheridan stared at Fatima and blinked. Hard. Her belly twisted into knots as she asked Fatima to repeat what she'd said.

Fatima didn't seem to hear the note of anxiety in Sheridan's voice.

"There is talk His Majesty will choose a second wife from one of the tribes, Your Highness."

"A second wife." How had she been in Kyr for over a month now and not considered that Rashid could have another wife?

"A Kyrian wife."

"I see." But she didn't. Fatima clearly thought this was not a problem because she went about her work as if she hadn't just upended the foundation of Sheridan's entire being. A second wife. A Kyrian wife. Why hadn't she seen this coming? And why hadn't Rashid told her it was possible?

After they'd returned from the hospital, she'd been angry and hurt by Rashid's sudden distance. But she'd known it would do no good to push him. She had to give him space, had to let him come around to it in his own time. He was an intelligent man and he would eventually realize he couldn't hide from life. He would miss her in his bed and he would want to continue the relationship they'd had. She'd had every faith they would grow together as a couple.

They might not have married for love, but that didn't mean love wouldn't grow.

But what if she was only fooling herself? He'd spent two weeks taking her to his bed every night and making love to her. He'd given her a puppy because he knew she'd never had one. But what else did he do that indicated his feelings for her might evolve?

He'd gone to the hospital with her so he could show his support, but he'd come away more distant than ever.

And now he'd gone into the desert without her. Could he possibly be looking for another wife? It didn't seem plausible, since he'd planned to take her with him up until the last possible moment. Would he really have gone wife shopping with her along?

His mood had changed so drastically after the revelation they were going to have twins that she couldn't be certain what was on his mind anymore. They weren't from the same world, and it certainly wasn't unusual in his to contemplate such a thing.

She grew chilled as she considered what it would mean for Rashid to have another wife. He would take another woman to his bed. Sheridan would have to wait her *turn* to be with him. She would grow big with his children and she would be shunned while he chose to spend his evenings with another.

In spite of the churning of her brain, Sheridan tried to go about the business of helping Layla to plan the wedding ceremony. It was to be a day of celebration in Kyr, a holiday for the people, and no expense was to be spared.

But she kept asking herself if she'd be helping to plan another of these events for Rashid and a second wife. And that was something she could not do. Not ever. Her stomach twisted in on itself until she couldn't even stand the thought of food. She grew shaky and hot and had to go lie down.

But she couldn't really rest. She kept thinking about how much her life had changed, how Rashid had come and snatched her out of Savannah with little thought to what she wanted, and then how he'd managed to woo her with hot kisses and silky caresses. She'd fallen deep under his spell.

But she had to be brutally honest with herself: it wasn't mutual. She wasn't sure it ever would be. And she couldn't live like that. She just couldn't. She was patient and she'd been willing to give him time—but if he brought home another wife? Hot tears fell down her cheeks and she swiped them away angrily.

No. Just *no*.

Sheridan got up and went to wash her face. She changed into a Kyrian dress and covered her hair with a hijab. She wasn't going to sit here and wait for Rashid to return with another woman on his arm. She'd been the good girl for so long. All her life, she'd given up things she wanted so that Annie would be happy.

It was the ultimate irony that she was here with Rashid *because* she'd been trying to make Annie happy. No other reason. And she'd been doing what she always did with loved ones, which was to be supportive and understanding and hope that they could come to happiness on their own. She'd tried to give Annie a baby, and she'd tried to give Rashid time and space.

Nothing she'd done worked. It was time she admitted that. And it was time she stood up for herself. *Past* time. Sheridan was done putting everyone but herself first. It was time she took action.

Time she demanded that Rashid make a choice.

Rashid sat through yet another meeting in yet another desert enclave, listening to his people's concerns and making plans for how to best help them. The nomads weren't quite the same as when he'd been a boy. Now they had generators, televisions, cell phones and satellite dishes. These things brought concerns of their own, so of course he promised to look into them.

And then there were the daughters. At every stop, he was presented with daughters who would, it was hinted, make fine wives. All of Kyr knew of his marriage to Sheridan, and of the upcoming national holiday in celebration. Soon they would announce the impending arrival of the royal twins, but not until Sheridan was safely into the second trimester.

Rashid's teeth ground together at that thought. Was there truly anything quite so ironic as safety during a pregnancy? So many things could go wrong. Babies were fine up until birth, and then they were stillborn. Mothers hemorrhaged to death. Things went wrong.

It made him break out into a cold sweat.

Not because he was in love with Sheridan, but he did like her. Against all his plans otherwise, he liked the woman he'd had to marry. She was so open and giving, so thoughtful. She'd been worried about his reaction at the hospital before anything had happened—and he'd proved her correct, had he not, when he'd been unable to handle the news she was pregnant with twins?

He'd hurt her by being so cold after, but he'd had to

escape. He'd had a sensation very like panic that had wanted to crawl up his throat and wrap its fingers around his neck. He hadn't known what would happen if that was allowed to occur. And so he'd planned his escape. He'd left her there and embarked on his trip without her.

And now he missed her. Missed her sweet scent, her sensual body, her soft hands and wicked tongue. He sat through meetings and pictured her naked, and then he shook his head and forced those thoughts away before he embarrassed himself in front of the tribal chieftains.

At dusk, Rashid returned to the tent they'd set up for him—an opulent tent adorned with the usual beautiful carpets, but also with most of the modern conveniences one would expect in the city, thanks to the generators that hummed efficiently nearby.

Rashid peeled off his head covering and shrugged out of the long robe, leaving only the light trousers beneath. Maybe he should call Sheridan, see how she was faring. He'd had reports from Mostafa that all was well with her, and the tight knot around his heart had slowly begun to ease.

He would go back to the palace in four days, and he would no doubt take her to his bed again. But he wouldn't let himself forget there were consequences to allowing a woman to get too close. Not ever again.

Yet part of him chafed at that restriction. Finally, he reached for his phone, determined to call her and see how she was doing.

But it rang right as he was about to dial. He answered to find a very breathless Mostafa on the other end. "Your Majesty," he said, and Rashid could hear the panic in his voice. The thread of utter chaos running through that familiar baritone.

Ice water ran in his veins then, flooding him with that familiar calm before the storm. "What is it, Mostafa?"

"Her Highness," he began, and Rashid's gut twisted. "She is gone."

Rashid was tempted to take the phone from his head and stare at it, but instead he forced himself to be cool. "What do you mean gone, Mostafa? Has she left the palace to go shopping? Gone to the airport in order to run away? Or is she hiding in the stables, perhaps?"

"She took a horse, Your Majesty."

Rashid blinked. "A horse?" Had Mostafa lost his mind? Had Sheridan? "Where is Daoud?"

"He is gone, too. When we discovered Her Highness had left on horseback, he went after her."

Daoud and Sheridan were on horseback. In the Kyrian Desert. But for what purpose? Why had Sheridan done such a thing? To get his attention? To bring him back to her side? The fear he'd tried to keep at bay broke through his barriers and flooded his system like a swirling tornado of sand. It scoured through him, raked him bare and filled him with utter dread.

And fury.

She'd taken a horse. She was pregnant and she'd taken a horse. Climbed on top of its back and rode it into the desert. Why? Why?

And then realization hit him. Hard. What if she wanted to harm herself? The desert was dangerous and she'd gone into it alone. Had he pushed her to the edge? Was she trying to get his attention—or trying to end her life?

That thought made the ice in his veins harder than ever—but for a different reason. He couldn't imagine Sheridan gone from his life. Couldn't imagine waking up without her in this world, without her smile or her touch or the look in her eyes when he entered her body and then took her with him to paradise.

She wasn't Daria but she was…she was *Sheridan*. And Sheridan meant something to him. She really meant something….

He was still reeling from the realization that he cared, that he'd not insulated himself from a damn thing by running away from her, that he couldn't control his emotions as if they had an on/off switch the way he'd always believed, when Mostafa said something that made his gut turn to stone.

Mostafa was talking about a search party and the coming night—and a thunderstorm.

A thunderstorm. Sandstorms in the desert were bad enough, but rain was the true danger. It was such a rare occurrence that when it happened, the rain created floods in the wadis—and the sand turned to sludge. Sludge that could trap anything in its path and annihilate it.

Rain was the true enemy of the desert, and a woman alone on a horse in unfamiliar territory—even if she did survive the brutality of a night exposed to the cold and sand, the jackals and scorpions and lions—was no match for a thunderstorm.

Rashid dressed quickly and then strode from the tent, calling orders as he went. Someone saddled a horse at the same time the Bedouin men emerged from their tents where they'd been preparing for dinner. Rashid and two dozen other men swung into saddles simultaneously. Arabian horses pranced and pawed and snorted, but ultimately they were ready for a ride into the night.

Sheridan could be anywhere out there, but Rashid

knew the direction of the city and he knew the most traveled routes. All who were raised in the desert did. Rashid spurred his horse into a gallop and twenty-four men did the same. It was still light, though only barely, the sky a pink stain across the horizon. The moon was full tonight and they would have it for a couple of hours once it rose, until the predicted storm swept in off the gulf and wreaked its havoc.

Rashid only prayed they would find Sheridan before that happened. Because if they did not, if she had to endure a storm in the desert alone... His breath caught painfully in his lungs as the truth hit him full force: if they did not find her soon, there was no way she would survive.

It had seemed like such a good idea at the time, Sheridan thought. She'd been going to the stables so often that no one had thought anything of it when she went again. Even Daoud had relaxed his guard because he was accustomed to her visiting the stables. There were still a couple of the puppies who were waiting for their forever homes, and she wouldn't stop playing with them just because Rashid had given her Leo.

It had been ridiculously easy to saddle a horse and ride out of the barn. She hadn't been thinking too much at the time, but she'd known from listening in the palace that the Bedouin were only a few hours away by horseback. Had she really thought she could ride out to the oasis and find Rashid?

Fatima had told her he was in a place called the King's Oasis, and she'd described it in great detail. Sheridan wasn't an idiot. She had a map and a compass—handy devices, those, and still quite necessary. She'd located one in the palace after a bit of inquiry. All smartphones had them these days, but of course there were battery and satellite issues to contend with.

So now she was riding along a ridge on a delicate Arabian mare, with the desert a sea of sand in front of her and the city a speck behind her, and beginning to come to her senses. Not only that, but darkness was also falling fast and she had no idea how she was supposed to keep riding in the night. To her left, there was a dark wall of clouds in the distance, and she didn't know if they were headed her way or not. They looked ominous, though, like thunderheads off the coast in Savannah.

The occasional brightening of those clouds told her that was exactly what they were as lightning sizzled through them and painted parts of the bank white and pink. She'd never realized there were thunderstorms in this area of the world, but why wouldn't there be? Her only comfort was that this was a desert and therefore they would lose their destructive power long before they arrived. Or so she thought, since a desert by definition was dry.

She was tempted to turn around, but the compass told her she had gone past the point of no return. If she stayed on track, she would reach the oasis in two more hours.

And Rashid would blow a gasket. Sheridan sank into the saddle as she imagined his face when he saw her. At first, she'd thought she would ride in like a general at the head of the army, triumphant and oozing righteousness. Now she imagined she would limp in like a worn-out puppy, her tail between her legs and her body aching from the punishment of a long ride.

In another hour, it was completely dark, except for the silver light of the moon painting the dunes. It was gorgeous and wild out here and Sheridan was at least partly enchanted by the beauty. But she was also worried, because the clouds were drawing ever closer. The moon would be blotted out before long, and while the flashing in the clouds would give light, it was a lot more worrisome the closer they got.

Not to mention the sand was beginning to blow in gusts, stinging her exposed skin. The horse trudged along sure footedly, but Sheridan wasn't certain how much longer that could last. She'd been so stupid. She'd behaved impulsively, rashly, and Rashid was going to be ashamed of her.

She could hear thunder in the clouds now—and something else. Something that set the hair on the back of her neck prickling. There was a howl somewhere to her right. And then another howl behind her. The horse snorted and kicked up her heels, and Sheridan snatched at the reins, desperate to keep the mare from bolting.

And then something snarled nearby and there was the sound of many animals moving at once. The mare tossed her head and reared onto her hind legs—and then she bolted forward while Sheridan cried out and tried to wrap her hands into the mare's mane.

But she'd been caught by surprise and she couldn't hold on. She fell to the sand with a scream.

CHAPTER FOURTEEN

THE ANIMALS BORE down on her quickly, snarling and thumping and snorting, and Sheridan rolled into a ball and tried to protect her head. She would die out here in the Kyrian Desert, her babies with her, and all because she'd been so tormented over a man that she'd lost her head.

There was another howl, and a shriek that was quickly cut off. And then the thumping grew louder and Sheridan realized there was shouting. Men shouting. She was afraid to uncoil her body, just in case the beasts were still there, but then she felt rough hands on her. She didn't even scream as a man jerked her up and against his body. He called out in rough Arabic and then she was flung onto a horse and the man climbed up behind her.

The hijab had fallen around her eyes and she couldn't see anything at all, but there was a man and a horse and she hung on to his waist for dear life as the horse bolted forward into the night. Around them, she thought she heard more hooves, more horses, but the sound became a dull throbbing as thunder split the night.

And then she felt the first cold drops of rain on her back and head. She was stunned as the rain began to fall harder. She would have never guessed. But the wind howled and the horses ran and the rain fell, and Sheridan had no idea where she was or who she was with.

But since the man was infinitely preferable to the beasts, whatever they were, she was grateful for the moment just to be where she was.

They rode for what seemed forever, the rain pounding down, the wind whipping, the horses straining forward, until finally they came to an abrupt halt and Sheridan knocked her head on the man's chest.

There was more Arabic ringing through the night, and then another man put hands around her waist and helped her down. The man on the horse followed, and then he swept her into his arms as if she was a rag doll and strode into a tent. Sheridan struggled to push the fabric from her face. Her teeth were chattering and her skin prickled with goose bumps.

The man dumped her unceremoniously onto her feet and began to remove her clothing. That was when Sheridan came to her senses. She batted at his hands and tried to scramble away. He said something, but the blood rushing in her ears prevented her from understanding. She just knew she had to get away from him. She had to find Rashid.

She drew in breath to scream—

And the man jerked her into his arms, his mouth coming roughly down on top of hers, silencing her.

Sheridan struggled for only a moment before she realized whose mouth was ravaging hers, whose arms wrapped around her, whose hands speared into her hair and tilted her head back for greater access.

She clung to him, her body softening, hands clutching his wet robes. When he realized she knew, he set her away from him, though she whimpered and wanted to stay in his arms.

"We have to get you out of that wet clothing, *habibti*," he said, his voice rough and beautiful.

Her teeth were chattering again and this time when he began to strip her, she didn't stop him. Her hands were too cold to help and so she simply stood there while he stripped the clothing from her body and then wrapped her in a warm blanket. He chafed her arms and then he picked her up and carried her to the bed, where he set her down and pulled a soft fur on top of her.

"Rashid," she said when he started to walk away, but he only turned and shot her a look that she couldn't read.

He was wet, too, his hair sticking to his head, his face streaked with moisture. He did not seem to be as cold as she was, however.

"I'm going to send for something hot to drink. I'm not leaving."

When he walked out, she huddled under the blankets, her brain whirling. She'd made a grave mistake coming here like this. He would be furious, and he would think her unbalanced for even attempting such a crazy thing. Why wouldn't he want another wife? A more sensible one who didn't act on her emotions without fully considering her actions first?

He returned soon with a brass pot and two cups. He poured tea for her, laced it with sugar and handed her a cup.

"I'm afraid the Bedouin don't drink decaffeinated tea, but this is weak. It shouldn't hurt the babies."

She dropped her eyes as she studied the cup, blowing on the steam curling over the top of the liquid. Shame rolled through her.

She could hear him pouring tea for himself, stirring the tiny spoon against the glass, and her nerves tightened as she waited for the explosion.

When it didn't come, she looked up and met a hot, dark gaze staring back at her. Her heart turned over.

"I'm sorry," she said. "I shouldn't have left the palace."

"No, you shouldn't have." He lifted his cup and she thought his hands were shaking, but then she decided it was just her who was shaking. "You could have died out there, Sheridan. The desert is very unforgiving."

"I know."

Strong fingers suddenly gripped her chin and lifted her face until she had to look directly at him again. His gaze was searching.

"Is that what you wanted to do?"

She blinked. "Wh-what?" It took her a moment to process it, but when she did, she sucked in a hard breath. "God, no! I wasn't trying to kill myself!"

"Then what were you doing?" He sounded angry now. Harsh. "Because you almost did just that, *habibti!* You and the babies were moments away from being mauled by jackals. If we had not come along when we did—"

The color drained from his face and he closed his eyes, his jaw tight.

At that look on his face, there was nothing she could do but tell him the truth. The reason she'd set out on a journey toward this oasis in the first place. Besides, she was too weary to dance around the subject any longer.

"I heard you were going to bring home another wife."

His head snapped up then, his black gaze boring into her. "Where did you hear this?"

"In the palace. The rumor is that you will marry one

of the chieftains' daughters." She lifted her chin. "I know that's not unusual in Kyr, but it's unusual for me."

"And so you decided to risk your life, and the lives of our children, to make your opinion known? Did it not occur to you to ask me about this when I returned?"

She snorted. "With a new wife on your arm? No, it didn't occur to me to wait."

"Sheridan." He shook his head. Said something in Arabic. And then he was looking at her again, his eyes filled with fury. "This stubbornness of yours could have cost you your life!"

"I realize that now!" she shouted back. "I behaved stupidly, I know it, and you're embarrassed and furious and no doubt the new wife is signing documents as we speak. Well, I won't live like that! I can't."

She put a fist to her heart, felt hot tears begin to roll down her cheeks and cursed herself for being so damned emotional. *Hormones,* she reminded herself.

"I won't do it, Rashid."

He looked stunned. "You do realize I am the king? That it's not your place to advise me on this?"

The trembling in her limbs was no longer only due to the cold. "Just tell me if it's true. Are you planning to take another wife?"

His jaw was marble. "Kyrian politics are complicated, Sheridan."

"That's not an answer." Her voice was a painful whisper over the lump in her throat.

He closed his eyes and put his forehead in his palm. "The council wishes me to take a Kyrian wife. But I did not come out here to do that."

"And yet it's only a matter of time."

"It would seem so."

She sipped the tea as if they were having a polite conversation rather than one that broke her heart and ripped out her guts.

"Well, thank you for being honest. If you could perhaps wait until the babies are born, I'll be busy enough then that I won't mind so much."

He growled. "You won't *mind* so much?"

She looked at him evenly, though her face was still hot with tears. "As you've taken pains to inform me from the beginning, I have no choice. And no say in the matter, either. If you take another wife, I'll endeavor not to disembowel you both with Daoud's sword."

If Rashid was amused or alarmed, he didn't show it. "He followed you, you know."

She didn't, but her heart skipped a beat at the thought of Daoud out there alone, too. Guilt filled her then. And fear. "Is he all right? The jackals didn't get him, did they?"

"He is fine. His horse went lame, which is why he didn't catch you. I sent men after him once we found you. They returned a few moments ago, and Daoud is well. For the moment."

She heard the dangerous note in his voice. "Rashid, it's not his fault. He trusted me and I gave him the slip."

"He should not have trusted you at all."

"Maybe not." She bowed her head. "Probably not."

"Apparently I should not, either. Or at least not with any swords."

She glared at him. "Are you making fun of me?"

"I'd rather do something else with you."

She sat there in shock for a moment. And then she shook her head violently. "No. I can't. Not ever again, Rashid. Not if you're going to marry another woman."

He reached for her, gripped her chin and forced her to look at him again. His eyes were bright. "Why not, *habibti?* Why would this bother you? Is it because you are American? Or is there another reason?"

Her heart thrummed and her throat ached and she wanted to sink beneath the covers and hide. He was holding her, demanding an answer, and all she could think was that she wanted him to kiss her. And then she wanted to strangle him.

"I've grown fond of you," she said as primly as she could manage under the circumstances. It was such a bald-faced lie, but she'd die before she'd admit that she loved him now.

She did not expect him to grin. "Fond? I like the sound of that."

She swatted at his hand. "I meant to say I *was* fond of you. I've changed my mind now. Who could be fond of a dictator?"

He took her teacup and set it aside. Then he moved closer, threaded his hand through her still-damp hair. "Who indeed?"

His head descended and she closed her eyes, aching for his kiss. But a hot feeling swelled inside her, bubbling up until she put her hand over his mouth and stopped him from kissing her. If he kissed her, she would sob her heart out and confess all her tragic feelings for him.

And she couldn't do that and keep her dignity.

"No, Rashid. You kiss me and charm me and make me forget myself, but this is where it has to stop. I can't do this anymore. I can't be with a man who runs away from his feelings, a man who can't even be with me without wanting to escape. I can't give you everything I have and only get part of you in return. I've spent too much of my life making other people happy and I'm not going to keep doing it with you when you can't even give me something so basic as a normal marriage between two people. I deserve better than that. I *demand* better than that."

She took her hand away slowly, expecting him to explode in arrogant pronouncements about being a king and her having a place, but he caught her hand and held it in his. His skin burned into her. She wanted to pull her hand away and she wanted to curl into his heat at once.

Why did she have to love a man who was so wrong for her on so many levels?

His brows drew together as he studied her. And then he lifted a finger and traced her mouth lightly, so lightly. She refused to whimper.

"When Mostafa called to say you were missing, I thought I was about to relive that moment when I lost Daria and our son. And I was terrified, but not because of what happened in the past and how much it hurt."

He pulled in a deep breath, his nostrils flaring. "I was terrified because it could happen again, and it would hurt just as much this time as the last. It would hurt because of you, Sheridan."

Tears filled her eyes then, but she shook her head and wished she could plug her ears. Because the beautiful words didn't mean what she so desperately wished they meant. They couldn't. Could they?

"Don't say that, Rashid. Don't say things like that to me when you intend to marry someone else someday."

He held her hard against him and she could feel his heart beating strong and fast. "I don't intend to marry anyone else, *habibti*. I said the council wishes it. I even agreed to it because it made political sense, but I am the king and I can change my mind. And I have changed my mind, Sheridan. I don't want any woman but you. I won't have any woman in my bed but you. You're all I need. You and our children."

Sheridan's fingers curled into his damp clothes as she squeezed her eyes tight shut and held on. It was as if she'd suddenly gotten onto a crazy merry-go-round and she couldn't get off. She was dizzy with the feelings ricocheting through her and confused about what was happening.

She pushed away from him until she could see his eyes. "What does this mean, Rashid? I need you to say it plainly. I need to understand."

He pushed the damp hair off her face. He looked so serious. So worried. "It means that I tried to harden my heart against you, but I failed. It means that I'm terrified about you carrying two babies, and that as much as I might like to spank you right now for what you did tonight, I'd much rather fall to my knees and worship your body and thank Allah that you are mine. It means that I love you, Sheridan, though I tried not to. I'm finished with running from this thing between us."

The lump in her throat was huge. "This thing between us?"

He laughed softly. "Have you not noticed? It's incendiary. I touch you, you touch me, and the room goes up in flame. But it's not just sex, Sheridan. I've had sex before, and it doesn't feel quite like that. With you, I can't get enough. Not just of sex, but of you. When I'm not with you, I want to be. And when I am with you, I want to be closer. I know you feel these things, too. You would have to in order to put up with me these past few weeks."

She smoothed her hand over his chest. "Oh, Rashid,

just when I think you can't say anything else that surprises me, you say this. I thought it was just me who couldn't get enough. I thought I was weak where you were concerned and I kept telling myself I needed to be stronger, that I should tell you no. But I couldn't."

"You haven't said you love me, *habibti*." He ran his fingers over her cheek. "And you don't have to. I already know. And if I had any doubts before, the fact you risked your life to come out here because of a rumor would have erased them all. I'm still angry with you for this, by the way. You should have called me."

"I wasn't sure you wouldn't run away from the question. I had to see your eyes."

He sighed. "Yes, I understand. But never do this again. If you had perished out there—" He swallowed hard. "I would have perished with you, Sheridan. Do you understand that? I would have perished, too."

Tears slid down her cheeks again, only this time she felt free enough to lean forward and kiss him. He was hers, really hers, and she wasn't hiding her feelings another moment. He caught her to him again and kissed her until she was on fire. She was no longer cold, but burning up from the inside out, her entire being filled with flame.

Somehow they got him out of his damp clothing and then he was under the furs with her, their hot limbs tangling together as they rolled together beneath the covers. She ended up on top, straddling him, sinking down on top of him until they both groaned with the rightness of it.

"Sheridan," he gasped, gazing up at her, his expression filled with so much more than simply heat.

She lowered her mouth to his, kissed him tenderly,

teasing it out until neither of them could stand it a moment longer. He gripped her hips and drove up into her while she rode him faster and faster.

They came together, gasping and crying out as the flame rolled through them. And then they collapsed into each other's arms with soft caresses and even softer kisses.

"I love you, Rashid," she said shyly, and he squeezed her tight. She could feel his smile against her hair.

"I love you, too, Sheridan. You keep me grounded."

"You mean I keep your ego in check," she said, laughing.

"That, too." He stroked his fingers up and down her arm. "I didn't know how lost I was until you entered my life."

"And I didn't know I would find home with a man who lived in such a different world than my own. But I did."

"Do you like it here?" he asked, and she thought he seemed a little hesitant. As if it worried him.

"I love it more every day. But the truth is I would love any place in this world so long as you were there. *You* are my home. You."

He squeezed her to him and they said nothing for a long while. But then they began to talk and they spent the evening speaking softly about so many things, and then they made love again, tenderly, before falling asleep curled tightly together.

They would return to the city in a few days and Rashid would issue the proclamation, at their public wedding ceremony, that Sheridan was to be his queen and not just a princess consort. He would deal with the council and they would learn to be happy. In time, they would come to love Queen Sheri, as they called her, as fiercely as if she had been born one of their own.

But tonight was precisely how the royal couple would spend every night for the rest of their lives. Curled together, complete in each other. First, last and always.

EPILOGUE

TWINS. RASHID STILL couldn't believe it, though he'd known for months they were coming. Sheridan had gotten huge and he'd worried himself silly, but his babies were born—a boy and a girl named Tarek and Amira—and his wife was safe. He watched her sleeping now, her hand held lightly in his as she rested after the long ordeal of giving birth.

Eventually her eyes fluttered open and found his. And then she smiled and his whole world lit up from within.

"Habibti," he said, his voice choked with emotion. Such incredible emotion. He'd never thought he could love so deeply more than once in a lifetime. But he did. He'd experienced it numerous times now, he realized. His wife. His children.

He was a lucky, lucky man.

"Have you been here long?" she asked.

He pressed his lips to her hand, her palm to his cheek, and reached forward to slide his fingers over her jaw. "Every moment."

Her eyes widened then. "Rashid! You have to get some rest. Go to the adjoining room and sleep. That's why they prepared this suite for us after all. So the king could rest with his wife in the hospital."

"I couldn't leave you."

Her smile was tender. "It's okay, Rashid. I'm not going anywhere. I plan to hang around and give you hell for the rest of your life. And I plan to give you more babies, too. Though maybe we'd better get used to two for right now."

His throat was tight. She understood his fears and knew just what to say to him. "I love you, Sheridan."

Her eyes were soft and filled with love. For him. It continually astounded him. "I love you, too, arrogant man. Now go and sleep for a while."

"I napped here in the chair. I'm fine. I also have some news for you."

Her gaze sparkled with interest. "What kind of news?"

"Your brother-in-law called."

Her eyes lit up with hope. "And?"

"The twenty-week scan shows a girl. A healthy girl."

Her eyes squeezed tightly shut. "Oh, thank God."

"He says your sister is very happy and she looks forward to talking to you when you feel up to it."

She pushed herself upright, wincing only a little. "I feel up to it now. What time is it?"

He almost laughed. "It's the middle of the night in Georgia. I think you need to wait a few more hours."

She sank back down again. "If I must."

"Kadir and Emily arrived a few hours ago. They're resting in the palace, but they will come by and visit soon."

Sheridan smiled. "I can't wait to see them."

"I believe they have some news to share, as well."

Her eyes widened. "Is Emily pregnant? Oh, that's so wonderful!"

He laughed at the way she didn't even let him answer the question before she exclaimed it was wonderful. "I did not confirm this to you, but yes. Kadir told me that Emily wanted to tell you herself, so you will act surprised."

"I promise I will."

There was a knock on the door and a nurse came in. "Your Majesty, are you ready for the babies? They're awake and hungry."

Sheridan's face lit up. "Yes, please, bring them here."

Two nurses came in and gently placed little Tarek and Amira on Sheridan's lap. Rashid watched his wife settle down with their children and his heart filled with emotion. He'd never thought he would experience this kind of utter happiness in his life, but he was so grateful he'd been given the chance. It continually astounded him that he had been.

When the twins were content and starting to sleep, Sheridan looked up at him, her eyes filled with love. "Would you like to hold one of them?"

Fear crowded him then, but he sucked in a breath, determined to be brave for his family. "Yes, I will do this."

She laughed. "You'll be a natural, Rashid. And you have to start some time."

He reached down and picked up a baby—he didn't know which one—and held it close to his chest, making sure to support the head the way he'd been told. The little face was pinched tight, the eyes closed, but the tiny creature's chest rose and fell regularly and the little lips moved.

"I don't know which one this is," he said softly, gazing with wonder at the baby and not wanting to wake it.

Sheridan laughed again. "That's Tarek. See the blue band on his little wrist?"

"Tarek." Rashid could only stare at the sweet little face. And then he lifted the baby higher and pressed a kiss to his cheek. "My son."

* * * * *

The dark blue of his eyes intensified, holding hers in a lock that made something inside her belly tilt and then spill.

'You're scared.'

Aiesha sent her tongue out in a quick darting movement to moisten her lips. 'Let me go, James.'

'I have a little forfeit to collect first.'

Something dropped off a shelf in her stomach. 'Forfeit?'

He spread his hands through the mane of her hair, his gaze moving from her eyes to her mouth in a slow and mesmerising fashion. 'You remember? Now I get to kiss you. Fair's fair.'

She affected a sneer but was pretty sure it was wide of the mark. 'Is that meant to be a punishment?'

'Why don't we find out?' he said, tugging her against him, and his mouth came down over hers.

From as soon as **Melanie Milburne** could pick up a pen she knew she wanted to write. It was when she picked up her first Mills & Boon® at seventeen that she realised she wanted to write romance. After being distracted for a few years by meeting and marrying her own handsome hero, surgeon husband Steve, and having two boys, plus completing a Masters of Education and becoming a nationally ranked athlete (masters swimming), she decided to write. Five submissions later she sold her first book and is now a multi-published, bestselling, award-winning *USA TODAY* author. In 2008 she won the Australian Readers' Association most popular category/series romance, and in 2011 she won the prestigious Romance Writers of Australia R*BY award.

Melanie loves to hear from her readers via her website, www.melaniemilburne.com.au or on Facebook: www.facebook.com/pages/Melanie-Milburne/351594482609.

Recent titles by the same author:

NEVER GAMBLE WITH A CAFFARELLI
  (Those Scandalous Caffarellis)
NEVER UNDERESTIMATE A CAFFARELLI
  (Those Scandalous Caffarellis)
NEVER SAY NO TO A CAFFARELLI
  (Those Scandalous Caffarellis)
HIS FINAL BARGAIN

AT NO MAN'S COMMAND

BY
MELANIE MILBURNE

MILLS & BOON

Published in Great Britain 2014
by Mills & Boon, an imprint of Harlequin (UK) Limited,
Eton House, 18-24 Paradise Road, Richmond, Surrey, TW9 1SR

© 2014 Melanie Milburne

ISBN: 978 0 263 24667 4

Harlequin (UK) Limited's policy is to use papers that are natural,
renewable and recyclable products and made from wood grown in
sustainable forests. The logging and manufacturing processes conform
to the legal environmental regulations of the country of origin.

Printed and bound in Spain
by Blackprint CPI, Barcelona

AT NO MAN'S COMMAND

To Nadine and Regan Drew.
Thanks for your friendship
and all the fun memories we share.
May there be many more to come! xx

CHAPTER ONE

AIESHA HAD BEEN at Lochbannon a week without a single whisper in the press about her whereabouts. But then, who would have thought of hunting her down in the Highlands of Scotland in the home of the woman whose marriage she had effectively destroyed ten years ago?

It was the perfect hideaway, and the fact that Louise Challender had been called away to visit a sick friend abroad meant Aiesha had had the place to herself for the last couple of days. And, being the dead of winter, there was not even a housekeeper or a gardener to disturb her idyll.

Bliss.

She closed her eyes and, tilting her head back, breathed in the ice in the air as fresh flakes of snow began to fall. The soft press of each snowflake was like a caress against her skin. After the traffic fumes and incessant noise and activity of Las Vegas, the cold, fresh, quiet Highland air was like breathing in an elixir, bringing her jaded senses back to zinging life.

Being up here on her own where no one could find her was like coming off a stage. Stepping out of a costume. Undressing the part of Vegas showgirl. She could feel it falling away from her like a heavy cloak. Up here she could take her game face off. The flirty vamp face. The face that told everyone she was perfectly happy singing in a gentlemen's club because the tips were great and she had the days free to shop, hang out by the pool or get a spray tan.

Up here in the Highlands she could relax. Regroup. Get in touch with nature.

Revisit her dreams...

The only hiccup was the dog.

Aiesha could babysit cats, no problem. Cats were pretty easy to take care of. She just filled their dish with biscuits and cleaned out their litter tray, if they had one. She didn't have to pat them or get close to them. Most cats were pretty aloof, which suited her just fine.

Dogs were different. Dogs wanted to get close to you. To bond with you. To love you.

To trust you to keep them safe.

Aiesha glanced down at the limpid brown eyes of the golden retriever sitting at her feet with slavish devotion, its tail brushing against the carpet of snow like a feathered fan.

The memory of another pair of trusting brown eyes stabbed at her heart like a knitting needle. Eyes that still haunted her, even though so many years had passed. She pushed back the thick sleeve of her coat and looked at the underside of her wrist where the blue-and-red ink of her tattoo was a vivid and permanent reminder of her failure to keep her one and only best friend safe.

Aiesha swallowed the monkey wrench of guilt in her

throat and frowned down at the dog. 'Why can't you take yourself for a walk? It's not as if you need me to show you the way. There aren't any fences to stop you.' She made a shooing motion with her hand. 'Go on. Go for a run. Go chase a rabbit or a stoat or something.'

The dog continued to look at her with that unblinking stare, a soft little 'play with me' whine coming from its throat. Aiesha blew out a breath of resignation and began trudging in the direction of the forest that fringed the stately Highland home. 'Come on, then, you stupid mutt. But I'm only going as far as the river. It looks like this snow's going to set in for the night.'

James Challender drove through the snow-encrusted wrought-iron gates of Lochbannon as evening folded in. The secluded estate was spectacular in any season but in winter it turned into a wonderland. The Gothic-style mansion with its turrets and spires looked like something out of a children's fairy tale. The frozen water in the fountain in front of the house looked like a Renaissance ice sculpture with delicate icicles hanging down like centuries-old stalactites. The thick forest that backed on to the estate was coated in pure white snow, the rolling fields were also thickly carpeted, and the air was so sharp and clean and cold it burned his nostrils as he drew it in.

The lights were on in the house, which meant the housekeeper, Mrs McBain, had generously postponed her annual holiday to look after Bonnie while his mother visited her friend, who had suffered an accident in outback Australia. James had offered to look after the dog but his mother had insisted via a hurried text before she boarded her flight that it was all organised and not to worry. Why his mother couldn't put her dog in boarding kennels like everyone else did was beyond him. It wasn't as if she couldn't afford it. He'd made sure she was well provided for after the divorce from his father.

Lochbannon was a little large for an older single woman with only a dog for company and a handful of staff, but he had wanted to give his mother a safe haven, a place that was totally unconnected to her former life as Clifford Challender's wife.

Although he had insisted the estate was in his mother's name, James liked to spend the occasional week up in the Highlands away from the fast lane of London, which was why he'd decided to come up in spite of his mother's assurances that Bonnie was well taken care of.

This was the one place he could focus without distractions. A week working here was worth a month in his busy London office. He liked the solitude, the peace and tranquillity of being alone, without people needing him to fix something, do something or be something.

Here he could let his shoulders down and relax. Here he could think. Clear his head of the stress of managing a company that was still suffering the effects of his father's mishandling of projects and clients.

Lochbannon was also one of the few places where he could escape the intrusive spotlight of the press. The repercussions of his father's profligate lifestyle had spread across his own life like an indelible stain. The newshounds were always on the lookout for a scandal to prove their theory of 'like father, like son.'

Even before he turned off the engine he heard the sound of Bonnie's welcoming bark. He smiled as he walked to the front door. Maybe his mother was right about her precious dog being too sensitive to leave with strangers. Besides, he had to admit there was something rather homely and comfortable about an enthusiastic canine greeting.

The door opened before he could put his key in the lock and a pair of wide grey eyes blinked at him in outraged shock, as if suddenly finding a prowler on the doorstep instead of the postman. 'What the hell are *you* doing here?'

James's hand fell away from the door. His body went stiff as if the snow falling behind him had frozen him to the spot. *Aiesha Adams.* The infamous, lethally gorgeous, impossibly sexy and outrageously wild Aiesha Adams. 'I believe that's supposed to be my line,' he said when he could locate his voice.

At a casual glance there was nothing outstanding about her features. Dressed in a loose-fitting boyfriend sweater and yoga pants and without make-up, she looked like your average girl next door. Midlength chestnut hair that was neither curly nor straight but somewhere in between. Skin that was clear and unlined apart from a couple of tiny scars that were either from chickenpox or the site of a picked pimple, one on the left side of her forehead and one just below her right cheekbone. She was of average height and of slim build, the result of lucky genes rather than effort, he surmised.

For a moment—a brief moment—she looked fifteen years old again.

But look a little closer and the unusual colour of her eyes was nothing short of arresting. Breath-snatching. Storm and smoke and shadows swirled in their depths.

The shape of her mouth had the power to render a man speechless. That lush, ripe mouth was pure sin. The bee-stung fullness, the youthfulness, and the vermillion borders so beautifully aligned it physically hurt to look and not touch.

What was she doing here? Had she broken in?

What if someone found out she was here…*with him*? His heart galloped ahead a few beats. What if the press found out? What if Phoebe found out?

Aiesha's chin came up to that don't-mess-with-me height James had seen her do so well in the past, her body posture morphing from schoolgirl to sultry, defiant tart in a blink. 'Your mother invited me.'

His mother? James's frown was so tight it made his forehead hurt. What was going on? His mother's rushed text message hadn't mentioned anything about Aiesha. Not. One. Word. Why would his mother invite the girl who'd caused so much heartbreak and mayhem in the past? It didn't make sense.

'Rather magnanimous of her under the circumstances, is it not?' he said. 'Has she locked up her jewellery and all the silver?'

Her eyes flashed gunmetal-grey fire at him. 'Is anyone with you?'

'I hate to repeat myself, but I believe that's what *I'm* supposed to be asking you.' James closed the door on the chilly air but, in doing so, it made the sudden silence and the space between them far too intimate.

Being intimate—in any sense of the word—with Aiesha Adams was dangerous. He dared not think about it. Would *not* think about it. Being in the same country as her was reputation suicide, let alone in the same house. She oozed sex appeal. She wore it like a slinky coat, slipping in and out of it whenever she felt the urge. Every movement she made was pure seductress. How many men had fallen for that lithe body and that Lolita mouth? Even with that smoky glower and that upthrust chin she still managed to look sex kittenish. He could feel the thrum of his blood in his veins, the sudden rush of sexual awareness that was as shocking to him as it was unwelcome.

He bent down to ruffle Bonnie's ears to distract himself and was rewarded with a whimper and a lavish licking. At least someone was pleased to see him.

'Did anyone follow you here?' Aiesha asked. 'The press? Journalists? Anyone?'

James straightened from ruffling the dog's ears to give her a sardonic look. 'Running away from another scandal, are we?'

Her lips tightened, her eyes burning with the dislike she had always assaulted him with. 'Don't pretend you don't know. It's been in every paper and newsfeed.'

Was there anyone who *didn't* know? The news of her affair with a married politician in the U.S. had gone viral. James had pointedly ignored it, or tried to. But then some unscrupulous newshound had unearthed Aiesha's role in the break-up of his parents' marriage. It had only been a sentence or two and not every paper or newsfeed ran with it, but the shame and embarrassment he had been trying to put behind him for a decade was back with a vengeance.

But what else could he expect? Aiesha was a wild child who attracted scandal and had been from the moment his mother had brought her home from the back streets of London as a teenage runaway. She was a smart-mouthed little guttersnipe who deliberately created negative drama, even for the people who tried to help her. His mother had been badly let down by Aiesha's disreputable behaviour in the past, which was why he was puzzled that she had allowed her to come and stay now. Why would his mother invite the unscrupulous girl who had stolen not only heirloom jewellery from her, but tried to steal her husband from her, as well?

James shrugged off his coat to hang it in the cupboard in the hall. 'Married men are a particular obsession of yours, are they not?'

He felt the stab of those grey eyes drilling between his shoulder blades. He felt the sudden kick of his pulse. He got a thrill out of seeing her rattled by him. He was the only person she couldn't hide her true colours from. She was a true chameleon, changing to serve her interests, laying on the charm when it suited her, reeling in her next victim, enjoying the game of slaying yet another heart and wallet.

But he was immune. He'd seen her for what she was right from the start. She might have got rid of her East End accent and chain-store clothes, but underneath she was a pickpocket whose aim in life was to sleep her way to the top. Her latest victim was a U.S. senator whose career and marriage were unravelling as a result. The press had captured a damning shot of her leaving his suite at the Vegas hotel where she worked as a lounge singer.

'No one must know I'm here,' she said. 'Do you understand? No one.'

James turned from neatly arranging the sleeves of his coat to face her. She was still looking at him with hatred but something else moved in her gaze, a flicker of uncertainty, or was it fear? She quickly disguised it, however. She jutted her chin and flattened those delectably full lips. Her mouth had always fascinated him. Ripe and soft and full, a mouth built for sin and sex and seduction. There was nothing innocent about her mouth or her body. She was a five-foot-eight knockout package of sinuous catlike curves that could wrap around a man until he was strangled by his need of her.

And she knew it.

James moved past her to stride to the warmth of the sitting room. Thinking about that mouth was a bad move. He could practically *feel* those plump lips clasped around him, drawing on him until he went weak at the knees. He suppressed a shudder of traitorous desire. He would *not* think about that mouth. He would *not* think about that body. He would *not* think of the lust that burned inside him.

'No one will find you here because you're not staying.'

She followed him into the sitting room, her bare feet padding over the Persian carpet like the paws of a light-footed lioness. 'You can't throw me out. This is your mother's house, not yours.' She stood with her arms folded across her chest, looking exactly like she had a decade ago, all pouty, sulky teenager even though she was now twenty-five years old.

He let his gaze run over her in a leisurely sweep as if inspecting a cheap and tawdry item he had no intention of buying. 'Pack your bags and get out.'

She slitted her eyes like a wildcat staring down a wolf. 'I'm *not* leaving.'

James felt his blood skip and then roar through his veins. It thickened in his groin, reigniting the embers of a fire that had never quite been extinguished. He hated himself for it. He saw it as a weakness. It reduced him to the baseness of a wild animal with no other instinct than to mate with whatever willing female was available.

He wasn't cut from the same low-quality cloth as his father. He could control his impulses. Aiesha had tried her seduction routine on him ten years ago but he hadn't taken the bait.

And he wasn't going to take it now.

'I'm expecting a guest,' he said.

'Who?'

'The woman I intend to marry is joining me at the weekend. You'll be decidedly de trop.'

She laughed out loud, even going so far as to bend over double to hold her sides as if he'd told her the most humorous of jokes. 'You mean to say you've actually *asked* that stuck-up frozen-faced heiress who doesn't do anything but spend Daddy's money on the High Street to marry you?'

James ground his teeth so hard he thought he'd have

to take his meals through a straw for the rest of his life. 'Phoebe's the patron of several well-known charities.'

Aiesha was still giggling like a naughty schoolgirl. It made the base of his spine tighten like a bowstring. How like her to mock the most important decision of his life. He had chosen his future bride after lengthy consideration. Phoebe Trentonfield had her own money, which meant he could rule out the gold-digging factor. It had plagued him for most of his adult life, trying to find a partner who wanted him for himself instead of his money. It was the first box he wanted ticked. He was thirty-three years old. He wanted to settle down. He wanted to build a stable home life—like the one he'd thought he had until his father's affairs had come to light. He wanted his mother to enjoy the experience of having grandchildren. He wanted someone who was content to be a traditional wife so he could rebuild the Challender empire his father had so recklessly frittered away. He wanted stability and predictability instead of scandal and chaos. His father was the impulsive one. Not him. He knew what he wanted and was determined and disciplined enough to get it and keep it.

Aiesha gave him a goading look. 'What's she going to say when she finds out you're here with me?'

His molars went down another couple of millimetres. 'She's not going to find out because you're leaving first thing in the morning.'

She hitched one of her hips in a model-like pose, a teasing smile still lurking around the corners of her mouth. 'So you're not going to be a big old meanie and throw me out in the snow on my toosh tonight, then?'

He wanted to bury her in the snow, at least ten feet deep so he wouldn't be tempted to touch her. And the less he thought about her curvy little toosh the better. How was he going to get her out of here? He could hardly send her packing at this time of night, with the roads so slippery and treacherous. He had only just made it through from the main road himself. The nearest village had a bed and breakfast but it was currently closed for the winter. The closest hotel was a half hour drive away…an hour in these conditions. 'Does your car have snow chains?' he asked.

'I didn't bring a car. Your mother picked me up from the airport in Edinburgh.'

What was his mother thinking? This was getting crazier by the minute. He hadn't known his mother had been in contact with Aiesha over the years. What was she thinking bringing the daughter of the devil back into her life?

Was this a set-up? A practical joke?

Surely not… How on earth could it be? His mother had insisted he not worry about the dog. Surely she knew how dangerous it would be to put Aiesha in the same house as him. She was a ticking time bomb. She courted trouble. She craved attention from anyone wearing trousers, making it her mission to get them out of them as fast as she could. She was ruthless and shameless and as sexy as a pin-up girl. *Damn it.* 'Right, well, I'll drive you back to the airport first thing in the morning,' he said. 'Your little stint as dog- and house-sitter is over.'

She sashayed over to him, deliberately trailing one

of her fingertips along one of the whitened tendons on the back of one of his clenched fists. 'Loosen up, James. You're as wound up as a tight spring. If you need an outlet for all that pressure—' she batted her impossibly long eyelashes at him '—just call me, OK?'

James forced himself to endure the electric shock of her touch without flinching. He forced himself not to look at her mouth, where the tip of her pink tongue had left a moistly glistening trail. He forced himself not to slam her against the nearest wall and slake the fireball of his lust by plunging into her hot, wet warmth and doing what he'd always wanted to do to her. Every cell in his body was vibrating with need, and what sickened him the most was she damn well knew it. 'Get the freaking hell out of my sight.'

Her eyes glinted with devilment. 'I love it when a man talks dirty to me.' She gave an exaggerated little shiver that made her braless breasts jiggle beneath her sweater. 'It makes me come in a flash.'

James curled his fingers so tightly into his palms he felt every one of their joints protest. 'Be ready at seven. Understood?'

She gave him another sultry little smile that sent another scorching flare to his groin. 'You can't get rid of me that easily. Didn't you hear the weather report for tonight?'

A fist of panic clutched at his insides. He'd heard it in the car half an hour ago but back then he'd welcomed the thought of a blizzard snowing him in for a few days so he could put the final touches to the drawings on the Sherwood project before Phoebe joined him at the weekend.

He glared at Aiesha with such intense loathing he could feel it burning through his eyeballs like hot pokers. 'You planned this, didn't you?'

She tossed the length of her glossy chestnut hair back over one of her shoulders as she laughed that spine-fizzing laugh again. 'You think I've got that much power that I can manipulate the weather to suit me? You flatter me, James.'

He sucked in a breath as she moved to the stairs with her swinging hip gait. Carnal lust roared in his body but he wasn't going to let her win this. They could be snowed in for a month and he would still resist her.

He would *not* give in.

He. Would. Not. Give. In.

CHAPTER TWO

AIESHA LEANED BACK against the door of her bedroom and let out a long ragged breath. Her heart was still flapping like a loosely tied flag in a gale force wind. This couldn't be happening.

James Challender wasn't just a press magnet. He was press superglue. Where he went the press followed, especially if anyone got a heads-up on his upcoming engagement. He was one of London's most eligible bachelors—the epitome of the Prize Catch. Every woman under the age of fifty panted after him. He was suave, sophisticated. Not a playboy like his father, but a classy specimen of modern sexy corporate man. Before she knew it, her sanctuary would be invaded by hundreds of journalists and prying cameras, hoping to get the latest scoop on him.

She would be hunted down. Found. Exposed. Mocked. Shamed.

The scandal she was trying to distance herself from would arrive on the doorstep. The shame of being at the centre of something so sordid wasn't new to her. She'd spent most of her life attracting scandals, encouraging them, relishing in them for the attention they gave her, which made up for the lack of attention she'd received as a child.

But that chapter was supposed to be over.

She wanted to put that part of her life behind her and move forward. The meeting with Antony Smithson—aka Antony Gregovitch—was supposed to have been her big break. The chance to get out of the club scene and nail the recording contract she'd longed for since she was a little kid singing into her hairbrush in front of a mottled mirror in a council flat. Instead, she'd found out he wasn't a music producer at all. He'd lied to her from the moment he'd sat down to listen to her sing through her shift. He'd come night after night, staying to talk to her between breaks, buying her drinks, telling her how beautiful her voice was, how talented she was. Fool that she was, she had sucked it all up and basked in his praise.

That was what angered her the most—the fact she hadn't seen through him. How could she have been so gullible, especially the way she'd been dragged up by a bunch of tricksters and sham artists? He hadn't been the handsome prince to rescue her from a life of singing to people who were too drunk to even listen to a word of her lyrics. He was a married man with a wife and family who was looking for a bit of cheap fun on the side.

Now she was painted as a heartless home-wrecker and her chance to prove she was so much more than a nightclub one-trick pony was over. She had no recording contract. She didn't even have a job. Antony's wife's smear campaign had seen to that. There wasn't a club in Vegas—possibly in the entire world—that would take her on now.

And now she had to deal with James High-and-Mighty Challender.

In spite of everything, Aiesha couldn't help a tiny smile of self-congratulation. She knew exactly how hard to tug on his chain. She had practised her moves on him when she was fifteen. He had a little more self-control than his sleazeball of a father, but she hated him just as much. But then she hated all men, especially superrich ones who thought they could have anyone they wanted just by fanning open their wallet. Sexually they were OK, quite useful for a bit of fun now and again, but as people? No. She hadn't met any she respected as a person. The men in her life had always let her down. Tricked her. Betrayed her. Exploited her.

James Challender might think he could control her but she wasn't leaving Lochbannon on his say-so. His mother had given her permission to stay for as long as she liked. She wasn't going to be pushed around by a stuffed shirt whose vocabulary didn't possess the words fun or spontaneity. He was a nitpicking, timekeeping workaholic who got antsy if the cushions on the sofa weren't neatly aligned.

And as for his so-called fiancée…what a joke! They deserved each other. Phoebe whatever-her-name-was did nothing but smile inanely at the cameras, showing off her perfect toothpaste-commercial smile and her perfect clothes and her perfect figure while her equally pampered and perfect parents pumped up her trust fund.

Bitch.

Aiesha tapped her fingers against her lips. Maybe there was a way for her to get this unexpected little speed bump to work in her favour. Why would anyone think she was hooking her claws into a boring old married politician back in Vegas when someone as staggeringly gorgeous as James Challender was spending the week cloistered with her up here in the Highlands?

She reached for her phone with a mischievous grin. *Twitter, here I come!*

James hadn't been able to get through to his mother but he left a message. A rather stern one, lecturing her on the pitfalls of harbouring a headline-grabbing harlot who was sure to pilfer the silver or trash the place with a wild party in her absence.

He rubbed a golf-ball knot of tension in his neck as he looked at the steady fall of snow outside the library window. For once the weather forecasters were spot on. It was snowing a blizzard and any chance of leaving now—let alone in the morning—was well and truly out of the question.

He dropped his hand back down by his side with a whooshing sigh. Thank God no one knew he was here with Aiesha. *Yet.* He'd checked on his phone earlier to see if anyone had tracked her down but so far they hadn't. The Vegas scandal was still generating plenty of comments, most of them unflattering to her on her part in destroying a perfectly respectable man's career and marriage. Personally, he thought some of the comments were a little harsh. Surely the man in question had to take some responsibility?

But then he thought of her little seductive moves downstairs. She was one hell of a temptation even the purest of monks would find hard to resist. His body was still reverberating with shockwaves of unbridled lust. She did it for the sport of it. It amused her to tempt and tease. It was a game, a competition to see who had the most willpower. He'd won that battle a decade ago. He'd been proud of his strength of will, but back then she'd been a kid. Now she was an adult and twice as dangerous. She'd had years to perfect her art of playing the courtesan.

James clenched and unclenched his hands. His skin was still burning from her sizzling touch and nothing he did would quell it. He had never thought of himself as a hedonistic sensualist. He enjoyed sex but there was an element to it that had always disturbed him. The closeness that came with sex and the out of control aspect made him uneasy. The idea of being vulnerable and at the mercy of another unnerved him and meant he always kept his passion on a tight leash. He was by no means prudish but he was uneasy with the thought of giving in to primal urges without thought of the consequences.

Like his father, for instance, moving from one relationship to another with a series of totally unsuitable women. His latest mistress was barely legal, yet another wannabe starlet looking for a sugar daddy to give her a good time. The shallowness of his father was a constant irritation to him. A constant embarrassment. A constant source of shame. He hated the assumption he was like his father because they shared the same features.

He wasn't the same.

He had drive and ambition where his father had none. He had focus and discipline. He cared about the company. He cared about the people who worked in the company.

Hard work and responsibility weren't words James associated with his father. Born to wealth, which he'd proceeded to dispense with as soon as it was bequeathed to him, Clifford Challender had all but destroyed the coffers and the reputation of the architectural empire James's grandfather had worked so hard to build.

Now the baton was in James's hand and he wasn't going to let it go until he had the company back where it belonged, up there with the top ten architectural firms in the country.

The Sherwood project was a pivotal step towards that dream. The multimillion-pound redesign of Howard Sherwood's London home and his Paris townhouse was small change compared to other projects the influential and well-connected businessman could send James's way. If James secured this contract then his dream of designing luxury environmentally friendly accommodation in select wilderness areas across the globe would be one step closer. It wasn't just the money that motivated him. The project was true to his values as an architect. He wanted to leave a legacy of buildings that enhanced the environments in which they were set, not exploiting or desecrating or destroying them. And it would be one step closer to proving he was nothing like his wastrel father.

Bonnie lifted her golden head off the carpet at James's feet and gave a soft whine. 'You want to go outside, old girl?' he asked. 'Come on. It looks like your babysitter's walked off the job.'

The snow was already up to his calves and the wind was howling like a dervish but fortunately the dog didn't take too long about her business. James dusted the snow off his shoulders as he came back in the back door leading off the kitchen. The back of his neck prickled when he saw Aiesha leaning in an indolent manner against the kitchen counter, her lushly youthful mouth curved upwards in a mocking tilt. 'I hope you're not expecting me to cook dinner for you.'

'I wouldn't dream of putting you to the tedious inconvenience of doing something for someone else.'

He opened the fridge and inspected the contents. The usual suspects were there—eggs, yoghurt, milk and cheese, vegetables in the crisper and Bonnie's meat in a Tupperware container.

'You can feed the dog now you're here,' Aiesha said. 'And you can walk her. I'm not going to freeze my butt off just because that overweight mutt needs to take a leak every five minutes.'

He closed the fridge to look at her again. 'So how *are* you going to earn your keep?'

Her grey eyes glinted as the tilt of her lush mouth went a little higher. 'Any suggestions?'

A rocket blast of blood slammed into his groin at her saucy look. His mind filled with images of his body rocking against hers, pumping, thrusting, exploding. He clenched his teeth, fighting the demons of desire that plagued him whenever she was within touching distance. She knew the effect she had on him. Knew it and relished it. But he wondered if it was not so much a game now but a tactic to get rid of him.

The more he thought about it, the more likely it seemed. She had hidden herself away from the press in the last place anyone would think to find her. His coming here had jeopardised the safety of her hideout.

He had no time for the press, especially since his father's exploits had sullied the family name so lamentably, but his own profile had attracted a fair bit of interest over the years. He had been in the gossip pages more than he wanted to be, but that came with the territory of being considered one of Britain's most eligible bachelors. The announcement of his engagement would bring a storm of interest his way, which was clearly something Aiesha was keen to avoid while she was holed up here with him.

James curled his top lip at her. 'You think I'd get mixed up with a cheap little two-bit tramp like you?'

She sent her smoky eyes over his body from head to foot, lingering on his groin for a heart-stopping, pulse-thundering pause, before re-engaging with his gaze with a mischievous twinkle of her own. She lifted the smartphone she was holding in one hand, tapping one of her slender fingers on the screen. 'You might want to check in with your fiancée. Fill her in on your current location and choice of company before she hears it from another source.'

James felt every hair on his scalp tighten at the roots as if being tugged out by tiny elves. But, before he could get his mouth open to speak, his phone started to ring. He took it out of his pocket, his stomach dropping as Phoebe's image came up on the screen. 'Hi, Phoebe, I was just about to—'

'You bastard!'

'It's not what you think,' he said, thinking on his feet and not doing a particularly good job of it. 'She's practically my...er...adopted sister. My mother is supposed to be here but she got called away at the—'

'Oh, for God's sake. Don't take me for a complete and utter fool. It's all over social media. You're having a fling with a—' the disgust and incredulity was starkly apparent in Phoebe's tone '—*a Vegas lounge singer?*'

James blinked. His heart thudded. His brow broke out in a hot prickling sweat. The Sherwood project flashed before his eyes. All the tricky negotiations he'd gone through to nail the pitch, all the work he'd done—hours and hours, weeks and weeks, months and months of his time—would be for naught if the ultraconservative Howard Sherwood heard about this before he could explain the circumstances. 'Listen, I can explain everyth—'

'It's over,' Phoebe said. 'Not that I was going to say yes if you ever happened to get around to proposing to me. Daddy was right about you. He said the apple never falls far from the tree and your family tree is particularly rotten. You're just like your jailbait-slavering father. I don't want my name to be dragged down to *that* level. Goodbye.' *Click.*

James curled his fingers around his phone so tightly he was sure the screen would crack or his fingers. Possibly both. He swung his gaze to Aiesha's smile. Not a cat-got-the-canary one. A cat-got-the-whole-contents-of-the-aviary smile. A red mist of anger blurred his vision. He had to blink a couple of times to clear it. 'You little game-playing bitch,' he bit out. 'What the hell do you think you're doing?'

She pushed her lips out in a pout. 'That's hardly the way to address your brand-new mistress, is it?'

He clenched his jaw so firmly it reverberated inside his skull like a slammed door. 'No one will believe it. Not for a New York second.' Mental gulp. *I hope.*

Aiesha held up her phone again, scrolling through the feed of tweets, and began reading aloud. '"WTG! About time. Always knew JC had a thing for you."' She looked up at him with that bad girl smile of hers. 'Guess how many retweets so far?'

James swung away, ploughing a hand through his hair. How would he ever live this down? Everyone in London—*everyone on the planet*—would be rolling about the floor laughing at his choice of partner. A sluttish club singer who was sleeping her way up the social ladder like a poisonous viper winding its way up a vine.

Everyone would be saying it, the words he dreaded the most: like father, like son.

But wait...

Maybe there was a way he could switch this around. It would reflect badly on him if their 'relationship' was viewed as nothing more than a casual fling or temporary hook-up. He would look exactly like his father if he didn't go into damage control and fast.

Think. Think. Think.

Aha!

What if his relationship with Aiesha was a little more serious?

James took out his phone again and typed a quick tweet and pressed send before he was tempted to think twice. This could work. It had to work. Please God, let it work.

'What are you doing?' she asked. 'You can't retract it now. It's too late. It's gone viral.'

'I'm not retracting it.' He gave her a payback smile as he slipped his phone back in his pocket. 'Congratulations, Aiesha. You just got yourself engaged.'

CHAPTER THREE

ENGAGED?

Aiesha hid her surprise at his countermove behind her trademark screen of streetwise brashness. 'Do I get a big, flashy diamond ring with that?'

His smile dropped away and his deep blue eyes glittered with disgust as they took in the impudent height of her chin. 'You're the last person on earth I would ever consider becoming engaged to and you damn well know it. You're the one who set this up. Now you can deal with the consequences. We'll stay engaged until the press loses interest. I give it a couple of weeks, tops.'

Aiesha folded her arms across her chest, the action pushing her breasts up so that a generous hint of her cleavage showed. She enjoyed watching him try to keep his gaze north of her neckline. He was so starchy and uptight, but she knew that inside those crisply ironed trousers with their knife-sharp creases was a hot-blooded man in his prime. 'How much are you going to pay me for this little pretend gig? You should know by now I'm not the kind of girl to do anything for free...

even for…erm…' she gave him a little wink as she put her fingers up in mock quotation marks '"…family."'

His savage frown brought his brows together over his eyes. 'Have you no shame?'

She laughed at his schoolmasterish-stern expression because she knew it would annoy him. She *liked* annoying him. He was always so serious and sober. So grave and so disciplined. It amused her to niggle him, to watch him fight to control his temper. She watched as a dull flush rode high on his sharp aristocratic cheekbones and a muscle flickered in his jaw, on and off, as if it was being tugged by a surgical needle and thread beneath the skin.

Yep. He was furious with her all right. He looked as if he wanted to shake her until her teeth fell out and rolled along the floor like marbles.

But there was something else throbbing in the air and it wasn't anger.

Aiesha could feel the echo of it pulsing in her own body. She became aware of every one of her erogenous zones as if his steely gaze had burned through the ice that kept each of them in a deep-freeze lockdown.

Molten heat pooled between her thighs as she thought of those clenched hands relaxing enough to reach out and stroke her flesh, for one of those broad, masculine fingertips to brush across the pebble of each of her nipples, to tease the puckered skin until she gasped out loud with the pleasure.

She glanced at his tight-lipped mouth. She had always wondered how it would feel to have that mouth lose its rigidly disapproving lines and soften in passion, to meld to hers in a fiery lock of lust and longing, for his tongue to stab through the seam of her mouth to plunder hers.

Aiesha suppressed an involuntary shiver. She wasn't interested in being overcome with passion. Unlike most women, she could *always* separate sex from emotion. She could get down and dirty, but her heart and her head were never in it, only her body. Her body had needs and she saw to them if and when the right opportunity came along.

But something warned her about getting physical with James Challender, like a foghorn sounding in the distance. She couldn't put her finger on it, or describe it accurately, but she knew if she stepped over the boundary of becoming involved with him sexually then it might not just be her body that would receive him.

No one but no one had access to her heart and she was going to keep it that way.

His slate-blue eyes seared hers. 'How long have you been in contact with my mother?'

Aiesha held his accusing look with a defiant hoist of her chin. 'She wrote to me the year after her divorce from your father was finalised.'

His brows snapped together. 'You've been in contact *that* long?'

'On and off.'

'But…but why?'

Aiesha had been surprised by Louise's first phone call eight years ago. With the benefit of hindsight and a little more maturity, she knew she had acted appallingly to the only person who had ever shown her a shred of genuine affection.

Louise Challender had always wanted a daughter; she was the type of woman who should have had a brood of children to love and nurture, and yet she'd been unable to have another child after giving birth to James. It had put an enormous strain on her marriage to Clifford, but then Clifford wasn't the type of man who would have been a suitable father for anyone, let alone a brood of kids. He was too immature and selfish, like a spoilt child who had been overindulged and always expected everything to go his way. Aiesha had seen that from the moment she had been introduced to him when Louise brought her home from the streets, where she'd been living since her stepfather had kicked her out a week after her mother had overdosed on heroin. She'd refused to take her mother's place in his bed so he'd turned her out of the house, but not before committing an unspeakable act of cruelty that still caused her nightmares all these years on. If only she had thought to get Archie out of the house first.

If only. If only. If only...

Watching as her beloved dog was strangled to death in front of her had destroyed her belief in humanity. Archie had only yelped the once but his cry had haunted many a sleepless night since.

Aiesha blinked the distressing scene out of her head as best she could. She wasn't that powerless young girl any more. She was the one in control now. She allowed no man to have an advantage on her.

Clifford Challender might wear bespoke clothes and

speak with an upper-class accent but underneath he was no different from her brutish, despicable, drug-dealing stepfather. She had proven it. It had only taken five minutes alone with him in the study to set it up. She had planned it to the last detail. They'd agreed to meet at a hotel in London's West End to 'begin' their affair. Clifford had taken the bait—as she had known he would—with the press waiting to capture the moment, but, looking back now, she regretted that Louise had been hurt in the process.

Although she had never told Louise, or indeed anyone, how deeply traumatised she had been from that last interaction with her stepfather, over time she had been able to understand why she had behaved as she had. She had been so angry, so viciously angry, at the injustice dished out to her and to poor little Archie that she had come into the Challender household with the sole agenda to cause as much mayhem as she could. Like a wounded animal, she had scratched and bitten at the hand that was trying its best to comfort and feed her.

Aiesha had apologised to Louise since and they had never mentioned it again by tacit agreement. But if Louise was bitter or still held any resentment she certainly gave no sign of it. If anything, Aiesha got the impression that Louise was much happier without the shackles of a marriage that had limped along for years for the sake of appearances.

But James's bitterness was another thing entirely.

He hadn't forgiven her for the attention she had drawn to his family. Drunk on the power of payback, Aiesha had sold her story to the press. Although no crime had been committed, for Clifford Challender hadn't done anything other than agree to meet her, the press had run with the Lolita angle and run wild. Selling her story hadn't necessarily been about the money—although it had come in very handy at getting her set up until she came of age—but about showing the world she would not be ignored or silenced just because she was from the wrong side of the tracks.

The impact on the Challender name in the architectural sector had been catastrophic. At the time she hadn't thought or cared how her actions would impact on James, but impact they did. Along with his father, he'd lost current and potential clients, and it had only been in the last year or so that he had been able to redress the effects of the fallout of the scandal.

No wonder he hated her.

And no wonder he couldn't understand what possible reason his mother would have for staying in contact with her, even sporadically, much less invite her to stay in her home for as long as she wanted.

Aiesha wasn't sure she understood it herself.

'Your mother isn't one to bear grudges,' she said. 'Unlike someone else I know, she's prepared to let bygones be bygones.'

His glittering eyes, his knitted brow, his flared nostrils and his iron-hard jaw visibly quaked with contempt. 'My mother's a fool to be taken in by you again. You haven't changed an iota. You're still a smart-mouthed, conniving little gold-digging tramp on the make. The fact that you want money to pose as my fiancée proves it.'

Aiesha tossed her head in a devil-may-care manner. 'Take it or leave it, James. It's your reputation on the line, not mine. I don't have anything to lose.'

His hands balled into fists as if he didn't trust himself not to reach for her and do her an injury. A perverse part of her was excited to see him teetering on the cliff edge of the iron-strong self-control he so prided himself on possessing. It made her want to push and push and push until he fell into sin. It was why she goaded him so shamelessly. She wanted to prove he was no different from all the other men she'd had dealings with throughout her life. He might have been surrounded by silver spoons and salvers, and slept on silk and satin sheets, but behind that stiff, upper-lip, straitlaced demeanour was a brooding, simmering passion that was as primal and earthy as any other sexually mature man.

His eyes nailed hers like blue darts, his mouth so tightly set it looked physically as well as morally painful for him to get the words out. 'How much?'

Aiesha pictured the cottage in the country she had dreamed of since she was a little girl living in council flats with walls as thin as diet wafers. She had dreamed of a place surrounded by flowers and fields and forest, of peace and calm instead of shouting and swearing and fighting. No pimps. No drugs. No violence.

Solitude. *Safety.*

She named a figure that sent James's brows shooting towards his hairline. '*What?*' he choked.

She folded her arms in an implacable manner. 'You heard.'

He frowned at her blackly. 'You're joking, surely?'

'Nope.'

He coughed out a disbelieving laugh. 'This is ludicrous.' His hand scored a jagged pathway through his hair. 'Am I even having this conversation?'

'Want me to pinch you?'

He quickly stepped back from her, holding his hands up in front of himself like a barrier. 'Don't touch me.'

Aiesha smiled as she deliberately stepped closer. It was thrilling to have so much sensual power at her disposal. The air vibrated with electric voltage; she could feel it lifting the skin of her arms in a carpet of goose bumps and wondered if his body was undergoing the same sensual overload. Was his blood thundering through his veins, thickening him? Extending him to full erection? Was he feeling that primal ache that consumed everything but the desperate need to copulate?

Maybe she should ignore that silly little foghorn inside her head. What would it hurt to have a little bit of fun to pass the time? He had always been the subject of her fantasies.

Now she could make them real.

She lazily stroked her fingertip over the thick and neatly aligned Windsor knot of his tie, close to where a pulse was beating like a piston in his tanned and cologne-scented neck. She breathed in lemon and lime and something else that was elusive and yet potently addictive. 'What are you afraid of, posh boy?' Her fingers slipped down from the knot to play with the end of his tie like a mean cat with a mouse's tail. 'That this time around I might prove to be irresistible?'

She heard his jaw lock. Heard his teeth grind. Saw

his pupils flare as his eyes flicked to her mouth for a
nanosecond.

'I can resist you.' His voice was so deep and so husky
it sounded as if it had been scraped along a rough surface and only just survived the journey.

Aiesha looked at the dark pinpricks of regrowth surrounding his mouth and chin. He had a strong, uncom-
promising mouth, his top lip neatly sculpted, but his
lower lip was fuller, rich with sensual promise. Something unfurled deep and low inside her belly, like a satin
ribbon running away from its spool.

Suddenly the game she'd been playing turned deadly
serious.

The battle of wills she was so sure she could win
shifted its power balance. She felt it in the immeasurable
beat of time where his gaze grazed her mouth again. It
provoked a visceral reaction inside her body, a lightning strike of lust that all but knocked her off her feet.

She sent her tongue out over her lips to try and quell
the fizzing sensation that was fast becoming an ache.
His warm, faintly mint-scented breath skated over the
surface of her lips as, centimetre by centimetre, millimetre by millimetre he ever so slowly began to close the
distance. Her own breath felt painfully restricted as she
drew it into her lungs, as if the space inside her chest
was already taken up by something big and suffocating.
She rose up on tiptoe, closing her eyes, waiting, waiting, waiting for that first blissful moment of contact...

Her eyes sprang open when she heard him take a step
back from her. His expression was as stiff and formal as
the wallpaper on the wall behind him. 'I'll deposit the

money in your bank account once I have a legal contract drawn up,' he said.

She arched a brow. 'The terms being?'

'If you speak out of turn to the press you'll have to repay the amount in full plus twenty per cent interest.'

Aiesha pushed her pursed lips from side to side. 'Twenty per cent seems a bit steep to me. Let's make it ten.'

'Fifteen.'

'Five, or I tell the press right here and now we're having a tawdry little affair that will be over once this snow melts.'

His jaw worked for a moment before he gave a curt nod of agreement. But she wasn't sure if he was agreeing because he thought the deal fair or because he couldn't wait to get away from her. His brusque statement suggested the latter. 'I'm going to the study to work for the rest of the evening.'

Aiesha hitched one hip higher than the other in her best femme-fatale pose. 'All work and no play makes James a very dull boy.'

His eyes held hers in a tight little lock that made the backs of her knees tingle. 'I know how to play. I'm just a little more careful than most over choosing my playmates.'

She curved her mouth in a mocking manner. He might find it easy to resist her now but she wasn't finished with him yet. She would bring him to his knees before the week was out. He would not be so straitlaced and sure of himself once she had him where she wanted him. She could hardly wait.

'I bet Phoebe Frozen-Face doesn't do it up against the kitchen bench or outside under the stars on a hot sweaty night. I bet she's a bed and missionary girl with all the lights off. Am I right?'

His lips came together in a flat white line. 'Please spare me the sordid details of your sexual practices. I'm not interested.'

'Yes, you are.' Aiesha all but purred the words at him. 'I bet you're wondering what it would feel like to do me right here and now. On the rug at our feet. So rough one or both of us gets carpet burn.'

The words were provocative, goading, tempting. The erotic images they triggered in her mind even more so. She knew she was being utterly brazen but something about his steely resistance fired her determination to have him finally admit his desire for her. It was the ultimate challenge.

He was the ultimate challenge.

James gave her a dismissive look but she noticed the hammer was back in the lower quadrant of his jaw. 'Keep your Vegas-showgirl tactics for someone who actually gives a damn,' he said. 'I have far better things to do with my time.'

Aiesha watched as he turned and strode purposefully out of the room, his back and shoulders as stiff as a plank, his hands balled into fists as hard as cannonballs at his sides.

An anticipatory smile turned up the corners of her mouth.

I am so going to win this.

CHAPTER FOUR

JAMES STARED AT his computer screen, but instead of seeing the designs he'd drawn up for the Sherwood townhouse he saw Aiesha lying naked on the Persian rug in the sitting room with him pounding into her. Her hair was fanned out over the rug, her beautiful breasts jiggling sexily, her feline back arching as she came with a primal scream that—

He gave himself a mental slap and refocused on the project in front of him. The plans, which had seemed so brilliant the day before, now looked like a boring set of angles and planes.

He pushed himself back from the desk and stood and stretched the stiffness out of his back. That wasn't all that was stiff…but the less he thought about that the better.

He stood in front of the window, staring at the moonlit white-out outside. His Highland sanctuary had become a prison of torturous temptation. A temple of sinful longings. He was trapped inside a house with a wanton woman with seduction on her mind. Aiesha was on a mission and he was her target. How was he going to resist her? She was a potent cocktail of sass and sensuality. He was already drunk on looking at her. On smelling her exotic fragrance that seemed to be in every room of the house, following him, haunting him, tempting him. He was mesmerised by those unique eyes, transfixed by that sinfully luscious mouth and that lithe body with its catwalk sway of hips and pelvis. His body throbbed with such raw longing he considered plunging himself in the snow outside to cool off.

Everything about her turned him on. Her wilfulness, her naughty pouts, the way she tossed her hair over her shoulders like a flighty filly tossed its mane. The way her grey eyes looked at him knowingly, smboulderingly, with that come-and-get-me-I-know-you-want-to steadiness as if she could sense his lust for her lurking, thickening him beneath his clothes.

James muttered an expletive and turned away from the window. It was well past midnight and he hadn't eaten. He would kill for a glass of red wine but bringing alcohol into a situation like this was asking for the sort of trouble he could do without right now. Falling into Aiesha's honey trap was exactly what she expected him to do. It was what every man she set her sights on did. She collected men like trophies, the richer and more powerful the better. He was just another prize to tick off her list. One she had wanted a long time. It was her unfinished business—the seduction of the son and heir to complete her set—the father and now the son. He would be discarded like yesterday's news as soon as she proved what she wanted to prove.

James could only hope the fervid interest in their

relationship would die away once some other couple was targeted. He loathed being besieged by the press. It brought back the cringeworthy memories of the days after Aiesha had sold her story. The cameras had been set up outside his parents' London home for over a week. He hadn't been living at home at the time but that didn't stop the barrage of attention. He was set upon at his apartment in Notting Hill. Every day microphones were thrust in his face as he left for work, asking him for comments on his father's behaviour. They followed him everywhere, even during work hours. The intrusion was so bad at one point that one of his most important clients had taken his business to a rival firm.

It had taken him this long to build up trust with a good clientele and now Aiesha was back and up to her usual mischief.

James took Bonnie out for a last pit stop before doing the rounds of turning off the lights downstairs. He came to the sitting room, where the door was slightly ajar, the muted light of the side-table lamps creating a soft V-shaped beam across the floor of the hall.

He pushed the door open to find the coffee table in front of the sofa littered with the remains of a snatch-and-grab meal: an empty wine glass, a side plate with cheese fragments and a browned apple core on it, a scrunched-up paper napkin, an empty yogurt container and a sticky teaspoon, a trail of crumbs. *Typical.* She was swanning about the place like the lady of the manor, expecting everyone else to pick up after her. He wasn't running a hotel, for God's sake. Who did she think she was, leaving his mother's sitting room in such a state?

His gaze went to the sofa and found…Sleeping Beauty.

That was exactly what Aiesha looked like. She was lying on her side facing the fire that had burned down low in the grate, her cheek resting on one of the velvet scatter cushions, her arms tucked in close to her chest and her slim legs curled up like a child's. Her hair was tousled and loose about her shoulders, one curly tendril lying like an *S* on her cheek. In sleep she looked innocent and vulnerable, far younger than twenty-five.

The eight years difference in their ages suddenly felt like a century. Make that an entire geological period.

Should he wake her?

No!

James looked at the fire. It would make too much noise getting that going again. The room, along with the rest of the house, was centrally heated but set on a timer. He could feel the slight chill in the air as the ormolu clock on the mantelpiece ticked its way to 1:00 a.m.

His gaze went to the mohair throw rug draped over the back of the wing chair. Should he or shouldn't he? He debated with himself for another thirty seconds as he watched her sleep. Her chest rose and fell, her soft mouth opening slightly as her breath came out on a sigh. Her eyelids with their spider-leg-long lashes fluttered and her forehead puckered as if something she was dreaming about had disturbed her. But after a moment or two her forehead smoothed out and she burrowed deeper into the sofa cushions like a dormouse curling up for winter.

James waited another half a minute before stealthily tiptoeing across the carpet like a burglar to get the throw rug—mentally rolling his eyes at the ridiculousness of his caution—and brought it back to gently cover her with it.

It was as if he had dropped a plank of timber on her.

She suddenly leapt off the sofa and struck out with her fists, catching him on the side of the nose in a glancing blow that made stars explode behind his eyes.

James swore and, stumbling backwards, cupped his hand over his throbbing nose, the blood dripping through his fingers to the carpet at his feet. Pain pulsed in sickening waves through his face, his skull and his stomach. He swayed on his feet as he fought against the dizziness as a school of silverfish floated before his gaze.

Aiesha reeled back from him, speaking through her hands that were clasped over her mouth in stunned horror. 'Oh, my God! Did I hurt you?'

'No,' he said through clenched teeth as he reached with his other hand for his handkerchief to stem the flow of blood. 'I have spontaneous nosebleeds all the time.'

Her eyes were still as wide as her discarded dinner plate. 'I'm sorry. I—I didn't know who it was.'

He glared at her over the wad of his handkerchief. His nose was still pulsating with eye-watering pain as it hosed blood. What was she thinking, swinging at him like that? *She* was the intruder, not him. 'Who the hell did you *think* it was?'

Her teeth chewed at her lower lip, her gaze falling away from his as she backed out of the room. 'Erm… I'll go and get you some ice…'

* * *

Aiesha held a hand against her juddering heart as she stumbled to the kitchen. The shock of waking to see a dark shape looming over her had made her react on instinct. Her primal brain hadn't had time to recognise it was not some predatory lecher after a quick feel. Her instinctive reaction to hit out was something she'd learned from a young age, having to dodge the inappropriate attention from her mother's collection of unsavoury partners. It was why she never spent the whole night with anyone. Ever. It was too awkward explaining her restlessness…or the nightmares. The last time she'd had a nightmare she'd wet the bed.

Try explaining *that* to a lover.

Aiesha looked at her reddened knuckles. If the pain throbbing in them was any indication, James was going to have a shiner by morning, if not sooner.

Her heart was not quite back where it belonged when she came back with a therapeutic ice pack she'd found in the freezer.

James was sitting on the sofa she had fallen asleep on earlier, his head tilted back, the strong column of his throat exposed. He opened one eye to look at her. 'That's a mean right hook you've got there.'

Aiesha averted her gaze as she handed him the ice pack. 'I took up boxing classes a couple of years ago. It's great for fitness. You should try it.'

He winced as he pressed the pack to the bridge of his nose. 'Somehow, the thought of thumping an opponent until they lose consciousness doesn't appeal.'

She bit her lip again. 'Does it hurt terribly?'

He gave her a look. 'That was the intention, wasn't it?'

Aiesha walked over to the remains of the fire and gave it a futile poke. She could sense his watchful gaze resting on her. He'd found her asleep. Off guard. Vulnerable. Had she given anything away while sleeping? Murmured anything? Revealed anything of the turmoil of her past?

She tamed her body language the way she'd been doing since she was eight years old. *Show no emotion. Show no fear.* 'I don't like people sneaking up on me.'

'I was trying to make you comfortable. You were lying asleep in front of a dead fire. I was worried you might be cold.'

Worried? Ha. When had anyone been concerned about her welfare? She was invisible unless she *made* people notice her. She had spent her life as an outsider. Not good enough. Not educated enough. Not posh enough.

The thought of him caring about her comfort disturbed her. No one cared about her. No one watched out for her. Not unless they wanted something.

Aiesha turned and squared her gaze with his. 'Why didn't you wake me up? Why creep around and scare the crap out of me? I'm glad I punched you. I should've hit you harder.'

He took the ice pack away from his face, frowning at her, but not in anger. There was something measuring about his gaze as it held hers. She looked away, flattening her mouth, locking him out.

He came over to where she was standing in front of the dead fire. 'You want to hit me again?' he asked.

'Come on. Put up your fists and clobber me with your best shot.'

She crossed her arms, flashing him a cutting glare. 'Stop making fun of me.'

Those dark blue eyes continued to penetrate and probe. 'I'm not joking, Aiesha. Get it out of your system. You want to hit me, then go ahead and hit me. I won't hit you back. I can take it like a man.'

Aiesha clenched her fists. She *could* hit him. She could probably knock him out cold if she put her mind to it. Trouble was, her mind was out of sync with her heart.

She hated that she'd hurt him. She loathed violence. Violence sickened her. She'd only taken up boxing as a precaution while living in Vegas. It wasn't called Sin City for nothing. Men with too much alcohol on board thought it their right to grope and proposition her each night as she left the club. She had never hit anyone before, just a punching bag in the gym. That punching bag had been the substitute for all the men she wished she'd been able to pummel back the way they had pummelled her mother. Hadn't she herself copped enough hits and slaps in her time to want to eradicate all violence from the world?

And then there was poor little Archie. He had trusted her to keep him safe from that despicable Beast Man and she had failed him. She tried to block the sound of that startled yelp inside her brain. She tried to block the sound of that fatal crack, as poor little Archie's neck was broken. She tried to block the sight of that poor little limp body hanging from Beast Man's horrible hand like a trophy.

Aiesha could feel her defences crumbling like the ashes of the log she'd poked in the grate a minute ago. James had seen her off guard. Unprotected by her outer shell of hard-nosed tart. Her fight-or-flight instincts were battling it out inside her chest. She could feel every moment of the struggle like fists landing heavy blows against her heart.

Flee.

Fight.

Flee.

Fight.

She was conscious of the silence...measured by the sound of the ticking clock on the mantelpiece above the fireplace. She was conscious of the dryness of her mouth and the unfamiliar hot moist prickling at the back of her eyes. She was conscious of a tight restriction as the deep well of her buried emotion bubbled up in her throat like a foul sewer.

She. Would. Not. Cry.

Aiesha blinked and quickly slipped her armour back on. She opened and closed her hands, testing him. Watching to see if he so much as flinched. 'I could really hurt you,' she said.

'Undoubtedly.'

She couldn't make out his expression. Was he testing her? Seeing if she would take up the dare? She brought her hand up but he didn't move a muscle. His gaze was steady on hers. She placed her hand on the side of his face, her skin catching on the graze of his stubble.

Something caught in her chest. A snag. A hitch. Then a letting go...

There was another heartbeat of silence.

He covered her hand with his, holding it within the gentle prison of his fingers. 'That the best you could do?' he said.

Aiesha looked at his mouth before flicking her gaze back to his. 'I don't want to ruin that pretty-boy face of yours.'

The dark blue of his eyes intensified, holding hers in a lock that made something inside her belly tilt and then spill. 'You're scared.'

She sent her tongue out in a quick darting movement to moisten her lips. 'Let me go, James.'

'I have a little forfeit to collect first.'

Something dropped off a shelf in her stomach. 'Forfeit?'

He spread his hands through the mane of her hair, his gaze moving from her eyes to her mouth in a slow and mesmerising fashion. 'You punched me in the nose. I get to kiss you. Fair's fair.'

She affected a sneer but was pretty sure it was wide off the mark. 'Is that meant to be a punishment?'

'Why don't we find out?' he said and, tugging her against him, his mouth came down over hers.

His lips were warm and firm, slow and deliberate. Purposeful. His tongue stroked against her top lip and then her lower lip without deepening the kiss. It sent every one of Aiesha's nerves into a frenzied clamour of want. She wound her arms around his neck, leaning into him to give more of herself to the kiss. She opened her mouth, inviting him in, teasing him with the flicker of her tongue against his lips.

He made a deep growling sound in the back of his throat and thrust his tongue against hers, wrangling and tangling with it, sending her pulses soaring. He tasted unique, not sour or beery, or stale or too mouth-washy or minty.

He tasted...*just right*.

Aiesha delved her fingers into his thick dark hair as he continued to explore her mouth in spine-loosening detail. Her body trembled with desire, great giant waves of it coursing through her as his tongue moved inside her mouth with erotic intent. His kiss was mesmerising, magical and intoxicating. Not rushed and greedy, but respectful and enticing. Her mouth responded to him like a flower opening to warm rays of sunshine. She had been kissed too many times to count but not one of them had been like this. Gentle and yet determined, passionate and yet controlled.

His pelvis was pressed against hers, his erection leaving her in no doubt of the effect she was having on him. She could feel the length of it against her belly, making her desperate to touch him skin on skin. She felt her inner core contract, the silky moisture of arousal anointing her in anticipation of his possession.

His breathing was heavy, as if he was only just holding on to his self-control. She felt the tension in him, the way his hands were holding her by the hips, set there, anchored there as if moving them to another part of her body would be dangerous.

She made a mewling sound as his teeth grazed her

lower lip, tugging on it before salving it with the stroke of his tongue. He repeated the process with her top lip, little teasing nips and tugs that made the hairs on the back of her neck quiver. He smoothly glided his tongue back into her mouth, sweeping hers up into a tango of lustful longings.

Aiesha wanted him so badly she could feel it writhing and coiling like a serpent inside her. Had she ever wanted a man more than James Challender? He was the ultimate prize. Rich, powerful, well-to-do. She had *always* wanted him. From the first moment she had met him when he came to visit his parents soon after she had come to stay she had felt a lightning flash of awareness arc between them. He had kept a respectful distance, making it abundantly clear he was not going to be seduced by a teenager. He hadn't been rude to her or cruel. He had been polite but firm. Implacable. And back then she had hated him for it.

Now…now she wasn't quite so sure what she felt other than rip-roaring lust.

She wanted him because he represented everything she had missed out on during her harrowing childhood. Success. Stability. Safety.

She made a move for his belt buckle but he stalled her hand, holding it against him as he fought to control his breathing.

'No,' he said.

No?

What man had ever said no to her? Ever since she was a kid she'd been fighting them off. Rejecting *them*, not them rejecting her. The shift in power was new and troubling...unsettling. She liked to be the one who said yay or nay. 'You want me.' She said it matter-of-factly. Without emotion.

He released her hand and stepped back from her. 'This can't go anywhere.' He pushed his hair back over his forehead. 'You know it can't.'

Aiesha hid behind her mask of brash bad girl. 'Too rough for your upmarket taste?'

His frown carved deeply into his brow as he moved away to the door to leave. 'I think it's best if we keep things on a platonic basis. It's...safer that way.'

She cocked one of her eyebrows at him in a cheeky manner. 'So we're friends now instead of enemies?'

He turned and looked back at her for a long moment. 'I suspect your only enemy, Aiesha, is yourself.' He punctuated his comment with a brisk dismissive nod and closed the door before she could think of a comeback.

CHAPTER FIVE

JAMES CLOSED HIS bedroom door with a self-recriminating curse. *Are you crazy? Kissing her? Touching her? Wanting her?* He pushed a hand through his hair in distraction. He should *never* have kissed her. He'd crossed the line. The line he'd put down a decade ago.

Aiesha was cunning and clever. For a moment there he'd sensed a softening in her. Her guard had slipped, or so he'd thought. But she knew exactly what she was doing. Which buttons of his to press. She wasn't the emotionally vulnerable type. She was too hard-boiled, too street smart. Hadn't her punch proved that?

He grimaced as he checked his reflection in the mirror of his en-suite bathroom. His nose wasn't broken but he was going to have a black eye for sure, all because he had come too close to her without her knowing.

He rubbed at the stubble on his jaw. She'd been soundly asleep; there was no way he had got that wrong. Her breathing had been deep and even, her whole body relaxed. Her reaction had been so extreme, so unexpected. *Why?*

He thought about her background…trying to recall

what his mother had told him about her in the past. Aiesha had been vague about her family of origin; the only thing she'd told his mother was that she was a teen-age runaway and it had been her choice to leave. She hadn't been with his family long enough to prise out any other details. As far as he knew, she hadn't been into drugs or heavily into alcohol, or at least not that he had noticed. She only had one tattoo, and a small one at that, on the underside of her right wrist—the name Archie with hearts and roses—but she had never said who Archie was or why he was so important to her that she'd felt compelled to have his name permanently inked into her skin.

James cursed again. Kissing her had been a mistake. A big mistake. A ginormous mistake. He'd known it but done it anyway. He hadn't been able to stop himself. As soon as she had put her hand so gently on his face he'd known he was going to kiss her. It had been inevitable. A force outside his control. He'd only planned to press his mouth to hers as an experiment, as a test for him-self. To prove he could do it without losing his head.

For years he had dreamed of kissing that mouth. He had fantasised about it. Hungered for it like a for-mer addict did a forbidden drug. Her mouth was as addictive as he'd imagined it—soft and sweet and yet hot and hungry. The blood had surged through him at rocket-force speed. Her deliciously feminine body had felt so...*so right* as he'd held her in his arms. The way her mouth had tasted, the way her tongue had danced with his in that sexy tango, the way her hips had been in the perfect position against his. He'd wanted her so badly he'd had to fight to keep his hands in one place so he didn't use them to tear the clothes from her body and ram himself into her wickedly tempting wetness.

He was not a man who acted on impulse. He did not indulge in casual affairs or shallow hook-ups. He had needs and he saw to them in a responsible and respectful manner. His life was carefully planned and detailed, organised and compartmentalised because that was the way to avoid nasty surprises. He had seen too many friends and colleagues—not to mention his father—come unstuck by succumbing to a reckless ill-timed roll in the sack. Careers, reputations, familial relationships were permanently ruined in the carnage of an illicit affair and he would not make the same mistake.

His father's double life had come to light during James's late teens. Throughout his childhood, whenever he was home from boarding school, his mother would do her happy-families thing and James had never questioned it. Hadn't thought to question it. Maybe he hadn't wanted to face it. On some level he'd known his parents weren't blissfully honeymoon-like happy, but neither had he thought they were utterly miserable. They were his parents and he liked that they were together and seemingly stable. But then, when he'd been in his final year, someone at school had made a comment about seeing James's father coming out of a hotel with a woman in the city and James's concept of a stable home life had been shattered. His mother had stoically tried to keep the marriage together for the next few years after his father promised to remain faithful, but of course Clifford had strayed time and time again, albeit a little more discreetly.

Ever since, James swore he would not live like his father, lying and cheating his way through life. He would not be swayed by temptation or sabotage his success and reputation by a lack of self-control.

But there were two things he couldn't control in his life right now—Aiesha Adams and the weather. He pulled back the curtains and looked at the flakes of snow falling past his window.

Fabulous.

Freaking fabulous.

Aiesha waited until James had left the house before she came downstairs the next morning. She saw him talking on his mobile as he headed to the river walk with Bonnie. He had his head down and his shoulders hunched forwards against the wind. He stopped a couple of times to glance back frowningly at the house but Aiesha kept out of sight behind the edge of the curtain. Even from this distance she could see the colourful bruise beneath his eye. Was he still wondering why she had gone at him like that?

She gave a long sigh when he disappeared into the fringe of trees along the river. Why should she care what he thought of her? What was the point of trying to whitewash her reputation now? He would never see her as anything other than a good-time bad girl.

She had to shake off this restless mood…and there was only one way to do it.

The ballroom was her favourite room at Lochbannon. It was next to the sitting room and overlooked the formal gardens at the front of the house. Watermarked silk curtains hung in large swathes at the windows, the bottoms lying in billowing pools on the highly polished parquet floor like the trains of elegant ball gowns. A central chandelier dripping with sparkling crystals hung from the ceiling and various velvet-shaded wall lights added to the sense of grandeur. The piano was a concert grand and had been recently tuned. Louise had always insisted the piano was regularly serviced but Aiesha had a sneaking suspicion Louise had quickly organised it once she had known Aiesha was coming to stay.

Louise was an accomplished violinist but had given up her musical aspirations to marry Clifford Challender. He had insisted on being the only star on the Challender family stage. Louise was required to be the supporting act, to grace his table with her congenial presence, to turn a blind eye to any extracurricular activities he indulged in from time to time, and to bring up his son according to the rules of the upper class.

It reminded Aiesha of her mother's fitting-in-with-men mentality. It had started with Aiesha's father, who had dominated her mother as soon as he got her pregnant. Her mother had done everything she was told to and yet was still punished for whatever he took offence to. It could be the way the housework was done or the way the meal was cooked, or the way she looked or didn't look. An opinion expressed that didn't tie in with the rules and regulations he set down. It had been impossible for her mother to gauge what was right or wrong. Her self-esteem had taken even more of a battering than her body.

And yet, after Aiesha's father had been locked away for armed robbery, instead of the new life Aiesha had envisaged, her mother had drifted into another relationship with the same old pattern developing within a matter of weeks. It happened repeatedly. Her mother would finally get the courage to leave and within weeks she would find someone else who was a carbon copy of the man she'd just escaped from. It was the drugs that did it. They were the lure each and every time. The mild addiction Aiesha's father had started with a joint had grown into an uncontrollable habit. Heroin, cocaine, alcohol—anything that offered a temporary respite from reality. Her mother had been charmed time and time again by manipulative men who promised her the world and gave her nothing but heartache, and finally death.

Aiesha looked at the walnut cabinet where row after row of musical scores were stored. All the classics were there as well as a selection of more modern pieces. She thought of Louise's talent, all those hours and hours of practice and personal sacrifice to make it to the top tier of musical performance, wasted on a man who hadn't appreciated her.

From the first moment Aiesha had stepped over the threshold of the Challender mansion in Mayfair she burned with envy over James's childhood. What she would have given for such luxury, for such comfort. For a full night's sleep without some sleazy beer-sodden creep sneaking up on her. For a roof over her head each night, for regular meals, a top-notch education, and holidays to somewhere warm and exotic and exciting.

But now she wondered if he, too, had suffered from neglect. Nothing like the neglect she had suffered, but the type that left other sorts of scars.

Growing up with a selfish, limelight-stealing father would be enormously difficult, if not at times downright embarrassing. Trying to please someone who could never be pleased. Trying to live down the shame of having his father's playboy behaviour splashed over every paper while his mother suffered in silence at home.

The weeks after Aiesha's story broke were intense for him and his mother. She had seen the footage of James being chased along the street outside his Notting Hill residence and again in front of the office block where he had his architectural business. His father's peccadilloes had brought enormous shame to him then and now.

Was that why James was so much of a workaholic and perfectionist? Driven and focused to the exclusion of all else, in particular fun? Was that why he had those lines of strain around his mouth and two horizontal ones on his forehead? He frowned more than he smiled. He worked rather than played. Was that why he had chosen such a boring and predictable woman to marry? Phoebe Trentonfield was probably a nice enough person, but she wasn't right for him. He needed someone who would stand up to him. To push him out of the nice little safe comfort zone he had created for himself.

Someone who would release the locked down passion in him.

Someone like me...

Aiesha pulled out the shiny black piano stool and sat down heavily on the thought. She wasn't the type of girl a man like James would settle down with. She didn't tick any of his neat little boxes.

She was from the wrong side of town.

She was from the wrong side of everything.

Men like James Challender did not get involved with Vegas lounge singers who had a father in prison and a stepfather who should be.

Men like James chose girls who were polished and cultured, women who had a blue-blood pedigree centuries long. Aristocrats who knew which cutlery to use during which course and who never put a high-heeled, designer-clad foot wrong.

Aiesha put her hands over the keys, opening and closing them to warm them up. Her bruised knuckles protested at the movement but she ignored them. She was used to pain. She knew all its forms. Physical pain was the easiest to deal with.

Emotional pain was the one she had to avoid.

'Are you out of your mind?' Clifford Challender roared at James via his mobile while he was out walking Bonnie. 'That little slut will ruin your reputation and laugh in your face while she's doing it.'

James refrained from disclosing to his father the truth about his relationship with Aiesha. It wasn't just because of the punch and kiss and make-up incident last night, which he was still trying to wrap his head around. Clifford was not the discreet type. The news of his sham engagement would be all over social media come his father's first vodka of the day. Although, judging from the tone of his father's voice, he suspected he had already sunk a couple of shots and it wasn't even 10:00 a.m.

'I keep out of your affairs. Please keep out of mine.'

'I blame your mother for this,' Clifford said. 'She's always been a sucker for a lame duck. That girl will take her for another ride. Just shows what a stupid fool she is to fall for it a second time.'

James was glad his father was close to a thousand kilometres away, otherwise he might have been tempted to give him a black eye to match his own spectacular one. He hated the way his father used every opportunity to trash his mother since the divorce. It was his father's way of shifting the blame off himself. In Clifford's mind, James's mother had ruined everything by 'making a fuss' about his occasional affairs.

Although James was furious with Aiesha about her methods, he was privately relieved the scandal had brought on the divorce that should have happened years before. 'I've already warned you about speaking about Mum like that.'

'You don't think she set this up?' Clifford said.

'No.' *Yes. No. Maybe. I don't know.* He hadn't told his mother he was coming to Lochbannon. He hadn't even told her he was thinking of asking Phoebe to marry him. It was coincidence. Happenstance. *Wasn't it?* 'Mum had to leave the country at short notice. I haven't talked to her since she texted me.'

Clifford made a scornful sound. 'I don't give your engagement to that little bit of trailer trash a month. You haven't got the balls to handle a chit like that. Stick to your nice girls, son. Leave the bad ones to me.'

James put his phone away, and then stopped and looked back at the house in the distance. He was assailed by two very different thoughts. First, sticking to a nice girl suddenly seemed very unappealing and second, the thought of Aiesha being anywhere near his father suddenly sent a shudder running down his spine.

James was coming back from his bracing walk to the woods when he heard the music coming from the ballroom. It was like nothing he had heard from there before. And it wasn't anything he would hear in a Las Vegas lounge bar, either. It was lilting and melodic and yet…strangely haunting. The cadences were deeply poignant, touching on a chord deep inside him, like someone plucking on the strings of a hidden harp.

He stood at the door of the room, watching as Aiesha's hands danced over the keys of the piano. She was dressed in a hot-pink velour tracksuit that had teddy-bear ears on the hooded top, which she'd pulled over her head, presumably to keep her own ears warm. The look was quaint, cute and endearing. It showed a side of her that was young and playful, as if she didn't care what people thought of her attire as long as she was comfortable. She had a fierce frown of concentration on her forehead, although there was no musical score in front of her. She seemed totally unaware of anything but the music she was playing.

He was transfixed by the sound. Rising and falling notes that tugged and twitched on his heartstrings, minor key chords that were like emotional hits to his chest. Feelings he hadn't encountered for decades came out of hiding. They crowded his chest cavity until he could barely breathe, like too many guests at a cocktail party.

She came to the end of the piece and closed her eyes and bowed her head as if the effort had totally exhausted her.

James stepped into the room and she jolted upright like a puppet being jerked back up by its strings. 'You might've knocked,' she said with a frown of reproach.

'I didn't realise it was a private performance.'

She got up smartly from the piano and crossed her arms over her body in that keep-away-from-me gesture he was coming to know so well. A faint blush was on her cheeks, which she tried to hide by turning her back to look out of the window, where the sun was trying to get its act together but making a lacklustre job of it.

Her teddy-bear ears looked even cuter from behind.

So did her toosh.

'Nice walk?' she asked.

'Did you watch me leave?' Was that why she had chosen to play such beautifully evocative music while he was out of the house?

She didn't turn around. 'Pretty hard to ignore that dog's crazy yapping.'

'That dog has a name.'

This time she did turn around. Her expression showed nothing. Zip. 'Your eye looks terrible.'

James shrugged. 'Just as well there are no photographers lurking around.'

'The roads are still blocked?'

'Well and truly.'

She didn't show disappointment or relief. She showed nothing. Her face was a blank canvas. But two of her fingers fiddled with the zip on her tracksuit jacket, the sound of metal clicking against metal as rhythmic as a metronome.

He moved across the floor to the piano, tinkling a few keys to break the silence. 'What was that piece you were playing?'

'Why do you ask?'

He turned and caught the tail end of her guarded expression. 'I liked it. It was…' he searched for the right word '…stirring.'

She walked over to the walnut shelving where all of his mother's music was stored, her fingers playing along the spines like a child trailing a stick along a picket fence. James wondered if she was going to answer him. It seemed like for ever before she let her fingers fall away from the spines with a sigh he saw rather than heard. 'It's called *An Ode to Archie.*'

'You composed that yourself?'

'Yeah, what of it?' Her eyes flashed at him. 'You think just because I'm a club singer I can't write music or something?'

'Did you write it for the Archie on your wrist?'

Her left hand encircled her right wrist protectively, chin up, eyes still glittering. 'Yes.'

'Who is he?'

'Was.'

She moved away from the cabinet to go back to the

piano. She closed the lid over the keys like someone closing a conversation…or a coffin. A shiver scuttled over the back of James's neck like the legs of a spooked spider. 'He's dead,' she said.

'I'm sorry.'

She gave a shrug but he couldn't decide if it was a 'thank you' or 'I don't need your sympathy' one.

'Who was he?'

Her eyes met his but there was no sign of anything resembling emotion. A curtain was drawn. A shutter was down. 'He was a friend I had once. A childhood friend.'

'What happened to him?'

Her gaze moved away again. 'Do you play a musical instrument?'

The swift change of subject alerted him to an undercurrent of emotion she seemed at great pains to conceal. He was intrigued by her shadow self. The side he had seen last night when she had sprung up from that sofa with her fists at the ready. The side of her he briefly glimpsed while she sat playing her music. She was capable of deep feeling. No one who wrote music like that could possibly be cold and indifferent, without feeling and depth. But, rather than push her, he decided to leave it. For now.

'I'm afraid I didn't inherit my mother's musical ability. I'm sure it was a bitter disappointment to her. I think she would've liked me to be a virtuoso of some sort.'

She pushed the hood back off her cloud of tousled hair to face him levelly. 'Your father was wrong to make her give up her career.'

James studied her expression for a moment. 'She told you about that?'

She pressed her lips together as if regretting having spoken. 'I don't think she's disappointed you didn't pursue music as a career. She's very proud of your work, as any decent parent should be. You're good at what you do. Brilliant, actually. Everyone raves about your designs. They're so innovative.'

He gave her a wry look. 'A compliment from the cynical Aiesha Adams. Well, I'll be damned.'

'Make the most of it. It won't happen again.'

She moved past him to leave but he captured her arm on the way past. He hadn't consciously realised he was going to touch her until he felt his fingers wrap around her slim arm. Even through the soft velour of her tracksuit sleeve he could feel the snap-crackle-pop shock of his touch on her.

She glowered at him. 'If you want the other eye to match your right one then keep on doing what you're doing.'

'What am I doing?'

'You're touching me.'

He kept his gaze locked on her fiery one as his thumb found the thud of her pulse. 'I thought you liked being touched by me. I thought that was your plan. To seduce me.'

She pulled back from his hold but his fingers tightened. So did his groin. 'I've changed my mind.'

Her game plan had changed. She was back-pedalling after coming on so strong. He had got too close. Seen a part of her she didn't want to reveal. He had never met a more fascinating person. She was all smoke and mirrors. Secrets and cover-ups. It made him want her all the more. She was unpredictable. Mysterious. Captivating.

He moved in closer, breathing in the exotic gardenia-like flowery scent of her, watching as her black pupils in that stormy sea of grey grew wider. Her nostrils flared as if she, too, were breathing in his smell like a she wolf did a mate. Primal need overruled his common sense. His body blanked out the warnings of his mind like a master switch turning off a source of power, rerouting it to where it was needed the most. Blood flowed thick and strong to his groin. He felt it surging there in a hot turgid tide that no sandbag of rationality was ever going to withstand.

He hadn't realised it would be so hard to fight it. To deny it. To ignore it. His desire for her had smouldered in his blood and body for so long it took nothing but a look or touch to set it raging. 'You don't like it when someone else is in control, do you?' he said. 'You like to drum up the action but you don't like being on the receiving end of it. That's way too submissive for you, isn't it?'

She continued to glare at him but every now and again her gaze would flick down to his mouth as if remembering how it had felt to have it fused with her own. The tip of her tongue passed over her lips, leaving them moist and shimmering. She could have moved away if she wanted to. He had deliberately relaxed his hold; his fingers were barely more than a loose bracelet around her wrist.

He brought his head down and heard the sharp intake of her breath as his mouth came down to hover above hers. Their breaths mingled. Her pulse raced beneath his fingers. His skyrocketed. 'You know I want you,' he said.

'So?' Her voice lacked its usual sassy edge. It sounded thready. Uncertain. As if she had somehow drifted out of her depth and wasn't sure how to get back to safety. But even so her body swayed towards his like a fragment of metal being pulled by a magnet.

He brushed his bottom lip against her top one, a teasing nudge. A come-and-play-with-me invitation. 'So maybe it's time I did something about it.'

'Enter a monastery.'

He smiled against her lower lip. 'There's a thought.'

'If you kiss me you're a dead man.'

'So shoot me,' he said, and covered her mouth with his.

CHAPTER SIX

OF COURSE AIESHA didn't kill him. She didn't even pull away. She opened her mouth to the first hot commanding probe of his tongue and let the lust that smouldered between them run free. It was like the flare of a struck match following a trail of fuel. It licked along at breakneck speed, consuming everything along its way. It didn't matter that she wasn't in control any more. She needed this—*needed him*—like she needed air to breathe.

His mouth plundered hers, deeply, erotically, thoroughly. His tongue tangled with hers, playfully and then purposefully. Demanding hers to submit to his. She whimpered at his masterful command; he had taken control of her mouth and there was nothing she could do but respond. The thrill of his kiss made her body shiver with delight. Her senses went into a tailspin. Her heart jumped and leapt and sprinted. Her breathing became laboured as she tried to keep up with the madcap pace of his untrammelled passion.

His hands weren't content to hold her by the hips this time. This time they were everywhere. Her hair, the small of her back to press her close against his erection, then cupping her breasts, then tugging at her clothes as she tugged and pulled at his.

She gasped as his hand uncovered her breast. His hand was still cold from being outdoors, but it didn't matter as her body was sizzling hot. She was burning up with molten heat. She could feel it coursing through her body like a red-hot tide.

His thumb rolled over her nipple, back and forth, round and round, making her flesh pucker and tighten and every nerve wriggle and leap in rapture. So few men knew how to handle a woman's breast. He did. Not too hard. Not too soft. He seemed to read her body, gauging its needs like a maestro did a temperamental instrument. The strings of her desire buried deep in her body tightened, hummed and sang.

His mouth left hers to suckle on her breast, drawing her nipple deep into his mouth, his tongue rolling and circling, rolling and circling while her legs all but folded beneath her. He switched to her other breast, lavishing it with the same wickedly arousing attention.

He moved to the underside of her breast where the skin was supersensitive. No one had ever kissed her there before. No one had ever moved their lips on her with such careful and gentle attention. His lips moved over her skin like a fine sable brush moving over a priceless work of art.

He came back to her mouth, sweeping her away again on a hot, drugging kiss. That was why he was so bewitching. He could be so gentle and yet so passionate. Her body responded with deep clamouring longing, her insides squeezing and contracting with pleasure at the thought of him finally giving in to his desire for her. He was not trying to disguise it. He was not trying to deny it. He was giving it full rein and it was exactly like a bolting horse—fast, furious and unstoppable.

But she wasn't letting him have it all his own way. She got his belt out of his trouser lugs and unzipped him in a matter of seconds, taking the hot, hard, pulsing heat of him in her hands, stroking him, caressing every inch of his potent length until he was oozing with pre-ejaculatory fluid.

He gave an agonised groan. 'You're killing me.'

She sent him a sultry smile. 'Told you you're a dead man.'

He sucked in a harsh-sounding breath and pulled her hands away, holding them in a steely grip that made her insides contort with restless need at the latent strength he possessed. 'No. Wait. Not like this.'

Was he having second thoughts? Pulling away from her intellectually as well as physically? *Rejecting her?* Aiesha kept her tone light and teasing even though disappointment stalked her. 'You're not frightened of a little carpet burn, are you?'

His dark blue eyes searched hers for a moment. 'I want you so badly I'd lie on a bed of sizzling hot coals or nails. Or both.'

'But?' Her heart sank a little further. 'There's a but coming, isn't there?'

His fingers loosened around her wrists, his thumbs moving over the backs of her hands in a slow, stroking motion, his eyes still holding hers. 'I never have sex outside of a formal relationship.'

'No one-night stands?'

'No.'

Somehow it didn't surprise her. He would always colour between the lines. There was no hint of rebel in him. He was cautious by nature, sensible. He led rather than followed. He controlled rather than being swayed by impulse. He didn't have to look back on all the wrong choices he had made. He probably slept through each night without a single niggle of doubt or self-recrimination to disturb him.

'You don't know what you're missing,' she said. *Loneliness. Emptiness.* 'Think of the money you'd have saved on dates if you just got the deed done on the first night.'

He kept holding her hands. Kept holding her gaze in that studied way of his that made her feel he was seeing through the brash layers of bolshiness to the sensitive and wounded girl within. Aiesha would have squirmed but she was too well trained. Years spent hiding her feelings had made her a master at keeping the facade intact. She might have lapsed last night while he found her sleeping, but the front was up again and it was staying up.

'I like to get to know a person before I have sex with them,' he said.

Aiesha gave him a bold smile. 'Hi, I'm Aiesha. I'm twenty-five, almost twenty-six, and I'm a Vegas lounge singer. Well, I was until a few days ago. I'm currently unemployed.'

'How did you end up working in Vegas?'

She could feel her smile faltering and worked hard to keep it in shape. She wasn't going to tell him she had followed a dream only to have it blow away on the Nevada dust. The audition she had thought would be her big break had turned out to be for a job in a lingerie bar. Playing the piano in her underwear wasn't her thing, nor was doing erotic dance tricks on a stripper's pole to eke out tips from gawping men, but by then her money had been running too low to fly back to London. She had taken the lounge-singer job instead, hoping it would be a springboard to getting noticed as a serious musician. But she'd soon found out no one cared a jot who was behind the piano as long as it got played. 'I liked the party atmosphere. And the weather. It was a change from cold and wet and dismal London.'

He studied her for another long moment, his expression hard to read. 'Favourite colour?'

'It's a toss-up between pink and blue. I can never decide.'

The left side of his mouth kicked up half a centimetre. 'Best friend?'

Aiesha looked at him numbly. 'Um…pass.'

His half smile was quickly replaced with a frown. 'Are you saying you don't have a best friend?'

'I have friends.' *None that I trust.* 'I just don't have a best one.' Not any more.

'How do you like to spend your spare time?'

Aiesha made sure she didn't have spare time. Any breaks she took were packed with activity. Spare time allowed thoughts to creep in and ghosts from the past to haunt her. But then, relaxing wasn't something she had learned as a child. Hypervigilance was the setting her brain was jammed on. Watching out for danger, keeping alert to exploitation, always on guard against attack. Nope, it didn't make for a chilled-out personality.

'Hey, don't I get to ask you some questions?' she said.

'Not until I've asked mine.'

'That's not fair.' She threw in a pout for good measure. 'You're getting a head start.'

He smiled that half smile again as he pushed her bottom lip back in with the tip of his finger, like someone closing a drawer. 'Answer the question.'

Aiesha's lip tingled where he'd touched it. Tingled and burned. Ached. 'I hang out.'

'Hang out where?'

She gave a negligent shrug. 'The gym. The pool. The barre.'

His brows met over his nose. 'The bar?'

Aiesha rolled her eyes. 'Not *that* sort of bar. I do a ballet class. It's really good for posture and balance.'

His frown hadn't quite gone away but it wasn't one of disapproval, more one of intrigue. Maybe even a little respect. 'Where'd you go on your last holiday?'

'San Diego.'

'Who'd you go with?'

She hesitated for a brief second. 'I…I went alone. It's a pain having to travel with other people. They always want to see stuff you aren't interested in. I like being able to do what I want when I want.'

His eyes moved between each of hers for a lengthy pause. 'What happened in Vegas?'

Aiesha gave him a bored look. 'You don't need me to tell you. You read about it, didn't you? Everyone on the planet read it.'

'I want you to tell me your version of events.'

She looked at their joined hands, the way his tanned fingers contrasted with her paler ones. He had strong hands, artistic and clever. Hands that were trustworthy and honest. Clean hands.

Aiesha pulled out of his hold. 'He didn't tell me he was married.' The shame washed over her again. The fact that she hadn't recognised Antony made her feel foolish and naïve. That she'd allowed him to kiss her, to touch her, to get close to her shamed her. The fact that she'd gone up to his room made her feel ill. 'He wasn't wearing a ring. I had no idea he was married until his wife texted me.'

'How long were you involved with him?'

'Not long…'

'How long?'

She hugged her arms close to her body. 'I had dinner with him a couple of times after my shift. And no, contrary to what the press said, I didn't sleep with him.' But she'd been about to, which made her feel even more of a fool.

'The press showed you leaving his room,' James said.

Aiesha bristled when she thought of how Antony had allowed everyone to think *she* was the one who had done something wrong. In the past she would have relished being cast as the bad guy. During her adolescence she had planted herself in the middle of scandal after scandal, actively seeking negative press, the more outrageous the better. To her disordered way of think-ing, it showed the world *someone* was interested in her.

But it was different now.

Over the last few months she had been planning her exit-Vegas strategy. She had become increasingly dis-enchanted with the life she was living. She lived and worked in one of the busiest and most fun places in the world and yet not a day went past when she didn't feel lonely and isolated and bored.

She was tired of the negativity associated with her image. Her tell-all interview about Clifford Challender had come back to bite her as the press had unearthed her history as a home-wrecker.

Now Antony had destroyed her attempt to make a fresh start. He had cast himself as the victim, the poor, misunderstood husband reeled in by an opportunistic seductress. But calling him out for a liar—even if any-one would've believed her, given her track record—would have hurt his wife and two school-age children. She had decided to disappear and let the dust settle instead.

'I went up to his room, but while I was in the bath-room I got a text message from his wife,' she said. 'I came out and told him what I thought of him and left.'

'That was a lucky shot for the press.'

'His wife tipped them off. She knew where he was and who he was with. The press did the rest.'

James was still frowning. 'You do realise by run-ning away the way you did it made you look guilty?'

Aiesha shrugged again. 'It suited me to get out of Vegas.'

'But what will you do now?'

She gave him a worldly look. 'Find myself a sugar daddy or a rich husband. What else?'

A flicker of annoyance passed over his face. 'Be serious.'

'I *am* being serious.' She stepped closer and tiptoed her fingers down his chest. 'How about it, James? You fancy hiring me full-time as your wife? I'll give good value for money. You can do whatever you want with me—' she smiled her tartiest smile '—for the right price.'

He captured her hand, holding it in a firm grip. 'I know what you're doing.'

Aiesha brushed her pelvis against his. This was much better. This was the language she was used to. Sex was much easier to handle than emotional intimacy. He already thought her an outrageous tart. The entire world thought it…and to some degree the world was right. She had been flirtatious and provocative to get where she was, even though she no longer wanted to be there. Why not make the most of his bad opinion of her?

'What am I doing, posh boy?'

His jaw flickered with a pulse as if his self-control was only just holding. But she could see the naked flare of lust in his dark blue gaze. 'You're hiding behind that sex-kitten mask you like wearing. It's not who you are. It's just a game you play.'

Aiesha laughed off his assessment of her but she worried he had seen too much. Knew too much. Sensed too much. She prided herself on being hard to read. No one got under her guard. No one ambushed her emotionally.

Not even smarmy Antony had engaged her emotions. She had seen him as a means to an end—a first class ticket out of Vegas.

But James Challender wasn't like other men. He was not easily manipulated. He didn't lie and cheat and lather on the charm to get his own way.

He didn't fight dirty.

He didn't play dirty.

She wanted to keep things physical between them but he kept pushing against her emotional armour. He wanted to uncover her. To expose her. To know her. The thought terrified her. Opening up to someone, laying it all bare was what weak people did. She was strong. Resilient. Self-sufficient. She relied on her wits and her body to get where she wanted to go. Her heart was not up for sale. 'You like playing, too, don't you, James? You want to play *so* bad.'

His eyes dipped to her mouth. She could read the battle playing out on his face. He wanted her but he was fighting it every step of the way. He took a deep breath and dropped his hold as he stepped back from her. 'I'm going out.'

'But it's snowing.'

He gave her a black look over his shoulder as he left. 'Good.'

James drew in a deep draught of icy air but it didn't do much to quell the fire of wanting burning in his flesh. It was like trying to extinguish a wind-driven wildfire by spitting on it. Aiesha was living, breathing dynamite when she put her mind and body to it. He was hanging on to his self-control by a gossamer thread. He had never wanted anyone the way he wanted her. It was all he could think of—how he wanted her. Ached for her. Needed her. Hungered for her. Every sultry look she gave him made him throb with intense longing. She was the ultimate tease, ramping up his need every chance she could, switching tactics so deftly he didn't know what to expect from her next. Temptress or doe-eyed innocent. Wild-child whore or lost waif. She did them all so well.

Last night had revealed a tiny chink in her armour but she was back to business now. He didn't like being played. He didn't like being a pawn in one of her mischief-making games. She got way too much power by playing the vamp. He had tried to get under her guard, to see the girl behind the mask, but she had pulled the curtain on him.

But he had seen enough to make him want to see more.

She had no close friends. She holidayed alone. She had taken the rap for a scandal caused by a wandering husband who couldn't keep his hands to himself. She had lost her job and pretended it didn't matter.

She composed music that was hauntingly beautiful for someone who had clearly meant a great deal to her....

Had anyone else heard that poignant piece of music? The depth of emotion in those few bars he'd heard had stopped him in his tracks. He could have listened to her for hours. She had looked so absorbed, so in the moment, she'd seemed to be lost in an internal world in which the music was somehow translating emotions she dared not or would not voice aloud. Those rising and falling cadences, those heartstring-pulling minor chords were still playing in his head, moving him, and haunting him still. The way the rhythm flowed, paused, and flowed again. But he had a feeling that particular piece was something she kept private. Why else had she looked so annoyed when he'd disturbed her?

There was so much about Aiesha he didn't know. There was so much she kept hidden.

There was so much he wanted to discover.

She was complicated and contrary. Beguiling and bewitching and beautiful and bold and brazen. Maddening.

And yet…likeable.

His instincts had been right. She had been genuinely upset after her knockout blow to his nose. Even though she tried her best to hide it, her gaze kept going to his black eye with a little flicker of concern. He saw the way she chewed at the inside of her mouth when she thought he wasn't looking. The way she deliberately tried to seduce him, but then pulled back whenever he took the lead. What was that all about?

James turned up his coat collar against the snow. He shoved his hands into his pockets and frowned.

It would be dangerous but he would have to get even closer to her to find out.

CHAPTER SEVEN

AIESHA WAS TRYING to get to Archie in time... She was running as hard and as fast as she could but her legs were useless, powerless. They were shaking so much they felt as if they were made of overcooked spaghetti. Fear clotted the blood in her veins, it stole the oxygen from her lungs, it churned her stomach contents, lique- fied and soured them in panic. She got a little closer. But then she stumbled over someone's skateboard, fell to her knees, her arms reaching out, her voice hoarse from screaming, 'Noooo!'

Aiesha sat bolt upright in bed, her throat raw from gasping and her chest pounding so hard she could hear the echo of it in her ears. The sound of her ragged breathing was deafening in the dead silence of the night.

She hadn't screamed out loud...or at least she didn't think so. Her room was a fair distance from James's and there was no sound of him stirring. There was no sound of a door opening. No footsteps running down the pas- sage. No voice calling out to see if she was all right.

She waited in the darkness, poised, tense, agitated.

Long minutes passed.

She lay back down and closed her eyes but it was impossible to relax, let alone sleep with those horrible images flickering behind her eyelids like an old black-and-white film set on permanent replay.

Aiesha threw off the bedcovers and reached for her wrap. A hot drink with a shot of brandy would have to do as James might not appreciate hearing her running through her scales at this hour. She hadn't seen him since he'd found her playing Archie's song earlier that day. But she could still feel the impact of his kiss reverberating through her body like the humming of a tuning fork.

When she got to the kitchen, Bonnie got up off her bed and looked up at Aiesha with a sheepish look in her brown eyes, her feathery tail slowly wagging back and forth like a metronome on three-two time.

'Don't even think about it,' Aiesha said and reached for the fridge handle. 'You'll have to cross your legs or something.'

The dog gave a little whine and padded towards the back door, looking back over her shoulder as if to say, *Come on—what's taking you so long?*

Aiesha closed the fridge and put the milk carton on the counter with a muttered curse. 'How come you don't use a pet door? I thought golden retrievers were supposed to be smart? You're the dumbest one I've met.'

She opened the back door, wincing as a blast of the icy wind whipped it back against the wall. The dog ambled out, sniffing the ground as she went, looking as if she had all the time in the world. 'Will you hurry up?' Aiesha said, shivering as the wind skirted around her bare ankles. 'Hey, don't go out of sight. I'm not going looking for you.'

The dog disappeared behind the low hedge that surrounded the vegetable garden. Aiesha swore under her breath as she reached for a jacket hanging by the door. She could smell Louise's perfume on it and for a moment she felt as if it were Louise herself wrapping her arms around her as she slipped her arms through the sleeves.

She stood for a moment in the darkness, wondering what life would have been like with Louise as her mother. Her music would have been celebrated, encouraged, nurtured... She would have been loved, celebrated, encouraged.

She would have been safe.

She looked up at the night sky, the sprinkling of stars and planets like peepholes in a dark blue velvet blanket. How many times as a child had she looked up there and wished upon a star? Wished for her life to be different? For everything to change?

She sighed and stuffed her feet into a pair of Louise's boots by the door. But before she had taken two steps the howling wind whipped around again and slammed the door behind her.

'*Shoot!*'

James woke to the sound of a door slamming. He thought he'd locked up everything securely on his last round downstairs. But the house was old and the wind was gale force so it didn't surprise him that a catch had come loose. He shrugged on a robe and went downstairs. Aiesha's bedroom door was closed and there was no light on, which meant Sleeping Beauty was fast asleep. He hoped.

When he got to the back door off the kitchen he could hear frantic knocking and swearing. He opened the door to find a shivering Aiesha on the doorstep. She was dressed in one of his mother's jackets with the hood pulled up over her head. Her body was quaking with cold but her eyes were blazing. She pushed past him with a savage imprecation. 'Took you long enough.' She stomped snow all over the floor. 'That stupid dog needs a tracking device. *You* go and find her. I'm frozen stiff.'

James caught the jacket midair before it landed on the floor where she'd kicked off the boots. She was in a towering rage, which seemed out of proportion to the circumstances. 'She won't stay out long in this wind,' he said. 'I didn't hear her barking to be let out. Did she wake you?'

'No, I was...already awake.'

Something about her expression was suddenly furtive. Secretive. What had she been doing downstairs in the middle of the night? He narrowed his gaze. She was backed against the kitchen counter, her chin at that defiant height, her cheeks pink from cold or guilt, or both. Suspicion crawled along his skin. Was she putting away a stash of his mother's jewellery or other valuables for when she left? A little bit here, a little bit there, hiding it away in incremental bits so as not to be detected.

The back of his neck prickled in anger. So this was how she was going to repay his mother for her kindness, was it?

'What were you doing downstairs at this time of night?'

The pink in her cheeks went a shade darker but her eyes remained diamond-hard. 'I was getting a drink.'

His gaze briefly went to the milk on the bench. 'Is that all?' he asked.

Her brows snapped together and the pink in her cheeks turned red. Angry red. Defensive red. 'What do you mean, "Is that all?" What—do you think I'm pilfering the silver while you sleep?' Her eyes flashed at him, her mouth flattening in a whitened line. 'Why don't you check each drawer to see if I've pinched any of your precious heirlooms?'

She started marching about the kitchen like an angry cop armed with a long-awaited search warrant. Opening cupboards wildly, banging doors, pulling out drawers with savage jerks of her hands. There was an air of mania about her. Of hysteria about to erupt. She pulled open the silverware drawer of the oak sideboard so quickly the contents landed in a clattering, deafening heap on the floor.

She stood looking at the jumbled mess of his mother's silverware in frozen silence.

And then, right in front of his eyes, she started to crack. It was like watching an ice sculpture fracture, centimetre by centimetre. Her eyes darted and flickered. Her tongue dashed out over her lips. Her stiff angry posture faltered. Her shoulders trembled. Her torso folded. 'I'm sorry…' She swallowed and dropped to her knees and began to reach for the silverware but he could see her hands were shaking almost uncontrollably and she barely managed to pick up a teaspoon before it dropped with a ping to the floor.

He crouched down beside her and put a hand over her trembling one. 'Leave it.'

Her eyes were trained on his chin as if she couldn't bring herself to meet his gaze, but her tone was resentful and snarly. 'Don't you want to count them?'

Something about her attempt to sound defiant when she was clearly so upset touched him. Ambushed him. She reminded him of a kitten puffing its fur up to look tough against a big scary dog. 'It can wait.' He searched her expression for a moment. 'Hey, are you OK?'

There was a whining at the back door and Aiesha's mask slipped back on like a glove. 'You'd better get that. Can't have your mother's dog carking it while she's under your protection, can you?'

It only took James five seconds to let the dog in but when he turned around Aiesha had disappeared.

Aiesha leant heavily on her bedroom door with bated breath, waiting for the sound of James's footsteps along the passage. Her heart thudded as each long second passed. What was he thinking of her after that crazy little show? What was he thinking of her brash attitude now she had let it slip? He had seen her at her worst. Out of control. Panicked. Upset. Vulnerable. She had lost it in front of him. She'd acted like some screwed-up nut job, throwing the contents of the kitchen around like one of her creepy mother's boyfriends in a drunken tantrum.

Would he mock her? Laugh at her?

Or, worse, would he try and understand her? *Know* her?

Aiesha thought of telling him…of finally being able to share some of the pain she carried like toxic waste in her bones. The shame of her childhood, the sense of being an outsider, the one no one wanted. The crushing weight of guilt she felt about not being able to protect her mother and Archie. The niggling despair that she might never be able to get her life on track. To reach her potential instead of being stymied by her past. How would James react to finding out she was not as tough as she made everyone think? That, underneath the brash facade, she was as sensitive and caring as his mother? Maybe even more so…

She heard the stairs creak as he came up them. She heard each of his footsteps, unhurried, steady and sure. She heard him pause outside her bedroom door. Heard the deep gravel-rough baritone of his voice. 'Aiesha?'

She clamped her teeth together to stop from calling out to him. She didn't need his comfort. She didn't need anyone's comfort. She had been on her own for the last ten years—for most of her life—and that was the way it was going to stay. So what if she'd got a little panicked over losing the dog in the dark? Big deal. The dog came back. No harm done.

The silence stretched and stretched and stretched along with her held breath. Aiesha wasn't sure which would break first—the silence or her lungs.

'Can we talk?' James said.

She clenched her hands into tight balls of self-containment. *No. Go away.*

'What I implied downstairs…' he paused momentarily '…it was uncalled for. I'm sorry.'

Another endless silence passed.

Then she heard him give a long sigh, as if he, too, had been holding his breath too long.

And then she heard the sound of his footsteps as he went further along the passage to his room, and then the soft click of his door closing.

Aiesha squeezed her eyes shut to stop the blinding stinging tears from escaping.

She. Would. Not. Cry.

When Aiesha looked out of the kitchen window the next morning she saw James clearing the driveway with a shovel. There had been a new fall of snow overnight but the sun was out and shining brightly, giving the wintry scene a sparkling brilliance that was blinding. James looked strong and lean as he loaded each shovel with snow and tossed it aside. He had taken off his coat and worked in his shirt and sweater. Even through the layers of fabric she could see the play of his muscles. He wasn't the gym-rat type but he still looked good. Damn good. He dug the shovel in the snow again and again, tossing its load to the side in a mechanical fashion, his brow deeply furrowed as if he was mulling over something…her, most probably.

Was he thinking she was a tantrum-throwing child in a woman's body? Was he thinking she was in need of a psychiatrist's couch? Was he thinking she was in need of a straitjacket?

She gritted her teeth. Best to get it over with. No point hiding away from him. If he mocked her then she would mock him right on back.

She pulled on her coat and mittens and wrapped a scarf around her neck. The cold air hit her face like the slap of an icy hand across her cheeks. She drew the scarf closer and wandered over to where James was shovelling with such vigour. 'Looking for my buried stash?'

He stopped shovelling to look at her with a rueful expression. 'I suppose I deserve that.' His eyes moved over her face as if searching for something. 'Are you OK?'

She made her gaze as direct and steely as she could. 'Never better.'

He gave a slow nod, which she took as an acknowledgement of her decision not to mention her meltdown episode last night. He went back to the task at hand, shovelling the snow. *Shoosh. Whoosh. Plop.* Spade after spade. Aiesha got the impression he was trying to distract himself from her presence. Did she disgust him? Did she repulse him with her out-of-control behaviour? Was that why he was keeping himself so busy? He didn't want to be with her. He didn't desire her now he knew how childish she could be. *Fine.*

'The forecast is improving,' he said without looking her way. 'We should be out of here by Friday. Maybe even earlier if the snowploughs come this way.'

She folded her arms. '*We?*'

He paused his shovelling to look at her. 'You'll have to come with me to Paris. I have a meeting with a client.'

She frowned at him. 'Hang on a minute. You said you were coming up here for a week and that what's-her-name was joining you at the weekend. Why the sudden rush off to Paris?'

'My client wants to go over the plans I've drawn up.'

'Why can't you email them to him?'

'He prefers to meet in person,' he said. 'He's old-fashioned that way. Besides, he wants to meet you.'

'Why on earth would he want to meet me?'

His look was still inscrutable. 'You're my fiancée, remember?' He went back to shovelling. 'We'll stay at a boutique hotel in Montmartre. There's a fund-raising dinner being held there for one of the charities my client is involved in.'

Aiesha swallowed a mouthful of panic. Staying in a hotel. One suite. One bed. *All night*. What if she had another nightmare? What if she…?

'I'm not going. I want to stay here. I hate Paris.' Romantic couples everywhere, walking hand in hand through the city of love. It was enough to make her want to puke.

He leaned on the handle of the shovel, his eyes meeting hers. 'You're the one who kicked this charade off. By the way, I did an electronic transfer of the funds into your bank account last night. Think of this as a job. You and I are engaged until such time as I call it off.'

He wanted to call the tune now, did he? Well, she was going to call her own. She planted her hands on her hips, straightened her shoulders and upped her chin. 'I want my own room.'

He stabbed the spade in the snow again. 'That would cause way too much speculation.' He tossed the snow before he gave her a crooked smile. 'Can't have everyone tweeting about that, can we?'

Aiesha threw him a caustic glare. 'I always sleep alone. I hate sharing a bed. I hate being disturbed by someone snoring or groping me when I'm trying to sleep.'

He leaned on his shovel to look at her with that pene-trative gaze of his. 'Do you often have trouble sleeping?'

She tried to keep her game face on but she could feel it crumbling around the edges. 'Just because I get up to get a drink now and again doesn't mean I'm an insomniac. This house makes a lot of noise at night. It's creepy.'

He continued to study her, his gaze unwavering. 'Just as well I'm here with you to keep you safe from all the ghosts and ghouls then, isn't it?'

Was he mocking her? It was hard to tell from his ex-pression. She let go of the inside of her lip and changed the subject. 'What about the dog? Who's going to look after it?'

'Mrs McBain has a nephew who said he'd take care of her for a couple of days.'

Aiesha tried another tack. 'I promised your mother I would do it. She was relying on me to house-sit until she gets back because Mrs McBain wanted to visit her daughter in Yorkshire. I don't want to let her down. Not after all she's done for me.'

His look was still searching. 'Have you heard from her since she left?'

Aiesha rolled her lips together. She hadn't heard a peep from his mother. She couldn't decide if Louise was annoyed with her or too preoccupied with worry over her friend's health to be concerned with what was going on—or not going on—at home. 'No, but I'm sure it's because she's busy looking after her friend. She might be in a remote area or something without a proper signal for her phone.'

'Do you think she cooked this up?' He pointed to her and then back at himself. 'You and me, stuck here together like this?'

Aiesha gave an uncomfortable little laugh. 'Surely you don't think your mother has the ability to summon up a blizzard to suit her own ends? And why on earth would she want you and me to hook up? She knows how much we dislike each other.'

Those dark blue eyes were still holding hers in a lock that made her spine feel like molten wax. 'What if she's playing fairy godmother?' he said. 'Waving her magic wand around to make everything turn out the way she wants it.'

'I hardly think your mother wants a Vegas lounge singer as her future daughter-in-law,' Aiesha said, trying to ignore the strange little pang below her heart. If her circumstances were different, Louise was exactly the sort of mother-in-law she would've liked....

'She has a soft spot for you. She always has.'

Aiesha kicked a little mound of snow away with the toe of her boot. 'Doesn't mean she wants me to be the mother of her grandkids.'

His gaze flicked to her abdomen as if imagining her swollen with his child. When his eyes reconnected with hers Aiesha felt her cheeks grow warm and her heart gave a funny little jolting movement that all but snatched her breath away.

James would be a wonderful father. He would be upright and steady, reliable and sensible. Kind and loving.

He would be patient and yet firm. He would take the time to understand his children, to get to know them. He would provide for them and never exploit or abuse them or the trust they had in him.

A vision slipped under a barrier inside her head...a vision of James holding a newborn baby. A tiny pink, dimpled little baby with scrunched-up eyes and a rose-bud mouth. Ten tiny fingers, ten wriggling toes, a little button nose and ears like miniature shells.

Something tightly wound up inside her belly began to loosen, unravel. Break free. Could James see the nascent longing she was fighting so hard to hide? The longing she hardly realised she possessed until now. It was a hunger that was buried so deep inside her she hadn't heard its voice above the babble of activity with which she had filled her life thus far.

The yearning she had for a family she could call her own.

To belong.

To be part of a family unit that was so strong nothing and no one could ever break it apart.

To be loved and to love in return.

Aiesha berated herself for her silly little pipe dreams, for those ridiculously fanciful imaginings that had no foothold in the real world. What sort of mother would *she* make? She couldn't even keep a dog safe from harm.

She swung away to go back to the house. 'I'm going to have breakfast.'

'How about making me some?'

She threw him a frosty look over her shoulder. 'Make it yourself.'

* * *

James came into the warm kitchen where Aiesha was sitting huddled over a mug of tea. She gave him a sideways glance that was two parts glower and went back to staring at her tea. He looked at the bowl of porridge she had set aside on the cooker and gave a private smile. He was right. She was not as tough on the inside as she showed on the outside. It was all bluster and posturing. She had a soft heart but it was hidden where no one could reach it.

Last night had shown him how much she cared. She had been genuinely worried about Bonnie going missing. She had come flouncing in with her usual you-fix-it-it's-not-my-problem manner but it was all bluff. She had acted childishly under pressure but rather than mock her for it, he felt drawn to her. She brought out every protective instinct he possessed. Getting to know her was proving to be the most fascinating and moving experience of his life.

What would it take for her to trust him enough to drop the mask? Would she ever feel safe enough to show her true self? Or would he have to be satisfied with rare glimpses, leaving him feeling frustrated and manipulated and dissatisfied?

'Is this for me?' he asked.

'I made too much.' Another hard little glare. 'No point wasting perfectly good food.'

He pulled out a chair and sat opposite her. 'Stop scowling at me. It's ruining my appetite.'

Her fingers fidgeted with the handle of her mug. She had slender fingers, with nails that were short but neatly manicured. The first two of her knuckles on her right hand were faintly bruised. His chest felt strangely tight, as if someone was turning a spanner on each of the valves of his heart. He hadn't realised she'd hurt herself when she'd landed him with that punch the other night. She hadn't said a word.

So many layers…

So many secrets…

'Is your hand OK? It looks bruised. Did you—?'

She slipped her right hand beneath the table. 'It's fine. I bumped it against something.'

'Aiesha.'

She gave him the sort of look an unrepentant delinquent did a correction officer. 'What?'

'Give me your hand.'

She looked as if she was going to refuse his command, but then she rolled her eyes and shoved her hand out to him. He took her hand gently in his and began brushing his thumb over the back of it. Nothing moved on her face but he felt her fingers shift inside the cup of his, a soft little trembling movement that made his body spring to attention. His groin throbbed as he remembered how those fingers had wrapped around him. Holding him. Caressing him until he had to fight every instinct to explode. She was blowing cold on him now but how long before she switched back to sultry siren? She was so complex, so deeply layered, like a lake or a pond that had hidden caves and canyons below the surface.

James released her hand and sat back and picked up his spoon. 'We need to get you a ring.'

She blinked at him. 'What?'

He pointed to her left hand with his spoon. 'An engagement ring.'

And, bang on cue, she did it.

One of her slim eyebrows arched and her grey eyes sparkled with her usual cheekiness. 'Do I get to keep it after we break up?'

'Sure.' He sprinkled some more brown sugar on his porridge. 'Think of it as a consolation prize.'

There was a moment of silence.

'It's not the one you bought for Phoebe what's-her-face, is it?'

He looked up from his breakfast to give her a lazy smile. 'No point wasting a perfectly good diamond.'

Her eyes hardened as she leaned across the table and pushed his spoon down away from his mouth. 'Listen up. I don't wear other women's cast-offs. Got it?'

James felt the tingle of her touch run all the way up his arm. The fire in her gaze lit a blaze in his pelvis. He could feel the blood surging through his veins, thickening him with lust that was like a raging fever. Her mouth was set in an intractable line but it still looked lush and plump. It was impossible for such a beautiful mouth to look anything else. He remembered the taste of her, sweet and hot and sinful. Her tongue swift and seductive as it mated with his. He wanted to feel her tongue, hot and wet, on his neck, on his chest, his abdomen, stroking and licking all the way down to where he throbbed the hardest.

'I'm not wasting my money on a ring you'll only be

wearing for a couple of weeks,' he said. 'What would be the point?'

She pushed back her chair and got up from the table. 'Fine. Whatever.'

James frowned as he watched her stalk over to put her mug in the dishwasher. 'What's wrong?'

She slammed the dishwasher door. 'Nothing.'

He rose from the table and went over to where she was standing with her arms folded across her body. Her expression was stormy and resentful and her eyes marble-hard.

'What does it matter what ring you wear when all of this is a sham?' he asked.

Her eyes glittered at they met his. 'Do you know how insulting it is to be given something that was intended for someone else?'

'Are we talking about engagement rings or something else?'

Her chin came up. 'What else could we be talking about?'

'Who gave you something that was meant for someone else?'

'No one.'

He studied her expression for a moment, watching as her grey eyes locked him out as surely as if a shutter had come down. 'Talk to me, Aiesha.'

'About what?'

He stroked a fingertip along the curve of her jaw, from just below her ear to her chin, but surprisingly she didn't jerk away. 'Tell me why you're upset.'

'I'm not upset.' Her lips barely moved as she spoke. 'I'm angry.'

James quirked an eyebrow. 'Angry about a few days in Paris, all expenses paid?'

She pursed her lips, firing another glare at him. 'I packed in a hurry to get here. I don't have the right clothes to wear.'

He stroked the underside of her chin, pushing it up so her embittered gaze couldn't escape his. 'So I'll buy you some clothes while we're in Paris. That's what sugar daddies and rich fiancés do, isn't it?'

'How are you going to explain that black eye to your business friend?'

James had wondered that himself. 'I'll tell him I walked into a door.'

Her look was scathing. 'Not very original.'

'Any ideas?'

Something shifted in her gaze, a fleeting shadow, but then she was back to her street-smart sass. 'I could give you some concealer to put on. Or I could do it for you. I'm a bit of an expert. Bruises are pretty easy to disguise. Cuts and swelling less so.'

He frowned. 'You've used concealer before? For covering bruises and cuts?'

'I should've been a make-up artist.' Her tone had a cynical edge to it. 'I had a long apprenticeship patching up my mother from all her sicko boyfriends beating her up. Should've put that on my CV. I wonder if it's too late for a career change?'

James's stomach contents churned, his heart contracting in disgust at what she must have witnessed.

At what her mother must have suffered. 'Did any of them hit you?'

She pushed her tongue into the side of her cheek before she answered. 'Couple of times.'

He swallowed a mouthful of bile. He thought of her as a child, all skinny legs and arms, being assaulted by someone huge and threatening. How could she possibly have defended herself? Violence in general was abhorrent to him, but violence against women and children sickened him to the core. Was that why she was so restless at night? What horrors had she locked away in her mind? What abuse had she seen or experienced first-hand?

'Is that why you ran away from home?'

She directed her gaze to the left lapel of his collar. He saw her draw in a breath, hold it for a beat, before slowly releasing it. 'A couple of days after my mother died of a heroin overdose, nobly supplied by her latest de facto, he decided I would make a good substitute in his bed. I declined.'

James swallowed thickly. Painfully. 'He tried to… to rape you?'

She didn't meet his gaze but kept staring at his lapel. 'I got out before it came to that.'

'So that's why you ran away.'

She nodded. 'Yep.'

James sensed there was more to it than that but she wasn't saying. He could read her better now. She put on that shield of brash armour, the tough-girl exterior that hid a world of pain. He heard it in the tone of her voice. He saw it in the brittleness of her eyes. It was a barrier she put up to make people back off from getting too close to her. She was like a junkyard dog, all bluster and bluff for self-protection. 'How long were you on the streets?'

'I couch surfed for a few nights but people soon get sick of freeloaders.'

'But you were fifteen, for God's sake!'

She shrugged. 'Yeah, well, they say charity begins at home but it wasn't at any of the homes I stayed in... except maybe your mum's.'

James frowned harder. 'Then why did you sabotage your stay with her?'

She met his gaze then. Hers was hard as steel. Cordoned off. Impenetrable. 'Your father was cheating on her. I overheard him talking to his mistress. I decided to show your mum what type of man he was. She deserves better. Much better.'

James looked at her in puzzlement. 'But surely you could've handled it without involving the press. You hurt my mother more than you hurt my father.' *And me.*

She gave another careless shrug of her shoulders. 'As you say, I was fifteen. I didn't know any better at the time.'

'What about the jewellery?' he asked. 'You do realise you could've been charged with theft if my mother hadn't pretended it was a gift?'

The tight set to her mouth softened a fraction. 'Yeah, well, I sent it back to her after I got paid for my story.'

James looked at her in a combination of frustration and admiration. She was a survivor. She fought her corner and fought hard. She used whatever weapons she had at her disposal. Wit. Charm. Artifice. Seduction. She was wily, as cunning as a vixen and as cute as a kitten, whichever suited her needs best.

But underneath all that he could see something else. *Someone* else. Someone who didn't let anyone get too close. Someone who didn't trust others not to exploit her or harm her. Someone who felt more than she cared to show.

'You said your mother died. What about your father?'

'I haven't seen him since I was eight.'

'His choice or yours?'

She gave him another cynical look. 'Her Majesty's choice.'

'He's in prison?'

'Yep.'

'For?'

'For being a jerk.'

James let it go. She clearly didn't want to talk about it. He was surprised she had told him what she had. He wondered if his mother had got as much out of her. He felt annoyed with himself for not understanding Aiesha better. Was that why his mother had resumed contact? She had understood there was much more to that brooding teenager with the challenging behaviour. His mother had seen the potential inside Aiesha to become a beautiful swan if only she had a chance to shine. She was not used to letting people in. His mother had been patient, spending the last eight years keeping in contact with Aiesha, letting her know there was a safe haven for her if ever she needed it.

'You don't have to feel ashamed of where you've

come from, Aiesha,' he said. 'None of that was your choice.'

She pushed her lips out in a what-would-you-know manner. 'I'm going to have a shower. Talking about my background always makes me feel dirty.'

Aiesha was still agitated after her shower. She stood staring out of the window at the whitened fields and forest, wondering why she had told James so much. She wasn't used to talking about her past. She *never* talked about it. Not to anyone. She'd didn't want people to think any less of her for being the daughter of a criminal and a heroin addict. She had spent most of her life trying to hide it.

It was hardly something you brought up as small talk at a cocktail party: *What does my father do, you ask? He's a career criminal. Armed robbery and assault with a deadly weapon. Drugs. Breaking and entering. You name it. He's either done it or has a mate who has.*

Aiesha had always been the outsider at school. The one everyone pointed at, whispered about, gossiped about. She had learned early on to mask her feelings, to armour up so no one knew how much those snarky comments hurt. But it had hurt to be the only one not invited to another child's birthday party. It had hurt to be the last one picked for a team. It had hurt to walk out of the school gate and see all the other mothers or fathers gathered to collect their children while there was no one waiting for her.

Her high-school parent–teacher interviews were the worst. Her mother would make an effort to sober up and drag herself there but Aiesha wished she hadn't bothered. The pitying looks that came her way from the teachers afterwards only intensified her feelings of being an outcast.

But then one day a couple of weeks before her fifteenth birthday she found Archie.

It was still the best day of her life. She had found him near the tube station close to where she and her mother and the Beast Man lived. They weren't supposed to have pets in the flat but Aiesha smuggled him in and out under her coat. He was terrier-small but of mixed breeding with a face only a mother could love. She didn't know how old Archie was or where he had come from, but from the moment he'd come over to her and looked up at her plaintively with those big brown eyes and wagged his tail she was smitten.

Archie would trot along to school with her each day and wait patiently in the alley behind the dry-cleaner's shop until she returned each afternoon. It was the highlight of her day to see him waiting for her there. His head would come up off his paws and his eyes would brighten and that stumpy little tail would wag so hard Aiesha was sure one day it would fall off. She would give him the scraps she'd saved from her school dinner and then they would walk to the park, where she would pretend she was like all the other dog-owners. Going home to a nice house with a garden, warm and cosy in winter, cool and smelling of flowers in summer. To food, not just on the table but also in the pantry and in the fridge. To a mother who wasn't stoned or drunk or beaten within an inch of her life. To a father—

or stepfather—who wasn't sending her leering looks through piggy eyes and smacking his thick wet lips at her.

Why had she told James—of all people—about her horrible background? How was she supposed to keep her emotions out of their relationship if he kept getting her to divulge stuff she had never spoken of to anyone before? Was it his steadiness? His centred calm that she envied so much? His self-control? His concern? His compassion?

Aiesha was used to being judged and vilified. Mocked and berated and excluded. She wasn't used to being listened to. She wasn't used to being understood. She wasn't used to showing a side of herself that had been hidden away since childhood. How would she re-assemble her armour if pieces of it were missing? The breastplate over her heart was no longer a thick layer of metal. It felt like a flimsy sheet of baking paper.

James would only have to hold her too close to the warm, firm safe shelter of his body and it would be totally destroyed....

CHAPTER EIGHT

'So you've finally decided to answer your phone,' James said to his mother later that night. 'What the hell do you think you're up to?'

'I could ask you the very same question, darling,' Louise countered. 'You're not really engaged to Aiesha, are you?'

'Of course not, but for God's sake don't tell Dad that. I let him think it was genuine…along with the rest of the world.'

'Your little secret is safe with me.'

James frowned at his mother's amused tone. 'You must've realised something like this would happen.'

'I had no idea you were planning to visit me,' his mother said. 'Last time we spoke, you said you were behind on the terribly important project you were working on and couldn't possibly spare the time to drive all that way just to—'

'So I'm a little task oriented at times,' he said, cutting off his mother's you-work-too-hard lecture. 'You'd be worried if I was lazing on some Caribbean beach with a bikini model half my age like someone else we know. Why didn't you tell me Aiesha was here?'

'You know why.'

He let the recriminating silence pass. Yes, he could be stubborn. Yes, he could be unforgiving when someone crossed him. But that didn't mean his mother should have kept her relationship with Aiesha a secret for all this time. She should have told him so he could have handled things a little better. He'd blundered in like a clumsy clown in a china shop. He didn't like the feeling. He was used to being in control. He was used to taking strategic measures to sort out difficult problems, not make them a hundred times worse.

'You don't know her, James,' his mother said. 'You don't know her the way I do. You've done what everyone else does when they meet her. They take her on face value and don't see the sweetheart of a girl hiding behind that don't-mess-with-me facade.'

James had seen the sweetheart girl; trouble was, he didn't know what to do with her. Well, he knew what he *wanted* to do with her. It was a constant ache to get on and do it. An overwhelming temptation he was finding very hard to resist. Wasn't sure he *could* resist. 'You still should've given me the heads-up on her being here. You know how much I hate surprises.'

'I hope you haven't been unkind to her.'

He gave an ironic bark of laughter. 'Unkind? I'm the one currently sporting a black eye.'

'Oh, my goodness! What happened?'

'You know that saying, "let sleeping dogs lie"? I should've taken note.'

Louise sighed. 'I'm sure she didn't mean it.'

James swung his chair so he could look at the moon rising over the tops of the forest trees. Australia suddenly seemed a very long way away. Another world away. A world without five feet eight of temptation torturing his every waking moment. 'When are you coming back?'

'Erm…darling, there's something I want to tell you but I don't want you to be upset.'

He swung his chair back round, his right hand gripping the armrest. 'You're not thinking of emigrating, are you?'

'No, darling, nothing like that.' He heard her take a quick breath before she added, 'I'm seeing someone.'

'Seeing someone as in *seeing* someone?' James said.

His mother gave an embarrassed laugh. 'You sound just like your grandfather when I was a teenager going out on my first date. Please don't be cross. I'm happy for the first time in years.'

'Who is it?'

'Julie's brother, Richard,' she said. 'I've known him for decades. Actually, I knew him before I met your father. He was involved with someone else back then, and then your father came along and…well, you know how that turned out. Anyway, Richard flew out from Manchester to be with Julie after her accident and… well…we've fallen in love.'

His mother? *In love?* 'How well do you know this guy?' he asked. 'You haven't seen him for years. What if he's turned into some wacko weirdo on the make who just wants you for your money? Come on, Mum, think about this for a bit. You can't just rush into a relationship without giving it some careful thought.'

'Like you gave it so much careful thought before you decided Phoebe was the one you wanted to marry?'

James frowned. 'I didn't tell you I was going to marry Phoebe.'

'You didn't need to,' Louise said. 'I figured it out for myself. She's totally wrong for you. I'm surprised you can't see it for yourself.'

He rolled his chair back and stood. 'I'm starting to smell a very big meddlesome rat.'

'I had nothing to do with what's happened,' she said. 'But maybe the universe is trying to tell you something. Don't ruin your life by marrying someone you don't love when I know the way you're capable of loving someone. Don't love with part of yourself, James. Love with *all* of yourself.'

James paced the floor, his fingers clamped on his phone so tightly the tendons in his wrist protested. 'Look, this engagement with Aiesha isn't the real deal. I hope you understand that? It'll be over as soon as I get this project with Howard Sherwood finalised.'

'Of course it will.'

'I'm not in love with her.'

'Of course not, darling.'

James frowned again at his mother's disingenuous tone. 'Don't get any funny ideas.'

'Darling, you're *so* cynical. I didn't orchestrate poor Julie to run her car off the road. And I certainly didn't have anything to do with the weather. Aiesha needed a place to stay and I welcomed her. The fact that I didn't mention it to you is neither here nor there. I don't tell you every time I invite someone to stay with me. But would you like me to do so in future?'

'Now you're being ridiculous.'

Louise gave a confessional-sounding sigh. 'Look, I must admit I've always secretly hoped you would one day have some face-to-face time with her, even if it was only for a few minutes. You haven't seen her for a decade. It's surely time to move on? The fact that you got stranded together is a good thing. It's like it was meant to be.'

'Have you been drinking?'

'Darling, you can be so terribly stubborn at times. You made up your mind about Aiesha years ago when she was a troubled teenager. That's not who she is now. I suspect that's not who she ever was. Please be nice to her.'

James wondered what his mother would say if she knew just *how* nice he was being to Aiesha. Nice enough to hold her. To kiss her. To want to make love to her so badly his whole body throbbed with it. 'I'm taking her to Paris with me. Is that nice enough for you?'

'Lovely,' Louise said. 'I knew you'd sort out your differences eventually. Now, will you be nice to Richard when I introduce you to him?'

'When do I get the chance to give him the once-over?' James asked.

'We'll have to have a double date or something when we get home,' Louise said. 'Won't that be fun?'

He rolled his eyes. 'An absolute riot.'

Aiesha was flicking through the channels on the television in the sitting room when James came striding in with a brooding frown on his face. 'My mother has hooked up with some guy and fancies herself in love with him. Can you believe that? She knew him years ago but she's only seen him for a few days since and now she thinks she's in love. Unbelievable. Freaking unbelievable.'

'Aw…how sweet.'

He glared at her. 'This is my mother we're talking about, not some young girl with stars in her eyes. She's fifty-nine years old, for God's sake. She should have more sense.'

Aiesha put the remote control on the ottoman before she got up from the sofa. 'Just because she's middle-aged doesn't mean she's dead from the waist down.'

His brows were jammed together over his eyes. 'What's that supposed to mean?'

She eased her hair out of the back of her sweater, shaking it free over her shoulders as she held his narrowed gaze. 'Sex.'

He sent a hand through his already tousled hair, suggesting it wasn't the first time he'd done so this evening. 'I don't even want to think about my mother and sex in the same sentence.'

'You're being terribly old-fashioned, James,' Aiesha said. 'Your father's getting it on with any female under twenty-five with a pulse, and yet you won't allow your mother to be in a mature and respectable relationship? That's hardly fair.'

His forehead was still furrowed. 'I don't want to see her get hurt.'

'She's in love. Of course she'll get hurt.'

His gaze met hers. Held it steady. 'Have you ever been in love?'

Aiesha laughed. 'Are you joking? I'm not the falling-in-love type. I use men and spit them out once I'm done with them. Surely you know that much about me.'

'I know you don't like people getting close to you.' He was suddenly close enough for her to smell his cologne. Close enough to see the flare of his pupils. Close enough to feel the desire wafting off him like a hot summer breeze. It warmed her from head to foot. Burned her. Scorched her. 'I know you like to show everyone how tough you are, when on the inside you're anything but.'

Aiesha goaded him with her gaze. 'You want to get close to me, James? Then get your gear off and let's do it.'

He took her by the top of her shoulders and slowly but surely brought her flush against his body. 'I think my mother has some weird notion that we'll fall in love with each other.'

'She's dreaming.'

He brought his mouth down to the corner of hers, his lips barely touching her top lip. 'That's what I told her.'

Aiesha's insides shivered as his warm breath skated over her lips. 'It would never work. You're too traditional. Too straitlaced and proper.'

'And you're too wild and unpredictable.' He moved his mouth to her lower lip, pushing against it in soft little nudges that made her legs threaten to give way. 'Too uncontrollable.'

She pushed her lips against his, teasing him the way

he was teasing her. Tempting her. Torturing her. *Why don't you kiss me, damn it?* 'Control is your middle name, isn't it? James Control Challender. Got quite a ring to it, hasn't it?'

He smiled against the side of her mouth. 'I think you secretly like that about me.'

She put her hands against his neck, leaning into his erection. 'What? You think I *like* you?'

He brushed his lips against hers, not a kiss, not a caress, but something in between. 'You don't want to like me. You don't want to like anyone. My mother is the exception… Oh, and Bonnie, of course.'

Aiesha jerked her chin back against her chest. 'That overweight and incontinent hair machine?'

He cupped her left cheek with the broad span of his hand, his sapphire-blue eyes holding hers. 'There was a chewy treat on her bed when I brought her in from her last walk. I didn't put it there, so that only leaves you.'

She hadn't realised he would find it before Bonnie. She had tucked it in under the cushioned bed so Bonnie could sniff it out later. 'Your mother gave me instructions on how to take care of her dog. I'm only doing what I was told to do.'

He put his hands on her hips, bringing her close again. 'I told myself I wouldn't do this. I promised myself I wouldn't complicate things by getting involved with you.'

'It's just sex, James. People do it all the time. It doesn't have to mean anything.'

His eyes searched hers for a beat or two. 'I want you, but that must surely be obvious by now.'

Aiesha brought his head down so his mouth was within a breath of hers. 'Then for God's sake do something about it.'

He covered her mouth with his in a long and passionate kiss that fanned the flames already burning inside her. His lips were firm and gentle in turn, a tantalising mix of dominance and reverence that made her wonder why she had thought him so uptight and starchy. His tongue tangled with hers, taming it into submission, only to let her have free rein to do the same to him. Desire raced through her, heating her core, turning it to liquid as he took back control of the kiss. His tongue stabbed and thrust, rolled and dived, flicked and darted and then caressed and soothed. His hands moved from her hips to skim over her breasts, the touch so light and yet it made her flesh shiver and sing.

He made a deep, growly sound as he slid a hand under her sweater and found her lace-covered breast. He cupped her through the cobwebby fabric, rolling his thumb over her tight nipple, swallowing her gasp as he deepened his kiss.

Aiesha felt his hands move behind her back and unclip her bra. It fell to the floor as she raised her arms to haul off her sweater. His eyes drank in the sight of her, his hands moving over her in a caress that was possessive and yet worshipful.

'You're beautiful...so damn beautiful.' He bent his head and took her nipple in his mouth, sucking on her with such exquisite tenderness she felt every nerve in her body tremble in response. His tongue circled her nipple and then he moved to the underside of her breast, dragging his tongue along her flesh, making her mind-less and breathless with want.

She *felt* beautiful when he touched her like that. Beautiful and desirable and feminine and…respected. There was nothing sleazy about his touch. He made her feel as if she was the only woman he ever wanted to make love with. The only one he wanted to share the intimate connection of body and soul.

He went to her other breast, exploring it in the same intimate detail, driving her senses into a wild frenzy as he subjected her to caress after caress, stroke after stroke, kiss after kiss. He moved back up to her neck, his lips playing with the sensitive skin there, lingering over her ear lobes and the delicate spot below.

He came back to her mouth, kissing her deeply and passionately while her lower body burned and ached for him with a need so strong it surpassed anything she had experienced before. She wasn't used to being swept away on a tumultuous tide of desire. She was used to being the one in control, mentally and physi-cally always a step or two ahead. But his kiss and his touch had a magical effect on her senses, sending them spinning and twirling in rapturous delight.

She undid his belt and unzipped him, taking him in her hands to stroke and titillate. To explore him, to make him feel the uncontrollable desire she was feel-ing. He made deliciously male noises of heavy arousal, his erection thick and hard in her hand.

His hands went to the waistband of her yoga pants, ruthlessly tugging them down so they fell to her ankles. She stepped out of them and her knickers as he shucked off his own trousers and underwear and shrugged off his shirt.

Aiesha fed off the sight of him with a hunger she had never felt with such intensity. He was lean and yet muscled in all the right places. His abdomen was washboard-flat, the pipelike ridges showcased beneath the tanned olive-toned skin. His chest was lightly covered in hair that spread from his pectoral muscles, down past his navel and to his groin, where his erection rose proudly.

'On the floor.' It was a gruff command that thrilled her as much as it surprised her. But she obeyed as meekly as a submissive to a master.

He deftly dealt with the application of a condom before he came down to join her. But he didn't rush to penetrate her. Instead he gently eased her thighs apart and brought his mouth to her intimately in a gentle caress that made her back arch in delight.

Aiesha had been pleasured that way before but she had never been able to let herself fully relax enough to orgasm. Her previous partners had performed the act in a perfunctory manner, as if they had realised it was what was expected but they didn't take the time to ask her what she liked, or what worked and what didn't. It had annoyed her that they thought they knew her body better than she knew it herself so she had cut it short by pretending to orgasm like a porn star, while privately she'd mocked them for their ignorance and arrogance.

But this was different.

James stroked her with his tongue, but then stopped

to ask if it was too strong or too light. 'Tell me what you like best. Hard or soft? Fast or slow?'

Aiesha could barely speak for the sensations that were coursing through her. 'Just like that…slow and gradually building up… Oh, God…*ohhhhhh.*'

Her body gave a convulsing spasm, every nerve quivering and then exploding like fireworks. The rippling waves gradually died away, her body feeling as limp and pliable as melted wax.

She felt strangely unguarded, unexpectedly vulnerable. He had unlocked her senses in a way no one else had. Sex was supposed to be just sex. He had taken it to another level…one she had never visited before.

He came over her, one thigh draped over one of hers, his hand brushing her hair out of her face. 'You OK?'

Aiesha snapped out of her daze. 'Sure, why wouldn't I be?'

He studied her for a moment. 'We don't have to do this if you're having second thoughts.'

Second thoughts? Was he kidding? But how considerate of him not to assume he had the right to continue. It made another layer of her armour peel away. She put a hand to his face, stroking it over the dark, sexy stubble, her core contracting with another wave of longing. 'We can't let that condom go to waste, now can we?'

He took her hand in his and brought it up to his mouth, kissing each of her fingertips as his eyes held hers. 'I don't know about you, but I hate unnecessary waste.'

She put her hand around the back of his neck and pulled him down. 'Me, too.'

His mouth fused with hers in a smoking-hot kiss that made her belly quake all over again. His tongue got busy with hers, teasing and stroking and tangoing until she was making soft little whimpering sounds at the back of her throat.

He put a hand below her bottom and raised her to receive him, entering her in a long, slow, smooth glide that made her shiver all over in delight. Her body gripped him tightly, the friction of his first slow thrusts making her senses go crazy. He rocked gently at first, taking his time as he let her catch his rhythm, letting her get used to the breadth and length of him. Then he gradually picked up his pace, bringing her along with him, the excitement building all over again in her body. The tightening of her core, the swelling and throbbing ache of her clitoris, aching and pulsing for his touch.

He rolled her over so she was on top of him, his hand firm on her bottom as he kept his thrusts going. How did he know this was the only way she could orgasm without direct stimulation? She felt the first wave of pleasure like an explosion in her body. She arched her back and rode him in a desperate, wanton manner, her hair flying about her shoulders as she followed the tantalising lure of a mind-blowing orgasm.

And then she was there. Flying off into the stratosphere with a panting cry as the pleasure rocked through her like a powerful earthquake. She shook and shuddered, she whimpered and cried. She clung on as the last waves washed over her, leaving her floating in a place where no thought could spoil the glow of ultimate pleasure.

James rolled her back over to her back, still thickly, powerfully encased in her body, his eyes glittering with the build-up of passion. 'Good for you?'

Aiesha moved her body against him, wanting him to finally let go so she could feel the vibrations of his release. 'You know it was.'

The dark blue in his eyes darkened to a shade short of black. 'You could be pretending. It's hard for most men to tell the difference.'

She cocked her head at him. 'But I suppose you can?'

He brushed his lips against hers. 'Let's put it this way. I don't stop until I'm absolutely sure.'

Aiesha shivered again as he began to thrust deeply and rhythmically. His pace went from slow, almost lazily so, but then he gradually upped the speed until he was rocking against her, sending shockwaves of pleasure through her like thrashing waves against a cliff face.

She gripped the taut curve of his buttocks, holding him to her, urging him on, delighting in the weight of him, the way he filled her, stretched her, tantalised her with the friction of male desire against female flesh. She was climbing towards the summit again, all of her nerves tight as a tripwire, all the sensations gathering again in the tightly swollen bud of her clitoris.

She wanted to come so badly but wondered if she should tell him what she needed to get there. But then he repositioned himself, shifting slightly so he could bring his hand down to her, stroking her with just the right pressure and speed.

It was impossible not to come. She threw her head

back and succumbed to it, letting it rip through her like a speeding train. It shook and rattled her from head to foot until she was gasping and just shy of sobbing.

And *still* he hadn't taken his own pleasure.

Aiesha marvelled at his self-control but another part of her felt a tiny bit irritated by it. Did he find her so easy to resist? Wasn't he the *least* bit overcome by his passion for her by now? In her experience, men got her orgasm out of the way, often times in a token fashion, and went for their own with a single-minded and often selfish determination. They shifted her to the position they wanted and pumped away, not checking to see if she was too tender or uncomfortable.

But James waited until she was breathing normally again. He even stroked her hair back off her face, watching her with those ink-dark eyes. 'Ready for round three?'

'I only ever orgasm a couple of times, if that.' *Sometimes not at all.*

The corners of his mouth lifted. 'First time for everything.'

Aiesha's belly quivered at the smouldering look in his eyes. 'What about you?'

'I'm getting to that.'

She stifled a gasp as he started those slow but deliciously rhythmic thrusts. 'Are you counting backwards or thinking of your mother doing it or something?'

He stroked a lazy hand over the curve of her breast. 'What's the rush?'

She gave him an arch look. 'What's the hold-up?'

A slight frown pulled at his brow. 'Are you uncomfortable?'

'No, it's just I'm not used to a guy taking so long to get the job done. I'm used to "wham, bam, did you come? Thank you, ma'am."'

He studied her expression for a long beat or two. 'You don't always enjoy sex?'

Aiesha wished she hadn't been so transparent. 'I didn't say that.'

'You implied it.'

She concentrated her gaze at the V-shaped dish at the top of his sternum. Why did he persist in trying to *know* her? She didn't want to be known. She wanted to be separate. Unknowable. Unreachable. *Didn't she?* 'Sex is sex.'

He tipped up her chin with a fingertip, locking his gaze with hers. 'Sex can be so much more than that.'

Aiesha was conscious of the length of him still buried deep inside her. He had stilled his movements, but he was *there*. Waiting. Wanting. She tried to disguise a swallow but she saw his eyes follow the up and down motion of her throat. She sent the point of her tongue out in a quick brush over her lips, but he followed that, too. Then he traced the outline of her mouth with the tip of his index finger in an achingly slow motion, every millimetre of her flesh tingling at the contact. Nerves she didn't know she possessed hummed and buzzed. Her body trembled, the need building to a level she hadn't encountered before. Was this how it was supposed to feel? Wanting someone so much it physically hurt? Needing their touch so much it was as important and as necessary as the air she breathed? How could she have sold herself short for all this time?

His eyes came back to mesh with hers. 'Sex is all about the destination.' He began to move, deep and slow, each movement triggering another wave of thrilling pleasure through her body. 'Making love is about the journey, as well.' He kissed her mouth lightly, once, twice, but the third time was deep and lingering.

Aiesha lifted her hips, rolled her pelvis, teasing him with the slippery friction of her body. He increased his pace but he was still in control. She stroked his buttocks, and then dipped her fingers between them to the supersensitive skin of his perineum. He stifled a groan against her mouth and drove harder. She rode with him, urging him on with little gasps and whimpers as the need rose to a crescendo in her body. She could feel the tension in his muscles as he poised in that pivotal moment before the primal force took over. He gave another raw groan, his skin peppering with goose bumps beneath her fingertips like fine gravel as he shuddered and then flowed.

Aiesha held him in the quiet aftermath, which was another new thing for her. She was normally the first to disengage, to disentangle, to gather her clothes and move on.

But she didn't want to sever the connection between them. Couldn't sever it. Not yet. Her body felt… at peace. Satiated. Floating in a sea of contentment, she had never felt quite like this before. Something about his lovemaking spoke to her deep inside her soul. Touched her. Moved her. His respect, his consideration and concern for her pleasure made her feel valued, treasured. *Safe*. His breath was warm against the side of her neck, his chest rising and falling with hers, his legs in a sexy tangle with hers. She absently moved her hands over his back and shoulders, exploring each contour of muscle and bone, each knob of his vertebrae, the dish in his lower spine, and back up again to play with the closely cropped hair on his head.

'How's that carpet burn?' he said.

Aiesha smiled as she met his teasing gaze. 'Either the carpet is too good a quality or you weren't going hard enough.'

The glint in his eyes intensified. 'I can fix that,' he said, and swooped down and covered her mouth with his.

CHAPTER NINE

In the early hours of the morning, James rolled over sleepily to reach for Aiesha beside him in his bed but instead his hand found a cool, empty space. He looked for a long moment at the indentation on her pillow where her head had lain beside his. The faint trace of her perfume lingered in the air, the same delicate but deliciously intoxicating fragrance he could smell on his skin.

He sat upright, listening for sounds of her moving about in the en-suite bathroom, but there was nothing but silence.

Empty silence.

He frowned as he pushed back the covers. He hadn't heard her leave. He hadn't expected her to leave. It made him feel like a gigolo who had served his purpose—a cheap hook-up that meant nothing to her. He didn't like the sense of being used. He had brought her upstairs because—all jokes aside—carpet burn wasn't his style, and he had a feeling it wasn't hers, either.

But then he remembered she'd told him she never spent the whole night with anyone. But surely *he* was different? He wasn't some nameless one-night stand she would never see again. He had taken the time to listen to her, to try and get to know her, to understand what put those shadows in her eyes.

He had *made love* to her.

He had taken the time to get to know her body as intimately as he could. She had responded to him with captivating fervour. Surely what they had shared meant more to her than a quick satiation of physical need?

He glanced at the bedside-table clock. It was 4:00 a.m. He shrugged on his bathrobe, telling himself he was only checking on her to see if she was all right.

Her bedroom was empty.

The bed had been slept in, or at least she had been in there because the sheets were all tangled and thrown back, the feather pillows crushed and misshapen. But whether she had slept or not was open to question.

How long had this restless bed-hopping been going on? When had it started? Why wouldn't she talk to him about it? If only he had realised at the outset how complex and traumatised she was he might have been able to get her to confide in him without all the game playing she went on with all the time. He still cringed at the way he had confronted her in the kitchen, accusing her of stealing. He had pushed her into a meltdown and in doing so he had lost his chance to earn her trust. How long would it take to win it back? Or was he fighting an unwinnable battle?

When he turned on the light in the kitchen Bonnie raised her head and blinked at him but didn't move from her cushioned bed near the cooker. She put her

head back down on her paws and closed her eyes as she
gave a deep doggy sigh.

James scanned the kitchen with his gaze. The kettle
was stone-cold and there were no crumbs or used plates
or discarded apple cores or milk cartons. He turned off
the light and went further along the passage to the ballroom. The door was open enough for the moonlight to
spill along the floor in a long silver beam.

The piano was a dark hulk in front of the windows,
and beside it stood Aiesha with her back to the room,
dressed in a silky ivory-coloured wrap that gave her the
appearance of a ghost.

Knowing all too well the danger of sneaking up on
her, James rapped his knuckles lightly against the door.
'Aiesha?'

She must have known he was there even before he
knocked for there was nothing hurried or startled about
her movements as she turned to look at him. It was difficult to read her expression, but with the moonlight sil-
houetting her slim body from behind he could see she
was completely naked beneath the wrap.

'What are you doing down here all by yourself?'
he said.

'Couldn't sleep.'

'Why didn't you wake me?'

She stepped out of the shadows, her eyebrows drawn
together and her voice sharp with an edge of irritation
to it. 'To do what? Make me a milky drink? Tell me a
bedtime story?' She curled her lip and added in a mut-
ter, 'Like that's ever happened before.'

James frowned. 'Sweetheart, what's going on?'

Her brows shot up mockingly. '*Sweetheart?* Isn't that taking this crazy charade a little too far?'

He came over to where she was standing so stiffly, so guardedly. 'What's the matter?'

A mask slipped down over her features. 'Nothing.'

'OK…so help me out here,' he said. 'Last time I looked, you were curled up in my arms and drifting off to sleep. Now it looks like you want to punch my lights out. Can you fill in the bits I've missed?'

Her eyes had that hard, streetwise sheen to them. 'Look, I don't mind sleeping with you, but I'm not sleeping with you, OK?'

'Want to run that by me one more time?'

'I'm not sharing a bed with you. It's too…intimate.'

James gave a wry laugh. 'And what we did a couple of hours ago wasn't?'

Two spots of colour rose high on her cheekbones. 'It was just sex.'

'What is it about being intimate that you find so terrifying?'

A frown of irritation puckered her forehead as she glared at him again. 'Why are you asking me these stupid questions?'

'I want to understand you.'

'And here I was thinking you only wanted me for my body.'

'I imagine most men do, but I like to think I'm a little less shallow than that.'

Her chin came up. Her eyes glinted. Challenging him. 'Well, guess what, *sweetheart*? My body is all that's on offer. Take it or leave it.'

James wanted to call her bluff. His mind told him to walk away. But his body craved her. Ached for her. Throbbed with a bone-deep longing that had not been assuaged by sleeping with her. Instead it fed his craving of her like an addict taking a hit. Desire was something he controlled, channelled.

But not with her.

He couldn't control it. He couldn't redirect it or tame it. It roared in his blood with the force of a tornado. 'Come here.'

Her chin went higher, those smoky grey eyes glittering with sensual heat. 'Why don't you come here?'

His groin pulsed with anticipation. 'I asked first.'

She tossed her hair back over her shoulders, the movement loosening her wrap so it revealed half of her left breast. 'You didn't ask,' she said. 'You commanded.'

'So?'

'So ask nicely.'

James was so hard he seriously wondered if he could even take a step. 'You want me to beg?'

Her lips curved upwards in a sexy half smile as she sauntered over to him, her wrap falling away from her to land in a puddle of silk on the floor. 'Would you?'

'I think you know me better than that.'

He sucked in a breath as she trailed a fingertip down the open V of his bathrobe. She got to his navel, circling it ever so slowly, her eyes locked on his. 'Want me to go lower?' she asked.

'How low are you prepared to go?'

Her naughty-girl smile made his insides quake with lust. Her touch was like a spreading fire. His heart pounded with excitement as she slithered down his body to drop to her knees in front of him. 'This low enough for you?' Her warm breath danced over his rigid flesh. Teasing him. Torturing him with the promise of her erotic possession.

He was swaying on his feet, struggling to keep himself steady as her mouth hovered so tantalisingly close. 'Wait. I need to get a condom.' He fished in his bathrobe pocket and handed it to her. 'Want to do the honours?'

Her eyes glinted. 'With pleasure.'

James held his breath as she ripped the foil packet with her teeth, spitting the piece to one side, before taking the condom in her hand and rolling it down the length of him. Her fingers smoothed it into place, driving him wild with each stroke and glide of her hand.

She moved in closer, breathing over him again, ramping up his anticipation, and escalating his excitement to fever pitch. Her tongue touched him, a tiny stab of a touch that even through the layer of latex was electric. She touched him again, a stroking caress that travelled the length of him, from swollen head to thickened base. Every hair on his scalp stood up. The backs of his knees tingled. The base of his spine fizzed.

Her tongue came back up, circled the top of him before taking him into her warm, wet mouth. He groaned as she sucked on him, slowly at first, but then she increased the pressure and suction until he was in danger of spinning out of control.

He gripped her by the head, his fingers clutching at handfuls of her hair, but she refused to relinquish her hold on him. She brought him to the brink and then ruthlessly pushed him over. He lost himself in the moment of climax, the waves of intense pleasure rippling through his groin as he surged, pulsed, shuddered. Emptied.

She gave him a smouldering smile as she crawled back up his body, her naked breasts brushing against his chest, her pelvis warm and tempting as it rubbed against him. She was every erotic fantasy he'd ever had: sultry, sinful and playfully slutty, and yet sensitive and sensual. 'Want to go another round?' she said.

James threaded his hands through her tousled hair. 'I need another condom first.'

She slid her hands over his pectoral muscles. 'I don't suppose you have another one conveniently placed in your bathrobe pocket?'

'Sadly, no.'

Her eyes brightened mischievously. 'Well, this is your lucky day because I've got one in mine.'

James watched as she walked over to the puddle of her silky wrap lying on the floor and retrieved a condom. Every one of her movements tantalised him. Made him hard. The way she bent down, giving him a full view of those long slender legs and that gorgeously neat bottom. The way she came back over to him with her pert breasts with their rosy nipples on glorious show. Her body was a temple of temptation. Long-limbed and slim, curved and toned, her head glossy and sexily tousled, her mouth shiny and moist. Every cell in his body responded to the sight of her. Throbbed and ached to be joined with her.

She did a repeat performance of tearing the packet

with her teeth, taking her time to roll it over him, holding his gaze in a scorching lock that made his body throb and burn anew with lust.

He took her by the shoulders and tugged her towards him, crushing her mouth beneath his in a fiery kiss. Her mouth opened under his, taking him in, devouring him. Her kiss was hot and urgent, as hot and urgent and desperate as his.

His hands moved over her body, her breasts, her hips, her feminine folds, touching, teasing, promising more but not giving it until she was making throaty little pleas. He was as ruthless with her as she had been with him. Ramping up her desire, making her beg for the release she craved.

'Now, oh, for God's sake, *now*,' she said against his mouth.

'Not yet.' He softly bit her lower lip. 'Don't be so impatient.'

She bit him back, harder, making his knees buckle. 'I want you inside me.'

He walked her, thigh to thigh, to the nearest wall, his mouth working its way around hers in teasing little nips and nudges. 'What's the big hurry?'

She clutched at his buttocks, pulling him closer. He could smell her salty and musky fragrance, the alluring heat of feminine arousal that made his need of her all the more overwhelming. He slipped a finger inside her, applying the lightest friction to her swollen need, swallowing her gasp as he captured her mouth beneath his. Her tongue moved with his in a combative dance, an exciting fast-paced tango of lust and longing and battle for control.

Holding her in his arms was like holding a powder keg and a match. She was the most exciting, thrilling lover he had ever had. He had never wanted someone as much as he wanted her. It was a driving need that dominated every waking moment. It was like being under a spell, a magical, sensual spell that was inescapable. Her flirtatious behaviour infuriated and inflamed him in equal measure. She was everything he avoided in a partner and yet she was everything he found so breathtakingly exciting.

She grabbed at his hair, her mouth breathing hot sexy fumes of lust into his. 'I want you. *Now.*'

James turned her so her back was against him, her hands splayed on the wall in front of her. He didn't have to nudge her thighs apart. She had already anticipated his intention. She gave a sexy little groan and wriggled her bottom against his erection, goading him on. It was an invitation he could not resist. He entered her in a deep, slick thrust, pleasure shooting through him like an electrifying pulse as her tight little body gripped him. He rocked against her, breathing in the fragrance of her hair that was brushing against his face. She made panting little noises, gasping noises, whimpering-with-pleasure noises, which made him drive all the harder and faster.

He gripped her by the hips, clenching his jaw to keep himself from coming too soon. She rose up on tiptoe, searching for more direct friction. He brought his hand around to stroke her with his fingers, the swollen nub slick and damp with moisture. He felt the contractions of her orgasm, each powerful spasm in time with her cries of ecstasy.

He drove himself over the edge, breathing hard, flying high in a whirlpool of sensations that made his body shudder all over with reaction.

He kept her pinned to the wall even though his erection was subsiding. Her hair tickled his cheek; the scent of her teased his nostrils. He lifted her hair out of the way and kissed the back of her neck in a series of soft-as-air kisses, delighting in the way she shivered under his touch. 'You like that?' he asked.

'Mmm…' She gave a dreamy-sounding sigh.

He kissed the cup of her shoulder, using his tongue to tease her soft skin. She made another purring sound of pleasure as he worked his way up the side of her neck, lingering at the spot just below her ear. He wondered if she was as responsive with other men. The thought was jarring. The image of her with other lovers stirred an uneasy feeling in his stomach. Jealousy wasn't something he had felt before. None of his partners had given him any reason to be jealous. He knew they'd had previous lovers; it was unfair in this day and age to expect anything else.

How many men had Aiesha been with?

Did it matter?

James stepped back and dealt with the condom, trying to get his double standard back in the Dark Ages where it belonged. It was none of his business how much experience she had. It wasn't as if their relationship was going to continue beyond a couple of weeks. How could it? She resented the world he came from. She didn't even *like* him. She saw him as a trophy to collect, a prize to show off. A box to tick. She might enjoy having sex with him, but that was all she wanted from him.

And it was all he wanted from her...*wasn't it*?

She picked up her wrap from the floor and slipped it over her shoulders, her grey gaze connecting with his. 'There haven't been as many as you think.'

James tied his own robe before he answered. 'How many what?'

'Men. Lovers.' She tied the ribbons of her wrap around her waist. 'The press make me seem like a tart. But it's not like I'm out there every night getting it on with someone. You're my first this year.'

He gave her a look. 'Not bad considering it's the tenth of January.'

Her lips tilted in a little smile. 'You hungry?'

'Are we talking about breakfast?'

She sashayed over to him, running her fingertips down the length of his forearm. 'Are you an early riser?'

James was rising now and she only had to move an inch closer to feel it. 'When I need to be. What about you?'

That smouldering look was back in her eyes, making his spine tingle at the base. 'Oh, I'm *very* flexible.' She untied his bathrobe and slid her hand down his abdomen in a slow caress. 'I take each day as it comes.'

He sucked in a breath as she took hold of him. The glint in her eyes drove him wild. Everything about her drove him wild. The way she ran the tip of her tongue over her lush mouth nearly sent him over the edge. Her sexily tousled hair tickled his chest as she pressed herself close. Her slender hips rubbed against his pelvis, inciting him, arousing him all over again. He placed his hands on her bottom and brought her even closer. 'Just as well this snow is on the melt because at this rate I'm going to run out of condoms,' he said.

She trailed a fingertip along his stubbled jaw and then over his lower lip, making every nerve twitch and dance. 'In future you'll know to be better prepared then, won't you?'

In future...

What future?

This couldn't go on for ever. How could it? Aiesha didn't develop bonds with people, not unless they served her interests. How could he be sure she wanted to be with him, other than for the prestige and protection his name and money provided? It would always play at the back of his mind. Did she care about *him* or what he could give her?

James slid his hands up her arms to hold her by the shoulders. 'You do realise this thing we have going isn't going to continue beyond the end of the month, don't you?'

Her mouth curved upwards, her grey eyes glinting mockingly. 'But of course. You're paying me to play a role.' Her fingers tiptoed up his chest. 'Am I giving good service so far?'

He dropped his hands and stepped away from her. 'Don't.'

'Don't what?' Her look was all beguiling innocence. 'Say it as it is? Come on, James. Don't be such a prude.

I'm your paid mistress. Don't all rich posh guys have one? Your father certainly does. She even looks a bit like me, don't you think?'

James clenched his jaw. He knew she was deliberately baiting him. It was her favourite pastime. But it annoyed him that she seemed not to be the least worried or conflicted by their situation. She wanted him and she'd got him. The trap had been set on day one and, like a fool, he had stepped into it. Now she was playing the hired hooker to make him squirm with guilt. She was well aware of how much he hated the thought of being compared to his father, of being tarred with the same cheap, dirty little brush. She was well aware of it and was maximising it for...for what? More money? Revenge? Just for the sheer heck of it? Didn't her behaviour prove how little she cared for him as a person? She was in it for what she could get and was shamelessly brazen about it.

'You are currently my fiancée,' he said. 'That's what the press thinks and I want them to continue to think it until such time as I inform them otherwise. Understood?'

She gave him a mercurial smile. 'Then you'd better get a wriggle on and buy me a big, expensive ring or no one will believe you.'

James muttered an expletive under his breath. 'Be ready by lunchtime. If we can't drive out I'll hire a helicopter to fly us out.'

CHAPTER TEN

AIESHA DECIDED JAMES'S anger was a good thing. He kept his distance on the trip over to Paris, barely speaking a word to her, keeping himself busy with his laptop, as if they were two strangers travelling together. But that was fine by her as she needed time to regroup. It was becoming confusing to be playing one role while feeling something else. *Feeling* was something she wasn't used to doing. Feeling was dangerous. Attachment was dangerous. *Bonding* was dangerous. She could be physical with someone without emotional engagement.

Of course she could.

Men did it all the time. Sex was a physical need like any other. She was not going to be stupid and fall in love. Not with James. Not with the one man who would never love her back. Why would he? She had all but destroyed his precious family. She knew he wasn't close to his father, but a relationship with her was only going to make his relationship with him so much worse.

His mother, Louise, might accept her but even that was stretching a dream way too far. The world Aiesha came from was so disparate, so foreign, so totally alien it was as if she had come from another universe. How could the chasm ever be breached? Everyone would look down on her, watching for her to make a slip-up. To say something she shouldn't say. To wear something not quite appropriate. To bring more shame and disgrace on the Challender name.

It was stupid to think of a future with James. He would never allow himself to love someone so unsuitable. She was a lounge singer from Sin City. Fairy-tale endings didn't happen to girls like her.

And the sooner she accepted it the better.

The press didn't show up until they arrived at the boutique hotel, a short walking distance from the Eiffel Tower. James took Aiesha's hand and led her through the foyer, answering in fluent French the barrage of questions from the crush of journalists and photographers. From her limited grasp of the language, Aiesha was able to pick up one or two phrases that communicated James's delight at their engagement and how he was looking forward to their wedding at some point during the year. He even managed to get her to the private lift to the penthouse floor without losing his urbane smile.

But once the doors closed he dropped his arm from around her waist and let out a stiff curse. 'This is ridiculous. How long are they going to hound us like this? It's not as if we're celebrities. Why are they so interested in us?'

Aiesha leaned against the waist-height brass rail on the wall of the lift. 'You're rich. You're handsome. People want to know what you're doing and who you're doing it with.'

He pushed a hand through his hair, his frown formidably dark. Aiesha knew he hated all the press attention because it made him appear like his father, holing up in a hotel with his latest lover. James was so private about his life it would torture him to have his every move anticipated and speculated and commented on. Her presence in his life was only intensifying that speculation. Was that why he was so brooding and prickly now they were back in the spotlight? At Lochbannon he could temporarily forget about the rest of the world, but now the world was after him for an exclusive on his engagement and wedding plans. No wonder he was looking antsy and conflicted. Which made her all the more determined to show she wasn't…even though she was. Desperately.

'I've organised an outfit for you to wear for the dinner tomorrow night and one for this evening,' he said into the silence. 'I've also arranged for a jeweller to bring some samples of rings to our room.' He pushed his sleeve back to glance at his watch with a preoccupied frown. 'He should be here in a couple of hours.'

'So…' Aiesha sent him a little smile. 'What will we do in the meantime?'

His mouth was pinched tight, although she could see the way his gaze slipped to the swell of her breasts and back again. 'Do you ever think of anything else but sex?'

She gave him an arch look. 'That's what you're paying me for, isn't it?'

He snatched her wrist as the lift doors pinged open, marching her out like a captor with a prisoner. 'I'm a little tired of you making those cheap little digs. We wouldn't be in this situation if you hadn't sent that first tweet, remember?' He jerked his head to indicate for her to enter the penthouse.

'Aren't you going to carry me over the threshold?'

'Get inside.'

She raised her chin. 'I want my own room.'

'I want you with me.'

'What if I don't want to be with you?'

A nerve twitched in his jaw, his eyes blue-black. 'This is your room. In here. With me. End of discussion.'

Aiesha fought her agitation by redirecting it into anger. She stabbed a finger at his chest, leaning her whole weight into it, but even so he didn't move a millimetre. She felt like a wispy blade of grass trying to push over a tree trunk. 'You do *not* tell me where I will sleep. Get it?'

He plucked her hand off his chest, holding it so firmly her fingers overlapped each other. He tugged her against him, his eyes holding hers in a tense little lock. 'I know what you're up to, Aiesha. You want me to lose my head. To lose my temper and act like a moron, like you believe all men to be. But it won't work. Push and defy me all you want. I'm not going to let you win. You will stay with me all night, no matter what.'

He stepped back from her, his expression enviably cool and controlled. 'I'm going to meet with my client. By the time I get back, the jeweller and the clothes will be here. Don't leave the hotel until I get back. The press are still out there.'

Aiesha threw him a mutinous glare. 'You can't tell me what to do.'

He opened the door, pausing to look back at her before he left. 'I just did.'

Aiesha waited until she saw James leave the front of the hotel in a cab before she picked up her coat and purse. She was not having him tell her what she could or couldn't do. She needed fresh air and she was going to go out and get some. He had no right to order her about as if she had no will of her own.

No man had that right.

She slipped out of a side door and managed to escape the attention of the press because a minor member of European royalty arrived and the cameras switched their focus on them instead.

The streets were slippery and icy from melting snow and a breeze that felt as if it had icicles attached sharpened the air. She put her head down against the cold and walked at a brisk pace to get warm. Paris was beautiful, no matter what the season, but with the Eiffel Tower and every building and bridge and cathedral spire painted white with snow it was particularly picturesque, giving it an old-world, timeless feel.

Aiesha walked along the banks of the Seine, where conical pines stood like powdered sentries along the whitened pathway. The park benches lined along the walk were encrusted with virgin snow, for no one had sat down and lingered there to take in the view due to the bitter cold.

She walked for over an hour and then began to retrace her steps and was only a few blocks from the hotel when she saw it happen. A man wearing a thick dark coat was dragging a small dog behind him on a lead. The little mutt didn't seem too happy on being pulled along and was wriggling and shaking its head from side to side to try and escape. The man said something foul in French and dragged the dog into a nearby alley.

Aiesha's blood ran as cold as the ice beneath her feet. Her heart started to thump so loudly she could hear it in her ears. Her stomach churned and, in spite of the freezing conditions, sweat broke out on her brow. Her legs felt as if they were stuck in the pavement, her ankles held there by steel vices.

But then she heard the little dog yelp and she was galvanised like a sprinter leaping off the block when the starter gun was fired. '*No!*' She ran screaming into the alley, slipping and sliding all over the place like a newborn foal on ice skates. She fell painfully to her knees and scrambled back up, her heart beating so frantically she could barely speak. 'No, please don't hurt him. Please don't hurt him.'

The man looked at her as if she were a crazed idiot. Even the little dog took one look at her and cowered behind its owner's legs. 'You are crazy, *oui*?' the man said.

Aiesha put her hand out for the dog's lead. 'Give me the dog.'

The man scooped the dog up and held it underneath his right arm, glaring at her. 'Get away from me.'

She took out her purse with hands that were shaking so badly several coins fell out as she opened it. 'Look, I'll pay you. Here, take this. It's all I've got on me. Let me have the dog. *Please*, let me have the dog.'

The man screwed up his face. 'You are mad. It is not even a pedigree dog. It's twelve years old and has teeth missing.'

Aiesha was shivering and sick and her head was pounding so badly she felt spaced out and light-headed. It was as if she were looking down at herself from above. It was someone else down in the alleyway begging and pleading with the man to hand over his dog.

But then another person appeared in the alley, his voice so familiar as he called out her name she stumbled towards him, sobbing hysterically. 'James, quick. You have to do something.'

'What on earth's going on?' James gathered her in his arms, opening his coat to wrap her inside it against the strong wall of his chest. 'Hush now. It's all right. I'm here.'

'He's going to hurt it.' She clutched at his shirt lapels in desperation. 'You have to stop him. He's going to kill it.'

'That lady is crazy!' the man said. 'She tried to steal my wife's dog, then she tried to buy it off me.'

James kept one hand on the back of Aiesha's head while he spoke to the man in French. 'My fiancée seems concerned you were going to harm the dog.'

'It's my wife's dog,' the man said. 'She's sick in bed so I offered to take the dog out. He doesn't like walking on the lead. But if I let him off he runs away from me and then I will be the one killed, *oui*?'

Aiesha looked up at James. 'What's he saying?'

'I'll explain later.' He turned to the man. 'I'm sorry for the misunderstanding. I hope your wife gets better soon.'

The man shifted his bulky body inside his coat like a bantam rooster after a fight with a rival who had outmatched him. He patted the dog, who subsequently licked his hand and looked up at him with bright button eyes. 'Come on, Babou,' the man said. 'Didn't I always tell you the English are mad?'

Aiesha bit her lip as she watched the man open a door further down the alley leading to a block of flats. 'I guess that's where he lives…'

'Yes, with his wife.' James looked down at her with a concerned expression. 'Are you OK?'

'I'm fine.'

'No, you're not. You're shaking.'

'Can we go back to the hotel?' She gave a long shuddery sigh. 'I'm cold and wet and…and I need a drink.'

He took her hand and led her out of the alley. 'I think I could do with one, too.'

James kept his arm around her on the way back to their hotel. She was still shivering and shaking but he wanted to get her warm and safe before he pressed her about the incident with the dog. He had thought her little tantrum the other night was bad but this was so much worse. He had never seen her so hysterical. So emotionally undone. At first he'd thought she was in danger. Seeing her in that alleyway confronting an angry-looking man had given him a visceral blow to his heart. The thought of her being attacked or harmed in any way had been like a knockout punch to his solar plexus. He tried to convince himself he would be just as concerned for a stranger but he knew it wasn't true. It physically *hurt* to see her in danger. His chest still felt tight, restricted. Painful.

He wondered what was behind her reaction. She didn't even like dogs…or so she said. What was she doing trying to rescue one that didn't even need rescuing? Did it have something to do with her past? Would she tell him if he asked or would she give him that hard, steely look and tell him to mind his own business? He could only push her so far. He had learnt that the hard way. When would she finally let him in? He wanted to know what put those dark shadows in her eyes. He wanted to know what gave her that sharp tongue and don't-mess-with-me air. He wanted to know what had made her so prickly and defensive that she pushed away anyone who showed the least bit of care for her.

'How did you know where I was?' she asked when they got back to their suite.

James took her coat off her. 'I was in a cab on my way back to the hotel and I saw you run into the alley. At first I thought you were trying to hide from me. I paid off the cab and got to you just as you were about to floor that poor man. What was that all about? I thought you didn't like dogs?'

She peeled off her scarf without meeting his gaze. 'I don't like seeing dogs mistreated. I thought he was being unkind to it. I overreacted. I'm sorry. My mistake. Can we forget about it now?'

'No, Aiesha,' he said. 'I want to know why you were so upset. Talk to me. Tell me why you got so hysterical.'

At first he thought she was going to refuse. She was rolling her scarf around one of her hands, the action mechanical, automated as if her mind was elsewhere. But then he saw the moment the screen came down. It was like watching a suit of armour being removed piece by piece. It started with her eyes, moved down to her mouth, her neck, and her shoulders—her whole body finally losing its tightly held stance.

'I should've known…' she said in a voice that vibrated with self-recrimination. 'I should've known he would kill Archie to get back at me.'

James's stomach plummeted and his heart lurched as if someone had shoved it. He swallowed thickly. 'Who was Archie?'

The sadness in her grey eyes was overwhelming. 'My dog.'

He was connecting the dots but it was a horrible picture that was forming in his mind. A ghastly scenario that he could see reflected in her pain-filled gaze. 'Your stepfather?'

'Yes…'

James gathered her close, his head resting on the top of her head as he tried to absorb some of her pain. 'Oh, you poor little baby,' he said in a shocked whisper.

She wrapped her arms around his waist and leaned against him as if he was the only thing she could rely on to keep her upright. She spoke in a muffled tone against his chest, telling him things he wished he didn't have to hear, but he knew how cathartic this moment was for her. She was finally letting him in. Revealing everything about her past. About her pain. Why she was the way she was. He thought of her as that terrified young teenager, traumatised beyond belief and yet hiding it behind a mask of come-close-to-me-at-your-peril. His mother had seen through it eventually, but it shamed him that it had taken him so long.

He continued to stroke her silky head, letting her speak of the unspeakable, letting her release the pent-up anger and rage that had festered inside her for so long.

Then there was silence.

James was loath to break it but he could feel her shivering from cold and reaction. He eased back to look at her face, ravaged by grief and anger and tears that had taken a decade to spill from her eyes. He was so glad she had chosen to tell him. So relieved. So honoured. It made him feel as if she finally saw him as someone she could trust. Not someone who would exploit her or betray her. It was a nice feeling. A good feeling. He blotted her wet cheeks with the pad of his thumb. 'Let's get you into a nice hot bath. I'll tell the jeweller to push back our appointment an hour.'

She put her hand over his and held it to her cheek. 'James…'

He looked into her tear-washed grey eyes. 'Yes?'

She chewed at her lip, looking so young and vulnerable his chest cramped. 'I've never told anyone that… Not even your mother.'

He brushed a wisp of hair off her forehead with a

gentle hand. 'I wish I'd known ten years ago. I would've tried to help you.'

She trained her gaze on his shirt button. 'I'm sorry about that thing with your father... I never intended to do anything other than show your mother what a jerk he was. I didn't realise how much it would impact you.'

James tipped up her face to look into her eyes. 'I knew my parents were unhappy. If you hadn't brought things to a head, my mother might have struggled on in silence for God knows how long. I guess you can tell she's not the type to give up easily.'

She gave a long sigh. 'I owe her a lot. And how do I repay her? By stuffing up your engagement to Phoebe what's-her-name.'

James was a little shocked to realise he hadn't thought about Phoebe for days. He struggled to think of what he had liked about her. *Liked?* Wasn't he supposed to have loved her? *Had* he loved her? He had liked that Phoebe fitted in with his lifestyle, that she was poised and well spoken, well read and cultured. That she understood the demands of his career and was content to stay in the background and support him.

But there were things he hadn't liked, annoying little things he had chosen to ignore. Phoebe was not adventurous or playful, in bed or out of it. She was even more staid and formal than he was. She had no interest in people outside her social circle. She didn't stop to talk to the housekeeper or the gardener.

And she would definitely not run screaming down a Paris alley putting her own life in danger to rescue a little dog....

He gave himself a mental shake. 'Phoebe is probably dating her childhood sweetheart, Daniel Barnwell, as we speak.'

Aiesha frowned. 'Doesn't that upset you? That she moved on so quickly?'

James was pleasantly surprised it didn't upset him. Not as much as it should have. 'They'd been dating for years. They'd only broken up a couple of months before I came on the scene.'

She gave him a wry look. 'Seems I did you a big, fat favour then.'

He searched her features for a beat, wondering if she felt anything of the confusion he was currently feeling. Their relationship was a complex mix of reality and pretence. It felt real when he held her, kissed her, made love to her.

She was a complex mix of reality and pretence.

For years she had been the enemy. She seemed to relish the role, maximising any opportunity to score points against him. She mocked him, laughed at him and goaded him. How much of that was real and how much of it was a defence mechanism? Was she hiding a sweet and sensitive soul behind that brash in-your-face attitude? Or was she too damaged and hardened from the past? What did she think of him, *really* think of him? Did she care anything for him or was she using him like she used everyone else?

'What will you do when our relationship comes to an end?' he asked.

She gave a little shrug of one shoulder. 'Find a new job. Not in Vegas. Maybe on a cruise ship or something.

I might meet someone filthy rich who'll set me up for life. An old guy who'll cark it after a few months and leave me all his money.' She gave him a slanted smile. 'How cool would that be?'

James locked his jaw. She was at it again. Deliberately pressing his buttons. Game playing. Making him believe she was something she wasn't. He could see through it now. It was all an act. A charade. 'You don't mean that.'

She walked towards the bathroom with her hip-swinging gait. 'Sure I do.'

'I don't believe you,' he said. 'You want everyone to think the worst of you because deep down you believe you deserve it. But that's not who you are, Aiesha. You're not the bad girl everyone thinks you are. My mother saw through it. *I* can see through it. Don't insult me by pretending to be something you're not.'

Her look was all glittering defiance and her tilted smile all worldly mockery as she stood framed by the bathroom door. 'You're a fine one to talk. I might have sent the first tweet but you're the one who took it a step further by setting up this pretend engagement. At least I have the honesty to call it by its real name. It's a dirty little fling. A smutty little hook-up.' Her eyes glinted some more. 'And you're loving every filthy minute of it.'

James flinched as she closed the bathroom door with a resounding click.

She was right. God help him.

He was.

CHAPTER ELEVEN

WHEN AIESHA CAME out of the bathroom there was no sign of James. But laid out on the king-size bed was a collection of clothes—a midnight-blue velvet cocktail dress and a gorgeous evening gown in black satin with spaghetti-thin straps and long black gloves with a white, fluffy stole. There were shoes and an evening purse and a velvet-lined jewellery tray with a collection of diamond rings. She chose the simplest one, a princess-cut diamond that winked at her as she slipped it on her finger.

A sharp little pain gripped her deep inside her chest. This was another part of the charade. The fancy props that turned her into Cinderella for the ball. She dressed in the velvet cocktail dress, swept her hair up on her head, did her make-up, put on the shoes. Turned in front of the mirror to see how the dress showed off her long legs and trim figure. She wasn't vain but she knew she looked good. Glamorous and elegant. Polished.

But underneath all the finery she was still a girl from the wrong suburb. With the wrong accent. With the wrong relatives.

She was wrong.

The door of the suite opened and James stood there dressed in a dark grey suit with a white shirt and red and silver tie. Her breath caught. Her heart jumped. Had he ever looked more magnificent? So tall. So sophisticated. So breathtakingly, heart-stoppingly handsome.

'You look—' he seemed momentarily lost for words '—absolutely gorgeous.'

Aiesha smoothed her hands over her hips. 'I hope you don't expect me to eat anything. And you'd better hope and pray I don't cough or sneeze because I don't think this zip will be up to it.'

'Did you choose a ring?'

She held her left hand out for him to inspect. 'Yep.'

He glanced at the ring before his eyes met hers. Penetrated hers. 'You didn't like the others?'

'Nope.'

'But it's the cheapest one.'

Aiesha held it up to the light, watching as the facets of the diamond glittered. 'Doesn't look cheap to me.'

'It's not, but—'

'Don't worry, James.' She flashed him a quick little smile. 'I'll give it back when this is over. You can give it to your real bride.'

He stood looking down at her for a long moment, his brow creased in a frown.

'Have I got lipstick on my teeth or something?'

'No.'

'Then why are you looking at me like that?'

He moved his thumb over the back of her hand in a rhythmic motion, his eyes still holding hers. 'I thought we could go somewhere for a quiet drink. I know a cosy little bar where the music doesn't thrash your ears. You can actually have a conversation without having to shout or mime.'

He wanted to talk to her? That could be dangerous. She had said enough. She had already told him too much. He *knew* too much. 'Won't I look a little over-dressed?'

'This is Paris,' he said. 'It's impossible to be over-dressed.'

The bar he took her to was in Saint-Germain-des-Prés, where a pianist was playing blues and jazz. The atmosphere was warm and intimate and, although the drinks were crazily overpriced, Aiesha indulged in a brightly coloured cocktail that made her head spin after two sips. Or maybe it was being in James's company. He wasn't so stiff and formal and brooding now. He was watching her fiddle with her straw with an indulgent smile kicking up one side of his mouth as if he had solved a difficult puzzle and was feeling rather pleased with himself.

She could only assume *she* was the puzzle.

He had been patient; she had to give him that. Waiting for her to drop her guard. Not pushing her too hard. And yet he had stood his ground with her on occasion, not letting her get away with manipulating him. 'Game playing' he called it. He was right. She did play games. It was her way of keeping people at a safe distance.

But she hadn't been able to keep him away from her secrets. He had discovered almost everything about her and yet he didn't push her away…or at least not until the end of the month when they would go their separate ways.

He would move on with his life and find a suitable bride. He would find someone who wouldn't play games. Someone he would be comfortable introducing to his friends and colleagues. Not someone who had the potential to embarrass him or destroy his reputation via an ill-timed comment to the press from one of her crazy relatives.

Why did it have to be this way? Why couldn't she be the one he chose? Why couldn't she accept him if he did?

Because that was the stuff of fairy tales and she wasn't a little kid any more, hoping that someone was going to wave a magic wand over her head and make everything turn out right in the end.

'I wouldn't drink that too quickly,' he said.

Aiesha gave her straw a couple of twirls before she took another sip. 'Don't worry, James. I won't embarrass you by suddenly jumping up and dancing on the tables.'

His smile was exchanged for a frown. 'Look, can you drop the armour just for tonight?'

Aiesha crossed one leg over the other and leaned back on the velvet sofa they were sharing. 'What armour?'

His dark blue eyes held hers. 'Let me see you without the brash bad-girl mask. Be the girl in the alley this afternoon. The one who loves dogs. The one who let me hold her as she told me stuff she's told no one before.'

She pursed her lips and reached for her drink, taking a generous sip that sent her blood-alcohol level soaring.

Or maybe it wasn't the alcohol. Maybe it was the chance to let her guard down and stay down long enough to connect with someone who was smart enough, intuitive enough to see behind the facade.

It was *so* tempting…

Could she do it?

Just for tonight?

What did she have to lose? It wasn't as if she had anything to lose or gain. James wasn't going to suddenly fall in love with her just because she showed him the side of herself no one ever saw. He cared about her, but then, so did his mother. It didn't mean he loved her or wanted to spend his future with her. He was too conservative, too sensible to fall for someone so far outside his social circle.

Aiesha kept her gaze trained on the pink-and-orange umbrella in her cocktail. 'Why are you doing this?'

'I don't want you to hide from me,' he said. 'I don't want you to play games. I hate it when you do that. I'm not going to exploit you. I'm not that sort of man. Surely you know that by now?'

Aiesha looked at him for a long moment. Everything about him was so incredibly special. His patience. His sensitivity. His kindness. Her heart felt so heavy at the thought of when this time together would be over. How would she ever find someone so in tune with her? How would she ever fill that giant hole of loneliness inside her once he was out of her life?

She took a little breath and slowly released it, her gaze going back to her drink. 'I hated everything about my childhood. I hated the poverty. I hated the cruelty.

I hated the fact I didn't fit in. For as long as I can remember, I dreamed of escaping. The only way I could
escape was with music.'

'How did you learn to play the piano?' he asked. 'Did
you have formal lessons?'

Aiesha kept looking at the tiny wooden spines on the
umbrella. 'There was a piano in the church hall a block
away from the estate we lived on. I used to go there and
play it for hours. The pastor didn't seem to mind. After
a while he started leaving a few music-theory books
lying around. I taught myself to read music. The tech-
nique of playing was much harder to learn. I listened
to CDs when I could but I'll never be good enough to
play anywhere but a dingy nightclub.'

'But you play like a professional.'

She screwed up her mouth in a self-deprecating manner. 'I wouldn't be brave enough to play in front of a
sober audience. Not my own stuff, that is.'

He leaned forward and took one of her hands in his.
'But you're so talented. That music you played the other
day. It was so emotional, so haunting. It was like a
soundtrack to a really emotional movie. Do you have
more like that? Stuff you've written yourself?'

Aiesha looked at her hand in his. The engagement
ring looked so real, so perfect for her finger. He was so
perfect. Why had she taken this long to realise it? Or
had she always realised it? He was perfect but she was
wrong for him. Bad for him. She would bring trouble
for him if she stayed around too long. Hadn't she caused
enough trouble in the past? She brought her gaze up to
his. 'You're nothing like him, you know.'

His brows met over his eyes. 'Who?'

'Your father.'

His expression clouded as he released her hand and sat back from her. 'I've spent too many years of my life trying to convince myself of that.'

'It's true, James.' She reached for his hand again, curling her fingers around his strong, capable ones. 'He doesn't care about anyone but himself. You care. Look at the way you looked after your mother after the divorce. She told me how you made sure she got a proper division of the assets. Your father would have swindled her out of her fair share but you stood up for her. You even paid the lawyer's bill. And you bought her Lochbannon. You visit her whenever you can. You worry about her hooking up with a guy you've never met. If that's not caring, I don't know what is.'

His mouth twisted as he looked down at their joined hands. 'I used to think my parents were doing OK. Not superhappy…but OK.' He looked at her again. 'I guess I didn't want to see my father for who he was. My mother, bless her for being so gracious, didn't want to ruin my relationship with him. But it cost her dearly. For year after year she put up with my father's affairs so I could have what she considered a normal upbringing. She came from a broken home and knew how hard it was for kids with shared custody arrangements.'

Aiesha stroked the length of his thumb where it was resting against her hand. 'It must have been a shock to finally find out the truth about him.'

'It was.' He flattened his mouth as if the memory disturbed him. 'I felt like my whole childhood was a lie. Everything I believed in was false. Love. Marriage. Commitment. It made me wonder if anyone was ever happy with their lot. That everyone was out there pretending to be OK when they were anything but.'

'I'm sure there are some people who get it right…' She looked at the way his thumb was now stroking the back of her hand. Her engagement ring—her fake engagement ring—glinted at her mockingly.

He turned her hand over in his, giving it a gentle squeeze. 'Want to dance?'

Aiesha slipped her arms around him as he drew her to her feet. She laid her head against his chest as he led her in a slow waltz on the small dance floor. Being in his arms felt safe. Made her feel anchored. Made her feel loved.

Loved?

James didn't love her. He cared about her. Like he cared about everybody. He was a responsible person who took others' welfare seriously. She would be a fool to conjure up one of her pointless little dreams. None of her dreams had ever come to life. None of her prayers had ever been answered. None of her planets had ever aligned.

James put his hand on the nape of her neck as he looked down at her. 'Where did you go just then?'

'Go?'

'You missed a step.'

'So? I'm a rubbish dancer.'

He held her gaze with the steadiness of his. 'No mask, remember?'

Aiesha chewed one side of her lower lip. 'This isn't easy for me…'

His thumb stroked where her teeth had been. 'I know it isn't.'

She looked at the knot of his tie. 'It's hard for me to let people get close. I push everyone away. I can't seem to help it.'

He cupped her cheek with his hand. 'Be yourself with me. Don't play games. Just be yourself.'

Aiesha looked into his dark eyes. 'I have nightmares. Horrible nightmares. About what happened to Archie. That's why I never share a bed with anyone. It's so embarrassing to wake up screaming or…or worse…' The truth came tumbling out in a rush but, instead of feeling ashamed, she felt relieved to have finally told him.

His eyes did that softening thing that melted her every time. 'Thank you,' he said.

'For what?'

His expression was full of tenderness, the sort of tenderness she had longed for someone to show her. 'For trusting me.'

Aiesha wondered if he knew how hard it was for her. She felt like someone had unzipped her wide open like a body bag. Everything was on show. Her doubts. Her fears. Her terrors. Her shame. But he wasn't repulsed. He wasn't pushing her away in disgust. He was looking at her with understanding and concern. Acceptance. She drew in a breath that rattled against the walls of her throat. 'How'd you get to be so nice with a father like yours?'

He gave her a twinkling smile. 'I can be bad when I need to be.'

She linked her arms around his neck and smiled back. 'Now that's something I'd like to see.'

James pulled the covers over Aiesha's sleeping form a few hours later. She was curled up like a kitten, her cheek pressed against the pillow next to his, her hair in a tumbled mass around her head. He stroked the wayward strands off her smooth brow, watching as her eyelids flickered in rapid-eye-movement sleep. She was so beautiful. So broken and yet so exquisitely beautiful it made his heart contract every time he looked at her.

Each time he made love with her he learned more about her. The way she expressed herself physically was an indication of the passionate emotion she kept hidden away. Was he fooling himself she felt something for him? How long would it take for her to feel safe enough to reveal her feelings to him? She had told him so much but not the words he most wanted to hear. He wanted to tell her how he felt but wondered if it was too soon. Would it spook her to have him reveal how deeply he cared?

She moved against him, snuggling up close, her eyes opening sleepily. 'What time is it?'

'Six a.m. Too early to get up.'

She rubbed one of her eyes with the ball of her fist, reminding him of a child waking up before it was ready. 'That's a big sleep-in for me.'

He took her balled-up fist and brought it to his mouth

and kissed the knuckle of her index finger. 'I liked having you beside me all night.'

Her expression faltered for a moment but then she gave him a slitted look from beneath her lashes. 'At least you didn't grope me.'

He rolled her on to her back and straddled her with his thighs. 'That was remiss of me. Is it too late to do it now?'

She laughed as he began to nuzzle her neck and he realised it was the first time he had heard her do so naturally. 'Stop it,' she said, batting him playfully with her fists. 'That tickles.'

He moved down to her breasts, kissing each one in turn. 'You don't really want me to stop, do you?'

She gave a little whimper as he moved down her belly. 'Not yet.'

'We could spend all day in bed,' he said. 'How does that sound?'

She gasped as he took a gentle nip of the tender flesh of her inner thigh. 'Don't you have terribly important work to do?'

He looked up and gave her a glinting smile. 'It can wait.'

When Aiesha entered the ballroom on James's arm later that evening, every eye turned to look at them as they walked to their designated table. All day, news feeds had run with the story of their engagement after the photos of them arriving at the hotel had gone around the world. Everyone was fascinated with the story of their romance. The former street kid and Vegas club singer and the Old Money talented architect falling head over heels in love. One journalist had even gone as far as calling it a modern day re-enactment of *My Fair Lady*.

But that was exactly what it was like. She was acting out a role in a play. She was dressed in the costume. She had all the moves down pat. James was perfectly cast as her leading man.

And tonight's event was their stage.

It was a highbrow affair with beautiful people dressed impeccably, the women dripping with jewellery, the men dapper in bespoke tuxedos. As well kitted out as Aiesha was in the black evening gown with its mermaid train, she still felt like a little brown wood duck surrounded by bright flamingos. She couldn't help feeling that any minute now someone would tap her on the shoulder and tell her to leave. Call her out for a fake. Mock her for pretending to be something she could never be.

She could see several women looking at her and exchanging comments behind their gloved hands. Were they questioning James's sanity in choosing her? Were they laughing at her behind their polite smiles? Nerves fluttered in her stomach like moths with razor-blade wings. What if she embarrassed James by doing or saying the wrong thing? What if she compromised his business deal? Hadn't she done enough damage to his name and reputation?

James had his arm around her waist as he introduced her to the host. 'Darling, this is Howard Sherwood. Howard, my fiancée, Aiesha Adams.'

Howard smiled a smile that made his light blue eyes

twinkle as he took her hand. 'You're every bit as stunning as James said. Congratulations on your engagement. When's the big day?'

Aiesha felt a hot blush steal over her cheeks. Couldn't he see how much of an imposter she felt? She felt as if it was emblazoned on her forehead: FRAUD. 'Erm… we're still trying to sort out dates. We're both so crazily busy. You know how it is.'

'Well, don't leave it too long,' Howard said. 'Never was one for long engagements, or for living together for years on end. Waste of time. Might as well get on with it, eh, James? Make an honest woman out of her.'

James smiled an easy smile. 'That's the plan.'

Aiesha waited until Howard had turned to greet some other guests. 'You're becoming a rather accomplished liar. It's got me worried.'

His look was now unreadable. 'What would you like to drink?'

'Champagne.' She took a steadying breath as more and more people swarmed into the ballroom, stopping to take photos with their phones of her and James. 'Better make it a double.'

'According to the latest news feed, we're the new "it" couple,' he said as he handed her a bubbling glass of champagne.

'I can't imagine why. Quite frankly, I'm surprised everyone's bought it. Just shows how dumbed down people are these days to believe everything they read in the press.'

Aiesha drank half a glass of champagne before

she realised he was still standing staring at her with a frowning expression. 'What?'

He brushed an idle fingertip down her cheek, his dark blue eyes suddenly intense. Earnest. 'What if it was real?'

She swallowed. 'What if what was real?'

'Us.'

She flickered her eyelids. '*Us?*'

'We don't have to pretend,' he said. 'We could have a real relationship.'

Aiesha licked a layer of her lip gloss off her lips. Her heart was banging against her breastbone like a window shutter in a high wind. Air was not getting down into her lungs. Her throat was as restricted as a clogged drinking straw. He was joking. He had to be. He had got her to take off her armour and now he was playing her at her own game. Leading her on, flirting with her, making fun of her the way she had with him. She gave a little laugh but it sounded grating. 'Good one,' she said. 'You nearly had me there. Can you imagine what your father would say if you brought me home? He'd disinherit you on the spot. I'm surprised he hasn't already done it.'

James frowned at her, about to say something further but stopped himself.

'James, sorry to interrupt.' Howard Sherwood came over with a flustered look on his normally congenial face. 'There's been a problem with tonight's entertainment. The feature act has suddenly come down with a migraine. I just got the message from her agent.' He swung his gaze to Aiesha. 'Would you fill in for her,

Aiesha? James told me you're an entertainer. It'd just be for an hour till the dance band comes on.'

Aiesha's stomach pitched. 'I—I don't think—'

'Do it, darling,' James said. 'You'd be brilliant. Everyone will love you.'

'Please, Aiesha,' Howard said. 'You'd be doing my charity and me a massive favour. There are some big international sponsors here and they'll be disappointed if the programme is cut short. I'm happy to pay you if that's what's—'

'No, of course not,' Aiesha said. 'It's not about the money. I would do it for free but—'

'Wonderful.' Howard beamed and clapped James on the back. 'You've got a good woman there, James. Oh, and about that contract. Consider it done and dusted. I'm also going to recommend you to some colleagues in Argentina. Have you heard of the Valquez brothers Alejandro and Luis? They have a big hotel and resort expansion in the pipeline. It'll be worth squillions.'

Aiesha felt James's hand tighten around hers. Who hadn't heard of the Valquez brothers? They were two of the richest men in South America. How could she refuse to play now? It would mean so much to James to secure the Valquez contract. It would rebuild the Challender architecture empire back to what it had been in his grandfather's day and expand it even further. She took a deep breath as she pushed her cowardice and self-doubt behind her. 'When do you want me to start?'

James sat at the head table and watched as Aiesha played the first bracket. Her fingers were light over the keys, her voice a clear bell-like sound that made the hairs on his arms stand up. The song she was singing was an original of hers, the lyrics poignant and deeply moving. It was a song about lost dreams, lost love and heartbreak. The ballroom erupted into applause and then she deftly changed key and went into another song. This time it was about secret hopes and yearnings that spoke to something deep inside him. Her lyrics were so timely. Hadn't he been ignoring his own hopes and dreams? He had been fixated on working, rebuilding all that was lost in the scandal blow-out ten years ago, but he had neglected the emotional side of his life. He had shut down. Locked away his feelings. Ignored his feelings. Become an automaton. He had chosen a bride who would not make him feel anything other than mild affection.

Aiesha made him feel passion.

She made him feel alive.

She made him feel like a man who could take on the world.

He loved her. He knew it as certainly as he knew he was sitting there watching her win over the crowd. She was tugging on everyone's heartstrings. He could see women dabbing at the corners of their eyes with tissues. He could see grown men swallowing. Choking on suppressed emotion.

This was what she was meant to do. To sing like an angel, to play her music to make people feel in touch with their emotions. What a waste of her talent to sing to a disinterested audience in a lounge bar. Why hadn't he stepped in before and got her out of there? Hadn't she been crying out for help since she came home with his mother? He had turned his back on her. Rejected her, just like everyone else had done.

All that was going to change. He would ask her to marry him, this time without interruption. He would get down on bended knee and tell her how much he loved her. They would build a future together. Have a family together. The family she had missed out on. The family he would have loved to grow up with if things had been different.

He thought of their children, a little girl with sparkling grey eyes and a cheeky smile, or a little boy with a serious expression and dark blue eyes.

He wanted it all.

He wanted to make her happy. To make up for her miserable childhood, for all the disappointments and heartbreaks she had experienced.

He would be her knight in shining armour. He would be her Prince Charming. He would be her defender. Her protector. Her best friend and her lover. She would no longer have to fight her corner with that hard don't-mess-with-me look in her eyes.

He would make her feel safe.

He would make her feel loved.

Aiesha stood and took a bow after her performance was over. The applause was rapturous. She had never heard anything like it. She wanted to check behind her to see if they were clapping for someone else. Surely it couldn't be her they were applauding? She had played her own songs. Why? Because she hadn't wanted to bring any hint of Vegas showgirl into the ballroom. This was her one and only chance to show everyone what she was capable of.

She had played each composition with her heart behind every word and cadence. She had never done that before. Opened her heart fully to the music, to the audience. *To James.* She had used her music to reach across the room to tell him what she couldn't say in person. Hadn't had the courage to say when he spoke to her earlier. Was he serious about making their relationship real? What did he mean? Did he want to make it permanent? Had she imagined the earnestness in his dark blue gaze?

What did it matter whether he was earnest or not? She couldn't bring him down by continuing their relationship. How long before a living skeleton popped out of her family closet and brought more shame and embarrassment to him? Even more was at stake now. He had the Valquez deal to consider. Her background was never going to go away. It would always be there. There would always be a journalist unscrupulous enough to rake over her past. It was better to leave before the real damage was done. Before her hopes got too high. Before she dropped her guard low enough for James to see how she felt about him…

Cameras flashed and the room was abuzz as she made her way back to the table where James—along with everyone else—was giving her a standing ovation.

He gathered her in his arms and held her close. 'You were amazing, darling,' he said. 'Truly amazing.'

Aiesha gave a self-deprecating grimace. 'I missed

a key change in that first bracket. I hope there were no musos in the crowd. *So* amateur.'

He held her by the hands, looking at her with a thoughtful gaze. 'You're always doing that.'

'What?'

'Putting yourself down.'

'Yeah, well, best to get in first is my take on that.'

'Miss Adams?' A man came over with a business card in his hand. 'I'm George Bassleton. I'm a talent scout for a recording studio in London. I manage recording contracts for up-and-coming musicians. Would you be interested in coming into the studio for a sound test?'

Aiesha took the card with a hand that was close to shaking. 'I… Thank you.'

'You could be the next big thing in music,' George Bassleton said. 'The new Amy Winehouse or Norah Jones. You have a lot of soul in your voice. It's unique. Call me when you're back in London. I'll set something up.'

James smiled at her once the man had moved back to his own table. 'See? What did I tell you? You're a star in the making.'

She whooshed out a quick breath. 'You reckon I could slip out and take a breather for a minute? All this attention is going to my head.'

'Come on.' He took her by the hand. 'I know just the place.'

Aiesha followed him to a quiet alcove behind a huge flower arrangement where two velvet-covered chairs and a small brass-inlaid drum table were situated. James had organised a waiter to bring an ice bucket and champagne as well as a long, cool mineral water with a twist of lime. He waited until she had drained the mineral water before he got down on bended knee in front of her chair. 'What are you doing?' she said, glancing around the legs of her chair. 'Have you lost something down there?'

He took her hands in his. 'I almost did lose something. You.'

Aiesha chewed at her dust-dry lips. Time to get the mask back on, even if it didn't feel as comfortable as it used to. 'Hey, I know my music is a tad sentimental and all that but you're really spooking me. It looks like you're about to propose to me, which would be a really dumb thing to do for a guy in your situation.'

His brows came together. 'Why?'

She gave one of her tinny laughs. 'You and me? Are you nuts? We'd kill each other before the honeymoon was over. Nice proposal, though.'

His hands gripped hers. 'Aiesha, I love you. I'm not sure when I started loving you. It just…happened. I want to marry you. I mean it. This isn't a joke or a set-up. I'm serious. I want you to be my wife.'

Aiesha got to her feet, almost knocking him off balance in the process. 'But here's the thing. I don't love you.'

He got to his feet and took her firmly by the shoulders. 'That's a lie. You *do* love me. I see it in your eyes. I feel it when we make love. You love me but you're too scared to say it because, hell, I don't know why. Maybe you've never had anyone love you before. But *I* love you. My mother loves you. You're the woman I've been waiting for all my life.'

Aiesha wanted to say it. She *ached* to say it. But the words were trapped in her chest. Years of heartbreak and disappointment and crushed hopes had buried them so deep she couldn't access them. She had loved her mother. She had loved Archie. But both had been ripped away from her, tearing her heart out of her chest each time, leaving a gaping, empty hole that still pulsed and throbbed with pain.

It was better to get out now while she still could. James would get over it. He would find some other girl from his nice, neat, ordered world.

'I'm sorry, James.' She steeled her gaze and iced what remained of her heart. 'Believe me, it's for the best. You're a nice guy and all that, but you're *too* nice. I'm already feeling bored.'

His frown was so heavy it closed the distance between his glittering eyes. 'I don't believe you. You want what I want. I know you do. Why won't you admit it?'

'Let's not make a scene,' she said. 'It wouldn't be good for your image. Howard Sherwood might change his mind about recommending you to his posh polo-playing pals.'

'Do you think I give a freaking toss for that?' he said. 'It's you I care about. I'd give it all up for you. All of it.'

Aiesha wondered if he knew how close he would be to losing it all if she stayed in his life. No one wanted bad blood. Not in their family. Not in their social circle. Not in their business dealings. What would happen to his squillion-dollar deal if her father or stepfather gave a tell-all interview to the press? She was surprised one or both hadn't already done so. There was money in it. Big money. The shame would be back in James's life. Shame she had brought in like dirty baggage. She couldn't escape her past. It would always be there like a horrible spectre just waiting for the worst possible moment to appear. 'I'm going to the powder room,' she said. 'I'll meet you back in the ballroom. We can talk about this later.'

His eyes took on a cynical hardness. 'You think I'm that stupid? You're going to run away as soon as I turn my back. That's what cowards do, Aiesha. I thought you were stronger than that. Tougher. Seems I was wrong.'

She stood straight and tall and determined before him. 'I'm not a coward.' *I'm doing this for you. Can't you see that?* 'Don't you *dare* call me a coward.'

'Go on, then,' he said through tightened lips. 'Go. Run away from what frightens you. See how far you get before you realise you've run away from everything that matters to you.'

'*You* don't matter to me, James,' she said with feigned cold, hard indifference. 'Your money matters to me. It's all I ever wanted from you or any man.' She put on her bad-girl smirk. 'Maybe I could look up your father. At least I'm legal now. Do you have his number?'

His jaw worked for a moment, his eyes turning blue-black with disgust. 'Find it yourself.' And, with that, he turned on his heel and left.

CHAPTER TWELVE

Two weeks later...

JAMES LOOKED AT his phone for the fiftieth time. No missed calls. No text messages. He knew he was being stubborn in refusing to reach out to Aiesha. But he wanted her to stop the game playing. He should never have fallen for that crack about his father. Of course she wouldn't contact his father—he was too busy sunning himself on the beach at an exclusive resort in Barbados with not one, but two girls half his age.

James pushed a hand through his hair. Even his mother was having a better love life than him. She was holidaying with Richard in outback Australia, camping under the stars while he was sitting here brooding over the one that got away.

The press had done their thing over his broken engagement with Aiesha. The speculation had been excruciating but he had done his best to ignore it. He had more important things to worry about. He wanted Aiesha to come to him. To reach out to him. He had offered her his heart and she had tossed it aside like a toy she had finished playing with.

Had he got it wrong about her? Had she been playing him for a fool the whole time? He thought of the way they had made love. Surely he hadn't imagined that once-in-a-lifetime intimacy. What about the way she had told him of her worst nightmares and fears? She had opened herself to him in a way she had never done to anyone else. He was sure of it. He *knew* her. He *loved* her.

He pushed back from his desk with a muttered curse. How long was this going to take? He was a patient man but this was getting way past ridiculous. He missed her. He ached to be with her, especially now as her career was about to take off. He'd read about her recording contract in the press. She had her first concert tonight in Berlin as a supporting act for a big-name band who was on a comeback tour. It was massive exposure for her. According to what he'd gathered from the press, if tonight was a success she would be joining the band on the rest of their world tour.

His phone flashed on the desk with an incoming message. He snatched it up but when he looked at the screen it wasn't a text, but a news feed coming through on social media. His gut clenched when he read through the article that had been tweeted. Aiesha's stepfather had given a warts-and-all interview to the press. It was nothing but a pack of lies. It disgusted him to read such trash about someone he loved so much. And of course the journalist had taken it one step further by including photos of his father and Aiesha's role in his parents' divorce.

There was even a photo of her biological father outside the court where he had been sentenced to prison. The shame of it might derail her on her big night. Who would be there to protect her from the fallout? Who would be there to comfort her? To stop her having a meltdown in case it all got too much?

He clicked on his computer screen to bring up a flight booking.

He would.

'Miss Adams?' The events manager, Kate Greenhill, popped her head around the dressing room door at the concert hall in Berlin. 'You're on in five minutes.'

Aiesha adjusted her droplet earrings, trying to fight the ants' nest of nerves in her belly. She would have to get used to this if she was asked to join the rest of the tour. Nerves. Panic. Doubt. What if she missed a note? What if her voice froze? What if the audience hated her? 'Thanks, Kate. What's the crowd like?'

Kate grinned at her in the light bulb-lined mirror. 'Massive. A sell-out. To be honest, I think they're here to hear you, not the band. The boys won't be too happy about that. This is supposed to be their comeback chance.'

Aiesha knew she should be feeling satisfied. Proud of what she had achieved in spite of all the setbacks in her life. She had been booked as the supporting act for the opening concert of the band's reunion tour. She had an album in production. She had the prospect of fans. Fame. Fortune.

But she was lonely.

Desperately, achingly lonely.

James hadn't contacted her. Not once. She knew it was for the best. He had to distance himself from her, especially now. Her stepfather had finally sold his story to the press. She suspected he had waited until now so he could go for collateral damage. He couldn't have timed it better. The lurid tale of her being a smart-mouthed teenage tease who had tried to seduce him had gone viral. The press had subsequently sourced photos from all over the place. It had stirred up renewed interest in the scandal with James's father, which would cause enormous embarrassment and hurt to Louise and James. There was even a photo of Aiesha's father being led out of court on the day he was sentenced.

Lovely. Just lovely.

Her business manager/publicist assured her that any publicity was good while she was building her career as a solo artist, but Aiesha wasn't so sure. She wanted to distance herself from her past. She wanted to be known for her music, not for her dodgy bloodline or step-relatives or her past behaviour. It would be different if she were a rock-and-roll chick. But she wasn't. She was a love-song and ballad singer with a hint of blues and jazz.

Louise Challender had sent her roses and a sweet message. Aiesha had held the card against her chest and cried so much the make-up artist had hysterics.

The card said: 'I always knew you would make it. Love you, Louise.'

But she hadn't made it. Not yet. Maybe not ever if the news of her past kept resurfacing like a bad smell at a perfume launch.

Kate popped her head back around the door. 'Two minutes.'

Aiesha let out a rattling breath. She hadn't done her vocal warm-up. She hadn't focused. She wasn't prepared. This was not how she'd thought it would be. She loved writing songs; she loved being in the recording studio working with the team to produce the best tracks she could. But singing her songs in front of huge crowds was not the thrill she'd thought it would be. What was the point of singing those heartfelt words when the only person she wanted to hear them wasn't in the audience?

The crowd roared as Aiesha came out to the spotlight, the beam so strong she could only make out the faces in the first few rows. She sat down at the piano, took a deep breath and went into the routine she had planned with her agent.

But then, towards the end of her performance, she turned on the piano stool and trained her gaze to the sea of unseen faces at the back. 'This song is a new one. No one has heard it before now.' She blinked to stem a sudden rush of tears. 'It's called "The Love I Had to Let Go."'

The roar when the song was over was deafening. Aiesha got up from the piano and took a bow. She had three standing ovations. As she performed each follow-up song she kept reminding herself: *This is what you wanted. This is your moment. You've wanted this since you were five years old. Enjoy it, for pity's sake.*

It was supposed to be the triumph of her life. But as she walked back through the bowels of the stage set to her dressing room she felt empty…like a deflated balloon at a children's party. Useless.

Kate came in while Aiesha was taking off her make-up. 'Um, there's someone here to see you.'

Aiesha put the discarded facial wipe in the bin next to her chair. 'I told you before. I'm not doing any press interviews.'

'He's not a journalist,' Kate said.

Aiesha swivelled to look at her. 'Who is it?'

'It's me,' James said from the door.

Aiesha swallowed. Put her hand on her stomach to stop it from falling even further. 'Erm...would you leave us for a minute, Kate? This won't take long.'

'Sure.' Kate smiled brightly. 'Nice to meet you, Mr Challender.'

'You, too, Kate.'

The silence was as deafening as the applause had been only a few minutes ago.

Aiesha rolled her lips together, searching for something to say. 'You should've told me you were coming. I could've got you complimentary tickets.'

His dark blue eyes held hers in an unreadable lock. 'You know me. I don't mind paying.'

Her cheeks still had a layer of bronzer on them but, even so, she was sure he would know she was blushing. 'So, what brings you here? Did you have business in Berlin? It's a lovely city, isn't it? I've always wanted to come here. It's weird because now I'm here I can't walk down the street without worrying someone will recognise me from the tour poster.' She was talking too much but at least it filled that ghastly silence. 'That's the price you pay for fame, huh?'

'Is it everything you hoped for?'

She painted on a smile. 'You would not believe the amount of money in my bank account. Oh, that reminds me.' She turned and fished in her bag in the drawer under the make-up counter. 'Ah, here it is. I knew I had it somewhere.' She held the engagement ring out to him in her open palm and stretched her smile a little further. 'I can buy my own jewellery now.'

He ignored the ring. 'How are you?'

'I'm fine. And you?'

'I see your stepfather sold a pack of lies to the press,' he said.

'Yes, I've been expecting that for a while now. It'll keep him in drink and cigarettes and drugs for a year or two.'

'Are you going to do anything about it?'

She shrugged. 'What can I do? Hopefully, it will blow away in a day or two.'

His brow was deeply furrowed. 'But it could damage your reputation before you get your career properly launched. You're only starting out. It could destroy what you've worked so hard for.'

Aiesha closed her fingers over the ring, barely noticing how it bit into the flesh of her palm. 'You shouldn't be here, James. People will talk.'

'So? Let them talk.'

'Your business will suffer.' She dropped the ring on the counter next to her make-up kit, turning her back on him as she straightened the cosmetic brushes in a neat line. 'Your reputation has a lot further to fall than mine. It could jeopardise your business.'

He let out an expletive and spun her around to face

him. 'Is that why you fed me that rubbish about not loving me?'

Aiesha looked into his glittering eyes. Tears were not far away in hers. They didn't look far away in his, either. 'Don't make this any harder for me. I don't belong in your life. I don't belong in your world. I'll bring you down, James. I'll ruin everything for you. It's already happening all over again.'

He pulled her up and crushed her to his chest. 'You silly little goose.' He kissed the top of her head, the side of her face, her chin, her nose and then finally a hot, hard kiss on her mouth. He held her from him, his eyes misty. 'That song. That was for me, wasn't it? I was the love you had to let go.'

Aiesha could barely speak for the emotions that were rising like a tsunami in her chest. A huge, emotional storm that was like a cauldron boiling over. 'I didn't want to hurt you. I figured I'd already hurt you enough. Letting you go was the hardest thing I've ever had to do.'

'I love you.' His hands gripped her shoulders so tightly it was close to pain but she didn't care. 'I love you so much. It's been so hard to stay away from you. Every day I wanted to call you. To beg you to come back to me.'

'Why did you come now?' Aiesha said. 'Why not before?'

'I was angry after what happened in Paris,' he said. 'But I stubbornly refused to make the first move, even though I realised soon after you'd only made that crack about hooking up with my father as a way to push me away.'

She gave him a sheepish look. 'I'm sorry about that. It was a pretty crass thing to say.'

He cupped her face in his hands. 'When that awful story came out this morning, I was sick with worry. I was worried there would be no one by your side to protect you. I want to be that person, Aiesha. I want to make you feel safe. I want you to feel loved. I want you to feel accepted. You're a part of me. I can't function without you. Just ask my mother. She's been tearing her hair out over me. You can't do that to her. You have to marry me, otherwise she'll never speak to me again. How bad would that be? You would have cost her a husband *and* a son.'

Aiesha felt a smile break open her face. It unlocked something gnarled and tightly bound inside her chest. 'I guess when you put it that way, how could I refuse?'

His hands tightened again on her shoulders. 'You mean it? You'll marry me?'

She laughed at his shocked expression. 'Aren't you going to ask me to say it?'

'Say what?'

'The three little magic words.'

He grinned as he pulled her close again. 'I heard you the first time.'

She wrinkled her brow as she tilted her head back to look at him. 'When was that?'

'On stage tonight,' he said. 'You turned to the audience and I knew you were speaking directly to me. I sat and cried like a baby through that song. I was surrounded by thousands of people and yet I felt like I was the only one in the audience.'

Aiesha blinked through tears of happiness. 'That's because you're the only one that matters to me.'

His eyes twinkled. 'What about my money?'

She twinkled her eyes right on back. 'I've got my own money.'

'What about my mother? She matters to you, doesn't she?'

Aiesha felt a warm rush of love flow through her. 'You know she does.'

'Have you ever told her?'

'Not in so many words, but I think she knows.'

He stroked her cheeks with his thumbs. 'You could call her and tell her. I think she'd love to hear you say the words. She's ridiculously sentimental like that.'

Aiesha put her arms around his neck. 'I want you to hear them first. I never said them to anyone else before.' She looked him in the eyes, her heart suddenly feeling too big for her chest. 'I love you.'

His eyes watered up. His throat moved up and down. His arms around her tightened. 'I love you, too. So much. I never thought it was possible to love someone this much. You will marry me, won't you?'

She gave him a teasing smile. 'I wonder if anyone's ever accepted a marriage proposal in a dressing room before?'

He brought his mouth down to within a millimetre of hers. 'First time for everything,' he said, and then he kissed her.

* * * * *

A sneaky peek at next month...

MODERN™

POWER, PASSION AND IRRESISTIBLE TEMPTATION

My wish list for next month's titles...

In stores from 18th July 2014:

☐ Zarif's Convenient Queen – Lynne Graham

☐ His Forbidden Diamond – Susan Stephens

☐ The Argentinian's Demand – Cathy Williams

☐ The Ultimate Seduction – Dani Collins

In stores from 1st August 2014:

☐ Uncovering Her Nine Month Secret – Jennie Lucas

☐ Undone by the Sultan's Touch – Caitlin Crews

☐ Taming the Notorious Sicilian – Michelle Smart

☐ His by Design – Dani Wade

Available at WHSmith, Tesco, Asda, Eason, Amazon and Apple

Just can't wait?

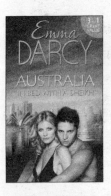

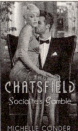

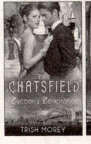
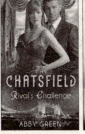

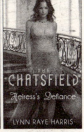

Make it a summer to remember with the fantastic new book from Sarah Morgan

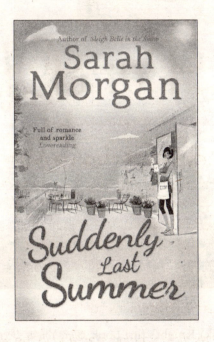

Fiery French chef Elise Philippe has just heard that the delectable Sean O'Neil is back in town. After their electrifying night together last summer, can she stick to her one-night rule?

Coming soon at millsandboon.co.uk

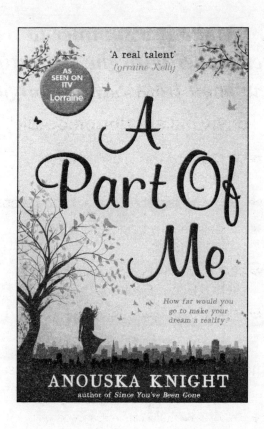

Anouska Knight's first book, *Since You've Been Gone*, was a smash hit and crowned the winner of Lorraine's Racy Reads. Anouska returns with *A Part of Me*, which is one not to be missed!

Get your copy today at: www.millsandboon.co.uk

Discover more romance at

www.millsandboon.co.uk

- ❤ WIN great prizes in our exclusive competitions
- ❤ BUY new titles before they hit the shops
- ❤ BROWSE new books and REVIEW your favourites
- ❤ SAVE on new books with the Mills & Boon® Bookclub™
- ❤ DISCOVER new authors

PLUS, to chat about your favourite reads, get the latest news and find special offers:

- Find us on facebook.com/millsandboon
- Follow us on twitter.com/millsandboonuk
- ❤ Sign up to our newsletter at millsandboon.co.uk

&B_WEB